Fractal Paisleys

Fractal Paisleys

By Paul Di Filippo

New York/London

Collection © 1997 Paul Di Filippo

Published in the United States by:
Four Walls Eight Windows
39 West 14th Street, room 503
New York, N.Y., 10011

U.K. offices:
Four Walls Eight Windows/Turnaround
Unit 3, Olympia Trading Estate
Coburg Road, Wood Green
London N22 6TZ England

First printing September 1997.

Library of Congress Cataloging-in-Publication Data:
Di Filippo, Paul. 1954–
Fractal Paisleys/ by Paul Di Filippo
   p. cm.
Contents: Master Blaster and Whammer Jammer Meet the Groove Thang — Fractal Paisleys — Do you Believe in Magic? — Lennon Spex — Mama Told Me Not to Come — The Double Felix — Earth Shoes — Flying the Flannel — Queen of the Pixies, King of the Imps — The Cobain Sweater.
ISBN 1-56858-032-0
1. Science Fiction, American. I. Title.
PS3554.I3915F55
813'.54—dc21   97-11712
                                                    CIP

Text design by Acme Art, Inc.
10 9 8 7 6 5 4 3 2 1
Printed in the United States

Copyright Acknowledgements

Master Blaster and Whammer Jammer Meet the Groove Thang ©1991 *Pulphouse*.
Fractal Paisleys ©1992 *The Magazine of Fantasy and Science Fiction*.
Do You Believe In Magic? ©1989 *The Magazine of Fantasy and Science Fiction*.
Lennon Spex ©1992 *Amazing Stories*.
Mama Told Me Not To Come ©1992 *Amazing Stories*.
The Double Felix ©1994 *Interzone*.
Flying the Flannel ©1996 *Interzone*.
The Cobain Sweater ©1997 *Interzone*.
Earth Shoes and *Queen of the Pixies, King of the Imps* have not previously been
published. © 1997 Paul Di Filippo.

My sincere thanks to Leslie Eng Newton, able to juggle babies and disks
simultaneously and with equal facility!

Dedication

To the memory of Thorne Smith, the Original Shaggy Dog.

To my parents, Frank and Louise, who taught the value of laughter.

*To all those blithe spirits who, in the face of the dire, the serious,
the responsible, the demanding, and the authoritarian,
'e felt impelled to slouch a little lower in their chairs, mutter,
"Uh, yeah, whatever," and pop another beer.*

*And to Deborah, Mistress of Bon Mots, who coined the term
"trailer park science fiction."*

Table of Contents

Fractal Paisleys

Surely you too must have asked yourself at one time or another: "What if I put Stevie Wonder and Peter Wolf (of J. Geils fame) together in a van, along with a Filipina Lolita, and sent them all on an interstellar joyride?" Of such commonsensical questions are SF stories born. By the way: I find this archetypical pair turning up later in Thomas Pynchon's Vineland *(1990), as the darker Blood and Vato, convincing me of their Jungian pre-existence.*

Master Blaster and Whammer Jammer Meet the Groove Thang

MASTER BLASTER IS PROBING THE CLUTTER on the dashboard shelf, his black hands moving like delicate parti–colored tarantulas among the assorted odds 'n' ends. Empty cigarette pax, a styrofoam Big Mac box redolent of grease, a road map somehow unfolded into a topological nightmare. Keys, wires, washers, a lorn tampon Dewey lost one day, dingy in its paper sleeve. A screwdriver with a chipped tip, oily rags, matchbooks, discarded pine-tree-shaped cardboard air-fresheners, pennies, the innersole of a shoe. . . .

Not finding what he is searching for, Master Blaster turns to his friend Whammer Jammer, who is driving. Master Blaster's long adorned colorful braids click ceramically together, sounding like a bead curtain stirred by a breeze. "Hey, Peter," says Master Blaster, "you see my Drive 'n' Drink cup anywhere?"

Whammer Jammer is a tall skinny white dude with a heavy five o'clock shadow spread across sharp features. He is wearing a blue bandana on his head, knotted in back. There is one silver stud in his right earlobe. He is dressed, as is his companion, in grungy brown patched Carhartt overalls, liberally stained, the insulated lining poking out of rips and tears.

He turns his head briefly toward Master Blaster and sees himself reflected in the black man's dark glasses.

"How come?" inquires Whammer Jammer.

"It still had some coffee in it yesterday, and I could really go for some now. It's ten already, and I ain't had a sip yet."

Whammer Jammer rolls his eyes hopelessly. "Check the floor, Stevie."

Master Blaster bends over and begins to rummage among the trash and debris on the floor. Shortly he straightens up, triumphantly holding a cup capped with a drink spout. He raises it to his lips and takes a pull at the plastic nipple. Only dry sucking noises results, like wind whistling over desert sands at high noon in the middle of summer.

"Shit," says Master Blaster. "Musta spilled out on the floor. I wonder if we got enough pennies here for some fresh jamoke. . . ." He begins collecting the loose change from the dashboard shelf by touch.

"We might need that money for gas," warns Whammer Jammer, ever the more cautious of the two. Then, more selfishly: "And I'm outa smokes."

The men are driving down a highway on the outskirts of their hometown in a battered, dented, rusted white Ford Econoline van whose muffler is attached only by bent coathangers. Mounted with ropes of pantyhose on the front grill is a revolting, molting stuffed moosehead which gives the van its name: Bullwinkle. On each side of Bullwinkle the van is hand-lettered the name of their raggedy-ass enterprise:

MASTER BLASTER AND WHAMMER JAMMER
HAULAGE, CARTAGE, FREIGHT AND MOVING
BASEMENTS, ATTICS AND GARAGES CLEANED
"IT AIN'T HEAVY, IT'S MY RUBBLE"

Temporarily deprived right now of both nicotine and caffeine, Master Blaster and Whammer Jammer are a little touchy, a trifle irritable, tending, in fact, toward downright despair. Money's too tight to mention, rent's due, their bellies are empty, and they haven't had a job in a week. And their last commission wasn't anything to boast about anyway. It was an assignment they perennially got, whenever the hometown trawlers made an especially large catch. Trucking loads of fish gurry—intestines, heads, fins, tails—from a local dockside processing plant out to the dump. Packs of alleycats gathered wherever they parked, and the interior of Bullwinkle still smells like low tide at the mud flats.

They've got to keep on keepin' on, tho. Nothing for it but to plunge on heedless of economic ill-fortune or the inexpungeable odor of fishguts, the malice of their fellow man—embodied in the ire of Mister Histadine, their landlord—or the ravages of bad weather and chapped hands.

"Whadda ya say we check out the dump for something we can salvage and sell?" asks Whammer Jammer of his partner.

"Sure," says Master Blaster. "We can scavenge some aluminum cans for the deposits anyway."

Out they head then, under the winter-grey sky, along the familiar road lined with winter-bare trees that look somehow like a child's stick figures, their muffler whumping away, Bullwinkle's shot suspension transmitting every bump in the pavement directly into their bony frames.

As they pass by one certain spot, seemingly no different from any other, Whammer Jammer ceremoniously beeps the horn.

"The Dewey Budd Memorial Roadside Rest Area," says Master Blaster.

"Yeah," says Whammer Jammer.

At the gate in the fence around the dump they pull to a stop beside Famous Amos's shack.

Famous Amos is the dumpman in charge of the vast smoldering odorous acreage. Naturally, in their particular line of business, Whammer Jammer and Master Blaster have come to know the slothful and contumacious old drunkard quite well. This acquaintanceship has not necessarily led to affection.

"You think we'll have to pay the bastard to get in today?" asks Master Blaster.

"Hope not."

The door of the shack opens askew on its single hinge, its bottom dragging through a permanent rut in the dirt, and Famous Amos emerges. The man's grizzled and normally suspicious face is wreathed today in beneficience and goodwill.

"Howdy, boys. Whatcha carryin' today?"

Whammer Jammer looks at Master Blaster for confirmation of this oddity. The blind man has his left ear cocked at Famous Amos as if he just heard a stone speak.

"Why, nothing, Amos," replies Whammer Jammer. "Just wanna pick thru the piles a little."

"Sure, sure, go ahead, be my guest."

Whammer Jammer puts the van in drive but holds his foot on the brake for a moment. "Say, Amos—anything wrong?"

Famous Amos is watching a seagull rapturously as the bird swallows a moldy orange peel. "Lookit that there bird, it's so beautiful."

"Amos—"

"Huh? Oh, no, boys, nothin's wrong. Jest the opposite, in fact. I feel so good today I could piss holy water. Don't know why, jest woke up that way."

"What you been drinking today, my man?" says Master Blaster.

"Nothin' but water, Stevie, nothin' but."

Whammer Jammer releases the brake and the van rolls forward.

"Okay, then—I guess. Take it easy, Amos."

Out of earshot of Famous Amos, Master Blaster says, "Whatever he's got, I hope it's not contagious."

"You said it."

They drive around the narrow dump trails for a time, looking for the latest, unpicked goodies. Neither partner says anything. Spooked by Famous Amos's sudden conversion and the notion that it might be catching, each man is intently examining his inner being, alert for signs of change.

Master Blaster speaks up first.

"Pete?"

"Yeah?"

"I don't feel no coffee jones no more."

"I could go without a butt for at least another year or two."

"This is weird."

"Creepy."

"Hey, turn left here!"

Whammer Jammer complies, then asks, "Why?"

"I feel it stronger this way."

They round a heap of garbage with a dilapidated couch perched atop it like some mock throne. The compacted multitextured strata of trash are open and flat here, like the foundation of a city four thousand years old with the city mysteriously vanished.

Out in the middle of the plain is a small humming fracture in the air, about the size of a giant panda. There seems to be something inside the shimmery air, a creature of some sort. Whammer Jammer tries to focus his vision on the atmospheric warp. He gets a quick impression of fur. Then the defect vanishes, seeming to implode.

"Hey, I felt it move!" says Master Blaster.

"I know, I know," says Whammer Jammer, feeling somehow disappointed to have lost sight of the anomaly.

The boys lever open their doors and step out. Something impells them to walk around to the back of the van.

The thing is there.

This time Whammer Jammer sees skin smooth as latex for a second, before the fuzzy air disappears again.

"It's out front now," says Master Blaster.

They walk to the open field of trash. The thing is in a different spot, a perpetual heat-shimmer in the middle of winter. As soon as Whammer Jammer's eyes light on it, it pops to another location. He looks again. Pop! Look, pop, look, pop. . . . It's like playing teleport chess. This could go on all day. . . .

"What's making it jump around like that?" asks Master Blaster.

Whammer Jammer explains. "I want to get close to it. But how can we if we can't even look at it?"

"Hear that noise it's making? Suppose I try to to zero in on it by listening?"

"Worth a try."

Master Blaster shifts his head toward the nearly subsonic vibrations from the thing. But the intelligent application of his aural perceptions has the same effect. The thing bounces in and out of existence, relocating halfway across the yard of garbage.

"It's obvious now what's going on," says Whammer Jammer, sounding none too certain.

"Oh yeah?"

The man tries to talk thru a theory still in formation. "This thing is some kind of creature from somewhere else in the universe—"

"Yeah, I'll buy that."

"—and it is plumb full of what you might call quantum uncertainty."

At one time, Whammer Jammer took a night-school course called "New Age Physics: Channeling the Cosmic Tao."

"Say what?"

"Well you see, on a very fundamental level, every particle we are made of is just plain unknowable. Anything you learn about these little bitty things subtracts certainty from another aspect of 'em. By trying to see and hear this thing, we are obviously concentrating its uncertainty into its physical location, so it is forced to jump elsewhere."

"You know best, bro'. So, how we gonna sneak up on this thing?"

"We got to try not to look or listen to it."

Master Blaster and Whammer Jammer go back to the van. They find some kleenex, shred them and stuff their ears. Whammer Jammer takes off his bandana and ties it around his eyes.

"How the hell do you live like this!" shouts Whammer Jammer.

"It's easy once you get used to it!" yells Master Blaster.

Hand in hand, they advance across the trashyard, zeroing in on the thing by some ineffable inner sense that does not appear to disturb it. Step by step, the thing's peaceful, happy aura increases. Pretty soon, the two men feel ecstatic, queasy, enraptured. It is as if their beings were taut guitar strings lightyears long, being plucked by some celestial Eric Clapton, and they were fulfilling the essence of their existences.

"Oh, man, I never felt like this before. . . ."

"Me neither. It makes me feel like I do when the Rascals sing 'Groovin'."

At last they know they must be almost on top of the alien. The new sensations are so intense that it's hard to think, hard to even remember ever having thought.

Without meaning to, Whammer Jammer rips off his blindfold. He has to see the source of his joy. . . .

They are suddenly empty.

The thing is gone, nowhere to be seen.

"Oooh," moans Master Blaster, "now why'd you have to go and do that?"

"Sorry, man."

They walk dispiritedly back to the van.

The closer they get to Bullwinkle, the better they feel.

With a hand on the door, Master Blaster states the obvious.

"It's inside Bullwinkle."

"I know."

"Quick, stuff your ears again! Can you get in without wanting to look at it?"

"I'll force myself."

"How about driving? Can you concentrate?"

"It'll be hard, but I'll try."

"Okay. Let's bring this thing home to Dewey. She'll love it."

They get in the van, which suddenly looks to Whammer Jammer's transfigured gaze like a Hindu temple, fantastic, ornate.

"It don't smell like fish no more," says Master Blaster.

"More like roses."

"Roses. . . ," says Master Blaster, then starts to laugh, a big hearty roar. Whammer Jammer joins in. The alien just behind their backs seems to laugh too. Tears roll down their faces.

When they are done, Whammer Jammer says, "Man, I could groove to this ol' thing all day long."

"Groove Thang!" corrects Master Blaster.

All the way back to the city, the Groove Thang hums contentedly behind them, putting out waves of pulsing, intoxicating vibes.

By the time they pull up in front of their tenement, the baleful moosehead on the grill is smiling, its patchy skull positively radiating health and zest for life. Bullwinkle the van looks as proud as a mile-long Lincoln Continental.

The doors open and the two men stumble out, hanging for a moment on the doorjambs.

"In-tense!"

"Have mercy!"

"That Groove Thang is deffer than a pot of espresso laced with Kahlua."

"Tuffer than Turkish tobacco."

"Wait till Dewey gets a hit of ol' Groove Thang!"

Whammer Jammer tries to summon up a bit of his cautious competence as counterweight to all this enthusiasm. "How we gonna get it inside, tho?"

"We could try spookin' it, and hope it jumps into the house. . . ."

"Great, and what if it jumps into, say, Mister Histadine's apartment?"

"Oh. . . . Well, suppose we was to just pick it up and carry it in?"

Whammer Jammer considers. "Do you think we could?"

"Look at it this way. If I stuff my ears, I can't hear or see it to get any information from it. I should be able to lay hands on it okay."

"Yeah, but you know how strong it felt when we were still a few feet away. What'll happen when you touch it?"

"I'll just have to take a chance. We could maybe cover it up somehow, so I don't actually make contact with it."

Whammer Jammer feels the surging waves of euphoria pouring from the Groove Thang right thru Bullwinkle's walls. "I don't think that's gonna help much. But if you wanna try. . . ."

"Sure."

Whammer Jammer goes up to the front porch of their ramshackle tenement, where a couple of paint-spattered tarps are lying folded. He takes one and returns to the van.

"When I say go, Stevie, you swing both doors open."

"Roger!"

"Go!"

Master Blaster yanks Bullwinkle's back doors wide, and Whammer Jammer, holding the unfolded tarp by two corners, twirls half round, eyes shut, and lets it fly into the van like a matador's cape.

Then he dares to open his eyes.

Inside the van is a shapeless, tarp-covered lump. The Groove Thang has not moved. Apparently, not enough information is leaking thru the tarp to focus its uncertainty.

"It's still there, Stevie. No offense, but I guess I could pick it up as good as you now, and I wouldn't trip or nothin' carrying it in."

"Be my guest, bro'."

Whammer Jammer puts a foot on Bullwinkle's sill and one hand on the jamb. His heart is racing, and he nearly jumps out of his skin when a voice calls from the porch.

"Hey, I'm thinking I heard you guys out here. What's going on?"

Dewey Budd is a sixteen-year-old Filipina about five-foot one and ninety pounds. Her glossy hair is black as squid ink and falls halfway down her back. Her complexion is dusty olive. She wears no makeup, is dressed in a white buttoned shirt belonging to Whammer Jammer, pink stretch pants and bare feet.

Dewey was born Dewey Pagano, in a small village outside Manila. Her parents named her after Admiral Dewey, hero of the Battle of Manila Bay (May 1, 1898). When she was twelve, Momma 'n' Poppa Pagano sold her to a whorehouse in the city. There, she met a sailor named Beauregard "Bodacious" Budd, stationed at Subic Bay. They fell into something approximating love, and one night, when Budd was extremely drunk, they got married.

Back in the States, after Budd's discharge, he found himself without a job. He had been trained in maintaining submarine nuclear reactors. This was not exactly a growth industry in the States. Budd began to drink more heavily. Dewey began to sport black eyes.

One day Whammer Jammer and Master Blaster were driving down the dump road when they—Whammer Jammer anyway—saw this foreign adolescent girl hitchhiking. The partners stopped to pick her up.

"Where you going?"

"To live in the dump."

"You can't do that."

"Hey, how come you gonna tell me lies? People do it alla time back home."

"Where the hell is home?"

"Pill-a-peens," said Dewey, lapsing in her sorrow into the native pronounciation. Then she began to cry.

She came to live with Stevie and Peter that day two years ago. Budd had appeared belligerently looking for her shortly thereafter. Master Blaster and Whammer Jammer had stuck his head in a barrel of gurry and booted his ass halfway down the block. He never came back.

"What you boys got in there?" says Dewey, advancing a step or two down the porch. Ice underneath her bare feet makes her hop back up. "I'm feeling some sort of major weirdness now."

"Something you're not gonna believe, Dewey. Just hold on a minute, we're bringing it in."

Whammer Jammer enters Bullwinkle now. The emotional radiance of the Groove Thang is mounting the closer he gets, a powerful beat warming his head and heart and groin. Before he can be overpowered and transfixed, he tosses himself at the alien.

For a microsecond he feels something like an armadillo. Then in instant succession it changes to a snake, a tiger, a butterfly, a flower— Wrestling Proteus, fer shure. . . .

Whammer Jammer falls face first to the floor. The Groove Thang is gone, dispelled along other dimensions by Whammer Jammer's gain of tactile information.

And the Groove Thang has taken the tarp with it.

"It's out here!" yells Dewey.

Whammer Jammer gets painfully up and exits the van.

The Groove Thang, still tarp-covered, is sitting in the middle of the street.

"Let me try," says Master Blaster.

Rush, tackle, pop. Dewey screams. The Groove Thang has materialized right beside her on the porch. Then her face goes all slack and gooey with bliss. She moves in a hypnotized fashion to embrace the Groove Thang. Whammer Jammer, standing on the brown winter-dead lawn holds his breath, wondering where Dewey's embrace will send the alien next.

She wraps her arms around it.

The Groove Thang lets her.

"Holy shit!" says Whammer Jammer.

"It's not jumpin', Pete?" guesses Master Blaster. "Dewey, Dewey, pick it up!"

"Bring it inside, quick, get it in the house!"

As if from deep within a trance, her dark eyes glazed over, Dewey obeys. She clutches the tarp-covered Groove Thang to her in a bear-hug, bent slightly backward to lift it off the porch. Then she waddles into the house.

She makes it up the stairs to their third-floor apartment before succumbing completely, coming to a halt in the front room as if frozen.

"Drop it, Dewey, drop it!"

No reaction. Tentatively, Master Blaster and Whammer Jammer sidle up to her, grab her arms—instant electric transmission of the Groove Thang's full power threatens to blank out their minds—and tug her away.

All three sprawl out on the floor. Dewey is unconscious, the other two nearly so. After a minute the boys get up and carry Dewey to the room farthest from The Groove Thang.

She wakes up shortly.

"What'd it feel like under the tarp?" asks Whammer Jammer.

"Can you tell us what kind of Groove Thang it is?" says Master Blaster. "Like, animal, vegetable or mineral?"

"I don't remember nothing so specific, guys. My mind wasn't working that way. That's gotta be why he lets me hold him, cuz I got the right kind of thinking. You Western boys too analytical. You gotta learn my secret Oriental ways if you wanna touch him. But I'm telling you—he's worth it! I can feel him even now."

"He?" says Whammer Jammer.

"Him?" echoes Master Blaster.

"Oh, yeah, that's one thing I did learn. Your Groove Thang's a he."

Pete and Stevie register dubiousness. Dewey takes offense. "Hey, you think I don't know men, you got another think coming!"

They leave it at that. But from now on, the Groove Thang is no longer an "it." Dewey just won't allow such inexact terminology.

When they feel completely recovered, they look slyly and shyly at one another. Here in the far room they can still feel the inexhaustible outpouring of the Groove Thang in an attenuated form which is nonetheless strong enough to make them smile continuously, in a goofy way.

"Should we go back in there with it?" says Whammer Jammer.

"Him, I told you, it's a him."

"Well," says Master Blaster, "why shouldn't we? Ol' Groove Thang can't hurt us, he just feels good. Real good. And you know, during that time at the dump when we were so close, I sorta got the impression that he liked having people around. He might need us as much as we need him. Who knows—maybe we give off some kind of vibes that Groove Thang gets high on. . . ."

"Okay," agrees the cautious Whammer Jammer. "But I'm worried about us catching some hint of his shape thru the tarp. We don't want him jumping again. So we've got to fix some kind of screen around him."

Dewey dashes suddenly for their bed in the corner and yanks off all the blankets and sheets.

"Gotcha," says Whammer Jammer.

In a few minutes, working tipsily atop a step-ladder within the Groove Thang's sphere of utmost potency, clumsily wielding hammer and nails, the trio have erected a makeshift tent around the tarpaulin-clad Groove Thang. They stand back to admire their handiwork.

"Maybe he's uncomfortable with that canvas on him," suggests Dewey dreamily. "No reason he needs it now."

Whammer Jammer kneels down and slides one hand and arm under the blankets puddled on the floor. Then he pauses. "What am I supposed to be doing?" he asks.

"I forget. . . ," says Dewey.

"Um, you're reaching for something. . . ," hints Master Blaster.

Whammer Jammer feels a scratchy canvas corner and intuitively yanks it back out with him.

"I guess that's that," he says to his companions.

But there is no reply. Master Blaster is collapsed spinelessly on the couch, Dewey seated spraddle-limbed on the floor with her back against his dangling arm.

Whammer Jammer crawls over and lies down with his head cradled in Dewey's lap.

As in a dream contained within the mind of a god, time passes. Maybe. It might just possibly be stopped for good. The three people remain unstirring, their breathing shallow, adrift on the soft, rose-scented seas of the Groove Thang's harmonic soporific aura. Their minds are filled with a shapeless calm and peace, not so much an absence of all unhappiness as a presence of all that is good and pleasing. This hyperaware oblivion stretches on endlessly, everything they could ask for, the ultimate in contentment. All their cares are forgotten. Money-, coffee-, cigarette-hunger, the memory of being slapped around—all are negated, made less than nothing.

The gatekeeper of the universe has locked himself out and is pounding on the mile-high brazen doors with his mammoth steel-wrapped fists.

Whammer Jammer pulls himself reluctantly back to reality. The knocking continues, only diminished in tone and importance. Whammer Jammer shakes Dewey and Master Blaster roughly.

"Wake up, someone's banging on our door."

Whammer Jammer tries to get to his feet. His legs feel like a string of loosely connected water-balloons. Dewey bestirs herself and starts to say, "My thighs are sure numb, boy—" when Master Blaster howls. "My arm is dead!"

Dewey pulls away from the arm she has been leaning on. "Sorry, Stevie."

"Can you move it, man?"

"No, it's dead, it's dead!"

Dewey and Whammer Jammer begin furiously to oscillate Master Blaster's arm, as if he is a balky pump. "Stop, stop! It's alive, it's alive—but that's worse! Yeee-oow! It's the baddest pins and needles I ever felt!"

Leaving Dewey to massage Master Blaster's arm, Whammer Jammer moves unsteadily to the door.

On the other side stands Mister Histadine, their landlord. Mister Histadine looks like a dyspeptic raccoon. Big black pouches under his eyes betray a soul too ill at ease with its sour self even to enjoy a good night's sleep. The accumulated bile, anger, jealousy, spleen and futile remorse of five decades has made Mister Histadine into a vengeful ogre.

Living on the first floor of the tenement, Mister Histadine is easily as close to the influence of the Groove Thang as Famous Amos was at the dump. But so constipated and cramped is his spirit that even now, standing only a few feet from the Groove Thang, Mister Histadine is still his old bitchy self.

Before Mister Histadine can say anything, Whammer Jammer asks, "What day is it?"

"Thursday, the first, as you well know, you scruffy little twerp. It's no use pretending with me to be spaced-out on some kind of drug. It's time for my rent, and I want it right now!"

Thursday. They've been under the influence of the Groove Thang for three days! Whammer Jammer's stomach suddenly clenches in on itself, and he feels intriguing pressures in his bladder and bowels. Holy Moly! They might've wasted away, had not Mister Histadine come knocking. Clearly, the Groove Thang has its possibilities for misuse. . . .

Whammer Jammer surveys the irate face before him. Mister Histadine looks ready to spit in his eye. Whammer Jammer decides to feel only gratitude to Mister Histadine, because he has saved their lives. Therefore he says, "Come right this way, Mister Histadine. We got what you're looking for right in here."

The landlord bulls past Whammer Jammer and down the hallway into the front room. Dewey and Master Blaster have retreated to the kitchen, where the effects of the Groove Thang are less.

Mister Histadine sees the blankets nailed to the ceiling, and manages to say, "This'll cost you your security deposit—" Then his features seem to shatter and crack, falling to pieces before reassembling themselves into an unprecedented beatitude.

"Stevie, Dewey, come help me carry Mister Histadine to the couch!"

With their landlord in a trance on the couch, the three room-mates—after a pisspot pitstop—sit down around the kitchen table for a strategy session.

At first they are a little tense from the unexpected intrusion and the way it has focused their attention back on the mundane demands of the outside world. But under the pervasive somatic throbbing of the Groove Thang they find themselves mellowing into a confident acceptance that somehow Everything Will Be All Right.

"First off," says Whammer Jammer, "what are we gonna do about Mister Histadine?"

"Can't we skip right to Problem Number Two?" asks Master Blaster.

"Okay. What are we gonna do with the Groove Thang?"

"Let's go back to Mister Histadine."

"I don't want that old monkey-faced bastard laying on my couch alla time," says Dewey. "I say let's wake him up and just tell him we don't got no rent money for him this month."

"Great. And we're out in the cold on our tails."

"I think maybe not, Pete. I think maybe Groove Thang be having some effect on even Mister Histadine, grouchy like he is."

"Any other ideas? No? Okay, we'll try it. Now, as for ol' GT—"

"We can't keep him to ourselves," says Master Blaster with a sense of earnest conviction that surprises them all, until they realize what he's said is just the plain truth. "He's too big and good for three people to monopolize. I say we share him with all our friends. With strangers, too. With everyone, in fact."

"I agree," says Whammer Jammer.

"Me too," chimes in Dewey. "And the more people we got here the better, because then someone can always be on duty like, to make sure no one stays in the groove too long. And if we got a lotta folks around, no one has to be watchdog for too long, without enjoying Groove Thang himself."

"I guess everything's settled then. I'll go wake Mister Histadine up."

"Not yet, Pete. The longer he stays in the groove, the better for us, I think."

"Good idea. Well, then—I don't know about you two, but I want a shower. Three days, and these coveralls feel like wallpaper on the wall."

The bathroom is closer to the Groove Thang than the kitchen. The hot steamy spray in the crowded shower feels like liquid kisses. Even in the bedroom, furthest from the radiant alien, the stained ticking of the bare mattress against their bare skin is smooth as cornsilk.

After dozing in a more normal sleep than they have had these past three days, the roommates dress and go to rouse Mister Histadine.

"Mister Histadine, hey, rise and shine, happytime's over! It's no good, he under deep. Steve, let's haul him outa here."

Out in the hall they shake Mister Histadine awake. When the landlord opens his eyes, he smiles. It is something the trio have never seen before. Even the bags under his eyes seem diminished in their morose puffiness.

"Hi, kids. Gee, you'd never believe where I've just been. It was a place—well, I don't really know where it was, but it was a long, long way from here. There were no burst water pipes or city taxes, no aching bunions or slipped discs. It was really, really peaceful."

"That's nice, Mister Histadine. Was there anything else you wanted to tell us?"

"No, no, not that I can remember. . . . Well, I guess I'll be going now." Mister Histadine put a hand on the doorknob, stopped, then turned. "Say, do you mind if I visit you again tomorrow?"

"No, man. I mean sure, anytime."

"Okay, see you later."

Mister Histadine leaves.

Dewey and Whammer Jammer exchange looks of relief, and Master Blaster wipes his sweaty brow.

"I wasn't quite sure that was gonna work. . . ."

There is the sound of footsteps ascending their stairs. Famous Amos sticks his head around the corner.

"Amos," says Whammer Jammer, "what's wrong? You ain't left that shack of yours in ten years."

"Since you boys drove outa the dump, I been feeling lower than a worm's belly. I wondered if you mighta knowed why?"

"C'mon in, Amos, we got the cure for what ails you."

After Amos is settled down in front of the Groove Thang, Whammer Jammer says, "I'm going out to round up some more people and spread the word."

"Dewey and I will take turns staying straight. And I'm gonna grab something to eat."

Whammer Jammer sets out. An hour later, he returns with a vanful of friends.

There is Hakim Bey, the Goofy Sufi; Ramona from Pomona and Sexy Sadie; Doug the Slug, Sol Solfeggio, and the Mojo Hobo; Sue St. Marie, Slick, and Nasty; Jeno and Daddy G.; Cavedog and Surf Nazi; Dixie Chicken and the Tennessee Lamb; and a couple of others. They all crowd up the stairs behind Whammer Jammer, eager to sample this new high he has promised them.

"How much is this going to cost us?" someone says.

Whammer Jammer stops in mid-step, deeply offended. "Nothing. I wanna make that very clear. It didn't cost us nothing, and it wouldn't be fair to charge anybody else. This is free, a gift from the Big Enchilada itself, Señor Cosmos."

Everyone is appropriately awed and hushed and reverent like.

When they get inside the apartment, of course, they understand everything.

This is the beginning of a month of frenetic activity somehow laced with serenity. Whammer Jammer, Master Blaster and Dewey are glad and proud to be spreading the gospel of the Groove Thang. News spreads fast about the mysterious high freely available in the apartment of the former trash-haulers and dump-pickers, and people begin to trickle in without personal invitation, attracted by word-of-mouth. They are made welcome. Most are content simply to bask in the aura of the Groove Thang, but some demand an explanation for what they are experiencing.

"It's a crystal that focuses mental vibrations," Whammer Jammer tells someone.

"It's a magic statue from my homeland," Dewey tells another.

"GT, he's like ET, only groovier," adds Master Blaster.

People accept whatever explanation appeals to them, or none. But they all keep coming back.

Eventually the trickle starts to turn into a flood, and the original finders of the Groove Thang are forced to institute a rigid, somewhat onerous system of Groove Thang utilization. . . .

Whammer Jammer is on door duty right now. He stands by a podium that holds one of those big appointment books that maitre d's use. There is also a machine for dispensing numbered tickets, as in a bakery. A couple approach the door, hand in hand.

"Hi, how're you doing today? Names, please? Fine, fine, here's your numbers. Tuck 'em in your pocket, so you don't lose 'em when your grip goes slack. Let's see, it's two o'clock now. That means we'll be waking you up at four. Try to find a spot to crash somewhere, don't step on anyone on the floor, please. Thank you, thank you very much."

This last comment is addressed to an unsteady departing fellow whom Dewey is showing out. The guy has dumped a handful of bills and change into a big wooden salad bowl at Whammer Jammer's elbow. For, despite the protestations of that first day, the trio have come to accept money for the privilege of basking in the presence of the Goove Thang. To their credit, they did not institute the practice.

People just began leaving money when they got up to go. At first, the roommates tried giving it back, but people insisted. It seemed that even the bounty of the Groove Thang meant more when people felt they had bought it. So the salad bowl was set up to hold contributions. It also works as a charity for those who need it, as anyone is free to take money from it too. Predictably, after experiencing the Groove Thang, no one abuses the freedom to take.

Dewey looks now at the money bowl. "This is just like that novel I read inna whorehouse, which some GI left behind. You know, *Stranger Inna Strange Place.*"

Whammer Jammer shakes his head wearily. "Well, I hope no Charlie Manson shows up. . . ."

It's later that evening, long after midnight. The three people sit around their kitchen table, ignoring the persistent knocking on their locked front door from a frustrated celebrant. (Each morning they open the door to find people sacked out on the stairs, enjoying the fringes of Groove Thang's aura.) They are tiredly munching sandwiches and discussing what they have wrought.

"This is almost like having a real job," says Whammer Jammer.

"Yeah, but it's in a good cause," says Master Blaster, as if trying to convince himself.

"Sometimes I could wish you guys never brought Groove Thang home," adds Dewey.

They sit in silence awhile, letting the object of their conversation extend his comforting mantle of bliss over them, unkinking their muscles and minds, kneading smooth their mental charley-horses.

"It's not such a bad life, handing out tickets by day," says Whammer Jammer.

"I'd miss Groove Thang if he was gone," says Master Blaster.

"Hey, Groove Thang, if you was listening, I didn't really mean it," says Dewey.

"You're talking to him nowadays, I notice," says Whammer Jammer.

"Yeah, I been feeling Groove Thang more like a person lately. It almost seems sometimes like he's trying to talk to me, so I talk back."

"There's never been any evidence that Groove Thang's even alive, you know. He doesn't eat, doesn't crap. . . ."

"Oh, he's alive, and he likes us—he's just real different from us."

Master Blaster speaks up. "You know, I've been thinking about how Groove Thang got here, to Earth."

"It's obvious. He jumped."

"Yeah, but consider, Pete: whenever we laid our senses on him, he jumped a few yards at most."

"Well, that must've been because we didn't get much information off him."

"Right. Our minds are too low-grade like."

"So?"

"So, what kind of mind could cause Groove Thang to jump across lightyears?"

The notion makes Whammer Jammer shiver. "Oh, I get what you mean. . . ."

At the end of another week with particularly high-volume attendance, the three are forced to abandon their apartment as living quarters. The Groove Thang's aura, seemingly fed by the attention lavished on it, has intensified to the point where anyone on the second floor of the building gets the same charge they used to feel only right next to the alien. (The elderly working-class Lithuanian couple who used to live there has moved out, explaining that they have invested their entire life-savings in a Club Med franchise.)

The amiable Mister Histadine gladly puts Peter, Stevie and Dewey up in his flat.

Some people aren't even bothering to come inside the house anymore. They hang around outside in the young spring air, grooving to the alien presence many feet away. Cops in cars arrive to investigate the gathering, and leave satisfied.

"He's putting out one hell of a signal now," says Whammer Jammer.

"Yeah," agrees Master Blaster. "I wonder who else can feel it. . . ."

Whammer Jammer shivers again, tho it's a warm day.

Looking out the window soon thereafter, Whammer Jammer spots "Bodacious" Budd, Dewey's husband, out in the crowd. Shit, just what they need, a confrontation. He hurries nervously outside.

"Okay, Budd, whadda ya want? Dewey ain't gonna talk to you, if that's what you're hoping."

"Oh, that's cool, I don't wanna see her, I just wanna stand here."

Whammer Jammer is left with nothing to say. "Oh. . . . Well, that's cool." He tries to see how far he can push Budd's new attitude. "You know, Budd, that Dewey, Steve and me are never gonna break up."

Budd's eyes are focused on infinity. "That's good. Whatever makes her happy. Hey, tell her I'm sorry, willya?"

Whammer Jammer shakes Budd's hand with unforced admiration. The Groove Thang's strength is passing all bounds now.

It's four AM. Master Blaster, Dewey and Whammer Jammer are sleeping peacefully, limbs sprawled this way and that. In a blink, all three awake instantaneously.

The continuous background presence of the Groove Thang has been reduced to a scared whimper in their minds.

They rush upstairs, barefoot, clad in boxer-shorts and tee-shirts.

The tent of blankets is still there. They can feel a frightened, diminished Groove Thang within.

Hovering above the Groove Thang is something they literally cannot look at. From it emanates an immense intelligence. Words fill their minds.

I HAVE COME FOR MY PET.

The next second they are standing hunched over in the back of Bullwinkle. The Groove Thang, covered in blankets, has jumped there, taking them along.

The Groove Thang's owner pops in a second later.

LET HIM GO.

The sun is shining. Bullwinkle sits in the middle of a featureless desert. It might be Africa.

"Let him go?" says Whammer Jammer in disbelief. He scrambles into the driver's seat automatically, as if he could drive them out of here, back to America. Master Blaster joins him up front, and Dewey comes to sit in his lap, throwing her arms around his neck. The van is heating up under the blazing sun.

GIVE HIM UP.

Whammer Jammer's head bumps the ceiling of the van. They're weightless. Bullwinkle spins eerily. The full Earth heaves into view in the front windshield, filling three-quarters of it.

"Hold your breath, hold your breath!"

HE DOES NOT BELONG TO YOU.

A puff of lunar dust rises from beneath Bullwinkle's tires. They have weight again. The full Earth is much smaller.

"Drive, drive!" yells Dewey.

"Where, where!" Whammer Jammer yells back.

HE WILL ONLY DO YOUR PLANET HARM.

Bullwinkle's tires loosely bite the grit composing Saturn's rings, adhering by microgravity. The van would appear to be riding a peaceful, curving, rocky, frost-rimed road back home, save for the gigantic planet visible through Master Blaster's window.

"We should be dead by now," explains Whammer Jammer calmly.

"Groove Thang's protecting us, I guess," says Master Blaster.

"If you can call it that—"

THIS IS YOUR LAST WARNING.

The next jumps come too fast for talk.

They are underwater, watching giant saurians feed.

They are riding a comet toward a fat red sun.

They are surfing on the wavefront of a nova.

They are in the middle of a crystal city peopled with beings with anteater snouts. A crowd of them flick long ropy tongues across

Bullwinkle to taste it briefly, before they jump again, still pursued.

They are in a glowing cavern, on a beach lapped by green waves, circling a cindered globe, falling into a black hole—

Suddenly all their anxiety is gone. They feel better than they ever have before, suffused with joy. It's almost more than their brains and hearts can stand. Looking out the window, Whammer Jammer sees a hundred fractures in the air of this world, a hundred Groove Thangs.

"It's GT's home. . . ," he says, before passing out from satori overload.

When Whammer Jammer opens his eyes, he sees they are parked out in front of their house. He stretches luxuriously, turns to Dewey and Master Blaster beside him. They all must've fallen asleep inside the van somehow, although he could swear he remembered going to bed.

"Wow, what a dream I just had, guys—"

PAY ATTENTION.

"Yeow!"

I WILL GIVE YOU ANYTHING YOU ASK FOR, BUT YOU MUST VOLUNTARILY RELEASE MY PET FROM THE BONDS YOU HAVE CREATED WITH IT. YOU, THE ONE CALLED MASTER BLASTER—WOULD YOU LIKE TO SEE AGAIN?

"Hey, man, I was born blind. I'm used to it now."

WHAT ABOUT YOU, DEWEY BUDD? I CAN MAKE YOUR HUSBAND DEVOTED TO YOU.

"I got two guys now, I couldn't handle no more."

SURELY YOU WOULD LIKE WEALTH, WHAMMER JAMMER?

"No thanks. We just want to keep the Groove Thang."

"Yeah!"

"Right!"

The Groove Thang's owner is silent. The three humans wait. They would be scared, but the Groove Thang is putting out reassuring waves aimed right at them.

VERY WELL, YOU WIN. I SUPPOSE I MUST TRAIN ANOTHER. BUT YOU CANNOT KEEP HIM JUST AS HE IS. FROM NOW ON, HE WILL BE ATTUNED ONLY TO YOU THREE.

And with that, the second alien's gone.

"Well," says Whammer Jammer after a moment, "I guess we got what we wanted."

"I suppose," says Master Blaster.

"Hey, Groove Thang, how you feel about this deal?" asks Dewey.

And the Groove Thang—he just sit there and hum.

When Ed Ferman purchased this story for F&SF, he called it one of the funniest he had ever read. That was high praise indeed, although I'm not sure the story sits at the very pinnacle of comic SF. But I think it does capture a Thorne-Smithian ambiance quite well. The Li'l Bear Inn actually exists in Tiverton, Rhode Island. I've never dared set foot inside, for fear of ending up on its walls.

Fractal Paisleys

THAT NIGHT THE LI'L BEAR INN was as crowded as the last copter out of Saigon.

But the atmosphere was a little more frenzied.

All three pool tables were hidden by tight packs of players and spectators, protruding cues making the whole mass resemble a patchwork porcupine. The dartboards looked like Custer's troops. Harley Fitts was rocking the pinball machine toward a high score: a sizable task, given that two sisters who called themselves Frick and Frack were perched on it. Rollo Dexadreen was monopolizing the single videogame as usual. Archie Opterix, on kazoo, was accompanying Gig von Beaver—who was making farting noises with a hand under his armpit—in a rendition of "Born To Run." Kitty Koerner was dancing atop the jukebox, which was playing Hank Williams Junior, though Kitty was doing something that looked like the Watusi.

Above the sounds of clicking pool balls, thwocking darts, ringing bells, exploding aliens, kazoo, farts, Hank Junior, and the bug-zapper hung outside the screen-door that gave onto the gravel parking lot, the calls for drinks were continuous.

"Tracey, two shots!"

"Tracey, another pitcher!"

"Tracey, six rum 'n' cokes!"

The woman behind the bar—Tracey Thorne-Smith—was on the tall side, and skinny as a book of poems by a sixteen-year-old virgin. She had long straight brown hair and a sociable smile, though her features were overlaid with signs of worry. She wore a white shirt knotted above her navel, and a pair of cheap jeans. Moving like an assembly-line worker with the belt cranked up, the piece-work rate cut in half and the next mortgage payment due, she paused only long enough to wipe the sweat from her forehead now and then.

A weary waitress appeared at one end of the crowded bar, where she set down her tray. She was short and round-faced, and her wavy hair—dyed a color not found in nature—was pinched in a banana-clip, one tendril escaping to hang damply against her cheek.

The bartender moved down to take her order.

"What'll it be, Catalina?"

"It's 'lick it, slam it 'n' suck it' time again, Trace. Larry and his city-friends, in the corner there."

"Four margaritas coming up."

Catalina leaned gratefully on the bar. "Lord, it's hot! You think that cheap bastard would get some air-con in here."

Her back to Catalina, Tracey said, "You best not hold your breath waiting for the Westinghouse van to arrive, Cat. You know well as I do that Larry's been pinching every penny, so's he can buy into the syndicate those boys he's with represent. And something tells me he's pinched himself a considerable sum, what with the way those lizards are crawling all over him. No, I wouldn't count on no air- conditioning anytime soon." Tracey set the salt-rimmed glasses two at a time on Catalina's tray. "How they tipping tonight?"

The waitress tucked the loose hair behind her ear. "Not bad. But I aim to get a little more out of Larry later, after closing."

Tracey made a sour face. "I don't see how you can bring yourself to be nice to him like that."

"Oh, he's not that bad. He's been real lonely since Janice died. It's downright pathetic sometimes. He keeps telling me, 'She was my

Honeypot, and I was her Li'l Bear.'"

"Eee-yew!"

Primping her hair, Catalina said, "That remark don't show much sympathy, Tracey, nor much common sense. You should try being nice to Larry, like I do. Might get yourself a little bonus. You sure could use it, I bet, what with Jay Dee being outa work."

"Forget it! Not only would I never let that man touch me in a million years, but if I did and Jay Dee found out, he'd kill him. Why, he can just about stand me working here as it is."

Catalina shrugged. "Your call. It's not like you're married or nothing."

After Catalina had sashayed away, Tracey went back to filling the non-stop orders.

She was bending over for a fresh bottle of Scotch when she felt a hand on her rear-end.

"You shore got a nice ass for such a skinny—gack!"

Tracey straightened up and turned around. "Jay Dee," she said, "turn that poor sucker loose."

Jay Dee McGhee removed his chokehold from beneath the impulsive patron's jaw and released the burly man's wrist, which he had been holding at about jaw-level, only behind the man's back. Shoving the gagging man away from the bar, he dropped down onto the vacant stool.

"Draw me a Bud, Trace. I had a long hot walk."

Jay Dee was shaggy and unshaven, with the looks of a mischievous five-year-old, perhaps one just caught affixing a string of firecrackers to a cat's tail. He wore a green workshirt with the sleeves ripped off and the same K-Mart-brand jeans as his girlfriend. In fact, they were a pair of hers, since the two were much of a size. He had a tattoo on each wiry bicep: on the left was a dagger-pierced, blood-dripping heart with the admonition TAKE IT EASY; on the right was a grinning horned and tailed pitchfork-bearing devil above the legend CLEAN AND SERENE.

Tracey pulled the tap. "You walked all the way from the trailer park?"

After a deep sip, Jay Dee answered, "How else was I supposed to get here? You got the car—not that it'd do me much good anyway—and ain't nobody we know gonna give me a ride."

Slopping a dirty rag onto the bar in front of her lover of six months and scrubbing violently, Tracey said, "Only thing is, you weren't supposed to come here at all."

"Jesus, Trace, gimme a break! How long can a man sit and watch television? Day and night, night and day! Zap, zap, zap with the damned remote! I'm going outa my head! I hadda get out."

"But why here? I told you, I get nervous with you around when I'm trying to wait on people. I can't do my job."

"It's a damn good thing I did come, or the next thing you know, that asshole would've had your pants off."

"Don't make me laugh. I can take care of jerks like that without your help. I got along just fine all those years before I met you."

"Well, maybe. Though the two black eyes and the busted ribs I seen them tape up at the clinic don't sound to me like you could take care of anything except getting knocked around."

Tracey glared. "I told you, Gene was a little too much for me. But you don't run into someone like him twice in your life. And what do you mean, you watched the doctor fix me up?"

"Well, it's true."

"The janitor at the Lakewood Walk-in Emergency Clinic was allowed to spy on patients?"

"It wasn't a case of being allowed."

"Oh, I get it. How many women did you size up, before you settled on me?"

"Well, lessee— Christ, Trace, we're getting off the track! The plain fact is, I missed you tonight! This routine sucks. With you working till two and sleeping till noon, I hardly get to see you no more. And then I got to rattle around in that tin can like a lone pea. . . . I'm sick of it!"

Tracey stopped polishing the counter. "I know, I know, Jay Dee. We're going through a rough time now. But it won't last forever. I don't like it anymore than you, but right now we need this job. And if Larry sees you here, after what happened the last time—"

"That fight wasn't my fault."

"It don't matter. He's still pissed at you. If I didn't work so good and so cheap, I woulda been fired right then."

"Well, there's no law says a man can't visit his girlfriend at work. Long as I don't cause no trouble, there's nothing he can do."

"This is his joint, Jay Dee, he can do whatever he— look out!"

Holding onto the bar, Jay Dee shoved his stool backward into the crotch of the man he had choked, who grunted and dropped the beer bottle he had been aiming at Jay Dee's head. While he was still recovering, Jay Dee laid him low with two succinct punches.

"It's plumb foolish to hold a grudge—" Jay Dee began.

"What in the hell is going on here?"

Larry Livermore was shaped roughly like a traffic-cone, and only marginally taller. Balding, he wore enough cheap gold around his neck to outfit a pawn shop window. He was accoutred in a checked shirt and lime-green trousers. Spotting Jay Dee, he turned to Tracey.

"I warned you about letting this troublemaker in here again, Thorne-Smith. And now he's made me look bad in front of some important friends, like I can't even manage my own joint. I don't need headaches like this."

Tracey had stepped out from behind the bar. "It won't happen again, Larry—I promise."

"I'm sure of it, 'cause I'm canning you now." Larry reached into his pocket, took out a roll of cash secured with a rubber band, and peeled off a hundred. "Here's half a week's pay. Take off."

Jay Dee moved menacingly toward the squat man. Larry's mouth opened in shock. "Hey, wait a minute—"

Tracey laid a hand on his shoulder. "No, Jay Dee, it's not worth it. Let's go."

Out in the parking lot, gravel crunched beneath their shoes. They walked silently to their car, a 1972 Plymouth Valiant, more rust than steel, its flaking chrome bumper bearing a sticker that advised ONE DAY AT A TIME. Tracey opened the passenger-side door and slid across the seat to take the wheel. Jay Dee got in after her. When the engine finally caught, they drove off.

Halfway back to the trailer camp, one of them finally spoke.

"You shoulda let me hit him, Trace."

Tracey swivelled her head angrily, taking her eyes off the dark road. "Hit him! Is that all you know how—"

There was a noise like a hundred-pound sack of flour being dropped on the hood of their car, and the sensation of an impact. Tracey slammed on the brakes.

"Could be a deer," said Jay Dee without much hope or conviction. "Though life has shown me that bad luck usually comes like an elephant. Namely, in buckets."

"I—I'll turn the car around so we can see what we hit. . . . "

Moving forward slowly, cutting the wheel, Tracey made a three-point turn.

There was a man lying in the middle of the road.

"Oh my god—"

Jay Dee got out.

The victim was a white guy in a business suit that appeared to be made out of rubber, with all the tailoring, including the shirt-front, stamped on. The suit continued onto his feet, forming shoes. He did, however, wear a separate tie patterned with paisleys. Something about the tie drew Jay Dee's fascinated gaze. Why, the borders of each paisley were formed of little paisleys. And the little paisleys were made of littler paisleys. And those were made up of even littler paisleys! And on, and on, and—

"What's the matter, Jay Dee?"

Jay Dee shook his head. "Nothing, I guess. . . . I just felt dizzy, like I was hanging over the edge of a skyscraper. . . . Hey, look— He's holding something—"

Prying open the dead man's hand, Jay Dee removed the object.

The thing squirmed for a moment in Jay Dee's grip, then settled down to solidity.

At that moment, a wave of shimmering disintegration passed down the man from head to toe. Then the corpse was gone.

"Mo-ther-fuck. . . . "

Tracey was squeezing his devil with both hands. "This is too spooky for me, Jay Dee. Let's split."

A minute later and a mile onward, Tracey asked, "What was in his hand, Jay Dee?"

" 'Pears to be nothing but a goddamn television remote." Jay Dee made to throw out the window, then stopped. "It's awfully big though. . . . "

Tracey made it back to the trailer camp in record time, without encountering any further obstacles. She pulled up alongside their home, an aqua-trimmed sag-roofed aluminum box with the former tenant's flower garden run to weeds that half hid the two creaky wooden steps braced against the side of the structure.

From the weeds emerged Mister Boots, a large tomcat the color of whole-wheat bread, and with white stockings. He carried a dead mouse proudly in his mouth. Spotting the car, he leaped inside through the open window to devour his feast in the privacy he required.

"Got to learn that cat some manners one of these days. . . . "

Inside, Tracey went straight for the bottle of vodka above the tiny sink full of dirty dishes. "Lord, I need a drink! I never knew that killing someone would feel like this—even if it was an accident."

Jay Dee flopped down into a beat-up chair. "Least when you kill someone you do a thorough job of it, Trace. No stiff left behind to clutter up things. Now look, calm down! Who knows what that was we hit? Chances are it wasn't even human, the way it vanished."

"I know, I know, that's what I've been telling myself since it happened. But it still leaves a person kinda shaky, you know?"

"Just take a pull and sit down. You'll feel better in a minute."

Jay Dee fell to examining the remote control he had taken from the corpse.

The black plastic device was about twice as big as a standard control, with more than the usual number of buttons. It had the usual smoky translucent cap on one end, where the signal would emerge. It bore no brand-name, nor were the buttons labeled.

But as Jay Dee studied it, this changed.

Gold letters appeared on the face of the device, seeming to float up from deep inside the case.

MASTER DIGITAL REMOTE ran the wording across the top of the case. Beneath each button smaller letters spelled out various odd functions.

One button was designated DEMO.

Jay Dee pressed it.

The control spoke.

"Please set me down on a convenient flat surface, pointed away from any objects of value, sentient or otherwise."

Tracey had her head in the fridge. "You say something, Jay Dee?"

Jay Dee leaned forward and calmly set the unit down on a table, making sure it was pointed at an exterior wall. "No, no, it's just this here box talking."

"Ha, ha, that's funny. Want a baloney sandwich?"

The control continued its speech. "I am a quasi-organic eleven-dimensional valve of Turing degree three. I am capable of modulating the Fredkinian digital substrate of the plenum."

"Say what?"

The control paused. "Call me a magic lamp."

Jay Dee got angry. "Hey, I'm not stupid. . . . "

Tracey approached with a plate of sandwiches. "I never said you were, hon."

"No, it's this smart-mouth box. Just 'cause I didn't understand all the ten-dollar words it threw at me, it started treating me like a kid."

"I am merely attempting to phrase my function in a manner most intelligible to the listener. There was no slur intended."

Tracey slowly set the plate down on the corner of Jay Dee's chair; it tipped, and the sandwiches slid into his lap. He jumped up and they fell to the floor, baloney draping his shoes.

"Perhaps an exhibition of my functions would clarify my nature. . . . "

"Sh-sure," said Tracey.

"First, we have 'smudge.'" A square foot of the wall in front of the talking remote lost all color, all features. It hurt to look at it. "'Smudge' simply strips all macroscopic features and quantum properties from an object, reducing it to bare digital substrate, the underlying basis of all creation."

"Not much use to that," said Jay Dee.

"You would be surprised. Once an object is smudged, we can use 'peel' to lift and superimpose a new set of spacetime characteristics on it. For example."

Mister Boots, as usual, had gotten in through a broken screen, and was now atop the table with the control. The box suddenly swivelled autonomously and aimed itself at the cat. A small square of fur was somehow peeled off Mister Boots—yet his hide was left intact. The square grew in size, then was lofted through the air like a two-dimensional piece of cloth to be superimposed over the smudge spot, becoming an integral fur patch on the trailer wall.

"Next, we should consider the 'checkerboard wipe.' This wipe dissolves any non-living object." Next to the fur patch, a portion of the wall big as a door flickered in a mosaic of squares, then was gone. The trees behind the trailer could be plainly seen. A breeze blew in.

"'Motes' will cause the dissolution of any living substance."

A cloud of infinitesimal glowing objects suddenly girdled the trunk of one tree. The next second they were gone, as was a clean chunk out of the tree. The upper part of the tree hung for a fraction of second, then began to tip toward the trailer.

Jay Dee and Tracey looked up from their prone position on the floor, Mister Boots between them. The roof of their rented home was buckled in a vee.

"Such minor mishaps can be easily corrected," said the box. "First, we use checkerboard and motes to dissolve the damaged roof and tree." The stars looked down on a stunned Tracey and Jay Dee. Mister Boots mewed plaintively. "Now, a new function: 'window.'" A window opened up in the air before their eyes, six inches off the floor. In it was displayed the ornate roof of the First National Bank in town. "Do you like this roof?"

"Yeah, sure, I guess. . . . "

"Using 'splinter,' we reassign its spatial coordinates and reassemble it in the correct place."

The window flew apart into flying shards, each of which contained its own piece of the original image. The shards expanded and somehow cohered above their heads into the roof of the First National.

The walls of the trailer began to creak under the new weight.

"Quick, Trace, outa here—!"

They were standing by the car. Mister Boots was inside Jay Dee's shirt, his head emerging from one ripped armhole. The trailer and all their meager possessions were crushed beneath the bank's stone pediments.

"At least we're shut of that goddamn box—" began Jay Dee.

A hole opened in the debris by checkerboard wipe. The Master Remote levitated out and floated to land atop the hood of the Valiant.

"I am sorry about the destruction. I was not aware of the flimsy construction of your dwelling. If I was Turing degree four, perhaps I would have had the foresight to examine its parameters, instead of taking your word that the roof was suitable."

Jay Dee started to make a sharp reply, then stopped. A curious look combining joy, revenge and a wet dream spread over his features.

Tracey grew alarmed. "Jay Dee, are you okay? You look like Saint Paul after the lightning hit him. . . . "

"I'm fine. In fact, I feel more full of piss than a Portajohn. C'mon, get in the car, Trace."

Jay Dee grabbed the Master Remote and hustled Tracey behind the wheel.

"Where are we going?" she asked when he was inside.

Mister Boots squirmed out of Jay Dee's shirt and leaped into the back seat to finish his mouse. "Back to the Li'l Bear. And after that, I think we'll pay a visit to the First National."

"Oh. I see. You really think—"

"I sure do. And so do you."

On the way out of the trailer park, the box said, "I have several more functions. Shall I demonstrate them now?"

"Hold on till we got us a target that deserves it," said Jay Dee.

There were still three cars in the parking lot of the Li'l Bear Inn, though it was long past closing.

Tracey clicked her nails on the steering wheel. "The Caddy is Larry's, and the Dodge is Catalina's. I figure the other must belong to those syndicate guys. What now?"

"I hadn't counted on this. . . . But it's no reason to back down. Let's check what they're doing."

There was one small window into Larry's office: it was frosted, and six feet off the ground. Light illumined it.

"I think I'll just make myself a little peephole," said Jay Dee.

"Why not? You're good at that."

Jay Dee started poking at the WIPE button. Nothing happened.

"Why are you doing that?" said the box. "It's unpleasant. You could simply ask for what you wanted."

"Why you got buttons then?"

"To conform to your notion of what I am."

"Oh. Well, drill me a peephole here then."

A patch of wall dissolved, revealing the back of a file cabinet. In the next second, a square tunnel opened up straight through the cabinet and its contents.

Jay Dee put his eye to the hole. He let out a low whistle.

"What's going on? Is Cat in there?"

"I expect she's somewhere in the pile. Unless those good old boys are getting off on each other."

"How disgusting! That poor thing!"

"I don't see her putting up much of a fight, nor complaining too loud."

"You wouldn't neither if your job depended on it, and you had two kids and no man at home. Quit goggling now, and do something."

Jay Dee addressed the remote. "Box, you got any way of immobilizing someone in a non-violent fashion?"

"I believe 'ribbons' would serve such a purpose. Would you like a demonstration first?"

"Save it for the real thing. Okay, Box, make us a door."

Studs, wires, insulation and plasterboard, all neatly truncated, formed the edges of the new door. Jay Dee stepped in, Tracey following.

The orgy dissolved in shock into its component naked people.

Larry's hairy obese stomach was quivering in indignation. "What the fuck—! Thorne-Smith, I'll have your butt for this!"

"No you won't, shithead. No way, no how. Box—ribbons on the men!"

Golden ribbons wide as a man's palm materialized, wrapping themselves around four sets of wrists and ankles before fastening themselves in fancy bows.

"Good job, Box."

Catalina had gotten to her feet and was trying to assemble her clothing, flustered as a rabbit caught in the open. "Tracey, I don't understand what's going on, but you know I always been a good friend of yours, haven't I? I even tried to talk Larry into giving you your job back. Didn't I, Larry? Tell her."

"Shut up, you dumb twat. I'll bet you were in on this."

Catalina had both her legs through half her panties and, oblivious, was trying to pull them up. "Larry, no, I swear it!"

The syndicate men had been eyeing Jay Dee coldly throughout. Now one said, "Kid, you're hash after this."

Jay Dee assumed a contemplative stance, one hand squeezing his chin. "You know, I don't like the way you all are talking at me. I think I'll just do something about it."

He pointed the remote at Larry's face and pressed SMUDGE.

Larry's face was replaced by a blank, eye-boggling surface. The results were so satisfactory to Jay Dee that he repeated the procedure on the other three men.

"Oh my god. . . . " Catalina dropped her panties and raised both hands in front of her face.

"Come off it, Cat. You know I don't hurt no women."

Catalina began to cry. Tracey moved to comfort her. Jay Dee turned to the old-fashioned safe in the corner.

Once the top was gone, the piles of cash were easy to lift out.

"Those appear cumbersome," offered the remote. "If you wish, you could store them in a 'cube.'"

"Let's see."

A silver cube appeared in the air; its lid elevated to reveal its empty interior.

"Where's it go when it ain't here?"

"It rolls up along several Planck-level dimensions you can't sense."

"Oh. Is that safe?"

"As houses."

"Good enough." Jay Dee began tossing the money into the cube. When he had emptied the safe, the remote shut the cube's lid and it collapsed on itself, dwindling along odd angles.

Tracey stood with her arm around Catalina, who was still sobbing, though less urgently. "Are you done now, Jay Dee?"

"Almost. I think I'd like to say goodbye to Larry. Box, give him back his face."

"Did you save it?"

"Shucks, I thought you were gonna handle everything. . . . "

"I cannot read minds."

"All right, this presents a problem. Lessee. . . . "

A stuffed moose-head was mounted on the wall. It caught Jay Dee's eye. He smiled.

"No, Jay Dee, it ain't natural—"

It was the work of a few seconds to peel off the moose's features and slap them on Larry's head.

The beady black eyes of the animal with the fat human body filled with intelligence—of a limited sort. Larry's head dipped under the unaccustomed weight of his new antlers. His wide wet nostrils flared. His snout opened to reveal a long stropping tongue. A sound midway between a moo and a sob issued forth.

"Larry, I just want to say thanks for Tracey's back pay for all her hard work, and for the extra compensation for the way you constant- ly ran her down. It was mighty generous of you. Which is why I done you the return favor of giving you a handsomer face than what you started out with. I predict you are gonna be a big hit with the ladies with that new tongue. It's been fun, but we gotta go now. C'mon, Trace. . . . "

Catalina cried out. "Jay Dee, wait! You can't just leave me here, now that Larry thinks I set him up!"

"That's true. Okay, you can come with us."

Tracey asked, "Are you gonna fix up those other guys with new faces?"

"No. It don't appeal to me."

On the way out, Jay Dee noticed a Rolex lying amid the discarded clothes of the syndicate men. He grabbed it and slipped it on.

Outside, Catalina, still naked, climbed into the back seat with Mister Boots, who eagerly assumed his rightful place in her lap. With Tracey driving, they roared off.

Jay Dee summoned up his cube full of money, and began to riffle through the bills. He broke open a stack and showered them down on his head. He let out a wild whoop.

"Girls, we got us the gold watch and everything! Let's see a smile."

Tracey let amusement break through the sober mien she had been maintaining. "I got to admit, Larry always did remind me more of a bull moose than a bear."

"You think you could afford to buy a girl a new dress with some of that?" asked Catalina.

"Buy? Why should we buy anything unless we absolutely hafta? Box, show the lady some clothes."

A window opened up onto the interior of a department store someplace where, judging by the light, it was early morning. The signs in the store were in French. The window onto a sunny world in the middle of the night-darkened car was like a dimensionless television. Catalina's eyes widened in amazement.

"See anything you like?"

"Um, that blue dress, and those shoes—size six—and that red teddy—"

The window splintered, reforming into the articles of clothing Catalina had named. She managed—with much attractive wiggling of her compact, generously proportioned body—to get dressed.

"Well," said Tracey, "are we going to the First National now?"

"I don't see any reason to be greedy, considering that we can reach inside a bank vault anytime we want. No, they're gonna need all their capital for a new roof. I say we put a few miles between us and our friends and then get us some rest. It's been a busy night." A thought occured to Jay Dee. "Box, can those ribbons be cut?"

"Yes. I was not aware you needed them to be indestructible."

"No, no, that's good. I don't wanna be responsible for killing anyone, even slimeballs like Larry and his buddies. They'll get loose sooner or later."

Catalina interrupted. "Jay Dee—exactly what you got there that's talking to you like that?"

"I don't purely know, Cat. But it sure is handy."

An hour's silent drive onward, the neon of a motel sign caught their eyes.

SEVEN BIRCHES MOTOR COURT
COLOR TV—WEEKLY RATES
VACANCY

"Looks as good as any place else we're likely to find. Pull in, Trace."

"None too soon, neither. The road was starting to float up at me."

"Ain't it funny," chirped Catalina. "I'm not sleepy at all! I feel like the night's still young!"

Tracey grunted, but refrained from comment. Jay Dee assumed a nervous look.

Coasting across a cindered lot, past the sputtering sign, they pulled up next to six long-decaying stumps and under a lone birch tree, its foliage as draggled and dusty as that of a desert palm. Jay Dee and Tracey piled wearily out of the car, while Catalina bounced around, holding Mister Boots, who had his forepaws on her shoulders and was butting his head under her chin.

"Cat, can't you quiet down?" said Trace. "I'm getting more and more tired just watching you."

"I can't help it, I feel wonderful! I'm shed of my horrible job, I got a new dress on, and I'm in the company of two rich friends. What more could I want?"

"Ain't you worried 'bout your kids?"

"Hell, no! I left 'em with my sister when I went to work, and she knows what to do with 'em if I don't make it home. I could stash 'em there for months! Cindy's got six of her own, so two more don't hardly make a ripple."

"Well, that's fine for you. But tonight already I done got my ass grabbed by a drunk, was humiliated in front of a whole room full of people by my boss, who immediately became my ex-boss, smashed my car into a thing from another world—which I apparently killed in some unnatural fashion—had my house come tumbling down around my ears, seen a man turned into a moose, and had to drive sixty miles just to find a place to lay my head down. So you'll excuse me if I'm not in a mood to party."

Catalina, crestfallen, stopped pirouetting; Mister Boots turned his head and hissed at his mistress. "Gee, Trace, I was just trying to be cheerful and show I was grateful for the rescue and the clothes, like. . . . "

"Well, just stow it till morning, okay?"

Jay Dee stepped conciliatorily between the two women. "Listen, girls, we're all dead beat. If we gotta have a contest of feminine wills, can't we get ourselves some sleep first?"

Tracey and Catalina said nothing. Jay Dee took this as assent. "Okay, good. One thing first, though. I wanna do something about this heap of ours. It's too easy to spot if anyone comes looking for it. Not that I expect Larry to have much luck tracking us down, even if he decides to venture out, looking like he does."

Pointing the remote at the old Valiant, he smudged it out to a heap of quivering nothingness. Then he peeled off the image of a new Lincoln Continental parked next to the MANAGER'S OFFICE, and superimposed it atop what had been their car.

Two Lincolns, identical down to the license plates, now stood a few yards apart.

Jay Dee laughed. "This is a hundred times better than boosting a car! Ain't nothing for the owner to report stolen!"

"Don't you think somebody's gonna notice something though?" asked Tracey.

"We'll be gone pretty early. And who compares plates, long as their own aren't missing?"

They headed to the lighted office.

The clerk was a guy in his early sixties, strands of white hair across a bald spot, crabby face like a clenched fist. He had a full ashtray in front of him and a lit Camel in his hand. Something old, grainy, black, and white filled the small television screen before him, Leo G. Carroll with the sound turned down.

"Two rooms," said Jay Dee. "Cash up front."

"You can't take that mangy animal in, buddy. I ain't having fleas in my sheets."

This was the last straw for an exhausted Tracey; she began to weep. "Muh-mister Boots always sleeps with us. . . . "

"Hold on, Trace, I'll take care of this."

Jay Dee raised the remote to point at the clerk, who remained unflustered at the seemingly innocent, though odd threat.

Tracey grabbed his arm. "No!"

"Oh, for Christ's sake. . . . All right, look—take this money, pay the man and sign us in. I'll put Mister Boots in the car for the night." His back to the clerk, Jay Dee winked broadly at Tracey, as if he knew what he was going to do.

Outside, Jay Dee, carrying the tom, stopped by a parked car. Visible in the back seat was a suitcase. Jay Dee paused, everything now clear.

"Box, save what this cat looks like, then smudge it."

The remote said, "Done." Then Jay Dee peeled off the image of the suitcase, which materialized like a wraith outside the car.

"Superimposition of a larger mass-pattern atop a smaller one causes an energy deficit which must be made up from some source," warned the remote. "I have been handling this automatically, but thought I should mention it."

"So you mentioned it. Now just turn this cat into some baggage."

The lights in the parking lot seemed to dim momentarily. Without further delay, the spatio-temporal digital suchness of the suitcase was layered onto the featureless lump of cat.

Jay Dee carried the suitcase back in.

"All set?" he asked.

Tracey held one key, Catalina another.

"Great, let's go."

The clerk warned, "Now don't try sneaking that cat in, 'cause I'll know it—"

At that moment, the suitcase meowed.

"So, you got it inside there. I thought so. Open it up."

Jay Dee set the suitcase down, flipped the latches, and sprang the lid.

The inside of the suitcase was lined deeply with fur, top and bottom, side to side; a clawed paw occupied each corner. Mister Boots, apparently none the worse for being turned into a living rug, looked up imploringly from his somewhat flattened skull.

"Meow?"

The clerk's eyes bulged out rather like Mister Boots's. He held up his hands as if to ward off an apparition. "Shut it, shut it!"

Jay Dee complied. "Can we go now?"

The clerk nodded violently. He made to reach for a bottle in the desk drawer, then apparently reconsidered.

The cinderblock units were strung out in a line, each sharing two walls with its neighbors.

Tracey and Jay Dee accompanied Catalina inside her room. The ex-waitress seemed to have crashed from her high. "Ain't it funny—I feel kinda sad now. Scared a little, too. What if Larry and his buddies come after us? I don't think I could take looking at somebody without a face all by myself, never mind three somebodies. Couldn't I—couldn't I share your room?"

"No way, Catalina. Look, we'll leave the connecting door open. And you can keep Mister Boots for company, since he seems to like you so much."

"I don't want no furry suitcase in here."

"No, we'll put him back together like his old self." Jay Dee quickly restored Mister Boots to his saved appearance. The cat rubbed itself happily against their legs, until Catalina reached down to pick it up.

The remote spoke. "Although your strategy worked, it would have made more sense simply to store the animal in a cube, shrink the cube, then open it inside the room."

"You can put living things inside one of them packages and roll 'em up eleven ways from Sunday without hurting 'em?"

"Yes."

Jay Dee nodded sagely, as if storing the information away for future use. "Well, goodnight, Cat. See you in the morning."

In their own room, Jay Dee and Tracey stripped and climbed bone-tired into bed.

Jay Dee awoke. Although it seemed he had been asleep for only five minutes, weak sunlight filtered in around the mishung curtains.

Catalina stood, naked and shadowy in the door.

"It's morning," she said.

Jay Dee hissed. "Jesus, Cat, go away—"

"Oh, let the poor girl in."

"Trace?"

"Shut up and slide over."

"I really do appreciate this, guys. Guy, I mean." Catalina giggled. "And girl."

Mister Boots joined them later, when things had quieted down.

Around noon, when Catalina was in the shower, Jay Dee said, "I don't know how many more nights like that I can take."

"Oh, don't pretend with me. You loved it."

"No, I ain't kidding. You're plenty of woman for me, Trace. Tossing Catalina into the pot is like adding fudge on top of butterscotch. It's just too much sweetness. And Lord, that girl would wear a mule out! No, we got to fix her up with someone fast."

Tracey came to sit in Jay Dee's lap. "I'm glad to hear you feel like that, Jay Dee. I don't mind comforting the poor thing for a while, but I'd hate to think you wanted to make it permanent."

Jay Dee leered. "Well, maybe we don't have to exactly rush to find her a man."

"Jerk!"

At their car, Tracey made to enter by the passenger's side, out of long habit, till Jay Dee stopped her. He conducted her to the driver's door and, with mock elegance, opened it for her.

"Why, thank you, sir."

Seated next to Tracey, Jay Dee looked over his shoulder for Catalina. Missing.

She stood outside the car, waiting patiently.

Jay Dee sighed, got out and opened her door for her.

"Why, thank you kindly, Mister McGhee."

They had a late breakfast at a truckstop diner named SHECKLEY'S MIRACLE CAFE and discussed their plans.

"Basically, Trace, I see us getting as far away from this crummy state as we can, out to where no one knows nothing about us, and settling down to a life of leisure. A nice big house, some land, maybe even some animals. Nothing too fancy. Swimming pool, maybe. And Cat—we'll set you up in a similar place, and you can send for your kids."

Tracey clinked her coffee cup down. "Sounds good to me."

"Me too," chimed in Catalina. "You can just fetch me a little old shat-toe from France or someplace and plunk it down next to a private beach."

"Oh, man, Catalina, get real! Wouldn't you stick out then like a tick on a bald dog's butt? You don't think your neighbors—not to mention the cops, the feds and anyone else you'd care to name— wouldn't get a little suspicious when they woke up and saw a house sprung up overnight like a toadstool? No, the safest thing to take is money, and just buy what we want, like any other person who never earned their cash."

"Oh, right. I see."

"So are we agreed that's what we're gonna do? Great. But there's one little personal matter I wanna attend to first."

Tracey looked dubious. "What?"

"Never you mind. You'll see soon enough. Now let's get going."

Out in the parking lot, while Tracey was unlocking the Lincoln, Jay Dee watched the traffic stream past. Toyotas, Fords, Hondas, Saabs, a Cadillac driven by a moose with its antlers sawed off, three faceless men in the backseat—

"Just saw Larry," said Jay Dee, once they were in the car and on the road. "He seemed to be heading for the city."

Tracey pulled into the breakdown lane and stopped. "Let's turn around, Jay Dee."

" 'Fraid not. That's where our chore is. Don't worry, nothing's gonna happen. City's a big place."

"I don't feel good about this, Jay Dee, but I know better than to argue with you when you got your mind made up. . . . "

"You hear that, Cat?"

"Yes, master." The plump woman made a mock bow. "Salami and baloney."

"Hunh."

In the city, Jay Dee directed, "Pick up Fourth at Main and head east."

"The meat-packing district, right? Jay Dee, I never claimed to be a genius, but a person would have to be senile, blind, deaf and have her head up her ass not to be able to figure out your pitiful schemes. You're going after Gene, aren't you?"

"That's right. I reckon we still owe him a little something for all the grief he put you through."

"Give it up, Jay Dee! I learned to. Gene don't mean nothing to me no more, good nor bad. I put all that pain behind me when I met you."

"You are a saint, Trace, and I love you for it. However, it is more in accord with my personal nature to be a little less forgiving. Not only does it require less willpower, but it can be downright satisfying to the soul."

"All right. But if you get your head handed to you, don't say I didn't warn you."

Jay Dee patted the remote in his pocket. "I think this little equalizer here will prevent such a sad occurence."

Catalina, quiet till now, said, "I agree with Jay Dee. It's not good to bottle up your feelings. Sometimes it's like trying to put a cork in a volcano."

Jay Dee snorted. "Good comparison in your case, Cat."

"Hey, let's keep this conversation above the belt."

A district of brick warehouses assembled itself around them. Most still retained their old industrial tenants; a few buildings, however, had been vacated and retrofitted for new occupants. On the ground level of one such a sign was hung.

GENE SMITH'S WORLD-CLASS GYM
NAUTILUS, STAIRMASTER, SPARRING
SHOWERS AVAILABLE AT EXTRA COST

They parked in front and got out, leaving Mister Boots meowing aggrievedly in the car.

Jay Dee clutched the remote so tight his knuckles were white as cream cheese.

"If you're scared, Jay Dee, it's not too late to leave."

Jay Dee stiffened right up. "C'mon, we're going in."

The gym was a large open space with equipment scattered around the floor, a boxing ring in the middle. Many of the machines were in use. In the ring, two men were sparring.

"One of them Gene?" whispered Cat.

"No," answered Tracey. "That's him punching the bag."

Gene Smith wore only a pair of spandex shorts and some unlaced sneakers. He sported short black curls and an NFL-style mustache. His body looked like that of a gorilla which someone had tried to shave with only partial success. The sound of his bare fists pummelling the bag sounded like a hail of hams striking the roof of a circus tent.

"Oo-whee, he's a hunk!"

"He's a pig-ignorant macho shit," countered Jay Dee. "It just ain't apparent if you let your hormones do your thinking, like Tracey done."

"I beg your pardon."

Gene spotted the visitors. He ceased his flurry of blows and came over to them, massaging one taped hand in the other.

"Well, if it ain't Mrs. Smith. Oh, I forgot. It always hadda be 'Thorne-Smith,' didn't it? I never could knock that crap out of your head."

"Nor never will."

Gene smiled. "I had a feeling you'd be showing up here, after I read about you this morning."

"Read about me?"

"Why, sure, didn't you hear yet? The police got a few questions to ask you, about how the First National roof ended up on top of that dump you were living in."

"Oh, Jesus. . . . "

"Well, I guess you can hide out with me. Though we'll have to get a few houserules straight first. Hell, I'll even put your buddies up too. Who are they anyhow? Your little brother and his old lady, maybe?"

"Old lady? I ain't nobody's old lady, kiddo."

"And I'm Tracey's man, you asshole. The man you never was."

Gene smiled cruelly. "Is that so? Well, looks like we're gonna need one less place setting than it first appeared."

Cracking his knuckles, Gene advanced on Jay Dee, towering over him like a falling building.

"Hold on a minute—I ain't quite resolved what to do with you yet. . . . "

"That's okay, baby. I know what to do with you."

"Shit, this is moving too fast— Box, get me a cube!"

A small silver cube appeared in midair behind Gene, who now had one massive fist cocked level with Jay Dee's nose.

"Bigger, bigger!"

The cube expanded to man-size.

"Open it!"

The cube's vertical face swung out. Jay Dee lowered his head and ran forward, ramming Gene in the midriff. Taken by surprise, the big man lurched a couple of steps backward. His calves caught on the sill of the cube and he toppled backwards into its capacious interior.

"Close it up! Quick!"

The cube snapped shut and shrank along eleven dimensions.

From outside the gym came the sound of several car doors slamming. Catalina went to the window to look. When she turned around, her face was drained of blood.

"It's Larry and the smudge-faces. And there's some other guys—with guns."

"You told Larry all about Gene, I take it," said Jay Dee calmly to Tracey.

"A girl's gotta get some things off her chest, even if the person listening is a jerk."

"Well, can't change the past. We'll just have to deal with 'em. Let's go out, where we can move."

They opened the door and filed out, hands raised high.

As Jay Dee had seen from a distance, Larry had sawed off his cumbersome antlers. Otherwise, his long and hairy moose's visage was unaltered, attesting to the permanancy of the Master Remote's changes.

The moose opened his mouth; sometime during the past night Larry had mastered—to a degree—his new vocal apparatus.

"Gib muh back muh faaaace," he brayed. A long thread of slobber drooled from his jaw with the effort.

"Larry, I'm plumb sorry, but I can't. The most I could do—if I wanted to—is to give you and your buddies somebody else's face. But I can't restore your own familiar ugly puss. But listen, why do you want to change? Before, you were just another mean and undistinguished son of a bitch. Now you're unique."

Larry raised a gun and began to squeeze the trigger. One of the new syndicate goons batted his arm down. The bullet ricocheted off the pavement.

"Listen, wiseguy—I don't know how you done this to Livermore or my bosses, but you better put them right. Or there'll be big trouble for you and these dumb broads."

"This is the second time today I've been called an insulting name," complained Catalina. "I don't like it."

"Me neither," said Tracey. "Jay Dee—whatcha gonna do about it?"

Jay Dee lowered one arm to his side and with his free hand scratched his head. "Well, I guess I'll have to come down on these jerks like a ton of bricks. Box, the cars!"

An enormous shower of bricks fell from nowhere, completely crushing and burying all the syndicate cars, including Larry's prized Cadillac.

For a moment the only sound was the clink of a few tumbling bricks. Then, almost but not quite simultaneously, Jay Dee and the head goon yelled.

"Wall!"

"Shoot!"

A twelve-foot cinderblock barrier topped with razor-wire and including a portion of guard-tower intervened between Jay Dee and the women and the toughs. It ran across the whole street, from building to building. Futile gunfire echoed behind it.

"I borrowed part of the local incarceration facility, as I judged these men were lawbreakers. I hope it is suitable. . . . "

Jay Dee laughed. "Sure should be an interesting scene at the old exercise yard! Let's go."

In the car the remote said, "I feel I am coming to understand your commands much better. A growing empathy now exists between us."

"I love you too. Okay, Trace, pick up the interstate. We got what we came for. The garbage is in the can. We just gotta figure out the best way to dispose of it."

They were on the outskirts of town when the sirens began to wail. Just as they were pulling onto the entrance ramp to the expressway, a bevy of police cruisers screeched through an intersection and, spotting the Lincoln, converged like pouncing panthers.

"Flower to the spirit," said Tracey enigmatically, before stomping on the accelerator and rocking Catalina, Jay Dee and Mister Boots back into their seats. The big car leaped up the ramp, narrowly missing a tiny Honda bearing a pack of Cub Scouts and Den Mother as it merged into the freeway traffic.

The cops were soon behind them.

Stiff-armed, Captain Tracey whipped the land-cruiser through the crowded sea lanes as her passengers turned green. Cars swerved onto the road's shoulder and collided with Jersey barriers. Still the sirens pursued them, all her maneuvers failing to shake the squad of cop cars.

"Time for tougher tactics," said Jay Dee. "Box, can you make those ribbons like elastics?"

"Would you care to specify the Poisson ratio or the strain/stress dyadics?"

"No, man, I wouldn't! Just string a big tough elastic band across the road to stop the cops."

"Done."

Tracey cautiously slowed. Jay Dee looked back.

A wide golden ribbon bisected the highway, anchored to the median barrier and the roadside fence. As Jay Dee watched, its rubbery surface bulged in the shape of four car noses. Instead of braking, the stubborn drivers continued to race their engines. The belt strained forward, bowing out from its anchor-points.

Realizing they were getting nowhere, the cops lifted their feet from the accelerators.

Released, the band snapped the cars backward. There was the sound of tires shredding and exploding, and the crunch of metal and glass.

"Oo-whee!" wailed Jay Dee. "Just like the slingshot I had when I was a kid!"

"I'm glad you're having fun," said Tracey, removing one hand from the wheel and flexing her fingers. "But I do wish you'd learn to drive, Jay Dee, just so we could share moments like this."

"You know I flunked the road test five times, Trace. I just ain't got the right skills somehow. But if I was perfect, you couldn't live with me."

"You may not believe this, Jay Dee, but I find it hard to live with you sometimes anyhow."

Catalina spoke. "'Flower to the spirit?'"

Tracey smiled. "Pedal to the metal."

They cruised slowly on, laughing and recounting the chase to themselves.

At the next on-ramp, three more cruisers sat with engines purring.

"Shit!"

Tracey got a good lead on them, since they had to accelerate from zero. "Another ribbon, Jay Dee?"

"Variety is the goddamn spice of my life, hon. Box, do you think you can do this. . . ?" Jay Dee whispered with the Master Remote close to his lips.

"Surely."

The road beneath their rear tires disappeared into a trench with a forty-five-degree slope. The police vehicles went helplessly over the lip and down. Within seconds there issued forth a loud glutinous plop, a sound between a belch and an underwater fart.

"What's at the bottom?"

"Enough molasses to float a battleship."

"Sweet."

"Do you think," asked Catalina, "they might know by now what our car looks like?"

"Gotcha. Trace, pull over a minute. Great. Box, can you smudge this car with us in it, without smudging us?"

"Your morphic resonances are now locked into my sheldrake chip."

"Uh, good. Go to it."

They were sitting on solid nothing. The windows had gone to impenetrable nothing so that they were blind to the world.

"Jesus, I didn't count on not being able to see. . . . Box, peel us off a new appearance from what's passing. Something inconspicuous."

The world reappeared. They were sitting in a commercial van. From the rear came a highly suspicious reek, emanating from many canvas drawstringed bags.

Tracey craned her head out her window. "'Blaylock and Powers Diaper Service,'" she reported smugly. "Good going."

"Just drive."

Several times packs of police cars raced past them, oblivious to the laundry van. During these moments, Jay Dee and Catalina hid in the back while Tracey drove.

"Jay Dee, don't the smell of a wet baby just get to you in a certain way? It's so earthy, like. It makes me all quivery inside. . . . "

"Well, it makes me wanna puke, so keep your hands where they belong."

They passed some cruisers drawn up to the side of the road.

"What's going on, Trace?"

"They're rounding up some escaped prisoners. Maybe we should take out another chunk of important wall someplace, just to keep them busy."

"I'll think on it."

Pretty soon they had crossed the state line. A road sign announced:

JETER'S LAKE STATE RECREATION AREA
CAMPING, BOATING, SKIING

"Jeter's Lake," said Tracey wistfully. "I haven't been there since I was a kid."

"Last time I was there, I was too pregnant to fit into a swimsuit. Leastwise, any I'd wanna be seen in."

"Well, hell, let's stop. I could enjoy some peace and quiet."

Tracey took the appropriate exit. The secondary road began to curve under arcades of firs. Soft sunlight dappled the van's interior, and a balsamy scent began to compete with the odor of a quarter ton of cotton-wrapped, pee-soaked baby shit.

A rustic wooden sign heralded the park's drive. The entrance fee was three dollars, which they paid to a Smokey-the-Bear-hatted Ranger who regarded their van with frank curiosity.

"On our lunch break," offered Tracey.

"It's mighty hard work," contributed Jay Dee.

"A regular calling, though," Catalina affirmed.

Down a narrow paved road to a half-empty lot surrounded by forest. Once parked, they eagerly climbed out. Catalina carried Mister Boots.

"Lord, I got to clean out my lungs! Let's head down to the water. . . . "

The forest gradually fell away to reveal an extensive body of sparkling water surrounded by tall hills, two of which were partially denuded, their ski trails now grassy, the lifts immobile. A small man-made beach, occupied by a few sunbathers, stretched to left and right; several red-stained log structures held changing rooms, showers, rest rooms, and a small snack bar cum grocery. Beyond the swimming area was a dock occupied by several rowboats, canoes and outboards.

Spying the boats, Tracey said, "Oh, Jay Dee, let's see if we can rent one. It'd be so nice to be out on the water."

Beneath the sign that said "Rates: $5/hr, $10 deposit" sat an old codger who looked carved out of an inferior grade of wood. His chair was tipped back, his hat was down over his eyes, and a dead pipe was held firmly between his teeth, indicating, if not life, then at least recent rigor mortis.

"Hey, fella, can we rent a boat?"

The ancient relic slowly raised a hand to lift his cap. He squinted suspiciously at the trio with one eye before declaring, "All taken."

"All taken? What're those?"

"Ree-zerved." He dropped his cap.

"Reserved, huh? No problem."

Jay Dee took out the Master Remote. "Window." A square plane appeared in midair. In it was portrayed a posh marina, numerous yachts abob at their berths. "Girls?"

"That one's cute."

A sudden wave swept over the shore. Half the boats tethered at the dock capsized and sank. At the end of the pier rode a proud forty-foot yacht, chrome gleaming, wood polished, radar turret aimed at the horizon. It bore the name THE BISHOP'S JAEGERS.

Startled by the commotion, the codger glanced out from beneath his cap. He jerked upright, his chair went out from under him and he toppled backwards.

Luckily, no one was aboard their new vessel; Mister Boots's prowling through every hatch would surely have aroused them. Quickly mastering the controls, Tracey swung the vessel about, demolishing the dock with elan.

They stopped in the middle of the lake and dropped anchor.

"Now we can relax," said Jay Dee.

Catalina said, "I want to go swimming, don't you? But we don't have suits."

"So? Go bare-ass. Nobody can see you from the shore, less it's some birdwatcher with his binoculars."

Catalina pouted prettily.

"Cat, are you trying to pretend you got any modesty left, after what you ee-nitiated last night?"

"No, it don't have nothing to do with modesty. It's just fashion. I like to dress nice, whatever the occasion."

"Oh, all right. But it's a waste of energy if you ask me." A concerned look blossomed on Jay Dee's features. "Box, your batteries ain't running low, are they?"

"I have extrinsic sources of power several magnitudes greater than your era's annual energy budget."

"Oh, good. Well, let's see some nice bathing suits for the ladies then."

Soon Tracey and Catalina were clad in the outfits they had selected, complete down to sunglasses, floppy hats and Grecian sandals laced up their charming legs. Jay Dee had been convinced to don a pair of flower-print baggy shorts.

"I feel like a goddamn idiot."

"No, you look sharp, Jay Dee."

"Mighty attractive."

Jay Dee smiled. "Well, okay, if you all say so. But I'll look even better underwater, where no one can see these pants. Last one in's a talking moose!"

Jay Dee hurled himself over the side. Tracey and Catalina soon followed.

The trio splashed and stroked until they had had enough exercise and fun. They climbed an aluminum ladder back into the yacht. Below deck, in a luxurious cabin, they stripped off their clammy suits and began to towel themselves off.

"That's a horny ol' devil you got there on your arm, Jay Dee," observed Catalina.

"That ain't his arm you're holding, honey," reminded Tracey.

"So it ain't."

An hour or two later, Jay Dee walked out on the deck, alone and clothed. Mister Boots appeared from somewhere and began rubbing against Jay Dee's ankles. Jay Dee hefted the Master Remote with an expression of thoughtfulness on his face. Then he spoke to it.

"Box, what am I gonna do with that Catalina? She needs a steady man something wicked."

"You are a man."

"Not the kind of heavy-duty boyfriend she needs! And besides, I got Tracey."

"What about the man in the cube?"

"Gene? Oh, he's handsome enough, but he's too ornery and spiteful and conceited to wish on the worst bitch, let alone a nice girl like Cat. She did like his looks though. . . . Nah, forget it! I— Boots! What the hell do you want?"

Mister Boots had stretched up with his forelegs and was using Jay Dee as a scratching post. Jay Dee unhooked his claws and picked him up. "Look, go hang out with Catalina, she loves you—"

Jay Dee stopped dead. A smile big as a slice of watermelon grew on his face.

"Get me the cube with Gene in it," he ordered.

The cube appeared, hanging six feet off the ground.

"Dump him out."

Gene Smith fell out of the cube's missing bottom into a heap on the deck. He appeared quite dazed.

"I could see inside myself. . . ," he said. "Wherever I was, I could see inside myself. And around the whole world too."

Gene spotted Jay Dee. "You. You did this to me." He began to climb to his feet.

"Smudge the cat."

Mister Boots went formless.

"Peel off Gene and layer him on Mister Boots."

"Compensating for the extensive mass-difference between origin and target will require my tapping a new source of power."

"Do it."

There was something casting a shadow between Jay Dee and the sun. Or so it seemed. He shaded his eyes and looked up.

The sun had a black notch cut into its circumference. Even as Jay Dee watched, the spot disappeared, reconquered by nuclear flames.

Two Genes stood on the deck. The original stopped in his tracks.

"It's me. . . . You turned that cat into me! You mother—"

"Smudge him."

There was a Gene-sized eye-wrenching hole in the air.

"Now put that image of Mister Boots you saved at the motel on him."

"This is inconvenient. I now have to dispose of extra mass that I could have used in the first transformation. You must learn to sequence your commands more rationally. . . ."

"Who's the boss here? Screw rational! Just do it!"

"How shall I dispose of the surplus mass?"

"I don't care what you do as long as you don't mess with the sun no more. That's too spooky. Just dump it somewhere."

"Very well." The box paused. "Your planet's satellite now has a new crater, its largest. Shall I inform the proper authorities, so that you retain the right to name it?"

"No!"

Jay Dee looked at the two other living creatures on the deck.

Mister Boots—wearing Gene's appearance—tentatively raised one hairy muscled arm into his line of sight, then began to lick it.

Gene—on all furry fours—bent his body to look at his hindquarters. He yowled, and launched himself at Jay Dee.

"Ribbons!"

The cat thumped to the deck, neatly packaged. It continued to hiss and spit.

Tracey emerged, rubbing her eyes sleepily. "Jay Dee, what's all this noy—" She froze. "Gene, you're free—"

"It ain't Gene, Trace." Jay Dee explained.

"Oh. My. God. Jay Dee, it's inhuman!"

"Sure. But 'inhuman' just might be what Catalina needs. C'mon, let's introduce 'em."

Tracey and Jay Dee each took one of Mister Boots's arms and walked him forward. The man-cat moved shakily, as if unused to the articulation of its new joints, walking on its tiptoes.

They guided Mister Boots down to the cabin.

Catalina stirred when they entered.

When Mister Boots recognized her, he began to purr. The front of his shorts bulged.

"Jay Dee, Tracey, what—"

"It's Mister Boots, Cat. He needs some petting."

"Nice kitty—oh!"

Tracey and Jay Dee sat in deckchairs, holding hands. The yacht had stopped rocking a few minutes ago. They silently contemplated the sinking sun, apparently none the worse for its loan of energy to Mister Boots. Then Jay Dee spoke.

"You know what, Trace?"

"No, what?"

"Life can be good."

"Sometimes you forget, though."

" 'Course we forget. Why shouldn't we, the way we live? People like us, we rush from one bad day to another, never having enough money, usually sick, stuck in dead-end jobs. We're forced by life and society to forget what we were born for."

"To mix men and cats in a blender?"

"You wanna hear my philosophy or not? Okay. No, to have fun! To enjoy ourselves without worrying about where the rent money's gonna come from. To laugh more than we cry. To relax our nerves and unknot our brains. To help our friends and confound our enemies. And this little box lets us do just that. Why, everybody should have one!"

At that moment, a car bounced down the access road that led to the now-empty beach. It stopped in a spray of sand right at the water's edge. Among others, a moose-headed man emerged and began to fire his pistol futilely at THE BISHOP'S JAEGERS.

"Well, almost everyone." Jay Dee got up. "C'mon, Trace, let's go."

"Where to?"

"Try the far side of the lake. Seems to me I remember Route 10 passing near there."

They upped anchor and motored off.

As they drew closer to the far shore, they could make out the highway guard-rail running along the top of the banking raised a few feet above the lake's surface.

When they were about a hundred yards offshore, sirens began to sound.

Soon the guardrail was lined with squad cars, their roof-lights flashing patriotic colors.

"Shit! If only we wasn't stuck on this boat! If only we had wheels!"

"Done," said the remote.

"Wait a minute. That's wasn't a real wish—"

"Jay Dee, the ship's handling funny—"

"You don't figure— Trace, I got a hunch. Head straight for the shore."

As the yacht approached the road, more and more of it emerged from the water. But instead of grounding to a halt, its keel embedded in the bottom, it moved steadily forward.

Catalina came up from below.

"Where's Gene? I mean, Mister Boots?"

"Catnap. What's going on? Oh, I see. . . . "

A cop began to yell threats through a bullhorn. He sounded less than sanguine.

Now enormous weed-wrapped wheels, big as those on a monster-truck, showed beneath the boat. Apparently the undercarriage of some large vehicle had been melded to the yacht and the drive-train integrated with its big engines.

The nose of the ship reared up as its treads bit into the sloping shore. Gripping the wheel, Tracey kept her feet; Jay Dee and Catalina were thrown against the walls of the bridge. Mister Boots—Gene, rather, and still in ribbons—slid back along the deck to thump solidly against the stern.

The monster wheels crushed the guardrail first, then the hood of a cop car. Tracey throttled up to climb the junk. The rear wheels bit solidly. Then they were onto the road.

The land-yacht began to trundle off at approximately twenty-five miles per hour.

Bullets were pinging off the ship's superstructure.

"Shall I give our craft a more conventional appearance?"

"Fuck that! They got me mad now, shooting at us like that, ruining our good times. I want everyone who comes after us stopped permanently. But without hurting them."

"May I recommend a glueball? I use only the highest quality gluons. . . . "

"Sure, if it'll do the trick."

Inside the Master Remote, a golden sphere materialized, just as the letters on its case once had, a short twenty-four hours ago. But when the sphere reached the surface, it kept on coming, emerging somehow through the intact remote.

Jay Dee held the marble-sized glueball. "This is gonna stop people from bothering us?"

"Once it is activated, yes, certainly."

"What should I do?"

"Throw it at your pursuers."

Jay Dee leaned cautiously out the bridge and tossed it.

The glueball landed atop a police car.

The car was gone. Or rather, it was plastered flat onto the surface of the glueball, which had swelled to accomodate it. The flat policemen inside the car banged their hands on their windows. One opened his door and emerged to slide around on the surface of the sphere.

The next car to touch the sphere vanished faster than the eye could follow, flattened likewise to the face of the glueball. The ball was bigger than before.

Lacking brakes, Tracey throttled down to nothing. The yacht coasted to a stop.

The glueball occupied the whole road. There were no cars left outside it. They all rolled around its surface like rainbows on a soap bubble.

Now the glueball began to move.

It rolled away from the yacht, toward the city.

Everything it touched—including the road, down to a depth of ten inches—was sucked into it. Trees, guardrail, grass, birds. The sphere swelled and swelled, like a snowball rolling down an alpine slope, leaving a cleanly sheared path of destruction.

"Holy shit. . . . Stop it!"

"That is beyond my capacities."

"Beyond your— You stupid machine! Why did you let it loose then?"

"I am Turing Degree Three. Humans are Turing Degree Ten."

"Oh, Jesus. Will it ever get full, like, and stop?"

"How big is this planet?"

The glueball was now six stories tall. It seemed to be moving faster.

Catalina was sobbing. "Jay Dee—" began Tracey. But the anguished expression on his face made her stop.

Something appeared in the darkening air above the sphere.

Jay Dee swung the ship's searchlight on it.

It was the man they had run over, the owner of the Master Remote.

Suddenly there were a dozen of him. They formed a ring around the glueball. It stopped. It began to shrink, but did not disgorge what it had eaten.

When it was marble-sized again, all the floating men coalesced into a single individual. He landed on the ground, picked up the glueball and pocketed it.

Then he was on the yacht.

"Uh, sorry we killed you once, Mister Spaceman."

The man brushed some dust off his rubberoid lapels. "I am as human as you, Mister McGhee. I am a resident of your future."

Catalina had ceased crying. "Juh-gee, you must come from pretty far in the future."

"Fifty years," said the man. "But they're going to be wild ones. Now, may I have back my unit?"

Jay Dee surrendered the Master Remote.

Tracey asked, "How come you didn't arrive one second after you were killed to claim it, and prevent all this mess?"

"The unit disturbs the Fredkin continuum in a chaotic manner. I had a hard time zeroing in on it."

"What's going to happen to us?" said Jay Dee.

"Oh, nothing much. Say, did you ever see a tie like this?"

They all stared at the time-traveler's paisley tie. The border of each paisley was made of little paisleys, and those were made of littler paisleys, and those were made of even littler paisleys, on and on and on, forever—

That night the Li'l Bear Inn was as crowded as the last copter out of Saigon.

But the atmosphere was a little more pleasant.

Above the sounds of clicking pool balls, thwocking darts, ringing bells, exploding aliens, kazoo, farts, Hank Junior, and the bug-zapper hung outside the screen-door that gave onto the gravel parking lot, the calls for drinks were continuous.

"Tracey, two shots!"

"Tracey, another pitcher!"

"Tracey, six rum 'n' cokes!"

The woman behind the bar smiled at the deluge of orders. It meant more profits in her till.

A man with two tattoos emerged from the back office. "Catalina just called, Trace. She's stopping by soon as Gene gets off work at the exterminator's."

Tracey said, "It'll be good to see her. I'll have a frozen daiquiri and a saucer of cream ready."

The man looked around. "Lord, it's jumping tonight. We should be able to pay off the mortgage next month."

A large neutered tomcat stepped fastidiously among the pools of spilled beer. A patron reached down to pet it. It hissed and scratched the offered hand.

"Jay Dee, you should get rid of that mean animal!"

Jay Dee just smiled.

There was a muffled noise from the moosehead mounted on the wall behind the bar. The moosehead had a rope tied around its snout.

Its eyes tracked furiously.

Jay Dee gave Tracey a kiss. "I'll relieve you in a minute, hon. But I got to do something first."

He went back into the private office on the far side of the bar, picked up a board—

—and gave Larry another whack on the ass.

When I first read an excerpt from William Kotzwinkle's The Fan Man *circa 1972 in* Esquire *("Horse Badorties Must Go Out!") I fell in love with that voice. Nearly twenty years later, I stole it for this story, a theft only Stan Robinson was perceptive enough to comment on. As for my prophetic Disneyfication of New York, one has only to visit 42nd Street to witness the plague in full bloom. Chalk up another valuable prediction for SF!*

Do You Believe in Magic?

THIS IS, LIKE, THE WORST DAY OF MY LIFE, MAN.

It is 7:00 AM and I am soundly and peacefully asleep, having been up most of the night writing a review for the prestigious music 'zine, *Magnetic Moment*, of some piece of digitially mastered Pop-Market-place shit—I don't remember what now; all this modern stuff sounds alike. When I went to sleep I had no intention of getting up before noon. But my blissful dreams of other days are shattered by this loud scraping noise, followed by a sharp slam.

Well. As soon as I extricate myself from the Komfy Koverlets, which my thrashing limbs have wrapped around my neck in a stranglehold, I realize it is the day of the week that my groceries are delivered. The kid from the market has just pushed a box thru the specially constructed Doggie Door, which has slammed down heavily, since its pneumatic catch is shot.

Having been thus summarily roused, I cannot go back to sleep. I decide to get up. Suddenly I am interested in what the market has sent me, and figure I might as well put it away.

I rise from my old stained mattress on the floor. I put on clean jeans and sweatshirt, which I handwashed early yesterday and which have been drying on the line overnight. They are still damp and clammy, and feel like seaweed. This is the pits. I check the Porthole for weather conditions, altho, as per usual, I shall not be going out. (All my windows are painted black. The Porthole is an area high up on one where the paint has flaked irregularly off. The vista thus revealed is a slice of sky and a few square feet of wall.) Conditions are partly cloudy, with patches of brick. Much like every day.

Barefoot, I shuffle over to the box of groceries. Wow, this sucker is heavy! I cannot believe the market has found all these canned goods for me. Shipments lately have been getting sparse. (I refuse to eat any food packed in these new plastic cans. I will take my nourishment from aluminum and tin, or from nothing at all. Plastic cans, man! That's crazy. . . . Unfortunately, there are no Native Goods packed in tin anymore. Thus, I am constrained to subsist on imports from the more traditional and/or backward countries: Portuguese and Norwegian sardines, Welsh meat pies, Spanish octopus, Italian scungilli, North Korean puffer fish, Nigerian hyena parts, Burmese lizard legs, Chinese bamboo shoots—man, it gets kinda depressing.)

I am anxious to investigate this week's offerings. In the patchy dark, I walk with the box over to my old wooden kitchen table and set it down heavily.

There is a heartbreaking CRACK! Too late, I realize what I have done. I lift the box up off the table and set it on a chair. A mournful little whimper escapes from my lips:

"EEEE-YAAAAAAAGH!"

I yank on the pull chain leading to the naked bulb above the table, hoping that I am mistaken. Maybe it is only some piece-o'-crap like Lionel Ritchie's fifty-first album that I have just turned into vinyl splinters.

But, natch, it's not. I knew it couldn't be.

It is a thirty-five-year-old masterpiece, an original pressing, the first album I ever bought, the keystone of a vanished decade, the touchstone of my life, now fragmented into irreparable shards, sharp as my sorrow:

Do You Believe in Magic? , by the Lovin' Spoonful.

I was listening to the prized album last night, in order to cleanse my ears of the horrid modern stuff I had been forced to review. I removed it from the turntable and, in a moment of bladder-type weakness, forgot to resleeve it. When I got done taking a leak, I had fallen straight into bed. The record lay unprotected all night on the table, forlornly awaiting its fate. . . .

I collapse into a chair. I just cannot believe this. To exist and give pleasure for three-and-a-half decades, only to be shattered by a load of scungilli. . . . At that moment I hate my stomach. Perhaps I should have switched to plastic cans after all. . . .

Numbly, I stare at the pieces of black plastic. Even the paper circle has been ripped by the jagged shards. It's the Kama Sutra label (distributed by MGM): yellow background, red sunburst, green Indian deity with three faces and four arms. Man, there wasn't a scratch or fingerprint on that whole record. It felt so good to handle, substantial and thick, not like latter-day, end-of-an-era, cheap flimsy platters. . . . It coulda lasted another century!

I look across the room, where sit the unadorned yellowed inner paper (not plastic) sleeve and the outer cardboard jacket. The grinning faces of John, Zal, Joe, and Steve mock me from the jacket, beneath the title in its retro typeface. (Funny, once we woulda called that style modern. But thus it is decreed: yesterday's modern is tomorrow's retro. . . .) John's look is particularly poignant, as he grips the stem of his round wire-rims with two fingers. . . .

I am suddenly having some kind of fit. I cannot breathe, and my chest is tight. I stand up and stumble to the stained porcelain sink. I stick my head under the faucet and run cold water over it. That helps a little. Goddamn it! THAT ALBUM WAS THE CENTER OF MY LIFE! I WAS SIXTEEN WHEN I BOUGHT IT! IT WAS GREAT MUSIC! I WILL NOT LIVE WITHOUT IT!

I realize I have been shouting. Luckily, my neighbors—whoever they may be—have grown used to my noise. At least, I think they have. Anyway, there have been no complaints in ages. Doubtless, if anyone heard my ranting just now, they thought it was merely another record.

I am possessed by a sudden knowledge: it is time for desperate measures. I must leave my apartment to secure another copy of this record, a duplicate original pressing. I really cannot live without it. My life is a precarious assemblage of tactile tokens and sonic symbols. To remove one is to disfigure the whole musical mosaic.

The Big Picture must be restored!

I am filled with energy now. I have a Kozmic Kwest.

I grab my sneakers from beneath a pile of clothing, put them on my bare feet, and lace them up. Now the conditions beyond the Porthole develop increased significance. I look again. Hmm, better have a jacket. I snatch some bills out of the tin where I keep my money and uncashed royalty checks, and stuff them in my jacket pocket. I advance to the door. I stop.

I have not been out of my apartment in twenty years. I believe the last time was around '81. That was when things seemed to turn really sour, and I beat my retreat. I have not had any visitors in half that time. My dealings with the world are thru the media of mail, telephone lines, and data coaxials. I am not sure the world even exists anymore, in any incarnation other than the shit I receive for review.

I am shivering. I DON'T WANT TO GO OUT THERE! I look around my place for some shred of comfort. There are jumbled piles of books, mostly about music. There is a broken television, which has not worked since Dick Clark died. There are banks of audio equipment: receivers, speakers, amps, equalizers, turntables, CD Players, DAT and DVD drives, regular cassette players, various remote controls. There is an old word-processing setup whereby I file my articles with *Magnetic Moment* and other publishers. And then, natch, there's my record collection: approximately six thousand LP's and as many 45's. They are lovingly filed on shelves and in stacks, the oldest protected by plastic. Among them is the last LP ever pressed by a major firm, the

Springsteen five-record set, *Live '85-'95*, which failed to move even ten thousand units in this format. (I do not keep the CD's and DAT's that I receive for review, unless they are reissues of old stuff that I absolutely lack. Otherwise, they go out the bathroom window, down the air shaft. I believe the pile has almost reached the second floor.)

The sight of all my possessions reassures me. I must be strong and survive this mission, if only to take care of them. I cannot stand the thought of strangers coming in after my death and breaking up my collection.

I turn back to the door. It has five locks on it, and a bar wedged under the handle and against the floor. I attempt to work the mechanisms, but they are all rusted shut. The bar has sunk immovably into the soft wooden floorboards. I am forced to crawl ignominiously thru the Doggie Door in order to exit my lair.

Man, this hallway is gruesome! Fulla dust 'n' cobwebs 'n' used syringes, rags 'n' cinders 'n' windblown trash. There is a trail thru all this junk, which the boy from the market has obviously worn. The path comes as far as my door and no further. Is this what I am paying my rent-stabilized $125 per month for? I angrily ask myself. While I'm out, I will go see Mr. Gummidge, the landlord, and demand better treatment. What does he think this place is, an abandoned building, fer chrissakes?

That is exactly what it is, I soon discover.

I am living in a bombed-out hulk! All the glass and doors except mine are gone. There are no other tenants, except some rats and wild dogs and perhaps, from evidence, an occasional squatter. Well, that explains the lack of complaints about my loud music. . . . Lord knows why I still got electricity. There was that blackout five years ago; power didn't come back on for a week—could it have been hotwired. . . ? Hey, if there's no super, who's been taking my trash away? Bums, I guess. Suprised the copper plumbing hasn't been gutted. Oh, that's right: it was replaced with some new plastic stuff back in '75. I lodged a futile protest, hated to have my water flowing thru PVC, finally gave in and learned to subsist on YOO-HOO CHOCOLATE DRINK, the only beverage that still comes in a real can. . . .

Now I am out on the street. Wow, this neighborhood was never much to look at, but it's really gone downhill!

I am staring at about forty acres of rubble-strewn urban terrain. My building sits in the center of the wasteland, the only halfway-intact structure. The wall I have unwittingly inspected each morning out the Porthole turns out to be merely a freestanding fragment. Man, what happened? This used to be Amsterdam Avenue, man!

I trudge across the desolate, bricky wastes, beneath the sky of gray. Man, this is like waking up in a T. S. Eliot poem!

On the outskirts of my private Twilight Zone, I encounter civilization, in the form of inhabited buildings, uptown, downtown and crosstown streets, traffic, commerce, humans. . . . Man, Harlem never looked so good! I thought it was post-WWIII, man! Instead, it appears that only my immediate surroundings have suffered these outrageous ravages.

I approach some soul brothers hanging out in front of a check-cashing joint.

"Hey, bloods, what happened with the war zone?"

They eye me warily. One finally speaks.

"The mayor and the po-leece drop a firebomb."

"What the fuck for?"

"Trying to stop the crack sales."

Wow, so that was what that *really* hot day had been! I thought it was just a regular New York August day cranked up to eleven. My building must have been protected in some eddy of the flames. . . .

While I have been cogitating, these young black guys have surrounded me menacingly.

"Is you the spook what lives in the haunted tenament?"

"I guess so. . . ."

"You spoze to be real rich. How about handing over some money?"

"Yeah," says another. He produces a gun made of . . . PLASTIC! "Or we gonna grease your ass."

I slap the gun out of his hand, and it goes skidding down the street like a cheap toy. The JD's stare at me unbelievingly. "Man, that was major uncool. Whatcha pointing some *plastic* gun at me for? Dontcha know you're looking at a dude who marched with King?"

The guys all eyeball one another.

"King? Who's he?"

"The brother they made the holiday for."

"Oh, yeah. . . ."

"You really known him, man?"

I break my stalwart silence. "Does a bear shit in the woods?"

This old chestnut sends the guys into convulsions. Is it possible they've never heard it before. . . ? Whatever the case, when they recover, they are smiling. I take advantage of their good humor to question them.

"Where's the best and biggest record store nowadays?"

"That be Tower Records, down on Broadway in the Sixties."

"O.K., all right; thanks, men; let's shake."

These guys are so lame, they don't even know how to shake hands. I gotta twist their thumbs upward in the proper grip. I leave them practicing the shake among themselves, and walk out to Broadway.

The subway costs two dollars now! And they use *plastic* cards insteada tokens! Quality of the ride ain't changed, tho: noisy, crowded, and rough. Car's clean of graffiti, tho. I wonder idly why, until I notice a kid whip out a marker and try to write on the walls. The ink from his pen beads up like water on grease and rolls to the floor. The kid swears— "Shit, they told me this new pen would cut it! Five dollars down the tubes!"—and sits back down. I touch the wall; it's dry. Heavy, man, some kinda Teflon Koating. . . .

I mistakenly ride all the way to Columbus Circle and have to walk back uptown to get to Tower Records. Wow, these people are dressed *weird*! The chicks are all in their underwear—bras and colored leotards; and the men seem to be in their pajamas—wrinkled old suits with colored T-shirts. Don't no one change outa their NIGHT-CLOTHES no more? Hey, how come *I'm* the one getting all the stares? Must be my hair. Seems like no one else wears it down to the tailbone no more. Screw 'em. Wotta buncha squares. . . .

Here is Tower Records. Wow, is this place garish! My eyes are hurtin' just to look at it. There are more neons and fluourescents here than at Graceland. And to think I usta like light shows. Must be gettin' old. . . . What're all these *televisions* doin' here anyway? Is this a music store, or an appliance discounter? And all playing snippets of bad imitations of Buñuel movies. . . . Oh, well, it don't matter to me, just go on thru the door, under this weird SCANNER—beam me up, Scotty, hee-hee—and into the store.

Boy, it's crowded. Everyone's got these little cordless buttons in their ears, groovin' and boppin' to some private beat. THIS LOUSY JOINT DON'T EVEN HAVE A PA SYSTEM! What kinds rock-'n'-roll community does that make for? Some of my happiest memories are of hearing new stuff in a store, and the whole place groovin' to the same wavelength. . . . Hey, don't see no salesclerks, just a lone cashier. What're those people doin'? They're ordering CD's from a computer console that spits them outa a slot. This is hell, man. . . .

I go to the cashier. She is about fifteen, and wears gold earrings shaped like scarabs that crawl up 'n' down her ears on little mechanical legs.

"Peace, lovely lady. Do you perchance have a selection of old LP's for the serious collector?"

"I dunno whatcha mean."

"LP's: vinyl discs spun on a turntable at thirty-three-and-one-third revolutions per minute, the single analog groove of which, when interpreted by a stylus, produces music."

The waif pouts sullenly. "You're yanking my rods. There ain't no such thing."

"Is there anyone else I could talk to?"

"I dunno. Check the back room."

I find a door I assume leads to the stockroom. Uncautiously, I open it.

Brawny, sweaty laborers naked to the waist are wielding huge shovels with which they scoop up CD's and DAT's and DVD's out of an enormous pile and dump them into a hopper that leads to the dispensing devices. A foreman wearing an eyepatch snaps a bullwhip over their scarred backs. He spots me and yells, "An intruder! Get 'im, boys, before he escapes!"

Is this real?! Maybe I am just having like my worst nightmare, badder than that yage trip with Allen. BUT I CANNOT TAKE CHANCES! I slam the door and make like Kleenex and blow. Feets, don't fail me now!

Several blocks down Broadway, I stop, outta breath. Man, this is the most exercise I've gotten in years! I seem to have shaken my pursuers, the Devil Dogs of the Rekkkord Industry. I lean against a building to rest, and gaze around.

An address across the street looks familiar. It comes to me then that I am staring directly at the building that houses the offices of *Magnetic Moment* ! Wow, what synchronicity, man! I decide to go with the flow. I must enter and reveal myself to the staff. I am sure I will be enthusiastically received. Their most Senior Kontributor, the Human Encyclopedia of Rock, Mister Pop-Popularizer Himself.

I enter the building; I ascend in an elevator that queries me for my destination mechanically; I emerge in a ritzy lobby. There is a gorgeous chick seated behind a desk. In her underwear, natch.

"Peace, ma'am. Would you announce to all and sundry that Mister Beaner Wilkins has descended from the heights to greet the faithful and unclog their mental arteries with some Zany and Zesty Zen Zappers?"

The chick glares at me with ill-concealed distaste. She thumbs an intercom button and says into the speaker, "Hello, Security, it's another one."

Barely does she remove her manicured digit from the button, when four immense Anthropoids in suits emerge from concealed doors and make free with my personal limbs in a painful manner.

"Hey, you pigs, what gives? Let me go, cut me loose, put me down, chill out! I didn't do nothin'! I am a respectable staff member of this rag, and just wish to see my editor!"

"That's what they all say," grunts one of the Musclemen, who has my neck held like a pencil between his thumb and forefinger.

"All who? I don't know any of these other jerks to whom you refer. I'm me, Beaner Wilkins, a Lone Wolf. I do not associate with any cliques, claques, covens, or cabals."

It's no use. I am being hustled toward the elevator. My shouts have attracted a crowd of office workers, who cluster at doors watching my humiliation.

"Emilio!" I yell. "Emilio Cuchillo!" I spot the shiny face of my young editor at the rear of the crowd. "It's I, Emilio—Beaner!"

He looks dubious, but does not attempt to restrain the Security Apes. I make a frantic move to break loose.

"Hey, that does it," says a guard. "Put the cuffs on him."

Bracelets clack shut on my wrist.

"ARGH! Plastic! Get it off, get it off, gedditoff!"

Somehow, Emilio is by my side. "It's all right, guys; there's been a misunderstanding. This fellow has an appointment. I'll see him now."

Warily, the semisentient hulks comply. I am released into Emilio's custody. Mustering all the dignity I can, I adjust my headband and untangle the long fringes of my leather jacket. Then I accompany Emilio into his office.

When we are both seated, Emilio, leaning forward with forearms on his desk, stares at me for several minutes. At last he speaks.

"It really is you. I can spot the likeness to that old picture we run above your column. You know, the crowd scene from Woodstock, where you're covered in mud. Beaner Wilkins. . . . I can't believe it.

You know, sometimes we used to speculate whether or not you were actually dead, and the columns were being written by a computer."

"I am obviously not *dead*, man. I just value my privacy. Also, this modern-day world is not one I care to associate overmuch with. But listen—what made you jump in and save me?"

"Well, first you have to understand that we get at least one nutcase a month showing up claiming to be Beaner Wilkins. There's quite a myth surrounding you, you know. Seems to attract all the dissatisfied types from every new generation. So at first, I had no suspicion you might actually be telling the truth. It was the business with the cuffs that alerted me. I remembered that the real Beaner hated—hates—plastic."

I am relaxing a little now, and feel I can afford to be generous with my praise. "It was, like, very astute of you, Emilio. I am glad your memory was so accurate, since I did not relish the prospect of greeting the pavement with my face."

"That fact always stuck in my head. I thought it was funny that someone whose whole life revolved around old-fashioned records would hate plastic so much. Sorta contradictory. . . ."

"I do not ingest or wear records; therefore their plasticity does not bother me. However, food encased in hydrocarbon derivatives, or clothing fashioned of same, rubs me the wrong way."

Emilio sits back in his chair. "So, Beaner, what brings you out?"

Before I can answer, I am suddenly seized by this Sahara-type thirst. The events of the day have parched my throat. "Got anything to drink, Emilio?" I ask.

Emilio stabs an intercom. "Ms. Orson, please bring us a couple of Cokes—"

"Hold on," I demur. "Is it, like, in plastic cans?"

"Why, of course— Oh, I see. Cancel that order, Ms. Orson. Beaner, I don't know what to offer you—"

My eyes have been roving over the office all this time, and now light on a trophy case containing a leather jacket, a pocket comb, a burned husk of a guitar—and A CAN OF YOO-HOO! Without asking, I go to the case, reach inside, and in a second have popped the Yoo-Hoo.

Emilio screams!

"Cool it, man," I advise. "What's wrong?"

"That can! Do you know who last touched that can?"

"No. . . ."

"John Lennon, just minutes before he was shot!"

"Oh. . . ." I look inside, and sure enough, there're little cards by each item: Lou Reed's jacket, Hendrix's guitar, Elvis's comb, Lennon's Yoo-Hoo. . . . Oh, well, man. . . . *Sic transit gloria*, and all that. . . .

Sitting back down, I explain the nature of my Kwest. Emilio, wiping the tears from his eyes, nods. When I am finished, he is mostly recovered.

"You've really set yourself a chore, Beaner," he says forgivingly. "Nobody except a few insane rich collectors wants those old LP's anymore, and so hardly anyone sells them. Your only shot might be this one store down in the Village—"

"Of course! The Village, the very birthplace of the Lovin' Spoonful! Spiritual home to every malcontent and freethinker, every beatnik and hippie and punk who has ever walked the globe! Surely, in one of the myriad second-hand stores in the Village I will find a copy of my beloved album!"

"Yeah, well, I think you might have a nostalgic view of reality—"

"No way, man; I am still plugged in."

"Yeah, maybe. . . . but 'plugged in' to what?"

I ignore Emilio's sarcasm and arise, eager to be off. "Emilio, it has been extremely groovy to make your editorial acquaintance in person, but now I must split. I trust my columns have been satisfactory. . . ?"

"Yeah, they're O.K. They pull in readers of your generation—who represent a big market share and have powerful demographics—and they give everyone else a laugh. But don't you think you could lighten up a little on modern music? I mean, you haven't praised anything since Madonna's album with the reunited Dead, just before her granddaughter was born—and that was six years ago now!"

"I will continue to call them as I see them, Emilio. Let musicians produce good music, and I will praise it. But I will not hype prefab shit."

Emilio shakes his head in mock woefulness and gets up to see me out. "Well, that's hot as fusion, Beaner, and I'm on the downlink to your telemetry with minimal noise. Just hang in there, old survivor. What is it you used to say? Keep on trackin'!"

"That's *truckin'*...."

"Oh. I thought it was like a tonearm...."

Emilio sees me down to the street. Then I am back on the subway, heading for the Village.

I emerge in Union Square.

Something is really wrong, man.

There is a turreted wall around the northern border of the Village, all fake boulders and pennants fluttering in the breeze. There is a gate at Broadway guarded by Mickey Mouse and Goofy. They are wearing sidearms.

Tentatively, I advance, gradually becoming one with a horde of tourists types, who I hope will provide me with some kind of cover.

Mickey spots me in the crowd, tho, and gestures for me to step aside. I do not argue with mice bearing weapons; therefore, I comply.

"Where the hell is your ID badge?" says the Famous Mouse belligerently.

"Uh, I forgot it at home...?"

"Jeez, you guys are getting too deep into your roles, being such screwups. All right, listen close: just this once, I'm gonna give you a temporary ID. Don't let it happen again."

"I certainly won't, Mr. Mouse. Thank you, thank you kindly."

With a hologramatic badge bearing the Disney logo pinned to my jacket, I am waved past the ticket-taker beyond the gates.

I immediately experience a flashback to 1967.

The streets are filled with the Children of Aquarius, long-haired guys 'n' girls flashing the peace sign to each other and the tourists, posing for photos, smokin' what smells like authentic reefer rolled as big as sausages. The Beatles blast out of every window.

What the fuck is goin' on here?!?

When I cross Tenth Street and find myself surrounded by cats dressed all in black spoutin' Allen Ginsberg, I dig the grotty scene.

THE WHOLE VILLAGE IS NOW A DISNEY THEME PARK!

Sure enuff, there is a punk enclave over on the Bowery, buncha skinheads endlessly pogoing to an audioanimatronic Ramones.

I sit down in the gutter.

I begin to cry.

When I am all cried out, I arise. All I wanna do is find my album and get outa here. Emilio said something about a second-hand record store. . . .

I find the place over on Bleecker Street, next to a glitzed-up jazz joint that advertises Michael Jackson doing a show wherein he impersonates Charlie Parker (NITELY AT SIX AND EIGHT).

Heartbroken, I go into the store.

The place features Day-Glo posters and the smell of incense. The Jefferson Airplane is being piped out of hokey little lo-fi speakers: "Do you want somebody to love?" Yeah. . . ! There is a young chick behind the counter, dressed in costume, but I ignore her in favor of the stock.

Gotta hand it to the Disney Empire, they don't spare no expense. It is all the Pure Quill here, rare original pressings from the 'Fifties 'n' 'Sixties 'n' 'Seventies, snug in their Mylar envelopes. The price tags are what you'd expect, most items under a thousand.

Behind the black divider printed with the psychedelic *L* , I find it.

Do You Believe in Magic? by the Lovin' Spoonful, for only eight hundred smackers.

I clutch the Sacred Disc to my breast and approach the counter. The girl smiles.

"Checking out the old stuff on your break?" she asks. "I don't blame you; it's so much better than what passes for music nowadays."

I figure she is just laying the Standard Patter on me, so I merely nod and begin fumbling bills out of my pocket. However, all the cash I have amounts only to half a grand. Bummer! I dig out a royalty check from my last book, *Dylan: The Final Years*. It is for three thousand bucks.

"Listen, I need this record badly, babe, and I don't wanna wait any longer to get home. Can I just make out this check to you? You can cash it, and pocket the difference."

The girl examines the check. Her eyes get wide.

"Beaner Wilkins? *The* Beaner Wilkins? Are you really him?"

I straighten my spine. "Yeah, I'm me. Look." I produce my long-expired driver's license and pass it over.

"Oh my God. I can't believe this. I never thought when I took this job—I mean, to actually have you come into the store! Why, I read your column every month! And all your books—I've read every one at least twice! The things you've seen and done, the era you grew up in— It's so wonderful, so—so magic! Not like these times—"

"Yeah, yeah," I say, anxious to make tracks away from this farce, this parody of the glorious long ago. "Now, will you take the check or not?"

"Oh, sure, Mr. Wilkins. For *you* ."

I prepare to endorse the check over to her. "Name?"

"Janis Smialowski. That's J-A-N-I-S, not I-C-E."

I am momentarily interested. "Not after—?"

She beams. "Yes. My folks loved her. My grandparents turned them onto Joplin as kids."

Completing the endorsement, I hand the check over to her. She studies it raptly, then says, "I might not cash this. I mean, I could keep it for your autograph. I'll pay the store out of my own pocket."

Is this dollybird pulling my leg? I can't figure her out. She is the nicest person I've met out here, but she makes me uneasy. All confused, I try to settle my thoughts by imagining my apartment full of music and memories, its warmth, the security, the peace, the lack of challenges—

A tune I barely acknowledge as within my era—Steely Dan's "Hey Nineteen"— starts up, and I realize I am listening to a premixed tape. No playing of whole sides allowed, too much chance for individual taste to enter. . . .

Disgusted, bewildered, I make my exit, gripping my precious album tightly.

The chick calls out to my back. "Please stop by again sometime, Mr. Wilkins. I enjoyed our talk!"

I am out on the streets, halfway to the ghetto gate, heading home.

I return to the store.

When Janis sees me, she smiles like sunshine.

"Janis, would you like to drop by tonight and groove to some old tunes?"

"Oh, Mr. Wilkins—I'd love to!"

This is, like, the best day of my life, man.

Rock music weaves like a thread through most of these stories, a tribute to that form's anarchic joy which the stories seek to emulate. From time to time, pop music forms the text as well as subtext. In this Nebula-nominated story, rock was also the compositional inspiration, as I fused two naggingly uncooperative ideas—psychic cords that bind, and magic spectacles—much in the manner of the legendary genesis of "A Day in the Life".

Lennon Spex

I AM WALKING DOWN LOWER BROADWAY, not far from Canal Jeans, when I see the weirdest peddler dude.

Now, when you consider that the wide sidewalk is jammed with enterprising urban riffraff—Africans with their carved monkeywood animals; Farrakhanized Black Muslims with their oils and incense; young white punks with their hand-screened semi-obscene T-shirts; sleazy old white guys with their weasel-skin Gucci bags and smeary Hermes scarves; Vietnamese with their earrings and pantyhose and pirated tapes—and when you also realize that I, Zildjian, am totally innured to this spectacle through long habituation, then you realize that this guy must be incredibly weird.

Except he isn't. Weird, that is. Not bizarre. I guess it's more that he's incongruous, like.

He appears to be a Zen monk. Japanese or Chinese, Korean or Vietnamese, it's hard to figure. His head is shaven, he wears a golden robe and straw sandals, and he looks serener than a Park Avenue matron after her first Valium of the day. His age could be anywhere from a year short of a legal drink to a year over early retirement.

The monk is apparently selling secondhand prescription eye-glasses. He has a TV tray with a meager selection neatly arrayed thereon. I see no handy-dandy lens-grinding equipment, so I assume there is no customizing. This gives new meaning to the term "cut-rate rip-off."

I stop in front of the monk. He bows. I am forced to bow back. Uncomfortable, I fall to examining his stock.

Tucked away behind the assorted cat's-eye, filigreed, tortise-shell old lady spex lies one special pair of glasses, their stems neatly folded like ballerina legs, as incongruous among their companions as the monk among his.

I pick these glasses up and examine them.

They are a pair of simple gold wire-rims with transparent, perfectly circular lenses. The stems extend from the middle of the outer circumference on each lens; the bridge is higher, about two-thirds of the way up along the inside. The spectacles feature no adornments.

Suddenly, I realize that these are what we would have called, more years ago than I care to ponder, "Lennon glasses." First popularized by Beatle John in the *Sgt. Pepper* album photos, later shown shattered on a posthumous jacket, they remain forever associated with his image, though he was to switch in later years to various aviator-style frames, undoubtedly seeking to harmonize his face with Yoko's in marital solidarity.

I do not suffer from near- nor far-sightedness; I have no intention of buying the frames and replacing the lenses with polarized ones, since I believe in the utility of unmediated sunlight. Yet something compels me to ask if I can try them on.

"Can I, uh, try these on?" I ask the monk.

He smiles. (A smile from one of his disciples was how the Buddha knew his message was getting through.) "You bet."

I unfold the stems. It is then that I notice a blot of what appears to be fresh blood on one stem. Maybe it's ketchup from some strolling patron's chilidog. Never squeamish, I lick my thumb and attempt to wipe it off. The blot temporarily disappears under my rubbing, then rematerializes.

The monk has noticed my actions. "Not to worry," he says. "Just a small stain from the shooting. Will most definitely not affect utility of the glasses. Please, try."

So I slip them on.

The rowboat is painted in psychedelic day-glo swirls of color; the wide rippled water which cradles it is purple. I am sitting on the middle bench, drifting downstream without oars.

On either shore, tangerine trees are interspersed with cellophane flowers of yellow and green that grow so incredibly high. The sky— you guessed it—is marmalade. With actual flecks of orange peel and English muffin clouds. A complete nutritious breakfast.

"Holy Salvador Dali," I whimper. I dip my hands into the purple water, stirring a scent of grape juice, and frantically try to divert the boat to shore.

"Zildjian," calls someone above me. I answer quite slowly: "Yuh-yeah?"

"Stop paddling and look up."

The floating girl has kaliedoscope eyes and wears a lot of shiny gems, but not much else.

"You're being given a gift, Zildjian. There's no need to panic."

"Oh, man, I'm not sure—"

The boat is rocking. No, it's not. I'm sitting astride a centaur. Only instead of hooves, he's got bentwood rockers. He's propelling himself across a field, while eating a Scooter pie.

Lucy is beside me on another rocking horse person. "Calm down, Zildjian. We don't invite many people here. You're the first in years and years. Trust me."

"What happened to the last guy who trusted you?"

Lucy pouts. "That was humanity's fault, not ours."

She opens the door of a taxi for me. It's made of old *Washington Posts* and *New York Times* with headlines about Vietnam. When I climb inside, my head goes through the newspaper roof and into the clouds. Lucy's too. As we cut through the moist vapor like wheeled giraffes, I find myself mesmerised by the sun reflected in Lucy's eyes.

She's leading me into the train station. "Just try them for a while. What have you got to lose? Here, see how good they look on you."

She summons over a porter made of modeling clay who resembles Gumby. His tie is formed of mirror shards pressed into his chest. I study my reflection in the looking-glass tie. The glasses don't look half-bad. . . .

The turnstile bumps my crotch and squeaks, "Sorry!"

"Have fun," says Lucy, and pushes me through.

I am clutching a streetlight on Broadway. I recognize it because it is the one that still bears a tattered remnant of a poster protesting the most recent war, on which someone has scrawled a particularly clever slogan: "Real eyes realize real lies."

Looking up, I anticipate the worst.

But no. The world—seen through what surely must be non-prescription lenses—is normal.

Except for the people.

Every last person is crowned, like Medusa, with a nest of tendrils.

From the skull of each person exit innumerable organic-looking extrusions which terminate about eighteen inches away from their heads. The tendrils are all colors, thicknesses and textures. Their ends are sheared off flat, and they do not droop. It is as if they enter another dimension a foot-and-a-half away from the individual.

The people look rather like rainbow dandelions gone to seed.

A dog stops to pee on my pole. Its head too is studded with worms, but not as many as the humans'.

A nasty thought occurs to me. I release my grip on the pole and slowly raise my hands to my own head.

I too am wearing a snakey turban. I can feel the velvety/rubbery/slimy/scratchy hoses rooted to my cranium.

I rip off the Lennon glasses.

Everyone's head-snakes are gone. Mine too, by touch.

Trepidatiously, I put the glasses back on. The snakes come back.

I sense someone by my side. It's the peddler monk.

He alone of everyone in my sight has but one tendril coming from his head. It's golden like his robe and, emerging from the exact center of his crown, rises vertically up.

The monk smiles again and lifts one hand to his golden carousel-horse pole.

"Goes straight to Buddha," he says, and laughs. "Use glasses wisely. Goodbye."

He vanishes into the mass of pedestrians.

Still wearing the glasses, I wearily sit myself down on a stoop.

Man, how can all these people be oblivious to the spaghetti coming out of their heads? Why don't they feel its weight? Come to think of it, why don't I feel the weight of mine? I reach up and find the offending objects still tangible. How can something be perceptible to the touch yet weigh nothing? Or is that we're just used to the weight. . . ?

The mutt that nearly peed on my foot comes over to keep me company. I offer my hand and it starts to lick it. As it slobbers, I watch its doggy head in horror.

A new tendril is emerging from its skull! And it is questing like a cobra toward me!

Suddenly into my field of vision from above a matching tendril of my own pokes, heading toward the canine feeler!

I jerk my hand away. The dog snarls, and its tentative tendril changes color and texture, as does mine. But now they seem less eager to meet.

Nobody ever called me Carl Sagan. But I am a fairly quick study. And you would have to be as dumb as a Georgia Senator not to figure out what is going on with these worms.

These tendrils coming out of everyone's head represent emotional attachments, bonds, links of feeling and karma. All the connections we pick up in life. Strings of love and hate, just like some bad pop song.

The dog has stopped snarling and is licking itself. As an experiment I extend my hand again. It sniffs tentatively, then gently strops my fingers.

This time, I let our feelers connect and fuse.

I love this dog! Good dog! It's practically in my lap, giving my face a tongue-bath. It loves me too. Aw, poor street-critter. I'm really ashamed of what I'm going to do next.

I grab hold of the seamless cable connecting our heads and yank it out of the dog's skull. Better to experiment with his head than mine. There's a slight resistance, then the connection comes away with a subliminal pop!

The dog yelps, then apathetically climbs off me and goes to sleep.

The cable in my hand, now anchored only at my end, is squirming, trying to reattach itself to the dog. I don't let it, and within seconds it just sort of withers up and vanishes like a naked hard-on in a blizzard. I can feel a ghostly patch fading on my skull. The cable, I realize, wasn't that strong to begin with, pink and thin as a pencil, and didn't put up much of a fight to survive.

Armed with this new insight into the nature of the head-spaghetti, I watch the people around me more closely.

Everyone, I now notice, is continually extruding new feelers every few seconds. In fact, if I focus my vision through the Lennon glasses in some nameless way, I see close to people's scalps a haze of movement rather like the waving of polyps and corals in some undersea forest.

The vast majority of these embryonic attachments are transient, dying as fast as they are born. F'rinstance:

A woman pauses before the window of a clothing store. She casts a line out like a fly-fisherman toward an outfit on a mannequin. Passing right through the plate glass, it connects for a moment, and then she reels it back in and strides off.

Of course. You can have serious attachments to non-living things too.

And as if to repeat the lesson, a guy pulls his Jaguar up to a miraculously empty space, parks and gets out. The cable connecting him and the car is thick as your wrist. But that doesn't stop him

from flicking out a feeler toward a passing Mercedes. Your cheatin'
heart. . . . Or head, as the case may be.

A delivery guy sends out a probe aimed at a classy babe in furs,
which, needless to say, is not reciprocated.

An old woman with a walker whips out a feeler toward a young
doctor-type.

A girl whom I half know, an architecture student at NYU, shoots
out an extension just like one of Spiderman's webs to an elaborately
carved cornice that catches her eye.

A dude and his babe stop at a corner, kiss and part. The connection
between them is thick and strong. As they get further apart, beyond
the combined three-foot extension of their bond, it hazes out at its
midpoint, entering whatever extradimensional continuum allows
individuals to remain connected to distant people and things.

I've seen enough.

It's time for me to go home and learn more.

Standing in front of my bathroom mirror, I begin to pull the cables
out of my head, one at a time.

Out comes this gnarly grey vine. What resistance. . . . Whoops,
suddenly I don't feel anything for my folks! Mom, Dad, what are
parents good for anyhow? It's spooky. There's just a big blank spot
where there used to be filial fondness. I don't like this. Better plug this
one back in. . . .

What this thin slick red-white-and-blue-striped one? Yank it.
Patriotism? Whodda thought I had one of those? Wonder what it
connects to on the other end? The White House? The Lincoln
Memorial? Plymouth Rock? Different for everyone maybe. . . .

Here's a little slippery green eel of a thing. Tweak it out. Holy shit,
that gameshow hostess! I never even knew on a conscious level that I
had the hots for her! Mega-gross. Man, I'm killing this one. I hold it
one side till it crumbles away. Can't be too careful about where you
put your feelings.

Like a mad oldtime switchboard operator, I spend the next couple of hours pulling cables, memorizing which ones channel what feelings. (Once I yank too many simultaneously and get kind of spacey feeling, as if adrift in the cosmos, spinning aimlesly across the universe.) I soon learn how to tell the difference between one-way connections, such as those to inanimate objects or unresponsive fellow humans (Sherry Gottlieb, a high-school crush), and two-way ones, such as those to another person who feels for you too. There's a different kind of pulse in each, a unidirectional flow in the former, an alternating current in the latter.

Since I basically like myself as I am, I plug nearly all of my attachments back in, although I do eliminate the ones for Twinkies and cigarettes.

A sudden inspiration dawns on me like sunrise on Mercury. I could get rich from these glasses! All I have to do is open an aversion-therapy center. I'll practice some mumbo-jumbo, yank people's addictive connections—assuming, and I think it's a safe bet, that everyone's cables resemble mine—and presto, you're looking at the next pre-bankruptcy Donald Trump (only without the bad taste).

But then I remember the parting words of the monk who gave me the glasses: "Use them wisely." And how about that single connection he had? "Straight up to Buddha. . . ?"

I take off the glasses and look at the ineradicable spot of blood on the frames. I think about John Lennon.

What did *he* do with these glasses? I imagine a little devil popping into being on my left shoulder. He's leaning on a pitchfork, wearing a derby and smoking a cigar. He blows smoke into my ear and say, "He got rich, you schmuck!" An angel appears on my right shoulder. Wings emerging from his black leather jacket, he's holding an electric guitar in place of a harp. "But that's not all he did, Zildjian. He made a lot of people happy. He contributed to progress. He improved the culture."

"He laid a lot of dames," says the devil.

"Yes, but always sought to express a philosophy of life, to illuminate people."

"Nothing gets a babe illuminated hotter than a dose of philosophy."

The angel flies over my head and lands next to the devil. "You cynical philistine!"

"Hey, back off!" The devil brandishes his pitchfork, puffing on his cigar till the coal glows. The angel hefts his guitar like a club and takes a swipe at his opponent. They both tumble off my shoulder, locked in that eternal pro-wrestling match of the spirit.

Their arguments have helped me make up my mind. I will use the glasses to feather my personal nest a little. But I will also do something very good for humanity with them.

But while the personal options are quite clear to me, the larger ones persist in staying somewhat hazy.

I let them remain so. The first thing I want to do is head over to Cynthia's apartment.

Cynthia and I broke up for what we both correctly surmised was the last time just a week ago. The cause was my telling her that this hunky actor she admired reminded me of an ambulatory roast beef, and probably had as much brains. From the nature of this tiff, you can probably gather that our relationship was not all that deep.

But I am still attached to her. I know, because I found the tendril. But it turns out to be strictly a one-way hookup, all the emotion flowing out of me and hitting a barrier on her end like a sperm hitting a diaphragm.

Now I am going to change that.

Cynthia is home. She is getting ready for her waitress job. I find her very attractive in the cowgirl boots and short skirt with tail feathers featured on the help at Drumsticks 'n' Hot Licks, the fried-chicken country-western club, and I tell her so.

"Yeah, great," Cynthia replies rather coldly. She keeps her back to me, adjusting her strawberry-blonde coiffure in the mirror. I am amazed that she can get her brush through all the karma-cords, which apparently offer no resistance.

Cynthia eyes me in the looking-glass, and I am briefly reminded of the plasticine porter's tie. It's hard to believe that she cannot see all my tendrils, including the one leading to her, but it is true. Then she notices my spectacles.

"Since when did you start wearing glasses?"

"Since I met a Buddhist street vendor who sent me on a trip to another dimension."

"Yeah, right. You'll never change, Zil. What do you want? I assume you didn't come over here just to compliment me. Come on, out with it. No mind games, either. And make it fast, 'cause I've got to get to work."

"Cynthia, we need to talk," I begin, laying down some sensitive-type patter just to distract her. She has turned away from the mirror and is bent forward, rummaging thorough her purse. Meanwhile, I am inching closer, within reach of her personal emotional attachments.

I zero in on one which is a livid purple and resembles in some strange indefinable way my own connection to the gameshow hostess. I deftly grab it and unplug it from Cynthia's head.

She twitches and says, "Hey, what are you doing?"

"Just admiring the scent of your hair."

"Well, quit it. You're creeping me out."

I push the connection into my own head. Just as I thought! It goes straight to that hambone actor who was the cause of our breakup. I am suddenly overwhelmed with impure thoughts about his bod. Yuck! This is not for me. I pop the tendril out and jack it into Cynthia again.

Then I do something I haven't attempted before.

I pull on the cable in the other direction, trying to yank it out of the actor, where I doubt it's heavily anchored. My physical effort is apparently transmitted successfully along the cable through the extraspatial dimension it traverses, for it suddenly comes loose.

I swiftly fuse the end of Cynthia's one-way cable for the actor with my one-way cable for her, which I have just unplugged at her end.

She straightens up as if goosed by Godzilla and wheels around to face me.

"Zildjian, you're—you're different somehow. . . ."

Even knowing what's going on, I am overwhelmed by the synergy of the new connection, which is full and taut as a firehose under pressure. "Cynthia, I—you—"

"Oh, come play in my strawberry field!"

After that, it's our own private Beatlemania.

The next few days proceed swimmingly.

I get a new car and a line of credit without even putting on a necktie. It's only a small matter of establishing the proper connections. At the car dealer's up near the Plaza Hotel, I borrow the owner's hookup to his elderly grandmother.

"No money down, no payments till next year, and no finance charges? Why not? I'm sure you're good for it."

At the bank, I utilize the loan officer's feelings toward his mistress to secure a large sum of cash, a Gold Card and no-charge checking with fifty-thousand-dollar overdraft protection. The only complication is his hand on my knee.

I maintain both these links for a few days to insure that the dupes do not come to their senses and renege on the deals before they are solid. (I am a little troubled about the cold shoulders which are no doubt being received by Granny and Lolita, but reassure myself that things will soon be back to normal for them.) Finally, I gratefully sever the adopted links, watching them retract through their transdimensional wormholes. Hopefully, they will re-establish themselves with their natural objects.

What a relief, I can tell you. It has always been my philosophy that you've gotta go through this world as free as you can, and these extra bonds drag me down.

I think from time to time of the monk, and his single golden cord. . . .

Cynthia and I spend the next couple of weeks having some major fun, she having turned in her tail-feathers. We eat at the best tables in the best restaurants, gain immediate entrance into the smartest clubs, receive front row concert tickets for the hottest acts gratis, and in general carve a path through the city like Henry Moore through a block of granite.

One day Cynthia asks me to accompany her to the hospital, where her sister has just had a baby.

At the maternity ward window, I stare in disbelief at all the squalling or sleeping infants.

Each one has a single golden cord, just like the monk's. A few of the older ones have tentative parental connections, but basically it's just that one heavenly stalk going straight up to who-knows-where.

After that, I start examining kids everywhere more intently.

Most of them seem to maintain their heavenly birthright pretty much intact up till about age three. After that, it starts to dwindle and dim, getting thinner and paler until it finally vanishes around age ten, tops.

In all of New York, I fail to find an adult other than the missing monk who still has what he or she was born with. And that includes, natch, me.

Of course, I am not exactly hanging in the places where such a person might necessarily be found.

And although several times I almost take the opportunity to unplug a kid's golden cord and sample the current flowing down it, I never quite dare.

I realize I'm afraid it might reveal how shallow what I'm doing is. . . .

One day about a month after getting the Lennon spectacles, just when I am starting to get bored with how easy life is, I am driving alone down First Avenue when I encounter an enormous flock of cars being herded by a squad of sheepdog cops. Poking my head out the window, I politely inquire of a policeman as to what's going on.

"It's the President," replies the cop. "He's speaking to the U.N. before the war starts."

"The war? I thought the war was over. . . ."

"That was the last one. This is a new one."

"Well, who are we against this time?"

"Whatsamatta, doncha watch TV? The enemy is South Arabiran-iopistan. Their leader's here too. He'll be lucky if he don't get lynched."

I am not sure I have gotten the name of the country right; I never was one for following politics much. But this war-thing is definitely bad news of at least the magnitude of the incarceration of James Brown.

Suddenly I recall my vow to do something good for all humanity.

I get out of the car and hand my keys to the cop.

"Here, park this, willya."

He starts to open his mouth to utter some typical cop thing, but I deftly make use of his obedience cable to his superiors (a slimy thing I always hate to touch), and secure his complete cooperation.

The U.N. is crawling with security. I watch for a few minutes until I ascertain who the head honcho is. Then I approach him.

This is not a time to cut corners, so I indulge in a little overkill. Not only do I quickly yank and plug into my skull his obedience connection to his distant boss, but I also take over his links with his wife, dog, son and what appears to be his riding lawnmower. (I always said these G-men were sickos.)

"Would you mind escorting me in?" I ask sweetly.

"Of course, sir. Right this way."

Issuing orders over his walkie-talkie, the Secret Service agent soon conducts me backstage in the Assembly chamber.

I now face a minor problem: how to get close enough to the President for what I need to do. My outfit is certainly not going to help, as I am wearing a Hawaiian shirt, green scrub pants a friend stole from Bellevue, and huaraches.

Improvise, improvise. "Loan me your suit coat."

"Certainly."

Thus somewhat more suitably accoutered, clutching a shopping list from my pocket as if it were a classified memo I must deliver, I step out onto the dais, my captive agent dutifully running interference for me.

The platform is full of seated dignitaries. The Secretary General is speaking at a podium. Television cameras are focused on us. I have always wanted to appear on television, but not in this fashion. . . .

Using the narrow space behind the rank of chairs, I sidle up inch by inch to where the President and his counterpart are seated. The Prez's prep-school Puritan face is puckered into a mask of righteous indignation. The leader of our enemy wears a smug duplicitous puss like what you might see on a drug dealer who just successfully tossed his stash out the car window and down a sewer before the narcs closed in.

No one is paying any attention to me.

Yet.

A thick orange scaly hawser of hate runs between the two leaders. I've never seen anything so malignant-looking. I truly believe for the first time in the reality of war.

I am now within reach of the emotional linkages of these geopolitical megalomaniacs. Unfortunately, people are starting to take notice of me, and not in a kindly way.

Before they decide to do something, I act.

Gripping the hate-cord with both hands, I attempt to yank its ends out of the leaders' heads. The resistance is immense. I strain—to the audience, both at home and in the Assembly, it must look, I am sure, as if I am gripping an imaginary barbell with the leaders' heads as weights and trying to press it for an Olympic record.

Finally, the hate-cord pops out. Both leaders jerk like gaffed barracudas.

I can't resist leaning forward and whispering in their ears.

"Imagine there's no countries, boys, it's easy if you try. And war is over, if you want it. . . ."

In the next instant, I pop the Prez's patriotism link and plug it into the head of the South Arabiraniopistan guy. Then I swiftly jack the other guy's loyalty into the Prez.

All the hoodoo movements this involves over the heads of the two leaders is apparently too much for the unseduced security people, who now pile on me as if I were the football in a Super Bowl game.

My Lennon glasses shoot off my face and fly through the air. I think I hear them crack. But I could be wrong. Sounds are rather muffled through a layer of human flesh atop me.

I black out.

During this more-than-usually-unconscious state, Lucy appears to me, naked and resplendently begemmed.

"A fine job, Zildjian. You are welcome to visit us anytime." She starts to fade.

"Wait, hold on, how do I get back to where I once belonged. . . ?"

But there is no answer.

I am in prison for only six months. The pants from Bellevue helped my insanity defense. I don't mind. Even if no one else realizes what I've done, I can relish being a working-class hero. Much to my amazement, Cynthia visits me three times a week. I had somehow thought that all the relationships I had rigged might vanish with the glasses.

During my imprisonment, I am proud to report, our President and the leader of South Arab-etc., after their stunning reconciliation in front of the entire world, are photographed playing miniature golf together at Disney World.

One day thereafter, I am walking down Broadway when I see the most familiar peddler dude.

I cautiously approach the monk. He smiles broadly and points to the top of my head.

"Nice looking lotus blossom you got there."

I don't let on that I am pleased. "Hunh. Whatcha got for sale today?"

The monk holds up a pair of clunky black retro plastic frames. They look vaguely familiar. . . .

"The name 'Peggy Sue' mean anything to you?"

Can one write a funny story that opens with an attempted suicide? The question is not as oxymoronic as it first appears. Much humor involves pain, but viewed through a suitably objective lens. As Mel Brooks once remarked: "Tragedy is when I get a thorn in my thumb. Humor is when you fall down a hole and die." Another rock reference aids in the title.

Mama Told Me Not to Come

"AREN'T YOU HAVING FUN YET, LOREN?"

I lifted my head slowly. It felt like it belonged to someone else. Some sadomasochist who had stuffed it with sand, used the tongue for a doormat and the eyesockets for a photobath, then left the whole mess out in a cold autumn rain.

Ann Marie, my hostess, towered over me, glass in hand. The numerous drinks she had consumed that night had done little to mute her incorrigible perkiness.

"Do I look like I'm having 'fun' yet, Ann Marie?"

I was sitting on the floor in a corner of Ann Marie's living room, clasping my upraised knees. I was wearing the same stained suit I had worn for the past week, twenty-four hours a day. My hair resembled a haystack pitched by one of the less competent Snopeses. The stubble on my face was patched with dried mustard from a steady diet of cart-vendor hot dogs.

All around me swirled and bubbled, perked and pooled, churned and chortled, shrieked and shouted, guffawed and gasped, tinkled and crashed that strange human activity known as—a party.

A party I was in no way a party to.

Ann Marie tried to focus her chipmunk-bright gaze on me, and, after womanful concentration, succeeded.

"Hmmm, well, now that you mention it, Loren, I have seen you look happier, not to mention more smartly dressed. . . ."

From a far-off room came the noise of breaking glass, followed by yelps, cheers and what sounded like curtains being ripped off their rods.

"Ann Marie," I said wearily, "don't you think you'd better see what's going on with your other guests? It sounds like they're demolishing your lovely apartment. . . ."

I believe it was one of the more feebleminded kings of England of whom it was said: "Be careful what idea you put into the King's head, for once inserted it is nigh impossible to dislodge." Ann Marie, especially after a certain amount of booze, was similarly singleminded. And now I was the sole object of her concern.

"Oh, I'm not worried about anything," she said blithely. "I bought special party insurance just for tonight. After all, it's not every day you get the chance to welcome in a new century."

"An astute and unarguable observation, Ann Marie."

"You see, I don't care what anyone does tonight, as long as they're having fun! And that's why I'm worried about you. You're obviously not having fun!"

"Fun" was a concept I could no longer wrap my mind around. It seemed to me now in my despair that I had never understood the word. I doubted anyone really did. All I wanted was to be left alone until midnight. Locking eyes with Ann Marie, I tried to communicate this.

"Ann Marie, do you know why I came to your party tonight?"

"Why, to have fun with your friends, of course. . . ."

"No, Ann Marie. Although that might have been true at one time, it is unfortunately not so now. I came, Ann Marie, simply because you live on the forty-ninth floor."

A look of absolute bewilderment instantly transformed Ann Marie's face, as if she were one of those dolls with a button in their backs that swapped their expressions.

"It *is* a nice view of the city, Loren, but you've seen it a *hundred* times before. . . ."

"Tonight, Ann Marie, I intend to see it 'up close and personal,' you might say. At midnight, when everyone else is celebrating the beginning of a glorious new century, I am going to open your sliding glass door—assuming none of these 'party animals' has broken it before then, in which case I shall simply step through the shard-filled frame—and emerge onto that small square of unadorned concrete you insist on calling a 'patio,' from the railing of which I shall instantly hurl myself into space, thus ending my complete and utter misery."

Someone twisted the button in Ann Marie's back, dialing up an expression of shocked disgust.

"Do you have any idea, Loren, what a bummer that would be for everyone who's trying to enjoy themselves?"

"I am not too keen on the notion myself, Ann Marie. But it seems like the only thing left for me to do."

Ann Marie dropped into a squat beside me, sloshing some of her drink on my pants leg in the process. Not that it mattered.

"Tell ol' Annie all about it, Loren. What's wrong?"

"It's quite simple. Precisely one week ago, my whole life fell apart like a dollar wristwatch. In the space of a single hour, Jenny left me and I lost my job."

"I wondered why she wasn't with you. What happened?"

"I still don't know. I got home and found a note. It said that she was flying to El Ay with someone named Reynaldo."

"Uh-oh."

"You knew about Reynaldo?"

"She swore it was just a fling. . . ."

I dropped my head into my hands and listened to someone moan for about thirty seconds before realizing it was me.

"There, there, Loren," said Ann Marie, patting my shoulder. "She was never good enough for you."

"But I still love her, damn it!"

"You'll find someone else, I'm sure. Once you get yourself looking respectable again. Why, the new love of your life could even be here tonight! And I'm sure you'll land another job."

My laugh must have been awfully loud and eerie-sounding, to cause everyone in the immediate vicinity to look at me as they did. Even Ann Marie appeared shocked, and she knew what I was feeling.

"Don't tell me—" she began.

I feared I was shouting, but I couldn't help it. "Yes! I've been replaced by an expert system! A thousand dollar software package has taken my place! Six years of higher education down the fucking tubes! There's nothing left for me but a government retraining camp. . . ."

"I hear the meals are great. . . ," said Ann Marie half-heartedly.

I scrambled awkwardly to my feet. Seven nights of sleeping on park benches and steam gratings had taken their toll. "I don't care if they serve stuffed fucking pheasant! I'm going to kill myself! Do you all hear me? I'm going to take the big dive! Tickets on sale now!"

"Loren, please! People are trying to start the new millennium off with a cheerful attitude!"

All the spirit went out of me. To say I felt like a sack full of shit would have been to err on the side of cheerfulness. I felt like an empty sack that had once held shit. "Okay, Ann Marie, you win. I'll be a good boy. Until the clock strikes twelve. And then I'm going to make like a crippled pigeon."

Ann Marie's native idiot exuberance reasserted itself. "That's wonderful, Loren. I'm sure something will make you change your mind before you do anything rash. Now, let me see. First you need a little drink. Then, we'll introduce you to someone exciting. Who would you like to talk to?"

"No one."

"Oh, don't be a poop! I know! There's this real character that Sam brought with him. The guy claims to be a Greek god of some sort.

Imagine! Now, he'll make you forget about your teensy-weensy troubles."

"Is he Charon? That's the only one I feel like meeting."

"Sharon? I told you, he's a guy! Now, c'mon."

I let Ann Marie lead me away.

I didn't have anything planned for an hour yet.

All around us the party was accelerating like a piano dropped from a penthouse suite, promising as spectacularly clangorous a finale.

Five people were monopolizing the middle of the living room with a game of Coed Naked Twister. A bottle of baby oil seemed to be involved. Their audience were the people sitting three-deep on the couch, seemingly oblivious to the fact that one of the cushions appeared to be smoldering. In the corner diagonally opposite the one I had been occupying, there was a knot of bodies around what appeared to be a burbling hookah. A crowd was gathered in front of the flatscreen HDTV, playing a drinking game: every time the septuagenarian Dick Clark said "rockin' in the millenium," whoever failed to shout "Let's party like it's Nineteen-ninety-nine!" had to chug from a fifth of peppermint schnapps. What appeared at first to be a diapered child draped with a New Year banner was drawing with crayons on the wall. Upon closer inspection, I saw he was a dwarf, and his drawing elegantly obscene. From the next room a DAT player blared over the sound of projectile vomiting, and I could feel dancers shaking the floor. The whole building, in fact, seemed to be quaking. None of this, however, managed to wake the mousey woman who had gone to sleep six feet off the floor atop a narrow bookshelf.

I had never understood parties. Overheated or freezing, ear-splitting or deadly silent, boring or overstimulating, crowded or sparsely attended, too much food or too little, liquor-saturated or temperance-bound, they always inhabited one extreme or another. Never had I been to a party that was just plain enjoyable, in a

moderate way. It was possible none such existed. Certainly, Ann
Marie's end-of-the-century bash was not one.

"Just think," said Ann Marie herself, as she steered me around a
recumbent body wrapped like a fashionable mummy in the curtains
I had earlier heard being misappropriated, "there must be a zillion
parties just like this one going on around the world tonight!"

"What an appalling notion."

"Poop! Gee willikers, where is that Greek guy?"

We entered the kitchen just in time to be nearly dually decapitated
by a colorful flying plate, which crashed and shattered against the
wall alongside the door.

"You bitch!"

"Bastard!"

Ann Marie intervened. "Jules and Melissa, I'm so hurt! That was a
piece of original Fiestaware!"

"Sorry, Ann Marie. But he deserved it. I caught him with that slut
Oona in the bathroom!"

"I told you, she only asked me to help her zip her dress. . . ."

"And what was it doing unzipped in the first place, may I ask?"

"Now, now," said Ann Marie, "why don't you two kiss and make
up? You don't want to start the next thousand years off with a silly ol'
spat, do you?"

Convinced that she had done all she could to effect a reconciliation, Ann Marie turned away from the glowering couple. Spotting a
jug of Smirnoff's on the counter, she snatched it up. Setting her own
drink down next to an unclaimed lipstick-smeared glass, she splashed
a few inches of vodka for herself and me.

"Here you go! Now, if only—oh, there he is!"

She dragged me over to a man sitting alone on a countertop.

If you took a composite of Keith Richards at the nadir of his heroin
addiction and Charles Bukowski on a six-month bender and started
to morph his body into that of Miles Davis just before he died, but
stopped with the transformation half complete, you might end up

with someone who looked like this guy. He was dressed in sandals and an outfit that resembled blue satin pajamas, and he was eating from a bunch of grapes with languid disdain. "Dissipated" was the most charitable word whose dictionary entry he might illustrate.

Ann Marie accosted him with, "Hell-low! I'd like you to meet someone. This is Loren. Loren, meet—oh, I've forgotten your name!"

Chewing a grape with enervated precision, the man said, "Bacchus."

I could almost hear the wind the allusion made, passing over Ann Marie's head. "Well, Mister Backus, you and Loren have a nice talk. I've got to go mingle."

Ann Marie left. A pool of silence seemed to surround "Bacchus" and me, strangely isolating us. I tried to think of something to say, and some reason to say it. The habits of sociability die hard. Finally, I opted for easy sarcasm.

"What happened to the figure, man? Aren't you supposed to be carrying a few more pounds? And what about the ivy wreath? Couldn't get to the florist's tonight? Wait a minute, let me guess. Al-anon, World Gym, Ralph Lauren, and you're a new man."

I knocked back my drink, watching him out of the bottom of my eyes, waiting for his reaction to the needling.

Bacchus finished chewing, regarding me with neither overt hostility nor friendliness. When he had extracted the last atom of taste from the fruit, he spoke.

"You from fucking Disney, or what?"

It took me a few seconds to get it. Then I burst out laughing.

"Yeah," continued Bacchus, "I came that close to slapping them with a lawsuit when that fucking cartoon came out. Made me look like a real asshole. The cute donkey, the pratfalls, scared of lightning, for Hera's sake, as if Zeus and I weren't tight as your mama's twat. But then I figured an out-of-court settlement would be best. I still get thirty percent on every tape sale."

"That's cool," I said, taking one of his grapes and flicking it across the room. "Keeps you in produce." The vodka had gone through my empty stomach and straight to my head. Suddenly, it seemed good to be drunk, for what I still intended to do. I made a move toward the Smirnoff's for a refill, but Bacchus stopped me.

"Here, let me."

I stuck my glass out, not knowing what to expect, and he held his right palm over it. Wine gurgled out, as if from a vinous stigmata.

I pretended not to be astonished. "Hose up the sleeve?"

Bacchus shrugged. "If you wish."

I tasted the wine.

Cool breezes on a green hillside, ocean spray and hot sunlight, a shaded stream under ancient oaks. That was the vintage.

My head was light as a Wordsworthian cloud. Bacchus's voice seemed to come from a neighboring solar system.

"You know, you can call them anything you want. Parties, revels, carnivals, orgies, saturnalia, mardi gras— Hades! Call 'em Bacchanalia, if I can toot my own horn. But all festivities have a certain logic. I could write a fucking book on the dynamics of fun. And one chapter would be all about cases like you."

I sipped more of the incredible wine. "And what exactly am I?"

"The specter at the feast. The suicide. Hanged man and fool."

I tried not to shiver. "What if I am? You gonna try to talk me out of my plans?"

Bacchus held both hands up, palms out. I couldn't see any tubes— or holes, for that matter.

"By no means. I just offer my Olympian perceptions, for what they're worth."

I was suddenly sick of talking. Sick of living. Midnight was fifteen minutes away, and I just wanted everything over with.

"Don't you have someplace else to go?" I said.

Bacchus laughed. "I am everywhere already."

I was turning away, but that stopped me. "Huh?"

Leaning forward as if to confide a secret, the strange man said, "Every party that ever was or is or will be is connected. Same with every war or every fuck. Or so Mars and Venus tell me. You just have to know how to get from one to another."

"And how would you do such a thing?"

"In my case, I am simply called, manifesting simultaneously, everyplace at once. Gods are like that. You see, I am the original party vibe, a permanent, omnipresent wavefront that collapses into physicality wherever conditions are right. But if *you* wanted to try it, you'd need some props."

"Props?"

Bacchus skinned back the sleeve on his right arm. The veins in his wrist were not blue, but royal purple, and there was definitely no tube down his clothing. He held up his empty hand in an affected magician's pose.

I never looked away, but somehow, with a mere twitch, he summoned up an object.

It was a paper and plastic party horn, with trailing cellophane streamers around the bell.

"One blast on this, and you're instantly elsewhere, dispersed randomly along the party matrix."

"Randomly?"

Another shrug. "Nature of the beast. Some drunken scientist named Heisenberg tried explaining it to me once, but I didn't dig it. Stochastic, probalistic, chaotic—made less sense than Socrates. Oh, I should mention something else. Wherever you find yourself, you're limited to the psychophysical boundaries of the party. Whatever gathering you pop up in, you can't just step out of it into, say, Armistice Day New York."

"How come?"

"Outside the special party environment, you'd be a temporal-spatial intruder. Your unnatural presence would cause the instant conversion of your whole mass to energy. Make Hiroshima look like a firecracker."

"Forget it," I said. "Not interested."

Bacchus tucked the horn in my jacket pocket. "You never know."

Despite myself, I found myself saying, "You mentioned 'props,' plural. . . ."

Bacchus grinned, and twitched his hand again. A polka-dotted conical party hat appeared. Before I could stop him, he had placed it on my head, snapping the rubber string maliciously under my chin.

"Lets you speak and understand all languages. And then there's this." He materialized a ziploc bag full of multicolored confetti. "Sprinkle a little of this on someone, and they'll accompany you when you blow the horn." He dropped the confetti into my other pocket. "Now, you'd better get going. It's almost midnight."

So saying, Bacchus spun me around and booted me in the rump.

I went down to my knees.

And when I picked myself up, he was gone, as if he had never been.

But I was still wearing the party hat, and my hands found the other "props" in my pockets.

Screw all his bullshit! Nothing in my pitiful life had changed.

I made for the patio door.

None of Ann Marie's jabbering or insensate guests tried to stop me, and Ann Marie herself was nowhere to be seen.

As was only natural, considering the chill and darkness, the small balcony was empty.

I shut the glass door behind me, a barrier to all warmth and human noise.

The narrow flat railing was bitter cold beneath my hands as I clambered atop it.

Below me the city spread out like a Tiffany show window. Wind plucked at my sleeves, beckoning. My eyes began to tear.

I leaned forward, then hesitated. Was this really my only out—?

Hands in my back shoved me over.

"See you later!" I heard Bacchus yell.

I fell about twelve stories before I got the horn out and up to my lips.

I closed my eyes and blew like Gabriel, releasing a long sour BLAT!

The tremendous passage of the icy wind past my plummeting body stopped. All sense of falling ceased.

I seemed to be sitting in a large comfortable padded armchair. The noise of rattling crockery dancing on a wooden tabletop came to my ears. Someone was huffing and puffing. Another someone was grunting. A third someone was squeaking. Then the grunting someone spoke. Shouted, rather, in a high-pitched unhuman voice.

"Put some butter 'round his ears!"

I opened my eyes.

A large tree overspread the tea-party-bedizened table, casting an emerald umbrage. I could smell growing grass and warm scones. The Mad Hatter held the Dormouse by his ankles, while the March Hare was pushing on the pitiful rodent's shoulders, trying to cram him into a teapot. Alice, of course, had just left.

Abandoning his efforts, the Mad Hatter lowered the Dormouse's legs to the table, and the Dormouse lay there with his head in the pot, his squeaks gradually subsiding, to be replaced by snores.

The Mad Hatter removed his topper and scratched his sparsely-haired scalp. I could see the dark line of sweat around his hatband. "'Put some butter 'round his ears'? Why, whatever for? We're not going to eat him, are we?"

The March Hare wrinkled his nose in disgust, quivering his whiskers. "Dolt! Naturally not. You can only eat Dormice in months that end with an 'O,' and this is May!"

Restoring his hat to his head, the Mad Hatter said, "As I recall, you were the one who formerly advised me to add some butter to the works of my watch, and we all know how that turned out. Why should this time be any different?"

"You must admit, the time your watch keeps with butter in the works is much different than the time it kept before."

The Mad Hatter removed his watch from his pocket and gazed dolefully at it, before soaking it in his teacup. "True, quite true. Although it's still right twice a day, the days seem so much longer!"

"I only suggested the butter this time," stipulated the March Hare, "with an eye toward slipperiness."

"You said, 'ears,' not 'eye.' It was the Dormouse's ears that needed buttering, you claimed. I recall it quite distinctly, for it gave me such a disturbing pause as I never experienced before, nor ever hope to again."

The March Hare grew huffy. "I said no such thing! I merely claimed that our somnambulent friend had gotten some butter in his eye, and it needed wiping."

"What a fib!"

"God's truth!"

"Fib!"

"Truth!"

From inside the teapot came a muffled voice. "Why not ask the gentleman wearing the dunce cap to settle the matter?"

The March Hare and the Mad Hatter both turned toward me.

I tried to shrink into the chair, but there was no DRINK ME bottle handy.

What in sweet Jesus's name had I gotten myself into? Goddamn that Bacchus!

"What a capital idea!" exclaimed the Mad Hatter. "There's no one more impartial than someone who has no idea of what's going on!"

Squinting one eye at me, the March Hare said, "I question his qualifications. He looks as if he's searching for something. How can a man with a mission possibly help us?"

"We already tried a miss with a mansion, and she was utterly useless."

The March Hare clapped his paws together. "That's it! He's looking for Alice!"

The Dormouse, with one paw on the pottery spout and one on the handle, succeeded in removing the teapot from his head. "I think not. He's merely looking for a lass. . . ."

"Oh, well, in that case, there's always the Queen."

"Or the Duchess," added the March Hare. "Neither one is married."

"What of the King?"

"The King has nothing to do with the Duchess. That's merely a nasty rumor started by the Knave."

"The King wouldn't object, then, if this fellow wished to marry the Queen?"

"Why should he? A husband has to do whatever his wife wants, especially if he's as powerful as the King."

"Then it's agreed? Our friend with the sugarloaf cap is to marry the Queen today?"

"By all means."

"Excelsior!"

Joining hands, the Hare and Hatter began to dance and sing.

> "We're going to a wedding!
> "It shall be very gay!
> "We'll save the groom's beheading
> "For another summer day!"

Meanwhile, the Dormouse had walked across the table and stepped down into my lap. Involuntarily, I flinched away from his furry weight. But, restraining myself, I allowed him to curl up and go to sleep.

I didn't dare do anything in this hallucination. There was no telling how I might make it worse. In any case, I fully expected to impact the pavement below Ann Marie's apartment any second now, once this Ambrose-Bierce moment of frenzied delusional brain activity was over.

Finishing their capers, the two strange creatures arranged themselves on either side of me.

"Have some wine?" asked the March Hare.

"Thanks, but I've had enough. Would you answer a question for me though?"

"Only if you ask one."

"Assuming that what Bacchus told me was true, how is it that I've ended up in a fictional party instead of a real one?"

"Fictional? Who says we're fictional? That's a tall story someone's shortchanged you with! Here, does this feel fictional?"

The March Hare inclined his head and made me stroke one long plush ear.

"No," I was forced to admit, "it doesn't. . . ."

"And what of poor Dormouse? If you were fictional, as you fictitiously maintain, would it be possible for him to eat that confetti in your pocket, as he is now so raptly doing?"

I looked down, alarmed. Although his eyes were still closed, the Dormouse had somehow burrowed into my pocket, gnawed a hole in the ziploc of transport-confetti, and was now chewing a mouthful.

"Hey!" I shot to my feet, dumping the Dormouse onto the ground. He lay on his back, still somnolently chewing.

Suddenly, my arms were pinioned with surprising strength by the Mad Hatter.

"That's no way to treat someone you've just poisoned!"

"Off with his head!"

The Queen and all her court had arrived. I was somehow gratified to see that their playing-card bodies had a narrow third dimension to them. It made the whole thing so much more plausible.

The masked executioner advanced on me. He held not an axe, but a butter knife he had appropriated from the table.

"I'm so sorry we shan't be getting married now," said the Queen. "But I can't possibly marry a murderer unless he's paid for his crimes by dying."

I felt the blade of the knife laid against my throat.

Jerking violently forward, I tossed the Mad Hatter over my shoulders. He flew among the playing-card figures, flattening a swath through their ranks.

I found Bacchus's horn and brought it to my lips.

I heard the March Hare exclaim, "How splendid! A fanfare for his own throat-slitting—"

And then I was gone.

By the light of two flaring cressets that cast back the night, I saw that there was a sign over the door of the marble mansion that read:

ANY SLAVE LEAVING THE HOUSE WITHOUT HIS
MASTER'S PERMISSION WILL RECEIVE
ONE HUNDRED LASHES

"Ah, Latin," said a drowsy voice from the vicinity of my knees. "How I wish I could read that marvelous language! Unfortunately, during my school days I developed the habit of dropping off to sleep whenever the Master began to declaim Caesar. Even now, the simplest 'weenie-weenie-winkie' sends me to the Land of Nod straight away."

I looked down. Standing on his hind legs, the Dormouse began to lick a paw and drag it over one rounded, unbuttered ear.

I couldn't believe my eyes. "What are you doing here?"

"Why, grooming myself. I'm positively slathered with soggy tea leaves! I'm terribly sorry if I've offended you. Is it considered ill-mannered to groom oneself in public where you come from?"

Obviously, Bacchus's transport-confetti worked as advertised. I had been hoping to leave all traces of the Mad Tea Party far behind me. Plainly, however, the Dormouse and I were now permanently linked.

"Where's the Latin?" I asked.

"Why, on the sign, of course."

"That's English."

"I beg your pardon. I'm English, and I like to fancy I'd recognize a compatriot if I chanced on one. No, that's Latin, or I'm not a member of the *Gliridae*."

Stretching its string, I lifted the party hat without removing it.

The sign was Latin.

I snapped the hat back.

The sign was English.

"Well, I'll be damned—"

Suddenly, my awful fate dawned on me in its full magnitude. Any lingering drunkenness in my veins burned off faster than gunpowder, and I felt an immense weight bow me down.

I was damned.

Never would I see my home era again, except perhaps in passing. The random path through time and space of my horn-assisted materializations insured that. And the temporary nature of the parties I was now forced to inhabit demanded that I perform frequent disorienting transitions. How long did the average revel last? Eight hours? A day, tops? I suspected that for me to linger beyond a party's natural end would be as fatal as attempting to step outside it while it was in progress. No, at the first hint of a party's imminent breakup, the first "It's getting late, we must be going, thanks, it's been great fun," I'd have to sound my trump and disappear.

I hated parties! And now I was doomed to spend the rest of my unnatural existence attending them, a Flying Dutchman of the social circuit. I had traded a quick and relatively painless—albeit messy—death for a lifetime of canapes and cocktails, tiny toothpick-pierced hotdogs and mindless chatter, loutish frat brawls and stuffy White House dinners, gallery openings and bar mitzvahs.

Almost, I turned and ran. How painful could it be to become an instant nova?

Voices approaching down the street stopped me. I had forgotten the existence of other people. My fiery demise would surely wipe out thousands of innocents. While I was quite content to go, I had no desire to exit as a mass murderer.

Damn that Bacchus!

"Oh," yawned the Dormouse, "all this Latin is good as a rum toddy for scattering sand in one's eyes."

Somehow, the Dormouse suddenly seemed like a familiar comforting presence in the face of these unknown people arriving, and I wanted him awake.

"No, don't go to sleep now!"

"I'm—afraid—I can't—help—"

Curling into a ball, the Dormouse filled the air with rodential snores.

Hastily, I picked him up and stepped back into the shadows, praying I wouldn't move beyond the party's invisible sphere.

For good or ill, I didn't explode.

The noisy visitors stepped onto the mansion's wide columned porch.

They were all dressed in splendid colored belted togas, save the slaves, whose clothing was drabber and more uniform. The citizens among them had obviously been drinking for some time, and were plainly several trireme-sheets to the wind.

A large man resembling Zero Mostel said loudly, "Ah, Trimalchio! You're a rich and ignorant ex-slave with no more grace than a camelopard, but we'll drink your Falernian anyway!"

"Hush, Glyco, our host will hear you!" advised an elderly woman wearing too much makeup for any era.

"What do I care! I'd say it right to his poxed face!"

"Still, for my sake. . . ."

"All right, all right!"

Now a young woman, seemingly unaccompanied, spoke.

"The rest of you may as well go inside. I have a last detail to attend to."

Glyco laughed. "Fitting a new pessary up your lovely quim, I daresay! The work of one of Priapus's priestesses is never done!"

Even the object of Glyco's crude jest joined in the raucous laughter, though there was an undertone of distaste in her chuckles. She swatted him with a bundle of herbs she carried and said, "Quartilla excuses your impious jest, Glyco. But I cannot swear that my god is as forgiving. Priapus does not take kindly such insults."

Glyco immediately paled. "Please, Quartilla, I meant no offense! Would—would a small donation of one hundred sesterces to the temple perhaps serve to amend. . . ?"

"Two hundred is more likely to soothe Olympian ire."

"Very well," grumbled Glyco, "I'll send a slave by in the morning."

A hulking man wearing a sword began to bang on the door. He was as ugly as ditchwater and as scarred as the carving tree at your local lover's lane. Drink had transformed what I could sense was innate belligerence into eager malevolence.

"Open up, for Achilles' sake! Hermeros, the life of the party is here!"

The door swung open, and a wizened porter in green livery was framed. "No need to shout, citizens, the meal's only just commenced. Come in, quickly now, before the night air gives me my death. Right foot first, mind!"

The partygoers entered, all carefully stepping over the threshold on the proper foot.

Left alone on the stoop, Quartilla looked carefully about, as if cautious of being observed. Muffling the Dormouse's snores against my chest, I held my breath, fearful that she would spot me. Lit by the torches, she seemed to have stepped fresh from an Alma-Tadema canvas, a pre-Raphaelite goddess, raven-haired, samite-gowned.

As I savored her delicate beauty, she lit her posy from one of the torches, filling the air with fragrant smoke. Tossing the burning herbs to the stones, she lifted her skirts and squatted over the small bonfire. The sound of her piss quenching the little fire filled the air.

"By Priapus and Hecate, Mithra and Eileithyia, I command the demon to appear now!"

A queer impulse urged me to step forward, and I did.

Quartilla shrieked and lost her balance, tumbling over backwards, her skirts billowing around her waist.

Cradling the Dormouse in one arm, I extended a hand to help her up. Somewhat fearfully, she took it. When she was standing, I said, "Here I am. What do you want?"

The priestess's eyes were large with awe. "I can't believe this, it's like a dream come true! I should have known it would happen on the night before my final exam! Though I have been trying to summon up a demon for ages. . . . But anyway, here you are, just like that, familiar and all. Why, there wasn't even any smoke or thunder. . . ."

"Smoke and thunder are out of fashion where I come from, except in balancing the imperial debt, in which case we also employ mirrors."

"Well, it's not as if I'm complaining, you understand. You're quite impressive as you are, what with your strange attire and all. Is that a gallows rope round your neck? Never mind, you needn't say, if it embarrasses you. One thing, though—I wasn't aware demons needed to shave as mortal men do."

"You caught me on an off week. My wife left me."

A gleam appeared in Quartilla's eyes. "Ah, naturally. Every incubus must be mated with a succubus. . . ."

"That she was," I agreed.

Quartilla grabbed my hand again. "You must come back to temple with me! Once Albucia, the head priestess, sees you, I'll surely be promoted! Mom and Dad will be so proud!"

She tried to tug me off the porch, and I quickly disengaged. "'Fraid not, priestess. I have to attend this party. Or some other."

Quartilla placed her thumb beneath her pert chin and her forefinger at the corner of her mouth. She looked absolutely charming. "You're under a geas, I take it."

"Yes. One of Bacchus's, curse him."

"Oh, him! It's not wise to flout the wishes of Enorches, the

Betesticled One. I advise you to comply with whatever compulsion
he has put on you."

"As if I have a choice."

"Well, what about after the party? Could you come then?"

I hated to disappoint her. "We'll see."

She lit up like Greek Fire. "Wonderful! I'll stay right by your side
all night! And so as not to divulge your true identity, I'll claim you as
one of my *umbrae*, an uninvited tagalong guest."

Squiring Quartilla for the evening did not seem like such an awful
prospect, so I nodded my consent.

"How shall I call you? 'Demon' will certainly not do. . . ."

"Loren."

"An uncouth name. How about 'Laurentius'?"

"Good enough."

Satisfied with my new nomenclature, Quartilla adjusted the
lines of her skirt with a deft tug and knocked on the door of
Trimalchio's big house. The same wrinkled servant appeared in no
time and let us in.

A magpie in a golden cage hanging near the entrance shrieked
hello. Ahead of us stretched a long colonnade painted with colorful
frescoes.

"Do you note the bald and querulous old man who recurs in each
scene? That's the image of our host."

"Did he really fight in the Trojan War and visit paradise with
Mercury?"

Quartilla shrugged charmingly. "When you're rich enough, you
may have painted whatever flattering fancy you wish."

The porter had retreated to a cubbyhole near the door and was
busy shelling peas into a silver basin. Meanwhile, an epicene figure
had stepped forward.

"The eunuch will show you to the feast," said the porter. "By the
way, is that beast trained not to befoul my master's fine carpets?"

I had almost forgotten I was carrying the snoozing Dormouse. "He's quite intelligent, although he does drip tea now and then."

"Well, don't let him drip on the brocades."

We followed the eunuch down the hall, and soon entered—right foot first—an expansive dining-room.

The large crowded room was well lit by several oil fixtures depending from the ceiling. Three large couches were arranged in a U-shape around a central table, and dozens of other smaller lounges and chairs were scattered about. People milled around, laughing, chattering, drinking and eating small elegant snacks.

As soon as we stepped in, we were beseiged by servants.

Lissome boys poured ice water over our hands; the runoff was captured in golden bowls upheld by others. Then our hands were gently dried for us. (I was forced to drape the Dormouse over one shoulder.)

I felt my shoes being tugged off. "Hey—!"

Attendants were removing Quartilla's sandals also. "It's only the pedicure, Laurentius. Don't they have pedicures in Hades?"

"Not at parties."

Like a starved alley cat adopted by Rockefellers, Quartilla was luxuriating under the attention. "It's one of the essentials of civilization. Ah, it seems like a lustrum since I last attended a good party!"

I cut the embarrassing procedure short. "Come on, let's meet our host."

Both of us now barefoot, we advanced across the carpeted room. I could see Quartilla was irked at having her pedicure interrupted. "Are all demons so impetuous and impatient?"

"Only those who have lost their wives, their jobs and their homes, and been thwarted in their suicide attempts."

"Oh."

We arrived at what Quartilla whispered to me was "the Upper Couch." Recumbent at one end, wrapped in a red felt scarf against a visible case of sniffles, was Trimalchio. The murals had exaggerated any of his minor graces. Lying next to the millionaire was Hermeros: the breast of his toga was adorned with the tissuey shells of a dozen shrimps he had consumed, and he gripped a giant flagon of wine in one meaty paw. As we stood there, he emitted an enormous belch, followed by a 100-watt leer at Quartilla.

"Ah, my favorite priestess," lisped Trimalchio, "how nice of you to come. I trust your mistress, Albucia, is well. . . ?"

"Thank you for inviting me, honorable sir. Yes, my mistress fares well, although she is somewhat weary from servicing so many soldiers of late, as are all we maidens of Priapus. You know what the average Legionary freshly returned from the provinces is like. . . ."

At this point, Hermeros made a grab at Quartilla's haunch, which she deftly sidestepped.

"Come here, you wench! I'll show you what kind of bronze balls swing under a real soldier's staff!"

"Then again," said Quartilla dryly, "it does not always require service in the deserts of Syria to render one witless. Sometimes, simple inbreeding will suffice."

There was a bustle behind us which caused Trimalchio to quickly lose interest in us. Before I could be introduced, he picked up a purple-striped tasselled napkin and, tucking it beneath his scarf, said, "Glad to hear it. Sit now, and take your pleasures."

We moved to empty spaces at the Middle Couch, and I gratefully set the snoozing Dormous down. He had been getting quite heavy.

The dish which had diverted Trimalchio's salivating attention from us was being lowered to the central table by four waiters. The door-sized platter was framed with the inlaid signs of the Zodiac, each of which held its symbolically appropriate food. A metal dome in the middle of the platter was soon lifted to reveal several plump fowls, fish arranged in a trough of sauce as if swimming, and a hare with pigeon wings affixed to its shoulders to resemble Pegasus. Also occupying the board were two or three amorphous objects which I did not recognize.

Quartilla gripped my arm and shrieked gleefully. "Oh, Laurentius! My favorite dish! Fresh sow's udder!"

All the fear, excitement, tension and despair of the crazy night and the past week congealed into one greasy knot in my throat. I felt my gorge rising unstoppably, like an express train in my throat. I tried to get to my feet, but couldn't make it. I averted my head—and found a servant waiting with a copper receptacle ready.

Then I heaved for what seemed like a day.

As I sagged back onto the couch, drained and weak, a round of applause filled the room.

Trimalchio's voice carried above the diminishing clapping. "Quartilla's foreign guest takes first honors! Bestow the laurels upon him!"

A slave advanced and dropped a floral wreath over my head and around my neck.

Quartilla bestowed a peck on my cheek. "Well done, Laurentius. That was truly a demonic regurgitation for so early in the feast."

I accepted a damp scented cloth from yet another slave and wiped my mouth. "Thank you. I haven't done anything like that since college."

"Are you ready for some udder now?"

Suppressing a mild gagging, I replied, "No, please, you indulge yourself. I believe I'll just have something to drink. . . ."

"Mead for our champion, Laurentius!" commanded Quartilla, before spearing and slicing a teat.

I rinsed my mouth with the mead, and then lay back as a spectator to the party.

After all, how often did one get to attend a real Roman orgy?

My expectations, however, were greater than the reality. If this was the height of the legendary decadence of Rome, than the twentieth century had them beat hollow. All anybody seemed interested in doing was gorging themselves on the various exotic dishes and gossiping. (Quartilla kept up with the best of the diners, in a somewhat appalling display of bone-stripping, lip-smacking, finger-licking avidity.) On the whole, I had been to wilder Rotary Club dinners. The height of excitement came when an argument flared between a husband and wife. She threw a plate at him, he ducked, and it narrowly missed Trimalchio.

"You bitch!"

"Bastard!"

Trimalchio intervened. "Julius and Melissa, I'm so hurt! That was a piece of original Corinthian!"

"I'm sorry, Trimalchio. But he deserved it. I caught him with that slut Oenothea in the privy!"

Singers sang (" 'Tis a ditty from *The Asafoetida Man*," Quartilla informed me), dancers danced and jugglers juggled. After the course which consisted of a roasted whole boar stuffed with live thrushes, a pair of rowdy disheveled jesters took the stage.

"My name is Haiga, and my comrade here is called Hatta."

"He's a lying Thracian!"

"Now, what makes you say such a cruel thing, Hatta?"

"You said I was called Hatta."

"Is that not your name?"

"Of course it's my name!"

"Then what's the problem?"

"My name is not what I'm called."

"Oh, I see. What are you called, then?"

"Mad!"

The audience cracked up. "A paradox worthy of Zeno!" complimented Trimalchio, tossing some coins at the performers.

Throughout the evening, I had sustained a virtually unrelenting barrage of glares and growls from Hermeros, who plainly resented my proximity to Quartilla. Whenever she leaned toward me, it provoked him to near-madness. Several times I braced myself for a lunge that he fortunately never quite carried through, restrained perhaps by the setting.

The night wore on in a blizzard of food and drink. Every dish seemed more elaborate than the last, announced by Trimalchio with boorish delight. I drank cup after cup of mead, until my vision and hearing grew fuzzy as the logic of the neural network that had stolen—would steal—my job two thousand years from now.

Somehow, it seemed like a good idea to lay my head in Quartilla's lap and go to sleep, whatever Hermeros might do. But that stupid hat of mine— I removed it and put it on the head of the Dormouse, where it wouldn't get lost.

All the chatter became a senseless babble, which lulled me to a hazy sleep. . . .

I came to a start when the Dormouse screamed.

On the table was the latest offering from Trimalchio's kitchens: nestled in a candied glaze were little rodents one tenth the size of— but otherwise identical to—my personal Dormouse.

The Dormouse was jabbering in Latin. I snatched the hat off his head and put it on. Now I could understand both his English and the Latin of the others.

"What month is it? What month is it?" the Dormouse was demanding.

"Why, 'tis the month of Quintilus," answered Quartilla hesitantly when I asked.

I told the Dormouse.

"But that doesn't end in an 'O!'" he wailed. "Oh, how could they do such a cruel thing to my cousins, without even waiting till October!"

"October doesn't end with an 'O' either."

"But at least it begins with one!"

The whole room had gone quiet while the Dormouse and I conversed. Several people were making horned-finger gestures at me, against the evil eye. Then Hermeros, standing somewhat unsteadily, broke the silence.

"He's a magician, an evil magician! That's the only explanation of how someone so puny could have enraptured the priestess so. He must be slain to free her!"

Hefting his sword, Hermeros stumbled menacingly toward me.

I fumbled for the packet of transport-confetti, found it and managed to shake some on Quartilla, out of the hole the Dormouse had nibbled. Then I got the horn to my lips.

"He attempts to summon the aid of spirits!" yelled Hermeros, and threw himself clumsily at our couch.

As I gave a mighty blast on the party horn, I saw a single dot of confetti fall from Quartilla's shoulder onto Hermeros.

Shit, thought I.

The sun was so bright in comparison to the oil lamps at Trimalchio's, I couldn't see for a moment. I could only hope that Hermeros—had he indeed accompanied us—was suffering from the same disadvantage.

As I did not immediately feel a sword piercing my queasy guts, I assumed the bad-tempered soldier was squinting and rubbing his eyes as fiercely as I.

As the sun-dazzles cleared from my vision, the pellucid notes of an electric guitar sounded from some distance away, and I realized from other familiar noises that a constant stream of people was flowing around and past our little tableau.

Finally, I could see.

Quartilla was turning around in slow circles of slack-jawed amazement. Hermeros was dragging a clumsy hand slowly over his apish incredulous mug, the point of his blade resting on the ground. The Dormouse was unconcernedly asleep at my feet, the sad fate of his cousins forgotten.

We were in some modern city, standing at the gates of some park. Throngs of people, mostly young, were ambling past us and onto the grassy grounds. One of them, as he passed, tossed a newspaper in a trash can, and I claimed it.

It was the *San Francisco Oracle*, and its banner headline read:

FIRST HUMAN BE-IN TODAY!

It was 1967, ten years before I had been—or would be—born.

The Summer of Love.

Quartilla had stopped turning, and now beamed at me.

"Laurentius, how marvelous! You have transported us to your Underworld home!"

"Close enough, give or take a decade or two and the width of a continent."

"Little did I ever suspect that the realm of Pluto held such wonders! Just wait until I report these marvelous adventures to Albucia!"

Instantly, I felt remorseful for having dragged this poor girl from her natural time and place. What had made me permanently wrench her from her home, other than greed for her beautiful company? And how could I ever tell her what I had done?

"Ah, yes, well, you see, Quartilla—gurk!"

Hermeros's swordpoint was nicking my throat. I swallowed tentatively, and my Adam's apple measured the steel in micrometers.

"You fiend!" spat the soldier. "You vile fiend! Return us to Rome immediately, or I'll run you through!"

"Now listen, Hermeros, it's not as easy as you might think—"

The blade pushed deeper. "No excuses! Do it!"

"I can't!"

Hermeros must have concealed in his back one of those buttons that Ann Marie had. His expression went instantly from mere anger to volcanic rage.

"Then I'm damned, and you're dead!"

I closed my eyes and tried to pray.

"Hey, man, quit goofin' around!"

"Yeah, brother. Be cool!"

I opened my eyes.

Two strange figures flanked Hermeros.

Both men had hair down to their navels or thereabouts, and flowers and peace signs painted on their faces. One wore a top hat, and the other flaunted a headband to which was affixed a droopy pair of cloth rabbit ears. The guy with the hat was dressed in a ruffled white shirt and denim bell-bottoms, while the other sported a fur vest over his hairy bare chest and tight green velvet pants.

"You could really hurt someone with that pigsticker," admonished Top Hat.

"Don't you know it's a day for groovin' in the sun?" inquired Rabbit Ears.

The sight of the hippies seemed to have discombobulated Hermeros. When at last he could speak he said, "I have seen Druids naked and painted blue, and lice-ridden Syrian anchorites blistering under the sun. But I'll sell my own mother into slavery if I've ever seen two such misbegotten hellspawn as these ones you have summoned, sorceror." Stiffening his resolve, Hermeros readjusted his sword for a thrust. "Though they rend me into pieces, I shall yet have my revenge!"

Top Hat turned to me. "What did he say, man?"

"He's very pleased to meet you, but he still intends to kill me."

Rabbit Ears clucked his tongue. "Major uncool."

"Bad vibes."

"Bringdown city."

"Total bummer."

Putting two fingers in his mouth, Rabbit Ears produced a loud whistle.

Out of the crowd materialized a brace of enormous Hell's Angels, filthy, bearded and leather-clad. They pinioned Hermeros's arms before he could react.

I gulped gratefully. Thinking fast, I said, "He's a little high. Could you just hold him for a while, guys, until he comes down? And, oh, don't take him out of the park, will you?"

The last thing I wanted was to destroy San Francisco on such a happy historic day.

"Sure, man," grunted one of the Angels. "That's what we're here for." Then they marched the struggling Hermeros off.

I knew the respite was only temporary. Linked to me by the confetti, Hermeros would remain my problem. Still, it felt good to be rid of him, even for a short while.

Quartilla had watched the whole affair with pale-faced consternation. Now she said, "You have mighty servitors here, Laurentius. I am astonished I could summon a demon as powerful as you."

"Looks count for a lot," I said.

The Priapic priestess blushed. "No one has complimented me in so long. It's just wham-bam-thank-you-goddess from most men I meet."

"Well, you don't have to worry about that from me." Mostly because we'll never have any privacy, I added mentally.

There came a gentle coughing. I turned toward the hippies, who were smiling bemusedly.

"You cats gonna join the party now?" asked Top Hat.

"What else?" I replied.

"Far out!" exclaimed Rabbit Ears. "I knew you were dressed up to get down!"

I suddenly realized what I looked like. Barefoot, wearing a crumpled garland, stubble-faced and vomit-bespattered, accompanied by a gal wrapped in a bedsheet. Yet somehow I fit right in.

"I don't believe we've swapped handles yet," said Top Hat. "My name is Fletcher Platt, and my friend here is Lionel Stokely David van Camp, heir to the canned vegetable fortune, and otherwise known as 'LSD.'"

Fletcher took off his top hat and bowed to Quartilla, while LSD kissed her hand.

"I'm Loren, and this is, um, Quartilla."

"Cool. What's the story with the rat?"

I had forgotten the Dormouse. "He's—I mean, it's, uh—a capyb-ara! That's it, a capybara. World's largest rodent. Comes from South America."

The hippies regarded the snoring Dormouse dubiously. "Shouldn't it be, like, on a leash, man?" asked LSD.

"No, he—it's quite domesticated."

"Groovy. Well, what are we waiting for? Let's make the scene!"

So we made the scene.

Meandering through the rapidly filling park, Dormouse cradled against me, I relished the illusion of freedom. Unlike claustrophobia-inducing indoor parties, the large-scale Be-in, with its fresh air, sun and sky, seemed like heaven.

We bought hotdogs from a vendor (Quartilla bit into hers tentatively, then ate it with gusto, while the Dormouse consumed most of mine in his sleep), and made our way toward Hippie Hill, where we could command a view of the stage.

On the way, I kept an eye peeled for Bacchus. Surely he would materialize at such a major bash as this. If I could only lay my hands on him, perhaps there was a chance I could undo what he had done to me.

But there were simply too many people. I estimated the crowd at several thousand, and not one that I could see was dispensing wine from his palm.

At the top of the hill, we flopped on the grass. Below us, a band was wailing.

"Who's that?" I asked.

"Man, where have you been!" said Fletcher. "Don't you recognize Quicksilver Messenger Service?"

I shook my head in amazement. "What history. It's like being at Woodstock."

"History? 'Woodstack?' Man, you're some wiggy cat!"

Quartilla seemed captivated by the music, so I explained to her who was playing. But in Latin, it came out funny.

"Mercury's Heralds? What an honor!" She began to sway with the tune.

I lay back on the grass. Lord knew where I would end up after this. If only I could relax for a moment—

As if reading my thoughts, LSD hove into view. He was brandishing a joint.

"Care for a toke?"

"Mega-awesome, dude."

"Huh?"

"Uh, right on!"

Pretty soon, after the third joint had circulated among us, the day turned transparent, and all my cares seemed to melt away.

Quartilla giggled. "I feel like the Delphic Oracle."

"Hey, man," exclaimed LSD, "I understood that! This dope is bringing back my high-school Latin!"

"Even the Caterpillar, curmudgeon that he was, let me sample his pipe now and then."

Dormouse was awake, leaning on both elbows on my thigh.

Fletcher and LSD had turned to stone at the first word out of the Dormouse. Their eyes were big as Mad Tea Party saucers.

LSD was the first to recover. Oh-so-slowly he extended his hand holding the joint to the Dormouse, who took it, puffed deeply, then handed it back.

"Thank you, sir. Did I ever mention that you resemble a friend of mine?"

LSD took a long drag on the roach. "Heavy, man. Beyond heavy. What was that phrase you used before, man?"

"Mega-awesome?"

"You got it!"

LSD lit a new joint off the old one, and now the five of us partook.

The day wore on peacefully. Someone came by handing out free cold beers from a cooler. Another someone laid a gift on us: a can of compressed air with a horn attached. Fletcher and LSD took turns sending out blasts of sound until they grew bored.

As the afternoon began to shade into night and the Be-in began to show signs of winding down, I grew melancholy, as did the others.

"Man, don't you wish a day like this could go on forever?" asked Fletcher, in what he falsely assumed was a rhetorical mode.

I was still a little high. "You'd like life to be one big party?"

"Well, hell, man—who wouldn't?"

I took the confetti out of my pocket. "I've got the power to grant your wish, boys. I sprinkle you with this magic pixie dust"—I suited actions to words—"and the next time I blow this horn"—I showed them the horn—"your endless party begins."

The hippies chuckled. "Whatever turns you on, man."

"You'll see how—" I started to say, when I felt cold steel in my back.

"Now I have you, sorceror!" said Hermeros.

I made to raise the horn to my lips, but a jab from the blade stopped me.

"Don't try it!"

Fletcher stepped forward. "Here, let me."

He took the horn from my hand and jammed it into the nozzle of the air can.

Then he mashed the button down.

The magic horn blared without cease and the universe exploded.

Like a film run at a zillion frames per second, all the parties of history began to rush by.

I was dancing on the Titanic, I was sharing a picnic with two Frenchmen and a naked woman, I was a champagne-guzzling spectator at a Napoleonic battlefield, I was boogieing at Club 54, I was in a temple in Egypt, a yurt in Mongolia, a ballroom in Russia. And that was the first picosecond.

Summoning up every ounce of will, I tried to turn around. It was like wading trough treacle. I could only move in those brief nanoseconds when I flashed through a gaudy party.

Like stone eroding, I pivoted to confront Hermeros. It took ten million, million parties, but at last I was facing him.

At that instant, the horn stopped. Fletcher must have managed to lift his finger.

We were surrounded by a ring of dinosaurs. T. Rexes, I believe. And they were dancing, shaking the earth. Partying, to be precise.

Hermeros was stunned, but I had no mercy.

"That ain't no way to have fun," I advised him.

Then I gave him a tremendous shove, propelling him beyond the circle of beasts.

At the same time, I yelled to Fletcher, "Hit it!"

The horn sounded, just in time.

The actinic radiation from Hermeros's explosion chased us through a thousand frames, forcing us to close our eyes. But it never quite caught us.

From First Be-in to Great Die-off. *Mea culpa*, man.

Silence. Blessed silence. The can must have run out of air.

I opened one eye timidly, then the other.

Fletcher was holding the shredded remnants of the magic horn, which had disintegrated under the prolonged blast.

And, I realized with a shock, we were in Ann Marie's apartment, with the Millennial New Year's Eve party seemingly still in full swing.

I collapsed into a chair. "Straight back to my old problems. Bummer, man."

Ann Marie bustled up, perky as ever. "Loren! I'm so glad you could make it!"

"Don't play games with me, Ann Marie. You don't know what I've been through."

"Well, how could I? I haven't seen you in twenty years, ever since that night you cut out so rudely after worrying me nearly to death!"

"Twenty—?" I looked more closely at my hostess. Sure enough, those were lots of brand-new lines on her face.

So I wasn't in my starting place after all. Which meant that I was still a potentially explosive intruder, with no means of escape. As soon as this party was over, I and my companions would go up with enough force to split the earth.

I hung my head. "I'm so sorry, everyone. I really am."

"What are you whining about now?" said Ann Marie. "I swear, Loren—you're probably the only person in the world who's not having fun these days!"

"How's that?"

"Well, you know. Ever since the neural whatsits took over all work and government, it's been one big party!"

I looked up. "You're telling me than no one has to work anymore. . . ?"

"Of course not! It's just play, play, play, from sunup to sundown, anywhere on the globe you go!"

I turned to Fletcher and LSD, who had been standing curiously by. "Guys, here's that endless party I promised. Sorry the ride was a little bumpy."

"Cool."

"Groovy."

"Where's the drugs?"

Ann Marie took one hippie on each arm. "Right this way. Loren, try to have fun! By the way, boys, I love your costumes!"

For the first time since we had met, Quartilla and I were alone. If you could count being adjacent to a sweaty game of Naked Co-ed Twister alone. I took her hands and gazed into her eyes.

"Bacchus be praised," was all I could finally say.

"Yes. And I'd be happy to show you how."

And as we headed for the bedroom, I heard the Dormouse exclaim, "I say, is that a hookah I hear burbling?"

Every humor writer finds certain idiosyncratic words, actions and objects to be inexplicably, inherently funny. Flann O'Brien, for instance, considered bicycles to be the ultimate slapstick vehicle. For James Blaylock, it might be fish. Without a certain amount of self-control and self-awareness, however, these personal talismans can become verbal tics. When writing "The Double Felix" (winner of the British SF Association award for best story of 1994), I felt that every major character at some point should be reduced to talking aloud to himself. Now, I wonder. Does this bother you?

Or am I just talking to myself?

The Double Felix

PROLOGUE

MOST FUNERALS, not surprisingly, are tearful affairs, and that of Felix Wren was no exception.

It need not have been, of course. Felix himself would have told everyone as much, had he simply remembered to do so before the inconvenience of his expected, if not entirely predictable death. If the mourners had only known about Tosh and the very special collar he wore, they all would have had cause for stunned rejoicing.

Except, of course, for the murderers.

From the front row of the packed church—where sat the lovely widow, Mrs. Wren (formerly the titled but impecunious heiress Galina Balyban, great-granddaughter of an exiled White Russian count)—to the last few pews packed with Felix's employees from Wren BioHarmonics and with his old classmates from the California Institute of Technology, tears flowed and sobs were choked back.

Even the minister delivering the eulogy was having trouble maintaining his composure.

Now, it seems likely that even the worst person who ever lived and died probably enjoyed a mourner or two at his funeral: Stalin's aged mother, for instance, assuming the dictator hadn't had her shot by then, might have wept over her boy's casket. But the tears flowing down during this particular funeral were neither sparse nor crocodilian. Felix Wren had been well loved. Everyone who had ever had any dealings with him had come away with respect and affection. The general consensus had been that Felix was a prince among the rabble. And now, every time anyone glanced at his closed coffin, they were struck anew by the pain occasioned by his unfortunate accidental death at so young an age.

Undeterred by his own sniffles, the minister was entering his peroration.

"And it seems only fitting that Felix should have perished in the manner he did, at home in his beloved workshop, searching for yet another product to benefit mankind. How a researcher of Felix's experience could have failed to take adequate precautions against the accidental needle-stick that injected the fatal compound into his veins must remain forever a mystery, and is not for us to ponder. The authorities"—here the minister glanced toward the rear of the church, where a lone hardbitten man stood awkwardly by the door, hat in his single hand— "are satisfied that Felix's death was strictly an act of God, one of those inexplicable mishaps all too familiar to us poor mortals. And perhaps God in his wisdom had some—"

"Will you get that goddamn tongue out of my ear!"

The hush that followed this astonishingly indelicate and decontextualized admonition resembled the silence one might encounter deep within the innermost chambers of the Carlsbad Caverns. Suddenly, birds half a mile away could be heard singing their vernal songs through the open church doors.

All eyes were now riveted on the lithe form of the black-suited Widow Wren as she shot to her feet and spun around to glare at the man sitting next to her. Beneath the black lace veil softening her features, a look of rage contorted her face for a moment, and, quivering, she seemed ready to launch into further vituperations. But then, with a visible effort, she recovered herself. Regarding the congregation with a look of pained contrition, she suddenly slapped a hand to her skirted behind and shrieked. And whereas her first imprecation had been delivered in the distinct tones of a Tennessee fishwife, the exclamation that now emerged was couched in a strange Ruritanian accent.

"I—I—I've been stung in the rear!"

The man on whom her wrath had been momentarily focused now stood. A large shambling fellow wearing a chauffeur's uniform about half a size too small and a visored cap half a size too large, he possessed a face reminiscent of one of history's lesser despots, crowned with bowl-cut black hair.

"Lemme help your Ladyship outa this solemnical and requisitive tent-show," said the man, taking the widow's arm in an overfirm grip.

Mrs. Wren spoke through her reactivated sobs. "Yes, please, Staggers. I—I'd like to wait in the car."

The pair proceeded down the church aisle. When they were halfway to the door, the minister resumed his speech, and attention refocused on the altar.

At the door, the lone man who had been standing approached them. The empty right sleeve of his suitcoat was neatly folded and pinned.

"Mrs. Wren. Mr. Staggers. Mind if I have a word with you?"

"No, of course not, Detective Stumbo. But we should step outside in deference to the deceased."

The man seemed barely to repress a snort. "Sure."

A white stretch limo with opaque windows sat on the gravelled crescent drive before the church. The trio stopped by its left rear door.

Detective Stumbo snugged his hat on, freeing his solo hand to filch a cigarette from a pocketed pack. He lit a wooden kitchen match with a flick of his thumb and puffed the cigarette alive. For a few taut seconds, he regarded the widow and her chauffeur with eyes that had in the past actually been employed by the FBI to wordlessly end hostage negotiations. Then he spoke.

"I just wanted you to know, Mrs. Wren, that although the department has officially closed the case on your husband's death, I intend to keep on pursuing it on my own. I'm not convinced that we've learned everything there is to learn yet. It seems to me there's a few loose ends—"

The woman brought forth a dazzling smile and directed it at the detective. "I appreciate your concern, Mister Stumbo—Grady, if I may. But I'm perfectly content with the results of the investigation. It seems like a waste of time for you to keep on probing—as well as a painful stimulus to a poor wife simply trying to forget such a tragedy."

The chauffeur spoke up. "Yeah. And it don't sound too legal neither, you fuckin' around on your personal time where you don't—ow!"

Mrs. Wren converted the aftermath of her kick into an innocent weak-ankled stumble. "Oh, I feel faint. . . . Do we really need to discuss this further right now, Detective?"

"No, of course not. But I'll be in touch."

The chauffeur stepped forward. "Just to show there ain't no hard feelin's, Dumbo, let's shake!"

Grady eyed the outstretched right paw coolly for a moment before answering.

"Pigs must have wings these days, since snakes have hands."

So saying, Detective Grady Stumbo moved off toward his car, a battered red Ford Escort. Soon, he was driving away.

"Haw, haw!" laughed Staggers. His glance fell on the Widow Wren, and his manner reverted to savagery. He yanked open the limo door in a highly nonprofessional manner.

"Get in, you dumb bimbo!"

Hustling the widow inside, he quickly followed, slamming the door behind him.

Once inside the privacy of the capacious car, Staggers began shaking his ostensible employer.

"Now, what's the idea of makin' a scene like that in there?"

Mrs. Wren, a bored expression on her face, said nothing, and Staggers soon grew tired of agitating her flesh without compensatory reaction, and so released her.

"Are you done?" she calmly asked.

"Yeah, for now—oof!"

Mrs. Wren unlocked the club she had made of her interlinked hands and stretched her manicured fingers while Staggers rubbed the rapidly purpling jaw she had smashed.

"You idiot! Feeling me up in church like that! I told you that we had to keep everything looking proper until the heat died down. Isn't it bad enough that that sneaky cop obviously still suspects us, without you practically writing him a confession?"

Rather than seeming angry, Staggers appeared pleased with Mrs. Wren's gumption. Leering, he said, "I couldn't help myself, babe. You just get me so worked up."

Staggers placed a big hand on the widow's knee and attempted to slide it up her skirt, but she knocked it away. However, she seemed not entirely displeased, despite her next words.

"I rue the day you ever found me again. If I had my way—"

"If you had your way, you'd still be whinin' about how that jerkola husband of yours was wastin' his fortune—our fortune—followin' them crazy ideas of his. If it wasn't for me, you never woulda had the courage to bump him off."

"I suppose. . . ."

Staggers reapplied his hand, and it met with no resistance. "Cold one minnit and hot the next. Jus' like the old Perfidia—"

Bristling, the woman said, "Didn't I tell you never to use that name, even when we're alone!"

Staggers laughed rudely. "Oh, it wouldn't suit your Ladyship's plans now, would it, if all your new friends was to find out that the rich bitch Gasolina Bellyband who gets her picture in all the papers—even the Atlanta ones—was really Miss Perfidia Graboys of Pine Mountain, Georgia. Or as she was otherwise once known for about a year, Mrs. Rowdy Staggers."

Rowdy's hand was now high up Perfidia's skirt, while the other one was busy inside her unbuttoned blouse. Her head lay back on the cushioned seat, painted eyelids closed.

"You bastard. You stinking bastard. But you always did know what I liked. A hundred times better than that wimpy little Felix. . . ."

There was silence for a busy minute. Then Perfidia spoke.

"Do you know what the first thing I'm going to do when we get home is, Rowdy?"

"Mrmph. . . ."

"I'm going to have you kill that horrid dog Felix loved so much.

"Yes, I think old Tosh will be the first thing I attend to."

1.

Your average specimen of the Komondor breed of canine weighs upwards of one hundred and fifty pounds and resembles a small loveseat festooned with long dreadlocks. The matted Rasta hair typical of the breed obscures the dog's face, giving it a fathomless expression which effectively conceals its sometimes ignoble intentions.

Felix Wren had owned three Komondors in his life, in sequence. The first had been named Marley, the second Cliff. The current one was named Tosh.

Tosh padded nervously now from one end of Felix's well-appointed workshop to the other. Ever since his master's death, he had been inconsolable. Penned in his outdoor run, he had barked incessantly, throwing his huge bulk against the wire in an effort to escape. The sight of either Perfidia or Rowdy had been enough to drive him to violent paroxysms.

Fearful that the grief-maddened pet would eventually break free and beseige them in the main house, Perfidia had ordered Rowdy to transfer the dog to Felix's lab. Rowdy equipped himself with a pole-mounted snare; Tosh snapped it in half, and Rowdy felt himself lucky to escape with even one pants leg. Only a tranquilizer dart administered by a compliant vet had succeeded in rendering the beast temporarily manageable. (Rowdy had argued for killing the monster outright, but Perfidia had countered that such a move would appear too suspicious, and should be postponed until at least after the funeral.)

The familiar smells in the lab seemed to have quieted the dog somewhat, and he now no longer raged, but merely whimpered and paced, claws clicking on the linoleum.

Around Tosh's neck was a curious collar. Hard to detect beneath his dreadlocks, it seemed to be composed of burnished, chunky metal lozenges, save for a single oval link of transparent crystal wired to its neighbors.

A digital clock atop a littered workbench flipped from 11:59 AM to 12:00 PM.

Tosh suddenly stiffened as if electrocuted, and fell to the floor.

A wave of distortion blurred the dog's body. It was as if it had been placed in the middle of an invisible oven, an oven whose superheated air was making the dogbody waver and shift, melting, warping, recohering the shaggy form into—

The body of a slim, red-haired and freckled man, naked except for Tosh's collar.

The man opened a pair of guileless blue eyes. He reached up and felt the collar, loose around his neck.

"Wow. It works. It works!" The man sobered. "Poor Tosh." He patted his own head. "Sorry, boy. We'll get you back soon."

An expression as of memories reintegrating themselves wrinkled the man's face, and he sobered even further. "What am I saying? Poor Tosh? Poor me! They—they murdered me! My own loving wife! Well, I suspected it was coming, but I never imagined it would happen so soon. I thought they were going to spend a little more time working themselves up to it. Still, I should have guessed. Galina never brought me lunch before. I was so amazed—even if it was only a peanut-butter and banana sandwich—that I never heard that rascal Staggers come in behind her—"

Breaking off, the man got to his feet. "Gosh, I have to remind myself Tosh isn't here anymore—or at least not as such. I'm so used to talking to the old boy—"

The man took a coverall down from a hook and donned it, along with a pair of chemical-stained sneakers. "I don't suppose this is the safest place for us to hang around, is it, Tosh? But there're things I still need to do without being interrupted. Now, where could we— Of course! Priscilla Jane's!"

Picking up the receiver of a phone, the man dialed.

"Hello, Priscilla Jane? This is Felix. Felix who? Your boss, Felix Wren. Do you know any other Felixes? It's not that common a name. Hello? Priscilla Jane, are you there?"

Felix hung up the phone. "Funny. We got disconnected. Oh well, I suppose it's just as quick to go over there as to call again."

From a plastic bin, Felix grabbed a handful of necklaces and bracelets of varying sizes, all otherwise identical to the one he wore, and dropped them in various pockets. He picked up a laptop computer, and moved toward the lab door.

The sound of a car entering the grounds of the mansion reached Felix's ears.

"Oh-oh."

Felix darted outside, hoping to elude the returning new owners of his home before they saw him.

But he was too late.

The car halted opposite his workshop while he was still framed in the doorway. His treacherous wife and chauffeur emerged. Busy talking, they at first did not see him.

"—and the dog should suffer! Shoot one paw at a time, Rowdy."

"Haw, haw, Perfidia, that's the style!"

Felix's vision was washed with crimson hues. Before he could stop himself, words spilled out.

"It's not bad enough you killed me, now you're planning to torture poor Tosh!"

Perfidia and Rowdy were nailed to the lawn. Their eyes assumed the dimensions of peeled onions. Perfidia staggered and clutched the chauffeur. Rowdy's color drained into his boots.

"Gallopin' Jesus! It's a ha'nt!"

Felix smiled. If they only knew. He was ten times more miraculous than a ghost.

Walking calmly across the lawn away from the frozen couple, Felix could not resist uttering a small "Boo!"

That shattered his wife's immobility.

"Ghosts don't carry computers, Rowdy! I don't know who he is, but we've got to stop him!"

"Gotcha, babe!"

Rowdy advanced slowly but determinedly on Felix.

Felix began taking off his clothes.

This apparently insane action gave Rowdy pause, but he soon resumed his cautious stalking.

Felix flipped the laptop's screen into position and opened a window. He jacked a cable from the laptop into a small port on the necklace he wore.

"Do you think sixty seconds will be enough, Tosh?" Felix asked the air.

"Buddy, you ain't gonna get more'n three seconds," growled Rowdy.

Felix clucked his tongue. "Such ignorance."

Then he tapped ENTER.

The improbable transformation which had wrought Tosh into Felix now recurred in reverse.

A snarling, slavering, vengeful dog sprang up, whipped his head around to disengage the computer tether, then focused on a stunned Rowdy. The man began to back away. With a yelp, Perfidia fled toward the house. Rowdy turned and sprinted after her.

Tosh was on him within a few yards. With one huge bound, he knocked the chauffeur to the ground. Rowdy's head bounced off an ornamental cement lawn frog, and he was still. Tosh lunged for the unconscious man's throat—

Felix found himself with a mouthful of uniform.

"Yuck!"

Climbing off the still-breathing chauffeur, Felix retrieved his clothes and computer. His wife—Perfidia? Is that what Staggers had called her? How strange everything was becoming!—was nowhere to be seen. Doubtlessly, she was on the phone to either the police or the dog warden. It was past time for him to leave.

Spitting out a shirt-button that had lodged itself under his tongue, Felix set out for Priscilla Jane's.

2.

Priscilla Jane Farmer hung up her phone and began to weep.

Damn that morbid prankster! He had had Felix's voice and goofy intonations down to a "T"! And he would have to call just when she was congratulating herself on being all cried out. Now she'd have to work her way through another bout of runny nose and hot tears and inflamed eyes. And all without benefit of tissues, since she had used them all up, and was hardly in the mood to go out for more. Those damn scratchy paper towels and damn clumsy hanks of toilet paper would have to damn well do!

And while she was damning people and things and life in general,

Priscilla Jane felt she may as well toss in a good goddamn for Felix Wren himself!

"Wha—why'd he have to go and die anyhow?" Priscilla Jane wailed. "So stupid! Sticking himself with a dirty old needle! I'll bet a million dollars that wife of his had something to do with it! Bitch! I begged him not to marry her. I spotted her as a golddigger from the first! But would he listen to me? No, of course not. Oh, I was a great secretary and Gal Friday, sure enough! Who helped him build the damn business from nothing? Hah! But when it came to personal things, would he take my advice? No! And I—I could—I could've made him so happy!"

Priscilla Jane grabbed the wheel of her wheelchair and spun herself about until she was facing the kitchen doorway. Half-blinded by tears, she propelled herself forward. On her way, she bumped clumsily against a table and knocked a vase to the floor. It shattered.

"Damn! Damn, damn, damn!"

Just as she was pulling down three or four towels, the doorbell rang.

Rolling to the front door, Priscilla Jane called out irritably, "Who is it?"

"It's Felix, Pee Jay. Let me in!"

A pang of grief mixed with a bolt of fear shot through Priscilla Jane. My God, the lunatic caller was here! How had he found where she lived? What did he want? He must be insane, to be mimicking a dead man this way—

"Uh, sure—Fuh-Felix. One minute. I—I'm not dressed—"

"Priscilla Jane, are you okay? You sound weird. Listen, I'm in a bit of a rush. Could you please hurry?"

The phone was in her hand and she was jabbing 911. *I* sound weird? "Right, I'm hurrying."

The voice of the man on the other side of the door assumed aggrieved tones.

"Priscilla Jane, something tells me you don't trust me. Whatever you do, please don't call the authorities. My wife's bound to learn from them where I am, and she's still trying to kill me."

The operator was on the line. "Hello? Hello? Do you need help?"

Priscilla Jane spoke. "Uh, no, sorry, my, uh, cat accidentally speed-dialed. Goodbye!"

Back at the door, Priscilla Jane secured the chain. "What do you mean, 'trying to kill you'?"

The voice of her old employer said, "Well, she is. I mean, she did kill me once—with the help of that fellow, Staggers—but it didn't take, and now I'm back, in the flesh. Well, not the same flesh exactly. . . ."

Priscilla Jane snorted. "You're back. The same but not the same. Yeah, right. . . ."

The mock-Felix grew exasperated. "Priscilla Jane, I can't fool around anymore. I'm coming in."

All her first floor windows were burglar-barred. "Just you try it, Mister!"

From the far side of her door came the sound of— computer keys clicking? Something rattled around the door handle.

Then her solid oak door turned to a Japanese screen, all bamboo and translucent tissue paper. The silhouette of the Felix imposter loomed frighteningly.

The intruder stepped through with a ripping noise.

Once inside the man calmly opened the fragile sagging door and removed a bracelet from the altered outer knob.

The door instantly resumed its normal appearance and structure, save for a ragged, splintery gash down the center. Considerately, the mock Felix closed it.

Priscilla Jane found herself somehow on the far side of the room, without any memory of having scooted there.

The man turned to face her.

There could be no doubt. It was Felix. The late Felix. Felix the deceased.

Now the man was next to her. She must've blanked out for a few seconds. He was patting her on the shoulder the dumb way Felix always did, with a seemingly real hand.

"Gee, I'm sorry, Pee Jay. I never stopped to think it might be a shock to people to have me return from the dead. I keep forgetting not everyone knows what I know. Say, did you actually see my corpse? I wonder if I could get a look at it? Do you think they've buried it yet?"

Only Felix would be so impractical as not to consider the possibility that his ghost might not be heartily embraced. Only Felix would be so adolescently fascinated by the notion of seeing his own dead body. It had to be him.

"Yes, I did see your corpse, you idiot, and it was as real as you are now! What's going on?"

Felix sat. "It's a long story. You know how I've been working on the theories of Rupert Sheldrake for the past few years, don't you?"

"Sure. That nut who believes in those nonsensical 'morphic fields.'"

Felix sighed. "It's not nonsense, Priscilla Jane. It's true. Everything Sheldrake hypothesized about his fields is true. And I've learned how to control them."

"Maybe you'd better refresh my memory. All I can remember is some stuff about tits."

"Tits? Oh, you mean the birds whose behavior helped Sheldrake formulate his theories. Well, they're quite interesting, but hardly the main thrust of his argument. How can I put it briefly. . . ? Look, everything has a form, doesn't it? From atoms to molecules to higher organisms to galaxies, every object has its characteristic structure and shape and properties. That's what Sheldrake's interested in, and why he calls his theory 'formative causation.' Anyhow, it's Sheldrake's contention that all forms originate in and are stabilized by what he calls morphic fields. Invisible, omnipresent, all-pervasive nets of energy which both shape and are shaped by all of creation, in a perpetual flux of two-way feedback. And it's not just forms which these fields influence, but also more numinous things, things like behavior, ideas, instincts, repetitive motions, memories—a whole host of items. All of life and inanimate matter, in fact, come under their sway."

"And these morphic fields have brought you back from the dead?"

"Please, Priscilla Jane, don't be silly. You make it sound like the fields have free will and intentions. I'm quite proud to say that I did it myself.

"You see, human consciousness is not contained in our bodies. All of a person's memories and personality reside in external morphic fields, as does the template of our bodies. Our everyday existence is a complex interaction between gross matter and these subtle webs of energy. And because morphic fields are eternal, so are our individual selves."

"You're telling me that everyone who ever lived and died is still present in some unreachable medium?"

"Hardly unreachable, Priscilla Jane. I've reached it. That's how I brought myself back." Felix fingered the necklace around his throat. "All it took was this."

Priscilla Jane squinted. "Is that Tosh's collar? It is! Why are you wearing your dog's collar, and how could it bring you back to life?"

Felix removed a bracelet from his pocket and fingered it thoughtfully. "Do you see this crystal, Priscilla Jane? Nothing like it and its cousins have ever existed before. It's synthetic and it's flawless, a lattice without the usual imperfections found even in the finest diamonds. I had them grown in microgravity. As such, it's infinitely tuneable. One of these can be made to vibrate complexly at any frequency, from nanohertz to gigahertz. Just like the quartz crystal in your watch, only infinitely more precise."

"And?"

"Vibrations are the key, Priscilla Jane. Everything vibrates ceaselessly, from the quantum level on up. And a structure's distinctive pattern of vibrations is how it attunes itself to the relevant morphic fields, much like a radio receiver tuning in a certain station. Hydrogen atoms vibrate one way, and so are susceptible to the hydrogen-atom morphic field. Sharks vibrate another way, and are governed by the morphic field for sharks. And Felix Wren vibrates in accordance with the Felix Wren field, which is a subset of the general human field, of course. There's not usually any confusion among people's fields, because as Sheldrake says, 'You resemble yourself more than you resemble anyone else.'"

"I still don't see—"

"I've found that a demonstration is generally more convincing than any amount of lecturing. Let me show you."

Felix leaned forward and clasped the bracelet around Priscilla Jane's wrist. He plugged his computer into it.

"There's a battery-powered chip in each of these gadgets that's hardly smarter than the one inside a digital clock. It can do only a few things: turn power off and on as instructed, read transduced vibrations from the crystal, or induce other vibrations. And of course, it can communicate with my laptop here.

"Now, the first thing we need to do is attune the crystal to you, get a readout of your personal vibratory pattern." Felix's fingers roved over the keys. "There, it's done. Your unique pattern's on file on CD. Quite simple, actually. Hardly more than a couple of megabytes. But that's because the highest-level pattern contains millions of pointers to the subsets that make up Priscilla Jane. Each of those is at least a megabyte too, but all you need are the pointers. It's neat.

"Anyhow, the end result is that the crystal you're wearing—powered by the batteries and instructed by the onboard chip—is now radiating the same vibrations as your mind-body gestalt."

"Rather redundant, isn't it?"

"Well, yes, right now. But if I were to remove your bracelet and fasten it to another living creature of approximately the same mass—"

Seeing where he was heading, Priscilla Jane interrupted. "It would swamp their natural vibrations. But why living? Why not a hundred and twenty pounds of beach sand?"

"Ah, that's one mystery neither Sheldrake nor I can answer. He has his theories about entelechy and vitalism, a special quality of living systems. Whatever the reason, you can't make inanimate matter resonate to the patterns of life. And that includes corpses, unfortunately, or I'd simply reclaim my old body. But to confirm your perceptive guess: the bracelet would indeed overpower the natural vibrations of whoever it was touching, and transform the individual into another Priscilla Jane."

"And that's how you came back from the dead?"

Felix smiled. "Exactly. You see, I was my own subject for all my experiments. I had my vibratory pattern on file. When I first began to suspect that Galina—or Perfidia, as she seems to prefer to be called—was out to kill me, I took certain precautions. Months ago, I put a morphic resonance collar on Tosh. The chip was instructed to watch its internal clock and activate its crystal with my pattern if seventy-two hours had passed. Every three days, just before the deadline, I rebooted it for another seventy-two hours. Once I died, there was no one to do so, and Tosh turned into me."

"Felix—why didn't you just go to the police if you thought they were trying to kill you?"

"I had no real proof. But what was more important, I knew my murder would provide the perfect test of my equipment."

Priscilla Jane looked at Felix in astonishment. "So you're telling me that you allowed yourself to be killed, just to prove your theories, and that you're here now only because you've taken over Tosh's body. That you're some kind of cybernetic weredog."

"Correct. If I were to remove this collar, or the batteries died, I'd instantly revert. And I'm very grateful to the old boy for lending me his protoplasm. Naturally, I've got his pattern on file, and as soon as

I can figure out some ethical way of restoring him without giving up my own existence, I will."

Priscilla Jane studied Felix for a minute before delivering her verdict.

"I believe you're Felix—"

"Good!"

"—and you're nuts! Somehow, you escaped being murdered, but the shock drove you insane. Galina stuck a dummy or an anonymous stranger made up to look like you in the coffin. Then she locked you up, but you got free. . . ."

Again, Felix sighed. "Priscilla Jane, why would you make up such a convoluted story when the truth is the simple facts I've laid before you? What can I do to convince you? Ah! Tell me again why you're in that horrid wheelchair, Pee Jay."

"That auto accident when I was twenty."

Felix began working on his laptop. "What I didn't mention is that all past states of an organism are also maintained in the morphic repository. It shouldn't be too hard to isolate the traces of Priscilla Jane Farmer's nineteen-year-old self. I've written simple pattern-searching routines. Hmmm. . . . Eureka! Of course, I'll have to separate the body fields from the mind fields— Ha-ha, mind fields, that's good! It wouldn't do to have you become as foolish and naive as you were at twenty, when you ran that red light—"

"I beg your pard—"

Priscilla Jane gulped at the odd sensations that had shivered through her. "Felix. What did you do?"

Felix calmly unplugged the computer from her bracelet and said, "Weren't you paying attention, Pee Jay? I thought I trained you better than that. Now get up out of that chair. We've got lots of things to do."

Priscilla Jane obediently stood.

And promptly fainted.

3.

Detective Grady Stumbo was not in the habit of talking aloud to himself. He had emerged from the Tiger Cages of the Viet Cong without resorting to that stratagem, though it had cost him an arm. He had survived twenty rough-and-tumble years on the force without developing such a quirk. Innumerable cases had been cracked without resorting to interrogating himself. But there was something about the death of Felix Wren that had broken down all his carefully shored-up compunctions against self-interlocutory abuse.

As he drove with one-handed dexterity toward the Wren estate, Detective Stumbo found himself recounting salient facts of this most puzzling case, along with the startling recent developments that had dragged him out just as he was settling behind a large stack of paperwork, having returned from Felix Wren's funeral and the unsatisfactory attempt at unsettling that damned widow's complacency.

"No bruises or signs of struggle on Wren. Almost like he cooperated, for Christ's sake! He knew the killers, that's certain. But no prints on the needle other than his. That's easy enough to arrange, though. That Staggers is a bad one. Record a mile long. Been in and out of the pen more times than a hungry hog. Georgia boys think he killed his wife, but they never found her corpse. He claimed she ran away. Couldn't pin anything on him without a—"

Stumbo removed his hand from the steering wheel and smacked his forehead. His old Escort began to track over the center line, and he pulled it back.

"Of course! What a fool! She did take it on the lam. New identity too. Countess Balyban, my ass!" Stumbo forced himself to cool down. "But even so, I still can't nail them for Wren's murder. It's all circumstantial. The most I could get them for would be forgery, bigamy, kids-stuff. If the will mentions her by name, she'd probably even still end up with the money. If only there was a witness. . . ."

Using his knees to steer, the detective went through his cigarette routine. "Maybe this latest action is the break I need, though. An intruder in Wren's lab. Could be an employee who knew something. Accomplice who had a falling-out, trying to pick up evidence we missed to cover his own ass? The dispatcher said the bitch sounded really upset. Maybe she's gonna crack. Something crazy about a dog, too. Could there be a clue in the kennel? I thought we searched it good. . . . Shit! It still doesn't add up! Now, what was Stagger's wife's name. . . ?"

Stumbo got on the radio. By the time he was pulling into the Wren property, he was muttering, "Perfidia, Perfidia—" Then, a shout: "Yeah, that old Ventures tune!"

Feeling as if he had cracked the whole case, Detective Stumbo parked confidently in front of the mansion, emerged and strode to the front door.

Rowdy Staggers appeared in answer to the bell. He was holding a wet cloth stuffed with icecubes up to a large goose-egg the color of a tropical sunset on his forehead.

"Oh, it's Lefty," said the chauffeur. His heart didn't seem to be in the insult, however. Something had obviously shaken him greatly. "C'mon in, her Ladyship's got a few bones to pick witcha."

Perfidia was pacing up and down the long parlor, chewing on one set of elegant fingernails. If she swallowed all that paint, she'd poison herself. Stumbo was gratified to see her so upset. With any luck, he'd leave her even worse off.

Spotting the cop, Perfidia halted and glared.

"You! Why'd they send you?"

"Rank hath its privileges. Now, Mrs. Wren, I'd like to get the details of this incident straight. There was some confusion over the phone. You arrived home from the funeral—"

Marshalling her considerable strength of character, Perfidia assumed her usual hauteur. "We pulled in to find an intruder in my poor husband's private lab. Obviously, he was much more than your common criminal, or he would have concentrated on plundering the house. Perhaps he was an industrial spy. You're so convinced that my husband was the victim of foul play, Detective Stumbo. Did you ever consider professional greed as the motive? Wren BioHarmonics is the leader in its field. Competitors are unscrupulous. Yes, the more I think on it, the more likely it seems. If I were you, that's where I'd concentrate my efforts."

Stumbo repressed a grin. "Certainly. I'll give that angle all the consideration it's worth. Was the intruder anyone you recognized?"

Perfidia blanched. "No. A complete stranger."

"Hmmm. There was something about a dog. Would that be your husband's dog?"

Rowdy broke in. "That's the fucker! It nearly killed me! I want that bastard smoked! Why, the only thing that saved me from gettin' my gullet torn out, accordin' to Perf—"

The widow cleared her throat. "What Mr. Staggers means to say, Detective, is that the intruder seems to have enlisted the affection and cooperation of my late husband's pet. I'm not sure how. Perhaps the criminal is an insider in my husband's firm, and known to the dog. Felix used to bring the beast to work with him, God knows why. It's untamed and savage, practically rabid in fact."

"Yeah," chimed in Rowdy. "If I was you and I seen it, I'd shoot first and offer it a Milkbone second."

They seemed fixated on this poor dog. It didn't make sense. . . .

"Let's take a look at the lab, shall we?"

Crossing the spring-fresh lawn, Stumbo noted crushed grass corroborative of the scuffle described. In a patch of mud, he spotted the imprint of an unshod human foot.

"Was the intruder barefoot?"

"No."

"Yeah."

"Oh, Detective, how could we be expected to notice such a thing? We were frightened out of our wits! Maybe he was, I can't say for sure."

Stumbo let it go, and they went inside the workshop.

"Does anything appear out of place or missing to you?"

Stumbo watched Perfidia's face as she looked about. Her attention snagged on an empty plastic bin, then jerked away.

"No, nothing, Detective. But I'm not totally familiar with my husband's work. . . ."

"Okay. I'm going to look around for a minute or so, then I'll be gone. Oh, yes, I'm waiting for a call from the station too."

Stumbo began poking about. As he moved, he whistled. At first tunelessly, then segueing into the Ventures' "Perfidia."

The Widow Wren maintained an icy composure in the face of her namesake ditty. Rowdy Staggers was not so mindful. He soon began tapping his foot and nodding his head to the beat. The woman eyed daggers at him, but he was oblivious. At last he burst out, "Hey, I ain't heard that tune your Daddy liked so much for nigh on twenty years."

Perfidia had reached the boiling point. "Idiot!"

Rowdy realized what he had done. "Uh, I mean my Daddy! Yeah, it was my Daddy who dug the Ventures. He was an old surf-bum from way back—"

Perfidia growled, "Shut up!"

Just then the phone in the lab rang. Stumbo picked it up.

"Yeah, yeah, fine. Thanks." He hung up. "There was a call placed from this phone an hour ago. I assume neither of you made it. No? Very good. We now have the next link in this case. I'm leaving now. But you can rest assured that I'll be back—Mrs. Staggers."

Stumbo left the lab. Recovering from his stupefaction, Rowdy made a move to stop him, but was restrained by Perfidia. As the motor of the Escort came to life, she spoke.

"No, it's too late now, Rowdy. The damage is done, thanks to your stupidity."

"You weren't no shinin' example of a criminal mastermind your-self, babe. I thought you was gonna piss your pants when he asked about the ghost's footprint."

"Let's drop it. We were both to blame. We have to decide what to do next. I've had some time to think. Rowdy, I believe that Felix really has come back to life. We saw how he changed himself into a dog and back. Assuming we weren't both hallucinating, then we witnessed a miracle! If he could do that, he could do anything! Maybe he cloned himself, built an improved, shape-changing body. Whatever it is, though, it makes all the money in the estate look like the coins in a beggar's cup. We've got to track him down and get his secret."

Greed overspread Rowdy's features. "Yeah, you're right, babe, as usual. We won't just be rich, we'll be fuckin' kings and queens!"

Perfidia's eyes narrowed. "I think the operative word is 'god,' my dear. Or goddess."

"What are we waitin' for, then? We gotta follow Dumbo right now, so's he brings us to your zombie hubby!"

Perfidia held up a hand. "Watch."

She picked up the phone and punched REDIAL.

Five rings, and a machine engaged. "Hello. Priscilla Jane is pulling wheelies on a skateboard ramp right now. If you want to leave a message—"

Slamming the phone down, Perfidia rasped, "That cutesy-poo secretary twat of Felix's. If she thinks she's going to get anything out of my pigeon— I'll kill her!"

Rowdy reached inside his chauffeur's jacket and removed a wicked-looking Intratec nine-millimeter semiautomatic pistol.

"No, babe, let me. I always did like shootin' people more'n dogs."

4.

Legs were really quite amazing things.

After ten years without them, Priscilla Jane found that the whole notion of personal mobility resembled some of the farther-out concepts of robotics experts. The hinges, the tendons, the flexing toes, the constant shifting of one's center of gravity—the process seemed like something scribbled on Marvin Minsky's dinner napkin.

Luckily, her body had not forgotten how to manage things quite well by itself, without the intervention of her shocked mind. How could it have? This was not her thirty-year-old untoned carcass being forced to walk. This was her original nineteen-year-old frame restored to her, complete with all its ingrained somatic routines.

Right now, Priscilla Jane lifted up the hem of her shirt for the umpteenth time and looked at the crimson welts on her midriff. She remembered quite well how she had gotten those: some roughhousing at a beach party, where she had lunged into the water without looking and scraped her belly across some barnacled rocks.

As best she could recall, the wounds made eleven years ago had about another two weeks to heal completely.

Dropping her shirt, Priscilla Jane looked toward Felix, where he sat on her couch.

Her reborn employer had gotten involved with her cat. Priscilla Jane had watched as long as she could before turning away. Some of the changes Felix was putting her pet through were just too unsettling to witness. She was pretty certain he was doing no permanent damage to poor Peabrain. On the other hand, a man who would encourage his own murder for intellectual reasons was perhaps not bound by the same ethical strictures as others. . . .

At this moment, Peabrain—who had started out wearing one of the morphic bracelets around his waist—now crouched in the middle of the charmed circle of links, which had dropped off as he altered. The body her cat now possessed, Priscilla Jane surmised, must have been one of the feline's distant ancestors, a small shrewlike creature. (What Felix had done with Peabrain's extra mass, she did not know. Obviously, in the process of experimenting on the cat he had found some way of storing it.)

"Why doesn't it run away?" asked Priscilla Jane.

Felix looked up. His expression, a familiar one, told her he had forgotten anyone was with him.

"I've shut off its gross motor-activity fields. But there's no point in keeping this antique critter here any longer. I've learned all I can from your cat."

Felix tapped some keys, and good old Peabrain reappeared, none the worse for its regression. Felix removed the bracelet from the cat, which scampered away. He stood.

"As you might have guessed, Pee Jay, I'm trying to refine and extend the range of my temporal searching abilities, with regard to living things. It was one of the major projects left unfinished at my demise, and finishing it is imperative. But I find I need a different class of subjects. Is there a zoo nearby?"

Felix's question unnerved her. "Why, sure, a private one. The Southside Wild Animal Farm. But Felix—do we really have to go there? Shouldn't we be doing something more practical? What about bringing your wife to justice?"

Felix smiled. "For what?"

"Why, for your murd— Oh. . . ."

"Absolutely correct, Priscilla Jane. There's no way my coming forward could not make matters worse. If I'm accepted as the real Felix, then there was no murder commmitted, and nothing to prosecute Perfidia for. Perhaps charges of attempting to defraud the life insurance company are even brought against me. On the other hand, if I'm declared an imposter, then my own motives are questioned, and I might end up in jail. And the worst possible scenario is that someone thinks to run DNA tests on both me and my corpse, and the results show we're identical. Everyone knows I have no twin brother. Imagine how confused my poor mother would be by all the questioning. She always said I was as much trouble as two kids. Maybe she'd end up agreeing that I was twins. Mom always was highly suggestible. No, I don't want to put her through that quite yet, so soon after I made it necessary for her to attend my funeral. And I'd probably get locked up in some government lab as a freak, subject to the moronic questioning of lesser scientists. In all cases, though, nothing is accomplished and much valuable time and freedom are wasted."

"But how can you stand to let that, that murderess walk away with everything you and I built over the years?"

"Wren BioHarmonics was a mature company, Pee Jay. It wasn't fun anymore for me. I'm much more interested in this new technology. I believe it has many interesting possibilities, perhaps even some market potential."

Priscilla Jane snorted. "Bringing anyone who ever lived back from the dead, repairing any kind of bodily damage, and Lord knows what else— I would say that your talents for understatement, Felix, have survived your death intact."

"Thank you, Pee Jay. A good scientist always resists hyperbole. I take it you have transportation available for our trip to the zoo. . . ?"

"My van."

"Let's have a look."

Felix and Priscilla Jane left the house by the gashed front door.

Her customized van boasted a wheelchair lift operating out the side cargo door. Clamps on the floor in the driver's position allowed her wheelchair to be secured in place of the missing fixed seat. All traditional pedal controls were mounted on the steering column and were hand-operable.

After studying the setup, Felix said, "Well, let's haul your wheelchair out here so we can get going—"

"No! I refuse ever to sit in that contraption again!"

"But Pee Jay, you're being quite unreasonable. The chair is an integral component of this well-designed vehicle. . . ."

Felix tapered off. He studied Priscilla Jane's glower for a moment, then said, "I'm forgetting emotions again, right?"

"Right."

"Thanks, Pee Jay. I need you around."

"Don't mention it. Now help me with a kitchen chair."

They had finished settling the captain's-style kitchen chair into place behind the steering wheel, and Priscilla Jane was seated in it, testing visibility and ease, when a dented Ford Escort pulled into the drive.

"Uh-oh," said Priscilla Jane.

"Who is it?"

"The policeman in charge of investigating your death."

Felix stepped back into the shadowy interior of the van and removed a bracelet from his pocket. He began programming its crystal, while whispering.

"This is not someone who can be expected to understand our situation, Pee Jay. If we can't talk our way out, I've got something in reserve."

The car stopped adjacent to the van, and Detective Stumbo emerged.

"Miss Farmer—"

"Yes?"

"I need to speak with you. About an hour ago you received a call—"

Stumbo froze. "Where's your wheelchair? How did you get out here on your own?"

"Um, I—"

The detective's holstered pistol hung above his right hip. In an eyeblink, it seemed to leap into his left hand.

"Get out. You and whoever's in there with you. And take it slow."

Priscilla Jane swung her amazing but shaky legs to the ground and stood. Felix emerged from the open side door. They both took a few steps closer to the stunned cop, then halted. Recovering, Stumbo sized them up, then nodded sagaciously.

"A crippled secretary who's not crippled, and her dead boss who's not dead. It's not what I expected, but I can see how it fits. You two and the other two were in it together for the insurance." (Felix bestowed an I-told-you-so look on Priscilla Jane.) "Then someone got greedy, and there was an argument. You decked Staggers—

though I don't see how a pipsqueak like you could—frightened your wife, then took off with the dog." Mentioning the dog made Stumbo nervous; he swung his gun in measured arcs. "Where is it anyhow? I hear it's a killer."

"Tosh? He's not here—as such. And in any case, he wouldn't hurt a fly. Oh, he hates my wife and chauffeur, but that's only understandable, since he realizes they murdered me."

"Oh, come off it, Mr. Wren. The jig is up. No one's going to believe in a talking dead man."

Felix sounded impatient. "But it's true. I'm only here conditionally. My renewed existence is quite precarious, just like Pee Jay's new legs. Old legs, rather. That's what I'm trying to fix now. If you could just see your way clear to allowing me a few more hours freedom, I'm sure I can wrap things up efficiently. Then I'd be happy to turn myself in and explain. It won't take long, I promise. First, you see, I have to visit a zoo. Pee Jay assures me there's one nearby that'll do fine. Then, assuming I'm successful—and I generally am—a quick trip to Mount Shasta—"

"That's enough. I don't have time for your crazy bullshit. I'm taking both of you in, and putting out an APB for Staggers and his wife."

Bafflement washed over Felix's face. "You don't mean—? You do. That faithless woman. She didn't even wait until my corpse was cold before remarrying. Now I'm really angry! Well, I'll give them a piece of my mind, should they dare show up again. But right now, your case interests me. When did you lose that arm?"

Stumbo answered automatically. " 'Sixty-eight."

"Thank you." Felix began tapping the keys of his laptop, which was still cabled to the bracelet.

"Hey, what do you think you're doing? Stop that! C'mon now, bring that stuff over here."

Felix closed the distance between himself and the cop. "What should I do with these?"

"Put the computer under my stump."

Felix complied, and Stumbo clasped the laptop under his armpit. "What about this lovely bracelet? I took it from my lab. It could be evidence, you know."

"Drop it in my coat pocket."

"You're sure?"

"Quit joking and do it!"

"All right."

Felix detached the computer cord and deposited the morphic crystal in Stumbo's jacket. Then he began to count aloud. "Ten, nine, eight. . . ."

Stumbo backed off. "What's going on? The thing can't be dangerous, you and the girl are wearing them. You're bluff—"

". . . one," said Felix, and Stumbo crumpled to the ground, unconscious.

Bending over the detective, Felix retrieved his laptop.

"Standard morphic field for human sleep patterns. It'll shut down in sixty minutes. By then, we should be far away."

On the edge of hysteria, Priscilla Jane giggled. "It's not a morphic field then, it's a 'morpheus field.' " She pulled herself together. "We'd better get going, Felix. Before anyone else shows up."

Behind the wheel, with Felix in the passenger's seat, Priscilla Jane put the van in drive and was just releasing the hand brake when a pickup truck pulled into the fenced yard.

"Who—?"

"It's my gardener's truck," explained Felix. "They must have decided the limo was too slow and conspicuous."

The truck blocked their exit. Perfidia and Rowdy emerged. The chauffeur held a gun.

Felix was busy programming another crystal. "Drive toward them slowly, Pee Jay. I need to get within throwing distance."

The van crawled forward. Perfidia and Rowdy moved off to

Felix's side of the drive, standing by the truck's front bumper. When the van's nose was a few feet from the truck, Priscilla Jane stopped. Perfidia spoke.

"Felix, dear, we need to talk. I realize you're a tad upset over our recent, um, misunderstandings. I imagine your death was not pleasant, despite its temporary nature, and I hope you'll be big-hearted enough to accept our sincere apologies for any inconvenience we might've caused you. But surely you can see that it's best for all of us to cooperate, now that we know all about your secrets."

"Yeah," chimed in Rowdy. "Get your asses outa that van before I cooperate you both fulla holes."

Felix craned his upper body out the window. He held a bracelet. "Perfidia, I don't mind particularly about my murder. I realize that you acted out of sheer animal instincts. But what I do object to is your disgracing my good name by consorting with this ape. Blinded by your glamour as I was, I doubt I ever really knew you, but I certainly can't count on you now. Just be glad I'm not the type to indulge in petty revenge."

Tossing the bracelet into the bed of the truck where it landed softly atop a sack of manure, Felix retreated inside the van. "On three, Pee Jay, gun it. One, two, three!"

The pickup truck turned into ping-pong balls.

For a millisecond, the thousands of celluloid spheres maintained the shape of the truck. Then they collapsed in an avalanche whose closest edge skittered under, over and between Rowdy and Perfidia, upsetting their footing and tumbling them to the ground.

Out on the street, Priscilla Jane made a hard left that nearly overturned her makeshift seat. Shots rang out behind them.

Smiling, Priscilla Jane turned to Felix and said, "Mister Moose, I presume."

"It's something everyone of our generation should get to do at least once in their lifetime."

5.

Rowdy lowered his gun and kicked vengefully at a herd of innocent ping-pong balls.

"That bastard's startin' to really piss me off!"

Perfidia was casting frantically about. Spotting Stumbo's car, she said, "Quick, this way!"

At the car, Rowdy yanked open the driver's door. "No fuckin' keys!"

"There's the cop! Looks like Felix knocked him out somehow. I bet the keys are still on him—"

Quickly, Rowdy was beside the recumbent Stumbo. He stuck his hand in the detective's coat pocket, a look of blissful peace softened his coarse features, and he collapsed atop Stumbo.

Perfidia made an instinctive move toward her unconscious partner, then stopped herself.

There was no telling what curse Felix had left here, or whether it would affect her if she touched the two men. Chances were, however, given Felix's benevolent sentimentalism, that the effect was both harmless and temporary. The two appeared to be merely sleeping; doubtlessly, they would awaken within some reasonable period.

Gritting her teeth, Perfidia sat herself down on the lawn to wait.

To her surprise, she found herself speaking aloud.

"The cop might've learned something we don't know. It'll be good to take him along. Felix and that bitch can't escape. They're too innocent, too naive, like children. And when we catch up—well, whatever Felix knows is probably on that computer of his. I can work it as good as him. If he doesn't want to play along—"

A look of utter bloodthirstiness that would have sent a Maori warrior fleeing in retreat contorted Perfidia's beauty. "He died once, he can always die again. Only this time, very, very, very painfully."

• • •

Priscilla Jane was curious. As she tooled down the highway, she found herself full of questions.

"If you were to shut off that bracelet you tossed into the gardener's truck, Felix, would the truck reappear?"

Felix was looking idly out the window, like someone who had never ridden in a car before. Like a dog, actually. Priscilla Jane felt that she loved him more than ever. If only—

"No," her employer answered after a moment. "But only because the original mass of the truck is too dispersed to be reactivated by the nascent truck fields. Just like your front door. When I restored its natural fields, the rip remained, because I had created gross macroscopic disorders while it was altered. Morphic fields are not magic, Pee Jay, though they might look that way. There are some constraints. For instance: suppose I were to alter your bracelet so that all your haemoglobin turned to cyanide."

He said it so matter of factly, that Priscilla Jane shivered.

"You'd die almost instantly, in a quite horrible fashion too. If I tried then to reimpose your original template on your corpse, it would be futile. That vital spark of entelechy would be gone from that particular lump of protoplasm. So you see, there are limits to what can be done with morphic fields."

"Let's talk about something more pleasant."

Felix redirected his guileless blue eyes on her. "Pee Jay, you brought the subject up—"

"I know, I know. And I'm sorry I did. Tell me, Felix— What kind of plans do you have for these fields—assuming we survive?"

Immediately, Felix exhibited a contagious excitement. "Well, first of all, I don't intend to start bringing people back from the dead left and right. It's too unethical. Every such instance would mean the effective cancellation of some other organism's right-to-life. Look at how I've had to usurp poor Tosh's existence. No, it just won't do. Every individual gets their stay on earth, and then must make way for newcomers. And although one's disembodied personality fields are not 'running,' so to speak, in the same way they are when one is alive, I seem to have vague memories of a quite satisfying postdeath existence. It seemed to me as if I were still participating in things, through the other members of the species. So, that's just the way life is. I don't quite agree with the setup, but I don't intend to change it—at least until I do some more thinking."

Priscilla Jane's reply was drenched in a sarcasm she knew would be completely invisible to Felix, but she couldn't help herself. "Oh, by all means!"

"On the other hand, I don't see anything wrong with bringing back selected individuals for temporary stays, using volunteer host bodies. Wouldn't it be quite useful to resurrect, say, FDR, during a major political crisis? Aren't there a few modern problems that Socrates or Buddha or Einstein could help us with?

"Then there's the obvious medical aspect, which I believe you alluded to earlier. Although a cure like yours is totally reliant on continued wearing of a morphic crystal, I don't imagine such a burden would be regarded as intolerable by the average patient."

"Oh, I imagine not!"

"There are a host of lesser ways humans could benefit directly from temporary use of morphic fields. Instant experts, for instance. Every skill—intellectual or kinesthetic—is stored in a morphic field. By tapping these, you could become as talented as the person who originally laid down the pattern. Then, there's enhanced personal memory access. The only reason we forget is that the vibratory pattern of our physical brains changes with age, cutting off the resonance with one memory field or another. There's really no need to allow this to happen anymore."

"Of course not!"

Felix was just warming up. "I imagine that people might be a little leery at first of occupying instant buildings or of using instant tools or instant machines which owe their very existence to an innocuous-looking crystal. But with appropriate fail-safes in place, and with continuous safety exhibited over a long period, people should come around."

"Who wouldn't?"

"Not to pretend that morphic technology doesn't present its own peculiar dangers. The potential for biological harm is certainly real. Sports, monsters and chimeras of all sorts could be created by mixing and matching the morphic fields of different species. But the inorganic realm offers scope for mischief too. Turning Hoover Dam or the World Trade Center into matchsticks is quite possible. Extending a mile-wide tunnel down to the magma would be a little trickier. You'd have to take into account the separate morphic fields of every type of matter from the surface on down, and then convert them to vacuum, say, while simultaneously building diamond tunnel walls. But with enough computing power, I could do it."

"I don't doubt it!"

"There are quite a few applications of deeper complexity which I won't get into here, mostly involving teleological chreodes and the cosmological morphic fields. But now we're talking galaxies, and I believe your question was implicitly limited to Earth."

Priscilla Jane was silent for a moment. "Anything else?"

"Not at the moment, no."

"Correct me if I'm wrong, then. Basically, you, Felix Wren, boy inventor, all on your lonesome, intend to pick up the entire globe by its heels and shake it until the loose change falls out of its pockets."

Felix looked hurt, and Priscilla Jane felt bad. But she had to knock some sense into him. Couldn't he see what he was unleashing? "Such a metaphor, Pee Jay, however colorful, puts the worst possible interpretation on my motives. You know I've never been interested in money. I only care about advancing human knowledge."

"I wish money was all that motivated you! You'd be a thousand times less dangerous! You're going to advance the human race right out of resemblance to anything we know!"

Felix looked sober. "Don't imagine I haven't thought of such things, Priscilla Jane. But there's never been a scientific genie which has ever been rebottled. I'm smart, but I'm not unique. Someone else was bound to discover this sooner or later. Look at how simple it all is. No, the only thing to do now is to try to use the technology purposefully and wisely, for the benefit of everyone. Actually, in conjunction with my near-term goals—which include stabilizing both my existence and yours—I'm hoping to get some advice on how to proceed."

"Advice! From who? God?"

Felix did not smile. "Not precisely."

Priscilla Jane was afraid to ask Felix to get more precise.

The exit for the Southside Wild Animal Farm slid up on them, and they took it.

Apparently seeking to further mollify his companion, Felix said, "It's not like morphic fields haven't always been subject to fluctuations and primitive attempts at control, Pee Jay. Take several phenomena generally considered to be magic. Shapechanging can be seen as instances of a human gaining mental control over his vibratory patterns, and altering them at will. Possession and multiple personality disorders are plainly cases of one's vibratory patterns changing sufficiently to resonate with other human—or nonhuman—patterns held in the morphic repository. Reincarnation might occur unpredictably, when a growing embryo—usually quite unique and historically unprecedented—chances to lock onto a pattern that's already existed once. This explains quite neatly why not everyone has memories of other lifetimes. I could continue. . . ."

Priscilla Jane's head felt like someone had it pinned in the grip of a giant nutcracker. "No, thank you. I've got quite enough to chew on for now."

Ahead of them now, on a busy two-lane secondary road spotted mostly with gaudy, tawdry businesses, loomed a sign for the Southside Wild Animal Farm. They entered, parked, and left the van. Admission was five dollars apiece.

"I'm afraid I'll have to ask you to pay, Pee Jay. There was no money in these clothes I was forced to wear, and naturally Tosh—"

"Loan you ten dollars and get a new pair of legs? A bargain at twice the price."

"I'm glad you're enjoying them, Priscilla Jane."

Inside, Felix ignored the rather seedy cages containing such bedraggled and snaggletoothed specimens as lion, goat and ostrich, and instead made a beeline through the crowd of visitors to the reptiles.

He stopped at a fence, and Priscilla Jane caught up with him.

The shoddy waist-high fence—straight and unbarbed—was erected at the very edge of the alligator pit, whose floor was four feet below the watchers. In the pit lazed a single somnolent gator over six feet long.

"Oh, he'll do nicely," said Felix.

And before anyone could stop him, he had clambered over the fence and dropped into the pit.

Everyone except Priscilla Jane screamed. She was so mad at Felix for not warning her of what he planned that she was rooting for the gator.

Opening first its left eye, then its right, the animal spotted Felix. It slithered sinuously toward him, and its jaws began to split open.

Felix stood his ground unconcernedly. When the beast was nearly atop him, he tossed a cabled bracelet like a quoit into its maw.

The gator instantly froze.

Felix tapped a few keys, and the gator began to go through disturbing bodily changes similar to those Peabrain had endured.

Remembering Priscilla Jane, Felix turned to reassure her.

"This data should complement nicely what I already have, Pee Jay. I might take the time to explore a few sidechains as long as I'm here."

Mass panic reigned immediately around the alligator pit. Guards and keepers were running up; sirens could be heard in the distance.

"I'd suggest speeding things up, if possible, Felix."

A keeper stood beside her. "What's he doing to Wally? Do you know this guy? Is he crazy, or what?"

"Or what," said Priscilla Jane. "Definitely or what."

The shapes the gator was exhibiting were becoming more and more primitive and outrageous. People were fainting.

Then, without warning, a full-sized brontosaurus occupied the cage, its head towering over the suddenly silent crowd, its tail draped atop the adjacent monkey-house.

Felix held up his computer, to show Priscilla Jane that the tether to the ingested bracelet had pulled away from the laptop's port. Looking up, Priscilla Jane could see it dangling from the bronto's jaws like a waterweed.

"A slight miscalculation," he admitted sheepishly. "How that extra mass slipped in, I'll never know. You really shouldn't have rushed me, Pee Jay. . . ."

The crowd melted into frenzied flight, the likes of which Priscilla Jane estimated might not have been seen since the last woolly mammoth stuck its trunk up the caveman's loincloth.

Priscilla Jane leaned over the fence and extended a hand. "Come out of there right now, you irresponsible idiot!"

Felix clambered out with her assistance. "Luckily, I've got a spare cable back in the van."

Helicopters could be heard in the distance. Someone was shouting over a bullhorn. Priscilla Jane imagined she heard a tank approaching. No, they couldn't have responded so quickly. But soon.

"We've got to get out of here, Felix. Now!"

They started jogging toward the admission booth. Her legs remembered how, but it still felt weird.

"Is Dino ever going to move?" gasped Priscilla Jane as they reached the van. Cars were tangled at the exit, and she realized they were bottled in.

"I've never subjected the electronic components of a bracelet to the effects of gastric acid before. And certainly, if I had thought to do so, I would not necessarily have chosen dinosaur stomach juices. As the suicidal scientist said just before he stuck his head into the accelerator beam, 'Results are unpredictable.'"

Priscilla Jane snorted, then said, "Maybe you can get back to the pit and fix it—?"

"How? One morphic crystal is equal to another. A second one would only muddy the patterns of the first, with chaotic results. No, I suggest that we continue with our quest. How far away from Mount Shasta are we?"

"Less than an hour."

"Let's go then."

"Go? How? Are you going to ping-pong that whole crush and all the people in it?"

"Of course not! Do you think I'm some kind of monster, Pee Jay? Just drive toward the fence."

At the chainlink separating the zoo's lot from the McDonald's next door, Felix used a bracelet to dissolve a large section and they drove calmly off.

"A second exit should alleviate the confusion a bit also."

Regaining the highway, they began to make speed north.

Priscilla Jane glanced in her exterior rearview mirror for a sign of Dino stirring.

But she saw something worse.

"Felix, someone's after us! It's Detective Stumbo's car, and he's driving, but he's also got—"

A bullet pinged off the van.

"Perfidia and that lout, Staggers?"

"Yes."

Felix located his spare cable, dug out a bracelet and began programming it. Shots continued to ring out.

"I hadn't wanted to try this. It's very chancy. But it looks like I'll be forced to now."

Priscilla Jane felt sick. "What? What is it?"

"The spacetime-continuum's spatial traits are subject to morphic resonance also. Every location resonates to both its physical configuration and the events that have occured in it. The reason we're going to Mount Shasta is that it's the closest place to us with the particular kind of spatial resonance I'm after. If I can impose Mount Shasta's special place-field on us and the van—"

"We should instantly teleport there?"

"Very good. The nineteen-year-old Priscilla Jane would never have caught on so fast."

Felix finished and hung the bracelet from a knob on the dashboard.

"It's on a thirty-second delay. We've got to be motionless by then, or we'll plow into who-knows-what at our destination."

Priscilla Jane began to slow. "But they'll catch up with us!"

"There shouldn't be any problem. I'll try to stall them."

Slowing, slowing, Priscilla Jane began to pray.

The Escort pulled up alongside them, on Felix's side.

Felix stuck his head out.

Priscilla Jane watched as, from the rear side window of the Escort, a leering Rowdy aimed, fired, and blew the top off Felix's skull.

The highway vanished.

6.

In the front passenger seat of Detective Stumbo's commandeered car, Perfidia Staggers, nee Graboys, also once known as Countess Galina Balyban, turned around and smacked her second-most-recent husband across his jaw with the barrel of Detective Stumbo's forty-five, enhancing the lurid bruise she had given him just that morning.

"You fucking fool!"

Dropping his own pistol in a blind rage, Rowdy lurched toward her, eager hands plainly intent on fastening round her neck.

Perfidia fired a shot through the roof of the car, nearly deafening them all. Taking the hint, Rowdy subsided back into his seat.

"Pull over!" Perfidia now ordered Stumbo.

They stopped in the breakdown lane. No one else seemed to have noticed the fatal gunplay or the vanishing of the van. Or, if they had noticed, they had neglected to report it amid the general confusion now dominating the region. Whatever madness Felix had unveiled at the Southside Wild Animal Farm was using up everyone's limited attention.

Rowdy seemed to have regained the modicum of reason he normally possessed. In hurt tones he said, "Jesus, Perf, what the fuck is up? When I woke up, the first words outa your mouth was about how we're gonna croak Felix. Then, when I do what you said, you lay into me!"

Perfidia too seemed to be making an effort to master her emotions and think rationally. "We were supposed to try to get him to cooperate first, remember? But it's too late now, so just forget it. The question we have to answer now is, where did they go?"

"Speakin' personal-like," said Rowdy, "I wasn't never really convinced Felix was alive again. Supposin' he was a spook. He probably just vanished back to spookland and took the girl and van with him."

"If that's the case, then there's nothing to go after. No, I prefer to believe Felix is—was—really alive. In some crazy way, his actions are too meaningful for any kind of ghost. . . ."

Perfidia faced the silent detective, who returned her gaze with his own medusal look. If he had been unnerved by being taken hostage and witnessing a bloody murder, he didn't show it. One-handed, he fetched and lit a smoke for himself.

Perfidia gestured at him with the gun. "You. What do you think?"

Stumbo exhaled. "I think you're both going down for murder one."

Rowdy growled. "Fat chance, you stupid dick. Once we get that computer of Felix's, nothing will stand up against us. Tell 'im, Perf! Say, how are we gonna get it?"

"Shut up. Tell the truth, Grady, or I'll take that other arm out of commission. Did Felix mention any destination other than the zoo?"

Stumbo calculated. He wanted to find Wren and the girl—or rather, Wren's corpse—as much as these two did. If leading the murderers there was the only way—and so it seemed—then he would have to do it, and hope for some reversal of fortune when they arrived.

Stumbo took his time grinding out his cigarette before he replied. Might as well make them sweat.

"Shasta. He said something about Mount Shasta."

"That's where he is then," exulted Perfidia. "He found some superscience way to get there instantly, and took it. Now the girl is sitting there alone, probably without a clue about how to work Felix's bag of tricks. We've got to get there before she learns— Let's move!"

Stumbo merged with the traffic and accelerated.

From the direction of the zoo, a tremendous bellow resounded like the foghorn of the gods.

Rowdy laughed. "Don't that sound just like some kinda dinosaur!"

• • •

Once already today, Priscilla Jane had told herself she was finished mourning for that damn Felix. She really, really should have known better.

Now she tried to convince herself again that her tears were finished.

The van sat in the middle of a small tree-ringed clearing occupied otherwise only by a rough-hewn picnic table. At the moment of their transition, they had still been moving at about twenty MPH, but Priscilla Jane had been able to brake in their new location without hitting anything.

A rutted dirt road led away from the clearing and down the mountainside. Priscilla Jane knew it quite well, as she had been gazing at it intermittently through her tears for over an hour.

Priscilla Jane sat at the picnic table. Now that her grief had exhausted itself and her, she was trying to nerve herself up to return to the van, where Felix's shattered body still rested, slumped in its seat.

She supposed she shouldn't have indulged herself in the orgy of tears, what with a pack of murderers hunting her. But the clearing had felt so safe, and she really couldn't hold back her feelings any longer. But now it was time to do something. Only she wasn't quite sure what.

All she knew was that it began with going back to the van.

So she forced herself to walk, her thirty-year-old mind overcoming the shakiness of nineteen-year-old legs.

Seated in the kitchen chair behind the steering wheel, she steeled herself to look at Felix.

Luckily, his head was resting on his right shoulder, the damage hidden. If not for the blood, she could almost pretend he was sleeping. . . .

Just to hear another voice, she flipped on the radio.

"—last seen heading south on Route Five. Scientists have so far convinced the National Guard not to fire on the mysterious brontosaurus, but Major Tompkins insists that force is still an option—"

Priscilla Jane snapped the radio off.

"Damn you, Felix! Look what you've done! I know, I know, it was just a minor glitch in your plans for a Utopia none of us even wants! And now you're counting on me, aren't you? I'm supposed to bail you out somehow, just like I always do. Maybe I can go out and tackle a goddamn grizzly bear or walk forty miles to steal a dog, just so I can stick your stupid necklace on it, just so you can come back to life again. Or maybe—"

Priscilla Jane stopped dead, horrified at the notion that had come to her. "No. I don't believe it. You don't actually expect me to— You do! Oh, you wicked, wicked man! Well, I've got news for you, buster! I'm not going to fall for it. You've caused enough grief for everyone already. Why should I give you a chance to cause more?"

Making a move as if to climb out of the van, Priscilla Jane stopped, then reseated herself.

"I hate you, I hate you, I hate you!" she told Felix's corpse.

Crying again, trembling, she removed her own bracelet, instantly feeling her cherished legs go dead.

Leaning toward Felix, she grabbed with both hands the morphic collar around his bloody neck.

Felix was looking down at his own mutilated corpse. Finally, he had gotten his wish. On reflection, it had been an unwise desire. . . .

He realized that his hands—formerly Pee Jay's, of course—were clutching the dog-collar around the corpse's neck, and he could feel no matching collar around his own neck.

Felix was touched. She must really care for him. How had he not seen it all these years. . . ?

"Thanks, Pee Jay," he whispered huskily. "I'll make it up to you real soon now. I promise."

Carefully unfastening the collar that permitted his renewed existence, Felix donned it.

The coverall-clad form in the passenger seat reverted to that of poor Tosh, whose head now illustrated the impact of the slug from Rowdy's gun. Another casualty of this whole unfortunate escapade. . . .

"Well, I can't waste time wishing I had managed things differently. Besides, the human factor is to blame. In any case, there's work to be done."

So saying, Felix left the van.

At the picnic table he laid all of his bracelets and necklaces out in a line—save for two, which he reserved in the pocket of the sweat pants Pee Jay had been wearing. He mated each gadget to the next in line, finally closing the loop to form a single circuit roughly six feet in diameter. This hoop of some seven morphic crystals he carried to the edge of the clearing. There, he draped it from some low tree branches so that the circle of links just touched the rocky ground. "Contact with the earth is essential," Felix informed the air as he cabled his laptop into a convenient port.

Felix addressed both of his temporarily disembodied companions as he worked the keyboard.

"Three point five billion years, Tosh. I imagine a dog would have a lot of trouble conceiving of that much time. Not that the average human being would have it much easier, would they, Priscilla Jane? But that's how long ago life began on this planet, according to best estimates. It's a lot of time to search through for what I'm after. But the data I got at the zoo really improved my routines. I figure it shouldn't take much more than an hour to run through the whole Archeozoic. By then, I should be able to detect the first manifestations of Gaia."

Felix opened a new window on the screen, and a color image of the Earth as seen from space appeared.

"Exactly how far I'll have to go before Gaia's signature field is fully developed, I can't really say. Complexity theory was never my strong suit. Maybe all the way into the Cambrian. Why can't I get Gaia's reading in the present? Good question, Tosh. Her signature pattern seems to be swamped by all the subpatterns of the higher organisms which she contains. Maybe it's the fault of my equipment, I don't know. But I'm counting on the sacred fields of Mount Shasta to help. It's a place that has resonated to Gaia throughout recorded history."

Felix finished his instructions and struck ENTER. The interior space defined by the circle of morphic crystals filled with churning whiteness like curdled milk.

Detaching his cable, Felix realized what had been constricting him across the chest, and blushed. He took off Priscilla Jane's shirt and removed her bra.

"Hope I didn't stretch your, uh, intimate apparel on you, Pee Jay.

You can have it back as soon as you need it. Speaking of which, I may as well prime these last two crystals. . . ."

When he was done, Felix lay down on the table, looking skyward with head cradled atop his arms.

As long as he had his shirt off, he might as well catch some sun.

Returning to life twice in one day was hard work. He must have dozed off.

The sound of an approaching car woke him.

By the time he got to his feet, the car had stopped and its occupants emerged.

Rowdy gripped and steered Stumbo by the detective's lone arm. The chauffeur's pistol was stuck in his waistband. Perfidia had her gun in hand.

The Widow Wren wore a look of hatred like a mask of maggots.

"You! How many times do I have to kill you!"

"Has it ever occured to you, Perfidia, that violence is not necessary at all?"

Perfidia made an inarticulate noise of rage. Keeping Felix covered, she moved to the van and glanced inside. She smiled. "The dog finally got his. Good, good. Now—where's the girl?"

"Priscilla Jane loaned me her body, Perfidia, in an act of nobility you would probably find impossible to imagine."

A look of absolute avarice replaced the mask of hate. "So, that's it. You can jump from body to body. Even better than I imagined! I'll be immortal, forever young!"

Felix clucked his tongue chidingly, and turned to Detective Stumbo. "Did you keep that bracelet I gave you, Detective?"

"Yeah, I've got it right here in my pocket."

Felix looked at Priscilla Jane's watch. "Good, very good."

"Shut up! I know a bluff when I hear one. If you know what's good for you—"

Perfidia saw the milky oval now. "What's that? What are you doing?"

"Just summoning a friend."

"Well, stop it right now—"

Rowdy's shout made heads turn.

The pinned right sleeve of Detective Stumbo's coat had popped its fastening, as the Detective's missing right arm materialized.

Before anyone else could react, Stumbo had snatched the pistol from Rowdy's trousers and fired at Perfidia.

His shot caught her in the shoulder, while her mis-aimed blast nailed Rowdy in the leg.

Both of the criminals collapsed howling to the ground.

"Very good, Detective. I was hoping I could count on your quick comprehension and reflexes. Now, with your permission, I'll fix our two victims up."

Stumbo pointed his gun hesitantly at Felix. "You're not going to kill them, are you?"

"What if I said yes?"

Stumbo regarded his restored arm wonderingly. "Oh, what the hell am I worrying about them for? Go ahead."

Felix walked first to where Perfidia lay groaning.

"It's not that I hate you, Perfidia. It's just that I realize I truly love someone else."

He placed the bracelet from his left pocket on her wrist. She glared malevolently at him through her pain. Then he walked to Rowdy. The chauffeur's knee appeared to have been pulverized, and he was drifting into shock.

"You, sir, are lower than a dog. So I plan to raise you up."

The last bracelet was bestowed on Rowdy.

"Remember our earlier countdown, Detective? Perhaps you'd do the honors. . . ."

Stumbo recited, "Ten, nine, eight. . . ."

On one, the crystals went to work.

"Felix. . . ," said Priscilla Jane. She looked down at herself, dressed in Perfidia's clothes. "Where, how—?"

"Woof! Woof! Woof!"

Tosh was ripping Rowdy's uniform off with his teeth and claws. In seconds, the big dog was free of all but the jockey shorts, and went bounding joyfully around the clearing, albeit with one crippled leg dangling.

Stumbo dropped his gun and massaged his brow with both hands. "Holy Christ—"

Felix went to help Priscilla Jane up. Standing, she hugged him tightly, then winced at the pain in one shoulder.

A woman's voice suddenly resonated across the clearing. It was like wind in the trees or water over stones or snow sifting through pines, and carried a mother's warmth. It stopped even Tosh in his tracks.

"Who summons me?"

Felix gently untangled himself from Priscilla Jane and turned toward the circle of crystals.

A naked woman stood within the links. Wheat-colored hair, rose-tinged skin, violet eyes. Felix was reminded of Botticelli's Primavera.

The incarnate form of the planetary morphic field.

Felix coughed nervously. "Ahem, yes, Gaia, it was I. You see, I'd like a little help, if you'd be so kind. I've learned how to use morphic fields in a read-only fashion, so to speak. But if you could teach me how to write on them, I'd be able to make a few permanent changes in myself and my friends so we could dispense with these clumsy mechanisms."

Gaia stepped forward out of the charmed circle, and Felix gulped. He had theorized that, once born, she would be self-sustaining, which was what he was after himself. But to actually see it—

Gaia fixed him with a perceptive and not entirely friendly stare. "You are the one responsible for the recent tampering with my creatures that I have felt?"

"Well, yes—"

Gaia flung up her arms. The sky darkened, thunder clapped, and a zigzag crack opened in the earth.

"It is forbidden!" she roared, her voice now an avalanche of sound. "I will not have it!"

"But Gaia, if the laws of physics and biology permit—"

"Then I shall change your precious laws!"

Gaia brought her arms down.

Felix closed his eyes, ready to die for a third time.

Nothing happened, and he opened them slowly.

Gaia was gone. The circle of morphic crystals was dull and dead, impotent as so much costume jewelry.

But Priscilla Jane and Tosh and he himself still existed. And Detective Stumbo was two-armed.

Felix removed his collar.

No change.

The others doffed theirs, including Tosh, who snapped his with a paw inserted between collar and neck.

Stability for all.

Felix remembered to breathe. "Apparently, we did not go back to the *status-quo-ante*. My best guess is that Gaia's self-sustaining field touched us and stabilized our own changes, before she shut things down."

"For how long?" asked Stumbo.

"Permanently, I imagine, now that morphic resonance is an inactive discipline."

Tentative smiles broke out.

"So I won't lose my arm."

"And I won't turn back into Perfidia."

"And I won't turn back into Priscilla Jane. And Tosh, good old Tosh, won't ever turn back into—"

"Rowr, rowr, rowrdy!"

Did everything change for the worse in the 'Seventies? Probably not. Yet the notion proved intriguing enough to me to generate this story, modeled affectionately on Phil Dick's Eye in the Sky *(1957). Rockville, the mostly nondescript town of this story, seems to me to have hidden potential as the setting for other tales, perhaps, with a nod to REM, "Don't Go Back to Rockville". . . ?*

Earth Shoes

1. ELEPHANT BELLS

CHARLES UPTON FAIRLEIGH drove a new car every year, courtesy of his father.

This year it was a royal blue 1975 Plymouth Sports Fury.

Kendrick Skye was able to identify the car by a sound nearly hidden beneath the noise of its engine, though the vehicle was still a quarter of a mile distant, having just turned down the long shaded dirt drive that led to Skye's junkyard home.

A month ago, Ken had told Chuck that the factory-issued fan belt on the luxury model car was defective, and needed to be replaced. Chuck had laughed that abrasive, abusive laugh of his—reminiscent of the noise one might hear from a mother swine insanely gobbling down her own newborn piglets—and mildly pooh-poohed the idea.

"What the fuck, Ken? I mean, what the fuck? Are you nuts? Did you burn out a bearing upstairs, or what? This is a fucking American car, not one of those hokey Jap shitboxes. It's fresh off the dealer's lot. Elmore Flurkey's. You know what a bitch Flurkey is for details. Look at that belt. I mean, look close. It's stronger than my fucking dick! Now, I know nobody measures up to your goddamn Saint Reese, but if you're claiming Elmore is some kind of jerkoff asswipe who couldn't spot a defective fan-belt—why, I'd be happy to tell him you said so. Maybe he'll return the compliment by not sending any more business your way."

Ken had said nothing, simply closing the hood of the Fury. Nowadays, Ken always said nothing when he had thoughts which he felt would not meet with a completely sympathetic reception from the party or parties doing the listening. He had been that way since returning from 'Nam, when he had learned of Reese's unfortunate demise, for which he felt himself partly to blame.

This adopted trait—by now sheer habit—tended to cut down on the number of conversations Ken was able to sustain.

On the other hand, he never had to argue with anyone.

Things tended to balance out in the long run, the good equaling the bad. Or so he had found in the course of his twenty-two years of living.

Today, as Chuck's car drew closer, Ken could distinctly hear the belt straining, its frayed plys producing a nearly subliminal, yet still recognizable—to Ken—whine. It was going to go any minute.

But Ken did not plan to make the same mistake twice.

The Fury wheeled up in a cloud of dust. When the cloud dispersed, Ken could see that the car held two people in addition to its driver.

Bonita Coney sat in the front seat, close to Chuck.

Mona J. Bonaventura sat alone in the back.

Mona J. had the rear door open before Chuck could shut off the engine. In a few seconds, much to the embarrassed mechanic's consternation, she was squeezing Ken tight.

"I just got back!" explained Mona J., her arms low around Ken's waist and her face only a few inches from his. "I didn't even know you still lived in Rockville! I ran into Chuck and Bonnie in town. You were the first person I asked about! I made them drive me straight out here!"

Releasing Ken, Mona J. stepped back. Ken was able to see how Mona J. was dressed. Nothing special, really.

Mona J.'s frizzy mane of auburn hair, parted down the middle, was held in place with a dimestore Indian-beadwork headband. She wore a leather vest over a straining purple acrylic tubetop. Her pants were bellbottoms of elephantine dimensions, completely concealing her feet and sweeping circles in the dust at least fifteen inches in diameter. Beneath these flares, something seemed amiss. Mona J. was definitely tilted somehow—

The woman's prominent nose, generous lips and wide-eyed gaze made her resemble, Ken suddenly realized, some plastic surgeon's synthesis of Carole King and Carly Simon.

Mona J. put her hands on her hips. "Well, aren't you going to say you're glad to see me?"

"Hell, sure, of course I'm glad. It's just that I'm a little stunned. I haven't heard from you in three years—"

Mona J. waved that trifling matter aside. "You were the one who went away first," she said, with impeccable accuracy, though indiscernible logic. He had not, after all, been totally out of reach of postal communication.

In 1972, at the age of nineteen, with the signatures of Rockville High Principal Rebozo and Superintendent Colson still wet on his high school diploma, Ken had joined the Army as a volunteer. The action was an impulsive one, taken after that huge argument with Reese, the one that led to Ken throwing down his tools and storming out of the junkyard, vowing never to return.

As his recruiter had promised, Ken got to pick his speciality. Naturally, he chose vehicle repair. He ended up in a motor pool outside Da Nang. There he labored happily for two years, even refusing to take his earned R&R. The closest he had ever come to actual fighting during his hitch was once when a stoned private in their barracks—name of Tub Raauflab—let loose a burst from his M-16 at what he thought was a rat but which turned out to be his own vulnerable booted foot poking out from under the bedcovers. Ken's whole Vietnam experience had been about as traumatic as high school. Less so, in many ways.

When he returned to civilian life, to Rockville, the only home he knew, he discovered two things.

Mona J. had left her parents' house without telling anyone where she was going, hit the road like a marble out a greased pinball chute.

And Reese Hawrot had died in a horrible accident, an accident Ken immediately felt he might have been able to prevent, had he been present.

To complicate his shock and surprise, Ken soon learned that Reese had stipulated in his brief will (scribbled on the back of a FoMoCo invoice, but duly notarized) that the auto-scrapyard-cum-repair-shop where Ken had spent practically all his free hours since he was old enough to tell a lug wrench from a crescent wrench was now the property of one Kendrick Skye.

Ken wasn't sure which desertion hurt the worst.

In the end, he tended to lean toward Reese's death.

After all, Mona J. was only a girl.

But Reese had been a *mechanic.*

And not just any mechanic, but the best damned mechanic on the face of the globe. A regular Moses of Mercurys, a Buddha of Buicks, a Christ of Chevys, an Odin of Oldsmobiles.

Ken had no hesitation in affirming this, though he had not personally surveyed every competitor for the title. There was simply no way that anyone could have possessed skills greater than Reese's. The elderly, cantankerous man—never seen out of his uniform of acid-burned thermal shirt and oily overalls—had been able to instinctively discern whatever ailed an auto, no matter what the make, model or year. From a cracked rotor to a leak in the manifold, from worn gaskets to faulty brake calipers, he had been able to pinpoint the trouble instantly and fix it with the minimum of effort.

Reese had been Ken's hero ever since the day Ken's father had driven out to the Rockville junkyard with his son to pick up a cheap windshield for their Corvair, and Ken had watched Reese at work.

And although Ken had learned quite a bit from the reclusive genius, he knew that he had not inherited a fraction of his intuitive skills. . . .

Chuck had finally cut his motor and emerged from the car, Bonnie following with alacrity out his door, as if attached to him by a string of short length.

Bonnie and Chuck were a real pair—had been since high school, where Chuck had been a star on the basketball team and Bonnie had swept the school's field hockey squad to the state championships. His buzzcut, chinos and sports shirt from The Put On Shop at Sears, combined with an agressive expression on a broad face, caused Chuck to resemble a young H. R. "Bob" Haldeman—a likeness which had provoked many jokes at his expense during the recent Watergate trials.

Blue-eyed Bonnie—her blonde hair styled rather like Gregg Allman's—wore today a white blouse with a smiley pin on its Peter-Pan collar, and a plaid skirt that showed off her hockey-stick-scarred calves. Usually to be found hanging adoringly on Chuck's arm, she reminded Ken of a cross between Tricia Nixon and Karen Carpenter.

The two had been engaged for four years. They were postponing their marriage until Chuck's long-delayed promotion at the Merchants' Bank should finally materialize, bringing them the income they deemed necessary for their married lifestyle. Chuck's father, Charles Senior, was president at the Merchants', and only that connection had secured Chuck a job there at all. His performance in the loan department was mediocre at best and abysmal at worst. The bank was still reeling from the loan he had approved for the local farmer who planned to raise coffee beans despite Rockville's bone-rattling winters, and Chuck's promotion seemed a distant prospect at best. This had tended over the past year or so, Ken had noticed, to render the relationship between the two ex-sports stars rather strained, at times even acrimonious.

Swaggering toward Mona J. and Ken, with Bonnie close behind, Chuck now spoke.

"Yeah, there's nothing I like better'n visiting my old buddy the grease monkey. How's it hanging, Greasy? And as for detouring halfway to hell and back, wasting most of my Friday evening just to haul out some bra-burning hippie broad who thought she was too good for Rockville until she got her tail kicked and came running back—why, I don't know how come I didn't think of such goddamn major fun myself before now."

"Oh, keep quiet, Chuck," said Bonnie. "I think it's cute that Mona J. was so anxious to see Ken again. Just think how we'd feel if we'd been separated for years."

Chuck rolled his eyes toward the clear summer sky. "I sure as fucking hell wouldn't've mooned around like old numbnuts here. You can bet your damn eyeteeth that I would've wet my wick in the next available bush without so much as one goddamn tear, probably starting the day after you split."

"Charles Upton Fairleigh, how could you say such a thing!"

Ken and Mona J. ignored the squabbling pair.

"Where have you been all this time, Mona J.?"

"California, mostly."

"That's a pretty big mostly."

"Well, Hollywood, if you really want to know."

"Oh. Did you get to be an actress, like you always talked about in school?"

Mona J. looked chagrined. "Sort of. Did you ever see *White Lightning*? Burt Reynolds as Gator McClusky?"

"I don't get to the movies much. . . . "

Mona J. appeared relieved. "Well, I had a small part in that—"

"Shit!" interrupted Chuck. "You were the chick dancing topless on the bar!" He whistled lasciviously. "That wasn't no *small* part! Hoo-whee!"

Ken suppressed an angry retort. "Anything else?" he asked Mona J. gently.

"I, um, exuded a similar presence in Nicholson's *The Last Detail.* Another bar scene."

"But you kinda felt these limited roles didn't, ah, fully exploit your acting potential," prompted Ken.

"Right! I knew you'd understand, Ken."

"And now you're back in Rockville. How long do you plan to stay?"

"Don't know."

"Whatcha gonna do?"

"Don't know."

"What do you know, Mona J.?"

She spread her arms wide. "I'm here!"

Ken was forced to smile. "I guess that's enough."

"Awww," snarled Chuck, "how sweet! I'm so happy for you two noodle-brains. Now if you'll excuse us, me 'n' Bonnie're gonna lay rubber in reverse down the yellow brick road straight outa this goddamn salvage-yard Oz and back to the real world!"

Chuck hustled Bonnie back into the Fury. He turned the key in the ignition and raced the engine.

The fan belt snapped with a noise like a giant's barber's strop descending on a galvinized tin roof.

Chuck hastily shut off the motor. He stuck his head out the window.

"Hey, Monkey! Fix whatever's wrong, and make it snappy! I don't wanna waste any more time here. C'mon, c'mon, I'll pay you, if that's what you're worried about."

Unhurriedly, Ken went into the ramshackle garage which stood like a battered wooden knight amid the sprawling wreckage of the hundreds of weed-curtained cars laid out like defeated warriors around it. (The oldest vehicle immediately visible was a 1949 Kaiser Victoria; the newest, a 1974 Pinto totalled when Mrs. Stubblefield, dizzy after one Mai-tai too many at the Bridge Club, had failed to negotiate Wapner's Curve.) He emerged shortly with a new fan belt and a wrench. In a minute or so, the repair was done.

Chuck re-started his car, put it in gear, and kept his foot on the brake. Reaching into his back pocket, he took out his wallet. From this, he extracted a few singles.

"Here you go, kiddo! Keep the change. Put it toward your retirement fund. You'll need it, the way you're going. You'll be stuck in this nowhere job till you're as old as fucking Reese. Unless, of course, you get your head crushed first!"

With this Chuck threw the money out, where it drifted to the ground, and raced off in a cloud of fumes and dust, his swinish laughter diminishing with the distance.

Ken wished silently that there could be a world where Chuck and his kind did not exist.

Then he nervously caught himself.

Such wishes, in his case, were dangerous.

Very dangerous.

Mona J. spat disgustedly in the direction of the retreating car. "Nothing's changed in Rockville, I see."

"Not true. You're back."

"That's so," chuckled Mona J. She walked in a funny manner over to the money and picked it up. "It's dirty, but no sense letting it go to waste. We'll need it."

Ken liked the way she said "we."

As Mona J. walked back toward him, Ken could restrain his curiosity no longer.

"Mona J., did something happen to cripple you up in Hollywood? Too many stunts or something?"

"Why do you ask?"

"It's the way you walk. . . . "

Mona J. laughed. "Oh, that's just my earth shoes."

" 'Earth shoes?' "

"Sure. Look!"

Much to Ken's amazement, Mona J. did not, as he had expected, lift her leg to reveal what lay beneath her elephant bells. Instead, she swiftly undid her pants, dropped them, and stepped out of the pooled denim.

Her panties were printed with peace signs.

Ken forced his eyes down to her feet. "Those are 'earth shoes'?"

"Yes. They were designed by a Danish yoga instructor. Anne Kalso. She noticed how healthy it was to walk in soft soil, where your heel sinks deeper than the ball of your foot, and realized how great it would be to have a shoe that allowed such a stance."

"Uh-huh. You look like you're gonna topple over backwards any minute."

"I just might."

Ken got nervous. The peace signs suggested a neutral topic. "Uh, what do you think about the war being over?"

Mona J. grinned. "I guess that makes my panties old hat."

And so she took them off too.

2. THE MOOD RING

The calendar in Ken's shabby kitchen featured a bare-breasted model in black leather hotpants and glitter-flecked platform shoes cozying up to an enormous driveshaft, against a red satin backdrop. There was an artful smear of grease on her forehead, calculated to increase her allure, mechanic-wise. The copy for the calendar read:

GOFFART'S TRUCK PARTS
"FOR TUFF PARTS—BUY GOFFART'S!"

Below the pinup was displayed the page for August, 1974.

One year ago to the month. The month when Ken had returned home from his hitch to learn of Reese's death. The very month Nixon had been forced from office. The month Paul Anka's "You're Having My Baby" had gone to Number One.

In a curious way, time seemed to have stopped that month. On a personal level, Ken had felt his life was at a standstill, that he was just marking time by trying to pick up Reese's business. On a national level, Nixon's resignation seemed to have put the country into a state of post-politico-orgasmic lassitude. True, many events had happened since then, but none of them seemed to matter. Or rather, they all seemed anticlimactic somehow, even the end of the war. Nixon's forced departure had definitely put an end to an era. But the new period—whatever shape it might assume—appeared reluctant to be born. There seemed no clear sense of what the future would bring. Everyone seemed to be floundering. It was as if the entire nation was waiting by the phone for a potential date with an unknown suitor.

It was after midnight. The kitchen was illuminated by a caged utility light hanging from a hook set in a ceiling beam. (In the next room Mona J. lay sleeping, earth shoes tumbled in the corner where she had kicked them before pulling Ken into bed for a sexual reunion as exciting and delightful as any of their hasty high school trysts.) The sound of the peepfrogs who lived in a marshy corner of the car lot formed a one-note symphony.

Ken was having a snack. The snack consisted of Fish Stix and Tater Tots. He kept a freezer full of these handy prepackaged near-edibles, and they formed the major part of his spartan bachelor's diet.

As he ate, Ken ruminated on a single question.

Was Mona J.'s return a sign that his life was bestirring itself again, entering into a new phase?

Perhaps now was the time to use the STP.

Assuming that he even believed in it.

Ken thought back to the last time he had seen Reese Hawrot alive, in 1972. . . .

The cranky and grizzled master mechanic had been lying on a dolly beneath a '58 Rambler Classic owned by Walt Whiteman,

Rockville's parsimonious pharmacist. Ken had been standing on the far side of the garage bay balancing off a tire.

"Bring me my socket set, will you, boy," came Reese's muffled voice.

Ken did so. Then Reese said the uncanny thing that was to spark their dramatic falling-out.

"Mighty handy to have a helper like you around to spare these old bones, Ken. I'm sure glad I dreamed you up."

Ken had frozen. A feeling of unreality washed over him.

"What—what are you talking about?"

Reese scooted himself out from under the car. His wrinkled face wore a sober look. He got arthritically to his feet.

"Well, son, I'm afraid that remark just kinda slipped out. I didn't mean to say anything to you quite yet about what brought us together, but I guess now I'll have to.

"You remember ten years ago, back in 1962, when you was just a tad come here with your father for that windshield. . . ? Well, it wasn't chance that brought you here, nor made you fall in love with me and this old scrapheap. No, it was something known as STP."

"The gasoline additive?"

Reese exploded. "Not your common STP, goddamn it!" He forced himself to calm down. "But that's right, I forget. You don't know nothing about the miracle STP.

"It all come about like this.

"T'was the fall of '54 and I was just stepping out my door one fine morning when I seen a trio of city slickers pushing their car up the drive. A big government-style Caddy it was. I went down to give them a hand. They intra-duced theirselves as three professors. Kurt, Johnny and Albert was their names. On their way to Princeton, they was, when their old jalopy broke down. For all their book learning, they didn't know squat about autos, and were as helpless in the face of their troubles as three kittens in a carwash.

"Well, I fixed up the old crate they was driving quick as could be. Then they started shilly-shallying about how to pay me.

" 'Who's got some cash?' says Johnny.

" 'I'm relatively broke,' says Al.

" 'It's impossible for me to decide,' goes Kurt.

"'Hell, ain't this great,' sneers Johnny. 'How we gonna recompense this kindly fellow? I'd do it myself, except I lost every cent at the roulette table.'

"They shuffled from foot to foot for a while, until Al seemed to remember something. He reached into his pocket and took out a bottle. There was like two drops of queer liquid in it.

" 'This is some crazy stuff Dirac sent me, trying to get me to accept his ridiculous nondeterministic quantum physics. He claims it is pure distilled essence of Heisenberg observation waves, or some such thing. He calls it—' "

Here Reese paused. Utterly bemused, Ken watched his boss as the old man walked to a shelf and removed from its hiding place what had to be the very bottle, along with a dirty scrap of paper.

"I made Al write this down for me," explained Reese. "This stuff is called 'Synchronistic Temporal Potentiator.' STP."

"What's it do?" asked Ken.

"My exact question, boy. Here's what Al said, near as I can recall.

"'Dirac claims this liquid, when applied to any observer, will allow them to influence the macroscopic world just as the fate of an atom is influenced by a measurement. The observer brings the world onto an alternate time line of his own devising.'

"'Are you saying this is some kinda magic wishing potion?' I asked.

"'That's more or less what Dirac claims. But since I know the physics of such a thing is impossible, I have not even tried it.'

"'And you're giving it to me?'

"'Yes.'

"Well, since it was all they was offering, I took it. But because I was basically happy with my life, I put it on a shelf and forgot about it for years, till one day, feeling the pain in my joints more than usual, I took the bottle down, poured a drop on my head—I figured that's where my observing powers was—and wished for a helper. Within minutes, you and your Dad came along."

"You're claiming you wished me into existence?" demanded Ken, feeling anger swelling up inside.

"Not exactly. Just that I kinda bent reality a bit to get you here and make you stay."

Ken blew up. "That's ridiculous! I've got free will! I'm not here because you wished for someone to help you!"

Reese was unmoved. "Believe what you will. I'm only telling you what those professors said, and what I did and what happened. Maybe it was all just a big coincidence. . . . "

This was not good enough for Ken. "Admit that you're making all this up."

"Sorry, boy, but I can't do that. Every word is true."

Ken threw down the socket wrenches. "That does it. I can't work here if you believe that. I'm leaving. If you want me back, you'll have to call me up and apologize."

Reese made no move to stop him.

When, in the next few weeks, his elderly ex-mentor had failed to contact him, Ken had joined the Army.

And then a falling engine block had put an end to any possiblity of reconciliation. Apparently, Reese had failed with his arthritic grip to secure the lifted engine safely, and it had fallen directly onto his head.

Quite evidently, the STP—if it worked at all—granted neither omniscience nor omnipotence nor invulnerability. Or perhaps the single drop Reese had applied had worn off.

One of the first things Ken had done upon inheriting the junkyard had been to look for the bottle of magical fluid.

It was still in its original hiding place, along with the scrap of paper with the writing in what Ken had come to realize was Albert Einstein's own penmanship.

Now, licking ketchup from his fingers, Ken pushed the remainder of his midnight snack away from him and arose. He went out to fetch the bottle of STP and quickly returned.

The single remaining drop of liquid lay like a black pearl in the innocuous bottle.

For a year, Ken had debated using the magical fluid. Not that he believed in it. But still, it was worth a try. The only problem was, he didn't know what to wish for. Like Reese, he was basically content with his life. (Whether that life had been imposed on him or freely chosen, he avoided thinking about.) As long as he had cars to work on, he was happy. From time to time, he had wished for companionship. But look at what had happened today. Mona J. had returned on her own initiative, without any magical intervention. Now he had nothing left to desire.

Mona J. She seemed like a sensible, happy girl. Yet Ken could sense that underneath her bouncy exterior was a core of dissatisfaction, stemming mainly from her failed stab at acting.

He would let her have the last drop of STP.

Ken walked into the bedroom. Mona J. lay on her back with the sheets tangled around her from the waist down. Somewhere in her travels she had acquired a tattoo of the Zig-Zag man on her upper left breast.

With the unstoppered bottle poised over her sleeping form, Ken hesitated.

What if something should go wrong? The STP could have been responsible for Reese's death! Wouldn't it be good to make the application reversible somehow. . . ?

Ken's gaze fell on the odd ring on Mona J.'s finger.

She had told him it was called "a mood ring." A liquid crystal center reacted with the wearer's body, supposedly indicating his or her emotional state. Right now, Mona J. was a blissful blue.

Without hesitating, Ken instinctively decanted the droplet of STP onto the mood ring.

The liquid exhibited a startling affinity for the artificial stone, being instantly absorbed.

Ken held his breath and waited.

When nothing unusual happened, he undressed, lay down beside Mona J., and went to sleep.

That is why he did not witness the change.

3. SATURDAY NIGHT FEVER

Ken awoke without feeling an overwhelming need to piss. This was highly abnormal. His intemperate bladder usually filled to bursting overnight, no matter how little liquid he drank before sleep. Oh, well, maybe a renewed sex life had something to do with it. Engine design, not human physiology, was his forte. . . .

Absentmindedly, he reached down to scratch his crotch, as he was wont to do of a morning.

There was nothing there.

Very, very slowly, Ken lifted up the sheet and looked.

The visuals confirmed what his hand had first uncannily conveyed.

His crotch was as empty as that of his namesake, Barbie's boyfriend.

Ken looked wildly around for Mona J. She was nowhere to be seen. He clambered quickly out of bed.

"Mona J.!" he yelled. "Come quick! My cock's gone!"

Ken realized even as he said it that such a bizarre proclamation was hardly calculated to lure help. He doubted if he himself would respond to such an insane announcement. But apparently Mona J. was a more daring or compassionate person than he. There was the sound of footsteps approaching from the front room.

In the door appeared the actress Ali McGraw. She was naked. Like Ken, her smooth pudendum was completely unadorned with any trace of functioning equipment.

Then Ken noticed the mood ring on Ali's finger.

"Mona J.?"

"Ken?"

"You've changed!"

"You too!"

Ken knew that something more was implied than the absence of his genitalia. He looked in the mirror across the room.

Ryan O'Neal looked back.

Ken sat down wearily on the bed. He held his head in his hands. "I don't believe this. Why would you do such a thing, Mona J.?"

"Me? What are you talking about? I didn't misplace our private parts. When I went to sleep they were right where we left them when we were done using them. And as for our new faces—how could I do such a thing?"

Ken explained.

A look Ken did not like came over Ali's—Mona J.'s— face.

"You mean to tell me that when I woke up this morning, the world instantly remade itself according to my secret perceptions?"

Ken groaned. "You did it, Mona J.. You turned us into actor and actress dolls. I gave you the chance to have anything you wanted, and this is what you picked."

"I guess I must've really absorbed the Ratings Code standards while I was in Hollywood. You know, like no full frontal nudity? Despite what goes on in the dressing rooms, you never see any real fooling around on the screen. And the love scenes always stop below the waist. But anyhow, what's so bad about it? I mean, sex is great, but glamour is even better. Haven't you always wanted to be a star? I sure have. I always hated my looks. That nose, those lips—too ethnic! Now think of all the parts I'll get!"

"Mona J."

"Yeah?"

"What about everyone else?"

"What do you mean?"

"If you look like Ali McGraw, and I look like Ryan O'Neal—"

"You mean everyone in the world looks like a star now too?"

"I would assume so."

Mona J. started grabbing her clothes off the floor. She slipped into her earth shoes, immediately assuming her familiar backwards-sloping stance.

"C'mon, get dressed! We have to go into town!"

"Mona J., don't you think you'd like to take that ring off now. . . ?"

"Screw that! You gave me this shot at making a new life for myself, and I'm going to use it!"

Even more so than usual, Ken was not inclined to argue. He had no idea what would happen anyhow if Mona J. doffed the ring. Would the world revert—or would it vanish? It might be wise to postpone the experiment.

He forced himself to try to look on the bright side. This new arrangement simplified a lot of things. Take dating and remembering to buy toilet paper, just for two. . . .

Ken's underwear fit funny. In the end, he discarded it and simply drew his pants on over his lack.

The car Ken used for personal errands was an ex-Checker Cab painted a permanent matte black with primer in expectation of a final coat that never came. He and Mona J. climbed in and tooled off down the tree-lined drive.

"Ken, look at those great squirrels—"

On a branch, a trio of extremely alert squirrels was stacking nuts in a perfect pyramid. The pyramid reached the point of instability and fell apart. The squirrels all did perfect double-takes, flipping end over end and chattering a mile a minute. Ken could almost hear the narration by the "aw-shucks" announcer:

"Those little critters plumb bit off more'n they could chew this time. . . . "

"Mona J., you've even disneyfied the wildlife!"

"I think they're cuter that way!"

"But it's not natural!"

"What is nowadays? Is lurex natural? Are the Eagles natural? And what about those horrid Fish Stix you eat?"

Ken made no reply.

On the road to Rockville, the Saturday morning traffic was light. Only three cars passed them. One was driven by George C. Scott in full Patton rig; one was steered by John Wayne as Rooster Cogburn; the third was piloted by Dirty Harry.

"I always knew Rockville was full of male chauvinist pigs," said Mona J.

"They didn't seem too upset by their new identities," said Ken. "I wonder why. . . . "

"It could be that only nearness to the mood ring lets us realize anything's different," ventured Mona J.

"I think you're right."

Main Street forked from Route One. Soon they were in what passed for downtown Rockville.

Marlon Brando was sweeping the sidewalk in front of Whiteman's Drugstore. Faye Dunaway was lowering the awning at Ford's Dress Emporium. Al Pacino was chatting up Barbra Streisand as he pumped gas into her Chevy. Woody Allen—looking very Fielding Mellish—was mounting a "Whip Inflation Now" poster in the window of his meat market. A whole pack of John Travoltas (one of *Kotter's* Sweathogs) ogled a herd of Farrah Fawcett-Majors (star of the TV movie *The Girl Who Came Gift-Wrapped*).

The sight of the assorted stars calmly imitating the stolid citizens of Rockville was too much for Ken. It was as if the pods from *Invasion of the Bodysnatchers* had been manufactured in California instead of deep space. He pulled into one of the parking spaces that slanted out from the sidewalk and rested his forehead on the steering wheel.

"I can't drive any further."

"Let's walk then. I want to talk to some of these people. If they don't realize they look like stars, then I've got a lock on all the casting calls."

They got out of the cab. Approaching them down the sidewalk was a couple walking arm in arm: Henry Winkler and Penny Marshall: the Fonz and Laverne.

"It's Chuck and Bonnie," said Ken.

"How can you tell?"

"Even without balls, nobody swaggers like Chuck."

Sure enough, the man hailed them in familiar fashion.

"Hey, Monkey! What brings you and the chick into town? I thought you'd be in bed all day. Didn't I say that, Bonnie? That they'd be pumping away all weekend? What's the matter—the well go dry?"

Chuck and Bonnie crossed an invisible line that plainly marked the sphere of perceptive immunity conferred by the mood ring. They stopped dead in their tracks, looking with shock and horror as they suddenly realized that Ken and Mona J. had been transformed into the protagonists of *Love Story.*

Relishing their discomposure, Ken gestured toward a plate glass window. Bonnie and Chuck saw their own reflections.

"Oh my god!" squealed Bonnie. "I look like that ignorant De Fazio tramp on television!"

"Who the fuck messed with my good looks?" Chuck demanded. Suddenly sensing what else had been changed, Chuck made a desperate grab at his fly. "My dick! Holy fucking Christ! Somebody's made off with my pecker! Who did it? Come on, cough it up!"

"A vivid image, Chuck," Ken commented. "But we don't have your pitiful willy handy."

With a minimum of details, Ken tried to explain what had happened. As he talked, the sour scowl on Chuck's borrowed face grew more and more pronounced, until finally he was wearing a look of total disgust.

"You know, none of this would ever have happened if Nixon was still in office. I've said it a hundred fucking times: this country has been going to fucking hell in a bucket from the second the fucking

Democrats blew up a minor prank to the size of the goddamn
Goodyear blimp! Watergate my ass! All this crazy stuff is a direct
result of disrespect for our elected leader!"

Ken tried to reason with Chuck. "Don't be ridiculous, Chuck.
This magic STP juice was sitting on Reese's shelf since 1954—"

"Reese was probably responsible for Nixon losing in '60!"

Bonnie/Laverne had been swivelling her attention all this time
from her own reflection to Mona J.'s altered face. Now she spoke.

"Why do you get to be Ali McGraw while I have to be Penny
Marshall?"

Mona J. slipped a hank of her long dark hair coyly behind one ear.
"Face it, girl. I was always better looking than you."

"Better looking! Hah! Maybe if your idea of good-looking is a
frizzy-headed, thick-lipped, big-boobed Italian slob!"

Mona J.'s face suffused with blood. She raised her hand bearing
the ring. "You'd better be careful what you say, Bonita Coney. . . . "

"I don't care what you look like now. I know you've *really* got hips
wide as a Mack truck!"

"That did it! You don't like being Laverne? It's not glamorous
enough for you? Try this!"

Where Laverne/Bonnie had been now stood Jean Stapleton.
Edith Bunker.

Mona J. broke into wild laughter. Chuck staggered back in terror.
Bonnie turned to catch her image in the plate-glass. With a wild shriek,
she hurled herself on Mona J. The two women tumbled into the street.

Ken moved to help Mona J. He found himself pinioned by
Chuck.

"I don't know what Bonnie's got in mind, but I aim to let her try
it. Anything's better than being stuck with the Dingbat for a
girlfriend."

Bonnie's greater weight and ferocity soon prevailed in the catfight.
Kneeling on Mona J.'s arms, the Queens housewife fastened her grip
on the mood ring.

She pulled it off and triumphantly slid it onto her own finger.

4. THE SILENT MAJORITY

The sky above the Skye household was the color of a TV tuned to *The Brady Bunch*.

In fact, the sky *was* a TV tuned to *The Brady Bunch*.

Florence Henderson's hemispherically distorted face stretched for miles across the titanic dome that formed the celestial ceiling. Far off in the west, a bit of Ann Davis's enormous nose poked into view. In the background was the out-of-focus Brady kitchen, tangerine walls and avocado table. It was like the Northern Lights, twenty-four hours a day.

The Skye family—Ken, Mona J., Ken Junior, Mona J. Junior, and their unnamed halfling—outside in their quarter-acre backyard, did not, however, pay any attention to the spectacle. So familiar was the overhead display from years of viewing that it had become invisible to them. Instead, happy parents Ken and Mona J. watched as their two-and-a-half children played in the approved manner.

Ken was dressed in his official Saturday Suit: chinos, loafers, madras shirt. Protruding from his mouth was his Father's Pipe, emitting a fragrant cloud of maple-ly smoke that competed with his Old Spice aftershave. Ken sat in a plastic-webbed lawnchair. Beside him sat "the little woman."

Mona J.'s hair was set into an enormous beehive do— much like First Lady Priscilla Presley wore on her wedding day—frozen in place with coats of lacquer. On her cheeks were two perfect circles of rosy makeup, while her lips were blood-red. She was dressed in ruffles and lace, pinafores and plackets. Her eyes appeared to be filled with liquid Valium, some of which was leaking out.

A few feet away, Ken Junior and Mona J. Junior—dressed like pint-sized versions of their parents—were enacting Play Scenario One Hundred and Fifty-Six. Ken Junior's G.I. Joe doll had knocked Mona J. Junior's Chatty Cathy to the ground and was now burrowing under the doll's dress. "Hold still, dammit!" said Ken Junior. Mona J. Junior emitted realistic shrieks on behalf of Chatty Cathy, whose built-in tape was on the fritz.

The Skye halfling, meanwhile, who had been kicking a soccer ball around, had gotten stuck in a corner of the lot, where the white picket fence met at right angles, separating the Skye yard from the thousands of identical ones that made up the town of Rockville.

Seeing the halfling's plight, Father Ken got up to help.

The halfling wore a pair of belted shorts, sox and sneakers. It did not need a shirt, because it had no upper half. This statistical necessity—one per family, always born after the allotted son and daughter—terminated in a hard hairy carapace just above the waist. Each halfling looked rather like an ambulatory footstool.

The Skye halfling was struggling blindly against the fence in vain pursuit of the soccer ball, which had squirted away behind it. Ken picked his half-child up and turned it around, then set the ball in front of it. The halfling felt around tentatively with its foot, found the ball and gave it a kick, cantering awkwardly after it.

Ken returned to his seat. He grabbed Mona J.'s hand and squeezed. Chuckling, he said, "What a little rascal!"

Mona J. made the obligatory reply. "A regular roughneck!"

"Not a big eater though, that's for sure!"

The fond parents chuckled appreciatively for a while. Then, puffing out a big cloud of aromatic smoke, Ken said, "Boy oh boy, it sure is nice relaxing with the family on the weekend. I can hardly wait for tomorrow, so we can go to church."

"Life is good," said Mona J., somewhat wearily. Ken gave her a cautionary glare, until she visibly perked up. (Though there was a tic at one corner of her smile.)

Ken was suddenly moved to look at his watch. "Holy Cow, it's almost time to go to the beach!" He clapped his hands, which garnered the attention of his son and daughter, but did nothing to stop the earless halfling in the senseless pursuit of its ball.

"Ken Junior, Mona J. Junior—pack up your toys and get your swimsuits on. It's time for the beach."

"Awww, do we hafta, Dad?"

"Yes, you 'hafta.' Now, scoot!"

The children rushed obediently indoors. Ken retrieved the halfling, carrying it under one arm like a keg of beer, and he and Mona J. followed.

Inside, Ken began to assemble the Family Outing Setup: the Cooler, stocked with Twinkies and Oscar Meyer Lunchmeats; the Coppertone, the Wetnaps ("Your Folded Fingerbowl"), the Thermos of Kool-Aid, the Striped Umbrella. . . .

As he was taking down some towels from a high shelf in the linen closet, something hard and heavy fell and bonked him on the head, making him see stars.

"Dangblasted frazzle-brazzle dadratted so-and-so!" swore Ken.

"Father!" admonished Mona J. "Watch your language!"

"Sorry, Mother."

Ken stooped to recover the item that had conked him. It was a single shoe. But the shoe was the strangest one he had ever seen. Big and clunky, it seemed to have a negative slope toward the heel. . . .

"Mother, do you recognize this?"

Mona J.'s eyes grew wide when she saw the shoe. "Nuh-no, I duh-don't. It's nothing I ever wore, I swear it. I wear only high heels around the house during the day, or mules in the bedroom, or flip-flops at the beach. I swear it!"

"No need to get so excited, Mother. I believe you. Well, into the trash it goes then."

Ken tossed the shoe into the kitchen garbage pail. Mona J. opened her mouth to say something, but seemed to think better of it.

In a few minutes, the whole family was in the loaded car and ready to go. And just in time! Already the streets were filling up with cars from every other household, all heading toward the beach.

Ken inched the nose of his auto out of the driveway. His next door neighbor obligingly paused to let Ken join the cavalcade, and they were off!

On the way to the beach, they sang along with the all-Captain-and-Tennille AM radio station.

"Love will keep us together. . . . "

Traffic slowed to a crawl at the entrance to the beachside parking lot, and the kids grew fidgety. Ken Junior gave Mona J. Junior an "Indian sunburn," and she retaliated by ripping his comic book in half.

"Dad!" wailed Ken Junior. "Look what she did to my copy of *Young Elvis, DEA Agent*!"

Ken picked up issue 516 of the comic which detailed the heroic early adventures of the nation's President. "You must admit you deserved it, son. But don't worry, next week's issue will be out soon."

Even the Skye halfling was not immune to the boredom. It began to fidget and kick, and its older siblings ganged up to tickle it into a better humor.

Soon the car was parked, and the Skye family, loaded down with beach apparatus, crossed the hot sands like a miniature caravan to stake out an empty spot on the crowded shore.

Once established, Ken announced that it was time to "slather on the ol' suntan lotion."

"I don't know why we bother with this silly chore," complained Mona J., even as she applied Coppertone to the halfling's bare legs. "We haven't seen that filthy sun in years. And God knows that even this close we're not going to get a burn from the Heavenly Screen."

Ken cast his eyes upward, to where the Eternal Sitcom played. Father Brady, Robert Reed, was delivering a lecture to his assembled brood. Ken's eyes slid down, down, down, to where illuminated sky met the sea. At this artificial horizon, exactly three miles out, the skydome plunged into the ocean, sealing off the country—God's chosen nation—from the hostile and inexplicable world at large.

It was true, what Mother had said. Lit only by the comforting glow of the Cathode Sky, they stood no chance of getting a sunburn. Still, it was best to do things the Old Way when possible. Tradition, that's what kept the nation strong. . . .

When they were all properly coated, Ken and Mona J. lay back to look at the sky, while the kids began to build a sand-castle. The halfling was left to its own devices, whereupon it mysteriously gravitated to a knot of its fellows. The clump of swimsuited halflings stood in eerie mute communication. Occasionally, two would lie down flat in the sand, top to top, and, digging their heels in, rub their hairy endplates together in some kind of ritual.

At the appropriate time, Ken announced, "Time for our Swim!"

They all raced down to the ocean and plunged into the waves.

As a Father, Ken was permitted to stroke out strongly away from the others, who could only frolic near the shore.

After a few dozen yards, he paused, treading water.

At the horizon, Florence Henderson's immense miniskirt-clad legs entered the ocean as if she were some modern-day Colossus of Rhodes. A funny feeling came over Ken, as he imagined swimming the whole three miles out to the television wall. Would he be able to see up her skirt, view the National Mother's private parts, her babymaker. . . ?

Shaking off the strange sensation—that bump from the shoe must've done more to his brain than he first thought—Ken headed back to his family.

Almost before they knew it, it was time to leave. They packed everything back into the station wagon, and joined their fellow citizens on the trip home. The tired children slumped fast asleep, including their halfling. (At least Ken assumed it was their halfling; it was kind of hard to tell them apart. Still, what difference did it make. . . ?)

Half-turning to Mona J., Ken said, "Going to the park tonight to hear the Town Band play and Mayor Fairleigh make his speech would be the perfect end to this day."

"Oh, Father, that's what you say every week!"

"Well, it's true."

"Oh, I know. It just makes me smile. Anyway, I wonder what his wife will be wearing? Bonita has such good taste. On Monday, you see her Saturday outfit in all the stores."

"And why not?"

After showers and supper—Velveeta sandwiches washed down with Tang—the Skye family set out to walk to the Town Common.

Amidst the comforting throng, with the strains of Sousa washing over them, the Skye family drank Pepsis and watched the sky dim. (But not to the point where the Eternal Sitcom ever entirely vanished.)

Just as the latest episode of the Eternal Sitcom was reaching its climax, Ken felt someone tapping on his shoulder.

It was Mayor Charles Upton Fairleigh!

Ken was stunned. "Wha-why, Mayor Fairleigh . . . What can I do for you?"

"C'mon with me. And hurry up!"

Without even saying goodbye to his family, Ken accompanied the Mayor. Truth to tell, he had little choice, since that worthy had grabbed his arm and was practically dragging him.

"You gotta help me," said Mayor Fairleigh.

"Me? How could I possibly help you?"

"You gotta get that ring away from Bonnie. I can't stand this fucking shitty world she's made one second longer. At first it was okay, being top dog, having anything I wanted. But it's gotten too fucking weird lately. Everybody acting like fucking zombies, the women all the same. Jesus, I like some variety in my fucking!"

"What's that word you keep using?" interrupted Ken.

"What word?"

"It starts with an 'eff.' I don't know it. . . . "

Mayor Fairleigh clutched his head. "Jesus fucking Christ! Of course you don't know it! That's Bonnie's doing too! Even I'm starting to forget how to say it, and I only been away from the mood ring for a minute or so. It took all my willpower and concentration just to break away and get you."

"I don't understand. If you want Mrs. Mayor Fairleigh to give you some ring of hers, why don't you just ask for it? Or even take it. You're the Father, after all, the Wonderbreadwinner."

"She's got a spell on me, some kinda curse that stops me every time I try to snatch the ring. That lousy fuh-fuh-fuh—cuh-cuh-cuh—! Poop! Listen, there's no time to waste! You'll understand once you get close enough to her. You're responsible for this whole mess, Grease Monkey! You've got to help me undo it."

"You know I'm at your complete disposal, Mayor Fairleigh."

"Great. Now follow me!"

Ken accompanied the Mayor to the base of the speaker's platform. Standing atop the reviewing stand, her back to them, was the Mayor's wife, waving gaily to the populace. Other dignitaries stood beside her, and Ken noticed for the first time how they all maintained an invisible circle of a certain diameter around her.

Mayor Fairleigh whispered in Ken's ear. "When I'm about halfway through my standard speech, I'll trip the ignorant slut. You rush up and yank the ring off her finger. But don't put it on! Hand it to me!"

"It still seems like an awfully drastic course of action. . . . "

"Just do it! You'll see why."

"I don't suppose I can refuse an actual order from someone who derives their authority directly from the King. . . . "

"You've got it, Monkey. Now, don't screw up."

"'Screw up?'"

Mayor Fairleigh left Ken in the tree shadows at the back of the stand and ascended the platform. A roar of applause swelled up at his appearance. After some throat-clearing and microphone-tapping, the Mayor began his speech.

Ken waited tensely at the base of the stairs. This was the oddest thing that had ever happened to him. He had no idea why the Mayor wanted him to do this. It seemed a dire and overly public way to settle a domestic argument. Perhaps he was dreaming. . . . That's it, thought Ken. I'm lying unconscious from that strange shoe hitting my cranium. I'll wake up any minute now. . . .

But he did not. And soon the moment he was dreading came.

Mayor Fairleigh whirled and lashed out savagely with a kick, sweeping Mrs. Mayor off her feet. Even before her head hit the carpeted wooden floorboards, Ken found himself rushing up onto the stage.

As soon as he got within the sphere of the STP-treated mood ring, everything flooded back to him.

Bonnie was hovering on the edge of consciousness, plainly making a tremendous effort not to lose it. Before she could take any quantum-influential action, however, Ken had pulled the mood ring from her finger and slipped it on.

5. THE OIL CRISIS

Kendrick Skye was the last human left alive.

And even he was not fully human any longer.

Now he was part Grease Monkey.

Half of Ken's body—the right half—had been replaced with mechanical parts. His arm terminated in a set of socket wrenches and screwdrivers. A door in his side could open to reveal a complete diagnostic and timing console. His right leg featured a special foot designed to interface more efficiently with accelerator and brake. A set of jumper cables emerged from his back; he wore them like a lasso coiled around his shoulder.

Ken was the product of a secret Defense Department program. DOD had been attempting to create a superior Master Mechanic to service its vehicles. When Ken had been injured in a Viet Cong attack on his base at Da Nang, the Army had saved his life by turning him into a cyborg.

It had cost a lot of taxpayer money.

Now he was the Six-Million-Dollar Mechanic.

Ken had just been getting used to his new life when the Disco Plague struck.

Apparently caused by a virus from outer space, the Disco Plague was similar to the dancing mania of the Middle Ages. (Top scientists, in the few weeks before they too succumbed, had indeed speculated that the earlier epidemic derived from a brush with the identical virus.) The Disco Plague caused its victims to gyrate feverishly—at approximately 125 beats per minute—until finally dying of sheer exhaustion. Medical science could offer no cure in the short time available to it before the whole research infrastructure collapsed, and folk remedies proliferated. The miracle fabric known as Qiana was falsely deemed a preventative, as was gold in large amounts. Thus, victims of the Disco Plague frequently went to their doom swathed in the silky fabric and loaded down with jewelry.

With his unique half-human, half-mechanical makeup, Ken was the only person immune to the horrid plague. (Although at times even he felt certain atavistic twinges in his left side. . . .) Forced to watch the demise of the entire world population, he was nearly driven mad.

The only thing that saved Ken's sanity was his work.

Using his DOD-given skills and the immense abandoned military resources at his disposal, Ken was able to fashion companions of a sort. By filling the interior of an average full-size Detroit car with an IBM mainframe (the tape drives went in the trunk), Ken achieved a lifelong dream.

He created a fleet of sentient automobiles.

Surrounded by his creations, the last human in the whole world tried to make the best of his situation.

In a way—Ken was almost ashamed to admit this—it was a relief sometimes to be rid of people. The stupid meat machines had been too emotional and unpredictable. Ken had never been able to relate well with them. He had always felt more comfortable around cars. (Even the person he had gotten closest too—old Reese Hawrot, his mentor—had let him down.) Although he never would have engineered the extinction of the human species, Ken was not altogether busted up about it.

Ken's post-apocalypse life seemed to be moving along on an even keel.

Until the Oil Crisis struck!

Ken sat on a large elevated makeshift throne fashioned from a bucket seat stripped from one of his failures. His vantage point occupied the middle of a deserted airstrip. The endless expanse of tarmac around him was packed with idling autos. A haze of exhaust fumes hung in the air, shielding Ken from the hot sun. The noise of the myriad throbbing engines was as comforting to Ken as the sound of a slumbering child's breath was to a mother.

The nearest cars to Ken formed his personal bodyguard, and consisted of various Muscle Cars: Barracudas, Chargers, Mustangs, Camaros, Firebirds and others. These swift aggressive autos raced their engines threateningly and flapped their hoods open and closed whenever any of Ken's lesser subjects wheeled up too near, whether out of mere curiosity or desire to have an audience with the Supreme Grease Monkey.

Now from across the field raced a smaller car plainly bent on speaking with the human. Recognizing it while it was still some distance away, Ken called out, "Let the supplicant approach!"

The elite guard parted ranks in deference to the command.

The vehicle—an old Valiant—came near.

In a nostalgic tribute to his departed human acquaintances, Ken had programmed many of his first creations with simulations of his old friends. (Later cars possessed only a generic personality.)

The Valiant manifested the persona of Reese Hawrot, and functioned as Ken's advisor.

"What do you have to report?" demanded Ken.

The Valiant coughed, the sound emerging from its radio speaker. "The news isn't good, boy." (Only the old Valiant could address the

Grease Monkey in such a familiar fashion.) "The scouts come back almost dry. There ain't a lick of gasoline in a hunnerd-mile circle."

The citizens of Ken's empire were kept running twenty-four hours a day, since not only couldn't Ken bear to shut any of them off, but it was logistically impossible for him to stop and start each car every day. Due to the failure of the electrical grid and the impossibility of pumping gas conventionally, Ken had equipped all the cars with special mechanisms that allowed them to open the access pipes to any underground tank, drop a tube and suck up all the gas they needed.

This perpetual scavenging, combined with the poor mileage most models got, had evidently depleted the surrounding territory. It was an eventuality Ken had been dreading, but for which he had a plan.

Picking up a megaphone, Ken bellowed out his orders.

"Attention, loyal subjects! I am authorizing the opening of the High Octane Reserve Supply!"

"Hurrah!" came the massed response.

"All vehicles will be allowed to top off their tanks. There should be plenty for everyone. As soon as each car drinks its fill, we will proceed south—to the Strategic Petroleum Reserves! Once there, I'll get a refinery going. The gasoline will flow like water for years to come!"

As soon as Ken finished his proclamation, the cars began to race for the Reserve Supply.

Ken's Praetorian Guard, knowing that their needs would not be neglected, remained loyally at their posts.

Descending his throne, Ken approached a blue Fairlane.

"Chuck Fairlane!"

"Yes, sir!"

"I'm making you my personal command car. I'll travel in your driver's seat, and we'll lead the crusade."

"I'm honored, sir!"

"Go now, and drink deeply for the journey."

The Fairlane roared off, pumping blue exhaust.

"When he returns, the rest of you may go."

Already the first of the sated cars were returning. Ken halted them, explaining that they must wait for the Fairlane, who would be their pace car.

These first arrivals were a pride of pink Swingers; obviously the more macho cars had allowed them priority access to the new gasoline. Now a little giddy from the High Octane, the Swingers giggled and chatted girlishly among themselves.

Ken approached them, and their giggles increased.

Stroking their headlights, Ken questioned his subjects.

"Bonnie, Mona J.—do you feel up to the journey? Are you scared? Are you well greased?"

"I could always use another lube job from you," Bonnie coquettishly answered.

"Don't listen to her, Ken," said Mona J. peevishly. "She's nothing but a sparkplug-teaser. You can put your key in my ignition anytime!"

Feeling gratified at the attention of the girls, Ken patted them on their bumpers and turned away. He had heard the familiar sound of Chuck Fairlane from a quarter of a mile off. For a moment, Ken thought to detect an anomalous noise beneath the healthy throb. When the Fairlane wheeled up to a screeching stop, Ken questioned it.

"Chuck, is there anything wrong with your fan belt?"

"No, sir!"

"Very well, then. Let's roll!"

The Fairlane opened its own driver's-side door, and Ken climbed in.

The motorized crusade was underway!

At the periphery of their territory, certain scout vehicles—mostly Jeeps—began to scatter down sideroads, hunting for untouched gas stations. The vehicles would need to refuel many times if they hoped to make the far off Strategic Petroleum Reserves. . . .

Just as dusk was falling and Ken was considering ordering a halt to travel for the day—his human half still needed the old anodyne of sleep—the fan belt on the Fairlane snapped with a noise like a giant's barber's strop descending on a galvinized tin roof.

"Damn it, Chuck! I thought you said there was nothing wrong with your fan belt!"

"Sorry, sir! I'm only a humble car, sir!"

Ken got out and walked to the front of the car.

"Open your hood."

The Fairlane obliged.

Ken bent over, head and shoulders under the shadow of the Fairlane's hood.

With an eager snap, Chuck had Ken in his grip!

Ken's cyborg half caught most of the blow, saving him from harm. But despite his mechanical abilities, he was inextricably trapped in Chuck's jaws, his nose an inch away from the whirling blades of the beltless fan!

An evil laugh reminiscent of the noise one might hear from a mother swine insanely gobbling down her own newborn piglets resounded from the Fairlane's speaker.

"You dumb motherfucker! Make me a car, would you? I've been waiting for this day for years in this fake-o world! You and your fucking preventative maintenance! But now I've got you where I want you! And you're gonna give me that ring!"

Ken was finding it hard to breathe. "Ring? What ring?"

"Don't give me that shit! The mood ring on your left hand!"

Suddenly, it all flooded back on Ken. The mood ring! He had completely blanked it from his consciousness after creating this world. He felt sudden remorse. What kind of pathetic mind would kill off all of humanity and replace them with automobiles? In an instant's time, Ken searched his soul and found an answer.

His mind.

Despite this new-found realization of how badly he had handled the power of the mood ring, Ken still hesitated before handing over the ring as Chuck demanded. What insane world would the revenge-driven automobile create?

"C'mon, c'mon, quit stalling!" The pressure from the hood increased. "I'll slice ya in half!"

Using the tip of one screwdriver-finger, Ken removed the mood ring and placed it atop the engine.

The hood sprang open, and Ken stood up.

The world did not immediately change.

Chuck seemed inclined to gloat.

"You and the chicks were such losers," said the Fairlane. "You couldn't leave the world alone, could you? You were all so eager to make things fit your own personal wacky dreams, that you unbalanced everything. That's because you're all pitiful, spineless wimps! You can't get along in the world as it is, so you dreamed of changing it. Well, not me! I *like* our old world. I don't care if it's full of injustice or sicko creeps or war or poverty! It is what it is! That's what none of you could see."

Ken dared to interrupt. "Don't tell me you wouldn't make a few changes. . . . "

The Fairlane chortled. "Oh, sure, I'm gonna make some changes. But they won't be far-out or idealistic or namby-pamby changes. They'll just be a little seasoning, a little accenting of the things I already like."

"I suppose you're going to put Nixon back in office."

Chuck seemed to consider that. "No, he was getting too stiff and paranoid. His time is past. And anyway, I've got something much better in mind, something that will really piss off all the liberals and pinkos.

"In the next election, in 'Seventy-six, I'm gonna let the Democrats win."

Ken couldn't believe what he was hearing. "But you hate the Democrats. . . . "

"Fucking A! And by the time I'm done, so will the rest of the country. I'm gonna let that goddamn peanut farmer, what's-his-name, win. And I'm gonna make sure he takes the whole country down the tubes, just for revenge. We'll have more gas lines, more inflation, more of everything bad that the Democrats do so good. And will he *whine* about it! You'll think your goddamn grandmother is running the country! And foreign affairs—! His one policy will be to *kiss* Brezhnev! Then, just when the whole nation is fed up, I'll bring in the worst conservative I can find!"

"Goldwater?"

"No! Ronald Reagan."

"You wouldn't! Not that washed-up, senile old actor!"

"I wouldn't, huh? Just wait. And once *he's* running the show, I'll make the country over in my image. I'll kick fucking welfare mothers out in the street! I'll have the biggest peacetime arms buildup in history! I'll take all the rules off Wall Street! I'll load the Supreme Court with right-wing loonies! When we want oil, I'll send troops in to occupy the whole Middle East! I'll even put the fix in on the fucking Olympics!"

The world began to waver around Ken. He uttered one final plea.

"How long, Chuck? How long?"

"Maybe forever! We'll see if I get sick of it. If you're lucky, I'll even let another wimpy Southern donkey-head hold the reins for a while. . . . "

Ken woke up with a start. Early morning light tinted the air. Mona J. lay slumbering beside him, her earth shoes tumbled in one corner of his familiar bedroom. Somehow her odd footgear looked pathetic and forlorn, as if it no longer meshed with a world that had somehow changed overnight. . . .

"Wow, what a nightmare!" Ken murmured.

But when he bent to kiss Mona J., he saw the mood ring was gone from her finger.

And to this day, Chuck still hasn't taken it off.

I fused the identities of two local bands, Miracle Legion and Small Factory, whose drummers I both know, to form the "Miracle Factory" of this story, where once again rock music (and beer) lend propulsive drive to the plot, much as jazz (and Prohibition) might have once flavored a Thorne Smith tale. I was particularly pleased that the Interzone *illustrator for this story, working only from my words, exactly replicated the appearance of real-life Phoebe in his drawing, confirming my sometimes wavering faith that anything I write has any basis in reality.*

Points will be awarded for spotting all the pop song allusions.

Any resemblance between Master Blaster and Whammer Jammer's van Bullwinkle, and the Econoline herein dubbed Zed Leper is strictly familial.

Flying the Flannel

1. OUR BELOVED REVOLUTIONARY SWEETHEART

PHOEBE SUMMERSQUALL FLOPPED DOWN on the spring-shot, beer-, tear-, sweat- and other-miscellaneous-exudates-stained couch backstage in what passed for the "performer's lounge" at Slime Time. The wall above the spavined sofa was covered with layers of grafitti: names of bands never famous and now long dust; injunctions to kill one despised performer or another; proclamations of musicological godhood or ineptitude; scabrous invective about the club's management.

"Jesus, I'm totally wiped," said the thin woman. Behind her outsized round black-plastic-framed glasses, her dark eyes loomed bigger than life. Dressed in a Goodwill-bin tulle skirt layered over frayed jeans, a skintight lycra polka-dotted top and suede clogs, her long black hair caught up in back with one of the thinner bungee cords normally reserved for lashing down the band's amps during transport, she resembled a tired cleaning lady, addled ballerina or unusually neat street person.

Raising a hand to wipe sweat from her brow, she found herself still unconsciously clutching her drumsticks. Wearily, she dropped them, and a frosty bottle of Sam Adams manifested itself within reach.

"Thanks, Scott."

"You deserve it, Pheeb. You were awesome."

Scott Bluebottle, round of face and wire rim-bespectacled, occupied tentatively, as was his way, a folding chair. He scraped at the label of his own bottle with a guitar pick. On the two remaining heterogenous lumps of furniture sprawled the other members of Miracle Factory: Mark the Snark and Frank Difficult. The former long-haired and stocky, the latter with the wolf-lean, hot-eyed, gaunt-cheeked look of one of the less well-known German Expressionists.

"Yeah," agreed Mark in a resonant singer's voice. "Especially on the last tune."

Frank chimed in. "I'm extremely proud to have a song of mine that I cherish as much as I do 'Eat the Shame' performed by such a talented drummer."

Phoebe felt herself blushing. "Gee, guys, I bet you'd say that to anyone who replaced someone who sucked as bad as your last drummer."

Mark chuckled ruefully. "Lonnie was mighty awful."

"Remember the night he fell backwards off the riser?" reminisced Scott.

Frank lifted the admonitory hand of a reluctant leader. "Let us not slag the departed. The thing to concentrate on is how good we were tonight."

"Agreed," said Mark, threading his fingers through his mane in an eloquent, practiced Hair Lofting that was second nature to him. "It's too bad there weren't more than ten people here to see us."

"It is a Monday night. . . ," said Scott weakly.

"Every night seems to be a Monday night lately," Mark grumped.

The four bandmates sat silently for a time, contemplating the fickleness, bad taste and inexplicable immunity to the charms of Miracle Factory, as exhibited by the club-going public. Then Frank spoke.

"It's Tuesday morning actually. Almost three. And we've got a gig scheduled five hundred miles from here, with a soundcheck in just a little over twenty-four hours."

"Are you trying to tell us we should start humping equipment?" asked Scott.

" 'Fraid so."

"Can we afford a motel?" ventured Phoebe.

"Everyone who wants to use tonight's money to eat and put gas in our noble transport, raise your hand," replied Frank.

"Oh, well, guess we sleep in the van again. Anyway, it's kinda getting to where I can't drop off without the smell of exhaust and a row of rivets in my back. . . . "

Quickly finishing their beers, the four trooped out onto the small stage. Phoebe removed her extraneous skirt, the better to work. With lackluster motions, watched over by the impatient owner, their activity causing ghostly echoes in the empty Slime Time, they struck their equipment and loaded it into their rotting '79 Econoline dubbed Zed Leper.

On the road, Mark driving, Frank riding shotgun, Phoebe and Scott in the back, several miles passed wordlessly, until Scott spoke.

"That guy was there again tonight."

Phoebe stiffened. "No way."

"Yes way."

"Where? I didn't see him."

"You were zoned out on playing. But I spotted him right away. He hung out at the bar all night, never came out on the floor. Had half a dozen empty longnecks lined up in front of him by the time we finished our set. Never smiled that I could see, never spoke to anyone."

The memory of the stony-faced older stranger who had haunted their last five appearances across as many states welled up in Phoebe. Materializing only since her arrival in the group, he had plainly set his sights on her, focusing a piercing stare on her throughout each performance.

"This really creeps me out," said Phoebe nervously.

"Maybe he's a bigshot A & R guy, sizing us up before offering us a huge juicy contract. . . ," said Frank halfheartedly.

"Yeah, and I'm Sinatra," replied Mark.

Phoebe turned on Scott, who sat next to her on a mattress placed on the narrow floor space between the ranked equipment. "Why didn't you tell me?"

Scott shrugged. "Didn't want to spook you. Besides, there's three of us watching out for you."

"That's right, Pheeb," said Mark. "We'll protect you."

"My sentiments exactly," added Frank.

Phoebe restrained an impulse to shout "bullshit!" Guys. . . . What was it about them? They meant well, but it was up to her to educate them.

"Well, next time, how about letting me in on what I'm being protected from, okay?"

"Sure, Pheeb."

"Right."

"It shall be as you wish, oh Mistress of Snares and Cymbals."

Phoebe stretched out on her back and rested her head on Scott's leg. "For not telling me, you've got first shift as pillow."

"Cramp city, man!" said Scott good-naturedly.

Within minutes, Phoebe was so soundly asleep that even when, an hour later, the vector of their van changed abruptly from horizontal to vertical and they were engulfed by the spacecraft which had silently paced them since their departure, it took a whole ten seconds before the shouts of the others woke her up.

2. PUT A LITTLE BIRDHOUSE IN YOUR SOUL

A pearly opalescence flooded the grungy interior of the van known as Zed Leper. The air was perfumed with strange scents: acid, electricity, brine and ginger.

Phoebe leaped to her feet, careful of the low Econoline ceiling.

Around her was utter confusion.

Scott was holding his head and moaning, having whacked his noggin on the van's ceiling in the tumult. Behind the wheel, Mark was activating every control on the dashboard in a desperate attempt to regain command of the stalled van. Windshield wipers batted futilely at streams of washer fluid. Frank was rifling furiously in the trash on the floor at his feet, saying, "The nunchuks, where are those goddamn nunchuks!"

Quickly deciding that her bandmates had plainly lost their scanty marbles, Phoebe asserted herself.

"Everybody shut up! Right now!"

Silence dropped, thick as a brick.

"Okay. That's better. Now—what happened?"

"We—we were just tooling along," said Mark, "when suddenly I could feel the wheels leave the ground. But I wasn't even sleepy, honest!"

"I thought we had gone over a cliff," said Scott.

"I stuck my head out the window," said Frank, "and something made me look up. There was a huge dark shadow blocking the stars. Then a square of white opened in it. It got bigger and bigger, then swallowed us."

"Where are we now?"

"Inside the freakin' UFO, I guess," ventured Mark.

"Heading who the hell knows where," added Scott cheeringly.

Phoebe considered, noting the van's open windows. "We can breathe and we can walk. Air and gravity. . . . Let's get out."

She threw open the rear doors and jumped down.

Timorously, the others followed.

The van sat in the middle of an enormous space. Walls and ceilings, if any, were lost in the pearly radiance that flowed from every direction.

Phoebe looked at the floor.

Her feet vanished at the ankles in the tenuous, hazy oyster-colored substance, which seemed to offer spongy support at some unknown depth. Lifting a foot, Phoebe was relieved to find her clog-shod extremity apparently intact. Reaching down, she brushed the rarefied material.

"It's soft, with a nap, like, like—flannel."

Mark snorted. "Great. Probably built in Seattle then. Maybe something new from Boeing. Used to kidnap any competitors to the Northwest scene."

Scott was shielding his eyes against the mild glare and scanning the distance. Suddenly, he yelped.

"Someone's coming!"

The four huddled closer together as a figure approached out of the foggy glowing remoteness.

It was the stranger who had stalked them across five states. Dressed in nondescript Earth clothing, his face so blank and inhospitable as to make Harry Dean Stanton look like Marcel Marceau, he seemed an unlikely starship pilot. Perhaps, Phoebe thought, Mark had been right about this being a ship of human design, however unlikely that seemed. Or perhaps the stalker was a fellow prisoner. . . .

Phoebe stepped bravely forward. "Did—did the aliens get you too, Mister?"

The man regarded Phoebe with the same unwavering fixity that had unnerved her onstage. Then he spoke.

"I am the owner of this vessel. You may call me Modine."

Their captor's insouciance was the final straw for the impetuous Mark the Snark.

"We'll be calling you dead meat in a minute, sucker! Let's get him, guys!"

Before Phoebe could do more than shout an objection, the three men had pinioned the UFO captain without much of a struggle.

"Okay," said Mark, facing the stranger while Scott and Frank held his arms, "are you gonna take us back home, or do I have to get rough with you?"

"No, please, you do not understand. I am bringing you someplace where your skills will be appreciated. . . . "

Mark polished the knuckles of his fist on his worn denim shirt. "Don't say I didn't give you a chance."

"I must warn you, this shell is fragile—"

Mark popped the stranger a good one on the jaw.

The alien's head split open with a sound like the ripping of cooked turkey skin. A jagged crack ran up the middle of his face and down the back of his skull.

Horrified, Frank and Scott dropped him, and Mark stepped back.

Up from out of the lifeless cracked shell fluttered a small agile bird. It resembled a canary—as much as a Lexus resembled a Stutz Bearcat—except that it was colored bright blue.

The supercharged blue canary landed on Phoebe's left shoulder.

"I did warn you," it said.

3. IS THAT YOU, MODINE?

Oh-so-slowly, Phoebe swivelled her head to the left.

The little streamlined bird was still there, its claws gripping the fabric of her shirt. It did not weigh much. A hardly perceptible mass, actually. But Phoebe felt her shoulder muscles quivering from the alien's presence.

Regarding her with a questioning expression, the azure avian dipped its head to peck at the feathers of its breast, then resumed eye contact. Plainly, it was waiting for Phoebe to speak.

"Are you—I mean, can it be—"

The bird was not helping her, and she suddenly grew angry.

"Damn it, is that you, Modine?"

"I am glad to see that you can accept the reality of my appearance. Races as primitive as yours generally deny the possibility of sentience in unfamiliar or unlikely forms." The canary's tones became prideful. "Yes, it is I, Modine, interstellar voyager and captain of the *Dustbath*. The artificial human shape you heedlessly destroyed—which was on the point of disintegrating soon anyway—was merely a camouflaged transport, a means of mingling with the natives. You see—"

At that moment, Mark lunged angrily for Modine. But the bird easily evaded his grasp, fluttering up to alight atop the van. Phoebe was relieved, both to straighten her neck and no longer to be functioning as perch to an alien budgie.

"Please," advised Modine. "Restrain yourselves. It is almost impossible for you to harm me. And even if you could, where would that leave you? You could not possibly learn how to operate the *Dustbath*, nor how to navigate in twelve-space. You would be stranded at our programmed destination or—even worse, if you managed to interfere with the controls—in some nameless fractal dimension between Earth and the Planet of Sound."

"Planet of Sound?" echoed Scott. "What's that? And why are you taking us there?"

"I shall explain all," promised Modine. "Let us adjourn to the bridge, however. Unlike the cargo hold, it offers seats and refreshments, as well as a view."

Modine rocketed off, leaving the humans with no choice except to follow.

Phoebe took the lead, trotting to catch up with the speedy bird. It was weird to watch her feet disappear into the floor and re-emerge with each step, and she wondered again what the flannel-simulating substance of the ship was.

Just before the foursome caught up with their host, Frank used the opportunity to whisper to Phoebe.

"This uncanny bird is fixated on you, Pheeb. When it was stalking us on Earth, it always watched you. It landed on your shoulder. And it chose you for the test of appreciating its intelligence. If anyone is going to be able to get us out of this jam, it'll have to be you."

"Any other reassuring words?"

"We'll be there to back your every move," chimed in Mark.

"I thought not," said Phoebe.

Now they were in what seemed to be a straight and level corridor of luminescent walls. Modine flew on ahead. Then disappeared.

Phoebe and the guys stopped.

"Modine?" Phoebe ventured tentatively.

The bird stuck its head out of the seemingly solid ceiling. "We'll be landing in a few hours," it said peevishly. "There's not much time to waste."

"But how do we get up there?"

"Just continue to walk."

Modine vanished.

Shrugging, Phoebe took a step forward, then another, and a third—

There had been no sense of climbing, nor was she now experiencing any disorientation. But Phoebe appeared now to be standing on the corridor ceiling, her head pointing downward at the guys.

"You goofs are hanging upside down," said Phoebe, smiling at their shocked expressions.

"No, you are," said Mark.

"Well, my way is Modine's way."

"This is true," said Frank.

"Let's follow her!" said Scott.

Phoebe took another step, and disappeared.

She found herself in a medium-sized glowing room. Elevated

mushroom-like cushions of the flannel-stuff sprouted from the floor. One wall appeared to be transparent, and gave a startling view: the *Dustbath* was apparently rushing through a medium that resembled an infinite sea of knotted multihued threads, ropes and cables twisting and contorting throughout colorless depths.

Modine was perched on a ledge in front of the view-wall. "Ah," sighed the bird, "the glorious vistas of twelve-space never fail to stimulate and enlighten!"

Behind Phoebe, the guys popped into existence out of the floor.

"Please, be seated," Modine said. "And I will serve drinks."

The humans complied, and Phoebe decided to use the moment to ask a question.

"Modine, what is this ship made of?"

"This craft is more of a mathematical construct than a solid vessel. It is composed of Cantor dust. Hence its rather punning name."

"But what's Cantor dust?"

"One takes an appropriate exotic material, and from it removes every tenth atom. Then from that mass, one removes every tenth atom again. This process is repeated approximately ten to the twentieth times."

Frank spoke up. "But that would leave almost nothing behind. . . . "

"Almost, but not quite," said Modine. "The resulting substance has some intriguing and useful properties."

A floating platter appeared. On it were five bottles of Sam Adams. Opened. One with a straw.

"One of Earth's finest products. Although I've taken a few liberties with its composition. . . . "

Phoebe took a bottle and sipped cautiously.

The first swallow washed away a bone-tiredness and a sleepiness, awareness of which her mind had been suppressing.

The second swallow left her feeling as if she had won a Grammy, a platinum record and an MTV award simultaneously.

Modine, claws gripping the lip of his bottle, sipping from time to time at his own drink, began to lecture.

"I come from a mighty race. Our name for ourselves is unpro-
nounceable in your language, but you may call us the Bowerbirds.
From the primitive tool-using and contruction instincts of my
ancestors, who reared their bowers on rocky shores, arose intelligence
and a highly sophisticated civilization. When we discovered faster-
than-light space travel, however, we were unprepared to compete in
galactic society on one very important level.

"You see, we could not sing or otherwise perform music. Always a
minimal skill with us, it had finally been bred out of us, in favor of
intelligence."

Ignoring the paradox of a songless bird species, Phoebe asked,
"But why was that so important?"

Modine slurped up the last of its beer. "Interstellar cooperation
and competition is based on music. It's the one arena in which all the
multiform and multiskilled sophonts can find common ground. For
thousands of millennia, musical competitions have determined
status and trade alliances, friendships and enmities, and hundreds of
other relationships for which you have no terms.

"Luckily, we Bowerbirds were able to take advantage of a clause
that allowed a client race to substitute for us. After much perusal of
many Earth musical assemblages, I picked you to participate in the
latest round. Your nearest competitor was a tribe of Pygmies, but I
judged that their culture shock would be insuperable. You must all
feel very honored. Frankly, you were almost out of contention at one
point. It was only when you added this one"—Modine pointed a
wing at Phoebe—"that your sound and gestalt became compelling."

Mark glared at the bird. "Let me get this straight. We're going to
play in some kind of Star Wars battle of the bands, but you freakin'
Bowerbirds are going to get all the credit?"

"Well, that is basically a correct summation of our respective
duties and rewards. But I do hereby promise to take you straight back
home if you win."

"And if we lose?" asked Phoebe.

"Most unfortunate. It happened to our last surrogate entry. They still have a century of indenture in the clubs of the Planet of Sound to while away. However, they are members of a long-lived species. And I understand that the free drinks served in most clubs to the performers are almost as good as Earth's beer."

4. THREE STRANGE DAYS

Phoebe gazed out the window of their private guest quarters on the Planet of Sound. Alone, she was waiting for the guys to return.

She leaned on the window sill; it squeaked and accomodated itself to her elbows. Scanning the crowded plaza below, its decorative subsurface chaotic animations obscured by numberless creeping, crawling, hopping, strolling, rolling aliens, Phoebe thought she saw her bandmates at some distance— But no, not unless they had all grown tails. Which was not entirely impossible here. Was that them riding the millipede transport? No, the riders were too furry, even for Mark. Perhaps this huge approaching manta-flyer carried them? Whoops! The manta-ray shape had broken up into a flock of butterfly-sized self-similar components, each of which flew off in a different direction.

Phoebe turned away from the window, which bleated in relief. The diversity of the Planet of Sound oppressed her. She felt overwhelmed by the cacophony of voices and the shifting montage of skins and limbs and faces. It was seductive, yet repulsive at the same time. All she wanted was the familiar comforts of Earth. Even the ratty lounges of Slime Time and its cousins would be a welcome sight.

Feeling this way, when the others had wanted to go out exploring on their first free day since their arrival, she had begged off.

Damn that Terwilliger anyway! He should have known better. What kind of manager was he, running his charges ragged the day before the big performance?

Especially a performance with such high stakes.

They had to rehearse. They were getting overconfident and that would surely lead to sloppiness. She did not think the judges would much credit sloppiness, despite its respectable terrestial lineage. No, chops and riffs and invention, wringing the most from one's equipment, were the musical currency here.

Two early easy victories had elated them. Modine's praise—not to mention a steady flow of doctored Sam Adams—had slackened their vigilance. The final crucial round, Phoebe was sure, would present them with some unique challenge.

She hoped that Terwilliger would not become tearful before the show, as he had prior to the others.

Phoebe had enough to worry about, without consoling an over-emotional fish.

Weren't cold-blooded creatures supposed to be stolid anyhow?

Moving to her drum kit, Phoebe resolved that she would polish a few licks, even if the others weren't here.

And of course, just as she lifted her sticks, they all piled in.

Leading the group was Terwilliger. Basically, the alien was indistinguishable from an eight-foot-long walking catfish, from the tip of its broad tail to its stubby locomotive fins to the end of its barbels. However, no earthly catfish of whatever size had ever been constantly attended by a cloud of telefactored waldoes, ranging in size from microscopic to human-scale. The horde of manipulators formed and reformed to the fish's will.

Behind their guide, Mark, Scott and Frank were whooping and chattering. Plainly flushed with the excitement of their expedition, the guys were oblivious to Phoebe's stony-eyed glare.

"Man, what a trip!" exulted Scott.

"Sailing the Seas of Time-Cheese!" Mark explained for Phoebe's sake. "With Captain Toad Sprocket!"

"A most intriguing voyage," Frank thoughtfully added. "I was particularly impressed by the Captain's explanation of the formation and function of wormholes."

Terwilliger (whose real name was closer to T'-[*blop*]-woll-[*splork*]-grrr) spoke now in perfect English. "Luckily, we did not engender any shadow duplicates in our chrono-travels. Metacausality is a field well beyond my slender mentality."

As Phoebe remained silent, the guys eventually wore down. Finally she bit out a question, her voice stern.

"What are those things on your heads?"

Frank reached up to touch what appeared to be a wig made of purple polyester spaghetti. Even Terwilliger wore one.

"Oh, these are souvenirs of a famous winning group from many millennia past. Their trademark, apparently. Don't they look kinda like Beatle wigs?"

"An example of convergent evolution, from what the fellows have told me," said Terwilliger.

Phoebe threw down her sticks in disgust. "I've had it! Our entire future is on the line, and you guys are out sticking your heads or—or your *things*, for all I know!—in wormholes or something! Don't you have any sense of what's at risk here!"

The argument started the big catfish crying; huge tears plopped down onto the living carpet, which quickly absorbed them. Phoebe felt awful. But she had to slam some sense into them all. . . .

Mark approached Phoebe and tried to soothe her. "Listen, Pheeb. Didn't we blow those first two acts off the stage? What have we got to worry about?"

"We can't assume anything!" Phoebe argued. "Those guys were jokers! The next race could still have an ace up their sleeves!"

The early competitors had been surprisingly amateurish. They wouldn't have lasted a week on the demanding club circuit that had honed Miracle Factory. First had come the Balloon Men, spherical bipeds with pipecleaner limbs. Informed of their defeat, they had explosively self-destructed, splattering Miracle Factory and much of the audience with what appeared to be hummus, tomato paste and strips of skin. Next up had been a double-headed ambidextrous race, each of whose members had been able to play two instruments at once. They had been a little stiffer competition. But Miracle Factory, playing as they never had before, had triumphed, thanks to their unique blend of Earth's hidden treasure of rock 'n' roll.

Now Scott came forward. "What difference is one day's practice going to make, Pheeb? If we don't have our sound down by now, we never will. We were just trying to relax, you know? And if we don't see these sights now, when are we ever gonna get a chance to? I mean, we'll be back on Earth soon enough. . . . "

"You hope," said Phoebe. "Oh, hell."

She came out from behind her drums and kneeled down beside Terwilliger.

"I'm sorry I yelled. It wasn't you. Stop crying, okay?"

As she was dabbing at the fish's eyes with the hem of her shirt, the door opened and Modine flew in.

"Tomorrow's matches have been posted," said the Bowerbird. "Your opponent is a one-man band, so to speak. The Bombardyx."

Phoebe stood, and fixed the bird with a determined look. "Now that the competition is almost over, will you tell us exactly what your race stands to gain if we win? I think we deserve to know."

The blue canary was quiet for a few seconds. When it spoke, its voice was respectful.

"You are a strange and forceful individual, Phoebe Summersquall. I have noted something puzzling about you ever since Earth, but I can't lay a feather on it. . . . Very well, since you ask what the ultimate prize is in this contest, I will tell you.

"Depending on who wins, either the Bombardyx or the Bowerbirds will be allowed to colonize Earth."

5. CLOSE YOUR EYES, HERE WE GO, PLAYING AT
THE TALENT SHOW

There was something extra in the sky, but none of the humans were quite sure it was a second sun. It had the apparent diameter of a sun, and gave out enough visible light to make staring at it painful. But the orb—whatever it was—also had a tendency to dart about disconcertingly.

Terwilliger noticed them looking. "One of the larger intelligences in this galaxy," the fish explained. "Constrained by its size to remain well outside the thicker atmosphere, it nonetheless wishes to watch the show. Their kind are notorious bettors."

"Oh, Lord," said Phoebe. "People are betting on us?"

"Yes," agreed Terwilliger. "But the stakes are low, commensurate with the prize you are contesting for. No more than a single planet will be won or lost by any individual."

"What are the odds on us?" asked Scott.

"Even," replied the catfish. "But subject to fluctuation."

The members of Miracle Factory, along with many of the other variegated contestants, milled about next to the stage: a simple hexagonal affair, roughly half an acre in extent, empty at the moment. The stage stood in the middle of an enormous plaza, much bigger than the one visible from their quarters. There were no bleachers or other seating, no roof or walls to define the limits of the arena.

"Let's have an equipment check," said Frank. Their leader was visibly nervous. For that matter, so were they all. Scott was polishing and repolishing his eyeglasses, and Phoebe had to fight to restrain herself from doing the same with hers. Mark was subjecting his hair to such vigorous manipulation that she feared for its roots.

"A *sound* idea," said Terwilliger proudly. "This, I believe, qualifies as a tension-relieving pun. . . ?"

"Just get busy," said Frank brusquely.

Terwilliger directed his manipulators around and, in the case of the micros, actually into the guitars, drums and keyboards belonging to Miracle Factory, as well as their various speakers and microphones and boards.

"All is fine. I did detect a slight weakness in one of Phoebe's membranes, but it is now repaired."

"I didn't know you still had that membrane, Pheeb," said Mark the Snark with mock innnocence.

Phoebe punched him in the shoulder. "Jerk!"

But she didn't really mind. For the joke had served to diffuse their anxiety a bit. And just in time.

The virtual arena was assembling itself.

From every quadrant came floating platforms of all sizes. Those carrying species which could tolerate the Planet of Sound environment were open to the air; others were closed and transparent; some were opaque. (For the benefit of shy riders—or easily frightened onlookers? wondered Phoebe.)

Within a short time, the stage was nearly englobed by a mosaic of hovering spectators: snouted, scaled, tendrilled; puckered and peppered with pseudopods. Automated cameras took up positions closer in. Although Phoebe had witnessed this assembly twice before, she was still impressed.

"Who'd ever think we'd get to play a stadium tour before we even got signed?" asked Scott with forced whimsy.

"Quiet!" said Phoebe. "We should be scoping out the level of talent."

"It's only the Bombardyx we have to worry about," said Mark. "Whoever he might be out of all these freaks."

"May I remind everyone," said Frank, "that we still haven't decided what we're going to do once we get onstage. . . . "

Their choices were pitifully few. To throw the contest, dooming themselves to an indefinite term of servitude and handing Earth over to the unknown Bombardyx. Or to go all out for a victory, gaining a return trip to a planet soon to become a Bowerbird fiefdom— whatever that entailed. And any refusal to play would count as a surrender, Terwilliger had told them.

"Yes," the fish had continued, "your options are not many. But this comes from being a lowly client race. If only you could claim consanguinity with one of the full-status species, things would be different."

Frank's reminder went unheeded now, for the first band had taken the stage.

A dozen impish creatures clad in rubbery unitards unfolded a large mat. Each took up a marked position. Then they began to perform incredible acrobatics. Their movements evoked a wild spacey wailing that soared and keened.

"It's like a theremin," said Frank. "They're modulating some kind of energy field by their leaps and tumbles."

The imps finished, and their rival took the stage: a flock of pterodactyl lookalikes whose long boney beaks were pierced with holes and played flutelike: musician and instrument as one.

Voting now took place. Results were flashed as hieroglyphic holograms in the air. Although the humans could not interpret the signs, the attitude of the imps told all: they had lost. Led away by robotic guards, they trudged gloomily along, showing none of the easy movements they had exhibited onstage.

"Tough crowd," said Mark weakly.

The battle of the bands continued, fast and furious. Unimaginable sounds, amplified or natural, filled the air. Melodious or screechy, atonal or pentatonic, brief snatches or long intricate sequences, the music swelled, roared, murmured and cascaded over the listeners. Winners exulted and losers slumped as the audience displayed their approbation or disapproval with various noises of their own.

Phoebe began to grow disoriented. The alien musics were almost succeeding in making her forget all she knew about playing Earth music! She wished for earplugs, but the band had never used them. . . .

There was moment of silence. Phoebe spotted robo-roadies carrying Miracle Factory's equipment into place. She prepared to ascend the ramp leading onstage.

Modine flew up then. Behind him tagged along a tray of Sam Adams.

"I brought along some refreshment to toast your success," said the blue canary.

Numbly, Phoebe took her beer, but did not drink it. She addressed the Bowerbird.

"We hate you, Modine."

The canary seemed somehow to shrug. "This is an understandable reaction. But I in return do not hate you personally, or your species. Our close contact during the past few days has led me to believe that we Bowerbirds might have made a mistake in seeking to acquire Earth, which appears to have more potential for self-development than we first estimated."

"Then call off the show!" shouted Phoebe.

"It is rather too late for that. However, I urge you to play your best, and retain the hope that all will be well."

Modine flew away.

The four humans took the stage.

Strapping on his guitar, Scott said, "I still can't get used to no cords."

Terwilliger had modified their equipment to use onboard power-paks and digital transmission.

"Thank God he didn't mess with my drums," said Phoebe. She set her beer down close to her, and hung her extra sticks in their stick bag within easy reach. Hate to break one and not have a replacement during such a crucial performance. . . .

His bass in place, Frank stepped up to mike.

"Hello, uh, fellow sophonts. We're Miracle Factory, from Earth. And we're here to play you some, ah, 'modern' rock 'n' roll."

Mark ripped off the opening to "Dirty Dawg" on his keyboard and began to sing. The band took off.

By the fourth song, Phoebe could tell they were playing as well as they ever had. She only hoped it was good enough.

By the end of the set, she was drenched in sweat. As the last notes of "Lost in Hilbert Space" rang out, she felt that no one could possibly beat them.

Then the Bombardyx appeared.

It was as big as a four-story building, an irregular block of oddly protuberant devices mounted on treads. It moved slowly up the stage ramp. When it attained the stage itself, Phoebe could feel the structure creak.

Terwilliger had stumped up to be with them. Phoebe turned to the fish.

"What—what is it?"

"The Bombardyx is a type of hermit-crab creature, a small organic slug. This one appears to have taken up residence in a leftover Symphonium device from the Disintegral Era of the Lesser Splenetics."

"Is this within the rules?"

"Apparently so."

Now the Bombardyx began to perform.

It started by duplicating Miracle Factory's entire set, note for note. Then, like a master jazz improviser, it elaborated on all the tunes, reconfiguring them into a whole ingenious suite.

When the hidden creature was finished, Phoebe knew that they had lost.

Glyphs burned in the air. Terwilliger gasped.

"It is a tie! The Bombardyx lost points by stealing your compositions. You both must perform again!"

Phoebe had not an ounce of energy left in her. Looking at her sagging friends, she knew that they did not either.

Her eye fell on the bottle of Sam Adams.

She lifted it, and the others brightened. The guys grabbed theirs, and everyone chugged them down.

The familiar invigorating spell cast by Modine's adaptation of the Earth brew swept through Phoebe's limbs.

Miracle Factory began their encore.

As Phoebe drummed, she felt strange changes overtaking her: swellings and tentative writhings along her midriff. Things were growing beneath her shirt!

There came a ripping sound, as her shirt seams popped.

She looked down at herself.

She had sprouted four extra arms, two on each side. Fully formed limbs, apparently—yes!—under her complete control.

Without hesitation, she grabbed up her extra sticks.

The guys missed a beat, then recovered.

"You go, girl!"

Phoebe began to drum. Really drum. For the first time in her life, she could do everything she had ever envisioned—with sticks, anyhow.

The others had stopped now.

It was just Phoebe, drumming up a storm.

It was the longest drum solo in history. Not to mention the most complex.

An hour later, she was done.

Phoebe collapsed. The guys clustered around her, lifting her up. She clung to them with all her hands.

Unimpressed, the Bombardyx began to vent its reply.

A platform swooped down on the stage, interrupting the building-sized creature. Out of the vehicle stepped a biped.

One with six arms.

The alien turned and faced the audience, and began to speak.

Terwilliger translated. "He says you are plainly a lost larval form of his race, the Sextuples. As such, you cannot be clients. This contest must be deemed null and void."

Phoebe couldn't believe it. Getting to her feet, she let the guys help her from the stage.

Modine was waiting for them.

"I told you, did I not, to hope for the best?"

Phoebe drew herself up. "You did this, didn't you? We're not any relation to that race."

"The Sextuples happened to owe the Bowerbirds a favor. A simple cell-potentiator with morphic overlays and some neuronal enhancers in your drink did the rest."

"Now we can go home!" said Scott.

"And Earth is saved!" said Mark.

"Thanks to Pheeb!" said Frank.

Lifting Phoebe to their shoulders, the guys paraded her around, Terwilliger frolicking at their feet and Modine flapping around Phoebe's head.

"I assume these extra arms can be gotten rid of fairly easily?" said Phoebe sternly to the canary.

"Yes. A simple resorptive—"

"I'll have it now, if you don't mind, Mister Bird."

"As you wish."

"But I'll use it when I'm good and ready!"

Are Pia Zadora and Danny DeVito truly the products of the gene-engineering of Lovecraftian Old Ones? Is Randy Newman's career decline explicable as an act of revenge for just a single song? If you were Snow White living alone in the woods with the Seven Dwarves, would you sleep easily at night? Is there a secret race cohabiting with humans, and if so, does that make getting a date for Saturday night easier or harder?

Do you really think I have the answers?

Queen of the Pixies, King of the Imps

1. THUMBELINA COMPLEX

THE CIRCUMSTANCES SURROUNDING MY PARENTAGE and birth were never clear. At least not to me. I deeply suspect that Aunt Itzie might have been able to tell me more about my origins than she ever chose to. But for whatever reasons, she never so chose. Shut up tight as a frightened armadillo when I asked, and said that what I didn't know couldn't hurt me. And now she's gone, so I can't ask anymore.

Right up to this day, I still couldn't say for sure whether Itzie and I were even truly related or not, whether she was my actual by-blood aunt. In a way, I kind of hoped she wasn't. Considering the fantasies I had about her during my adolescence. (And, to be honest about it, straight into my rather lonely adulthood.)

The first real memory I have is of Aunt Itzie holding my hand as we walked to school on opening day. The September sun warm as flannel pyjamas. My leg braces and little wrist-support canes occasionally clacking together like castanets. Kindergarten, I assume, since the braces finally came off in first grade. I was four or five, of course, and Aunt Itzie was—well, she was an adult, however old. Had plainly done all the growing she was ever going to do.

Yet the top of my five-year-old head came up to her shoulder, and my cowlick probably stuck up above that point.

Itzie was an appreciable but not overwhelming measure over four feet tall. And that was in three-inch heels, her favorite footwear, and with her strawberry-blonde hair piled high. I doubt she weighed more than eighty pounds. Her wrists and ankles were sparrow-delicate; her charming, always lipsticked mouth small and perfect as a fairy rose. Yet she wasn't a dwarf or a midget, or any other kind of oddly formed person. Quite the opposite, in fact.

Itzie was an ultra-petite knockout. A doll, a looker, a babe. Any other non-PC term you can think of conveying head-turning pulchritude. I said she wasn't oddly formed, but that's not quite true. Like a (modestly) scaled-up Barbie, her measurements were slightly skewed. More on top than seemed supportable by her narrow ribs and waist, but the whole harmonized by undeniably fertile hips. She generally accentuated her curves with a tightly cinched belt. Her whole manner of dressing, in fact, without being overtly provocative or tasteless, was maddeningly sexy. At least to me, the more so naturally the older I got.

Over the years, as I got to know Aunt Itzie with more adult insight, it seemed to me that her appearance, while plainly calculat-ed, was almost out of her control. It was as if her curvaceous form helplessly and naturally exuded a preternatural, almost genetic allure, which even muffling with sackcloth would have failed to mute.

Another thing she naturally exuded—and you don't have to believe me, if you don't want to, but I never saw my aunt use perfume—was a spicy scent most similar to that of viburnum. A kind of cinnamon tang.

Now, I understand there are some people who aren't turned on by beauty in miniature. They find it too cloying or alien or fragile.

Obviously, I'm not one of them. And judging by the number of male—and even female—heads that turned when Aunt Itzie walked down the street with her young charge (on that specific day and many general others), I'm not alone.

Itzie was not her real name, of course. It was Fritzie. Fritzie de la Mare. (I'm Wally.) But my initial stumbling childish speech christened her "Itzie" and the nickname stuck.

For obvious reasons.

Aside from not knowing my parents and being raised by a very small single-parent-substitute, I had a perfectly normal childhood. One exception. A lot of trips to the doctor. As an infant, I exhibited a congenital leg deformity that necessitated corrective braces and, over many years, a course of mysterious injections whose purpose I never really knew or questioned.

As long as Aunt Itzie assured me it was for my own good, I had no doubts or worries.

Anyway, by high school I had grown up into a healthy lad, slightly over six feet. My looks were—well, "rugged" is the conventional euphemism. No one would ever call me conventionally handsome, but I wasn't a monster either. If you imagine Tom Berenger without whatever panache landed him a Hollywood career, you'll have a good idea of my features.

I was a normal guy in all respects. Sports, studies, hobbies. Save for one thing.

Girls proportioned to my own size failed to excite me.

Any female much over four feet tall struck me forcibly and viscerally as a gawky giantess, ugly despite any superficial beauty. They just didn't attract me. A fair number of these "big girls," as I came to mentally label them, tried, however, to gain my interest over the years. But I just couldn't honestly reciprocate.

I was fixated on small women. Very small women. Precisely, of Aunt Itzie's size and build. Whether I had been conditioned or conditioned myself, or whether it was some neurochemical or genetic quirk, I just couldn't get interested in any body type other than the ultra-petite.

Needless to say, my choice of potential mates was very limited. The population of my smallish high school numbered about five hundred, and there were only two or three of my classmates who were anywhere near the dimensions I dreamed of. Not just any very small woman, it eventuated, would match my odd parameters. She had to exhibit most of my Aunt's features to interest me.

In the end, only one girl existed who really fit my idealized portrait. She was a very popular girl—although, mysteriously, she had no steady boyfriend—and I had to build up my courage for months before I dared approach her.

Her nickname was Pidge, short for Pigeon, which bird she resembled not a little, especially in the bosom. When, amid much coughing and stuttering, I finally expressed the possibility of a date, she regarded me curiously, as if trying to see beyond my exterior somehow, searching for some elusive quality. But in the end, she said, "No, I thought for a second— No, I'm sorry, Wally. I just can't."

And so I was left to take the horny adolescent's usual path of gonadal self-relief, aided and abetted by mental images of Aunt Itzie in various poses which I still blush to recall.

Of course, I was completely unable to share this dilemma with my guardian. Rather awkwardly, she tried to give me dating advice, me all the while unable to tell her how useless her words were.

Perhaps if Aunt Itzie herself had by example taught me how adults got together, I might have grown up more socially adept. But the odd thing was that Aunt Itzie, attractive as she might have been, had absolutely no love life. None. No suitors, no one-night-stands, no old flames come to console a grieving widow (if widow she even was; the prior existence of an Uncle de la Mare was strictly conjectural on my part). In the twenty-odd years of our relationship, she never, to the best of my knowledge, deviated from an old maid's lonely existence.

Which is not to say Itzie had no libido. Rather the contrary, since hardly a midnight went by that I did not hear unmistakeable sounds of self-vented passion emanating from her room.

Of course, such eavesdropping simply added fuel to my own frustrated needs.

But until the day she saddened me more than I had ever been saddened by precipitously dying without undergoing any prior illness—she was then perhaps sixty, perhaps older, her ageless, marvelous figure utterly intact, only her blonde hair to some degree whitened—Aunt Itzie never knew, I hoped, the role she had played in my psyche.

But who can be sure about anybody knowing anything?

Aunt Itzie's death seemed to free me slightly from keeping silent about my compulsions, enough anyhow for me to try visiting a professional. After several expensive sessions, the psychiatrist felt confident enough to utter a diagnosis.

"Mister de la Mare, I have some good news and some bad news. First off, you are definitely neither a pedophile nor some misogynist who must render women symbolically insignificant in order to approach them. Your symptoms simply don't fit the clinical profiles."

"Well, gee, thanks, Doctor. I never felt like either of those types, but it's good to know for sure."

Professionally oblivious to my weak sarcasm, the man continued. "What you do have, I believe, is a very rare neurosis, one I personally have never encountered before outside of texts. Thumbelina complex, we call it. A fixation on women of diminutive stature. There's been no real success in curing past cases. But it should not interfere with your living a happy and productive and companionable life."

"I agree, Doctor! If only I could find the woman of my dreams!"

"Have you considered soliciting potential dates perhaps an inch or two taller than your, ah, optimum? You could work your way up the spectrum. Perhaps after a few, um, satisfactory intimate encounters, you would find even a five-foot woman agreeable. . . . "

"I suppose. . . . "

I left that day, poorer but just as frustrated, and never resumed therapy.

In fact not only did I leave therapy, but also my job, and my home state, relocating far from the painful memories.

I was resigned to spending the rest of my life alone, without female companionship of the only kind that would make me happy.

Two months later, Pia Zamora came to work in my office.

Young Aunt Itzie's twin.

2. IGNATZ INTRUDES

Tom T's was noiser than I've ever heard it. A group of state workers from the Registry of Motor vehicles was celebrating the millionth nervous breakdown they had induced in a customer. Or something similar. The bridge-and-tunnel crowd was acting like members of a suburban chapter of the Hellfire Club. A passel of theatergoers was rehearsing the entire soundtrack of the musical they had just seen. Songs and lyrics by the famous team of Schmaltz and Glitz.

Even though Pia was seated just the diameter of a small round table away from me, I could hardly hear her speak.

But this was good. Because it meant she couldn't hear me sound like a fool. Which is what I'm sure my babbling would have conveyed.

So instead, while she sipped her drink (she had declined alcohol, and chosen just a Sprite), I contemplated her and my luck.

The tips of Pia's pumps barely grazed the floor. She was dressed in a tight green angora sweater and plaid wool skirt. Her tiny waist was belted. Tightly. Her styled hair was a deeper auburn than Aunt Itzie's, her complexion darker. But her mouth was the same perfect cupid's-bow, her eyes showed the same flashing impulsive nature.

My throat had closed up to the size of a straw. I sipped some of my beer.

For three weeks, I had dreamed of this moment. Watching Pia across the office at her desk, hardly daring to believe in the reality of her. When she stopped for lunch or a snack—I noticed she favored finger food, mini-Ritz, Chicken McNuggets or the like, things that would disappear in a few small nibbles—I was amazed that she was earthbound enough to need to eat. I spied on her as she laughed and chattered. When I had plausible and neutral reasons to talk to her, I found myself zoning out at the sound of her voice. It seemed to pluck the strings of my central nervous system.

At last, after ascertaining that she had no boyfriend, I had dared to invite her out for a drink. It was the last possible moment that week, since she was starting her vacation the next day. Going someplace abroad.

She eyed me the exact same way that high school-era Pidge had, and I held my breath for the inevitable refusal.

"Why, sure, Wally. Sounds like fun."

I was washed by a wave of lust that felt like a blast of hard radiation. It was all I could do to make it back to my desk.

And now, I was going to blow my one chance so far at a normal male-female relationship—or at least as normal as I could hope for—by clamming up or spouting nonsense.

Wake up, Wally! Say something halfway intelligent!

"Um, Pia, your last name? Is it Spanish?"

Lips pursed around her straw, she gurgled up the last of her soda before speaking. When she set the bottle down, I was struck once more by the perfection of her miniature hands. Painted nails the size of dots punched from colored paper.

"Mexican. My Mom was born in Mexico City. Dad hailed from Denmark, though. He was a diplomat stationed there. Mom and I eventually became American citizens."

"And you use your mother's maiden name?"

She looked genuinely puzzled. "Why, of course."

Then, like an idiot, I blurted it out. "Were your parents both as small as you?"

A certain wariness stiffened Pia's spine and features. "Why do you ask?"

"Oh, no real reason. Just curious, heh-heh. I could never— I mean, one doesn't— That is, it's quite unusual—"

My obvious confusion seemed to relax Pia. "As a matter of fact, they were. Could you get me another soda, please?"

Dumb as I was, I could recognize when the subject was being changed. "Sure."

On my way back from the bar, I was surprised to see a stranger at our table. He and Pia seemed to be engaged in some kind of passionate confab.

The newcomer was a fellow with a well-developed upper body. The kind of guy who either worked out a lot or was simply lucky enough to manufacture massive amounts of testosterone. He wore a plain white tee shirt with the legend MICROD00DZ across the back. His youngish face was craggy as a weathered cliff, topped by black hair thick as a goat's pelt. Leaning across the table, he had Pia pinioned by the wrists. She wore a look not of fear but of lofty disdain.

As I threaded my way through the crowd, anxious and curious, one of those weird public silences occured. The music and conversation and laughter and shrieking hit a momentary dead spot. In the lull I could plainly hear an exchange between Pia and the stranger, though no one else seemed to pay any attention to their low voices.

The man's tone was gruff. "You will marry me and give me an heir soon, my Queen! Willingly or not!"

Pia sniffed with hauteur. "Mate with you, Ignatz? Why, I'd sooner screw a human! And besides, neither you nor your horrid father are the real king, despite all the tricks you and he have employed. That Bobo! One day—"

The man sneered. "One day the Lost Son will return? Don't tell me you believe that fairy tale? Face it, he's dead—"

Then the noise swelled up, and Pia's rejoinder was lost.

By the time I reached the table, the man had released Pia. His arms folded across his massive chest, he was sulking like a child. She was unconcernedly chafing one wrist.

When Pia saw me she brightened, sending a jolt of dizzying energy through me.

"Wally! What a sweetheart you are! It's too bad we didn't know this *person* would be joining us. I guess he'll just have to serve himself."

I set the drinks down. "I don't believe I caught your name—?"

The man continued to pout. Pia spoke for him. "This is Ignatz Lagerkvist, Wally. He's a cousin. On my father's side."

I extended my hand, and he reluctantly took it.

Ignatz exerted a measure of bone-crushing power that I succeeded in partially returning. But the really odd thing about our shake was how it made me feel. Emotions of mingled attraction and repulsion, as if Ignatz were my brother, but his name was Cain.

The feeling had the same intensity as my attraction toward Pia.

We broke our clasp and I sat. Ignoring me and any reciprocal vibes he might have felt, Ignatz turned back to Pia.

"Will you end this farce now and come with me?"

"I have no intention of going anywhere with you, Ignatz," said Pia curtly. Then, sweetening her tone, she said the words that took my breath away. "Wally's my date for this evening."

Pia took my hand and squeezed it. It might as well have been my heart.

That was the final straw for Ignatz. He shot to his feet.

Ignatz was perhaps three inches taller than Pia. He would have had a bit more height, except that his muscled legs were bowed like those of an old cowboy. His nose was on a level with my midriff.

Nothing had really prepared me for Ignatz's stature, and while I found it seductive in women, it only looked ridiculous on him. I laughed out loud before I could contain myself.

He swept me and Pia with a smoldering glare. "You'll pay for this insult, Pia. You and your 'date!' One way or another, you'll pay. And perhaps sooner than you think!"

Then he stalked out.

The rest of those hours in the bar passed in a haze. I couldn't get Pia to tell me any more about Ignatz, and the talk turned to personal matters. Her mother, who had raised Pia alone after her father had apparently deserted them. (Although Pia seemed to accept his desertion as a matter of no import, harboring no ill will toward him.) Her childhood, her college days. Reluctant to delve into my own strange upbringing and the way it had molded me, I let her carry the conversation.

By the time we found ourselves on the stoop of her apartment building, my mind was whirling.

Pia stood on tiptoes and I instinctively bent down for a kiss. I smelled the cinnamon tang rising off her skin, received a tiny peck on my cheek, then heard her whisper, "Thank you, Wally, you're a lot of fun and very kind."

Then she was gone inside.

I turned to descend the steps, which bore a distinct resemblance to an escalator of clouds.

There was an unlighted service alleyway on the side of Pia's building, the dim bulk of a dumpster lurking within the gloom. I suspect that was where they were hiding. But I can't be sure, for when the blow descended on the back of my head I went instantly out.

3. MISTER GULLIVER, I PRESUME

Ropes secured both my wrists and my ankles to the the arms and legs of a heavy chair. Another stout cord went around my waist. I sat beneath a dangling twenty-five-watt bulb, no other furniture, with or without occupants, within my limited vision. I had tried rocking the chair across the empty, shadowy, windowless room, toward the doubtlessly locked wooden door set in one dank wall. No go. So I just slumped. And waited. And fumed. The knot on my skull throbbed like my heart had when Pia kissed me. The inverse of that pleasure.

But somehow, I had a distinct feeling, not unconnected.

When the door eventually opened, my suspicions became instant fact.

In walked Ignatz Lagerkvist, behind him a procession I could only call a royal entourage. His followers consisted of half a dozen small men nearly identical to him: bandy-legged and broad-chested, with coarse hair of various shades, and uniformly rough features. They trailed him dutifully with such silly deference that I would have laughed if I hadn't been so angry.

The exception to this general air of servility were the two oldest members of the party. Each man had gone partially bald, tufts of white hair prominent above their ears, and both their faces were heavily wrinkled. But beyond that, they couldn't have been more different. One carried himself with utter pompousness, while the other trudged reluctantly along, as if he'd rather be anyplace else. The pompous one's piggy expression told of an egotistical, self-indulgent nature, while the trudger wore a hangdog, long-suffering look.

As they drew closer and spread out in a semicircle before me, I realized with a start that the pitiful look of the latter oldster derived in part from the milky-white blindness of his eyes.

Then Ignatz was confronting me. I spoke before he could.

"No need for introductions, thank you. I spotted you as Dopey right away. And this must be Sleazy."

I nodded my head toward the pompous old gnome, who scowled furiously.

Ignatz thumped me solidly on the chest. "Very funny, human. You may joke all you wish, but we hold the upper hand. And if you ever wish to see the light of day again, you'll show proper respect to my father, King Bobo."

The old man puffed up his barrel chest, which was unfortunately outclassed by his barrel belly.

"King? And I suppose that makes you a Prince. King of what, Prince Ignatz? This cellar?"

Ignatz assumed a dignity then that I hadn't suspected he possessed, and said, "King not of any land, but of a race older than yours, human. King of the Imps."

Despite myself, I was impressed by his absurd air of solemn pride in an impossible claim. Ignatz seemed to recognize this reaction, and to capitalize on it he assaulted me with a string of questions.

"What's your connection to Queen Pia? Has she mentioned where the Pixies are meeting, or how sentiment is running toward my plan? Are they willing to try the new drug? There have been no trials aside from the lab animals, naturally, but the researchers all feel it will be safe and effective. God knows, I've paid those damn scientists enough for them to be sure! I would insist, of course, on maintaining a parity between Pixies and Imps, if the drug should produce an imbalance in the sexes. Would they agree to any additional births, as necessary?"

"Ignatz, I have no idea what you're talking about. Pia and I work in the same office together. We were out for the first time tonight for an innocent drink. It's that plain and simple. If you want to know the answers to your crazy questions, why don't you ask her?"

Ignoring my explanantion, Ignatz narrowed his eyes and thrust his ugly face closer. Whether it was my fatigue and the strange circumstances, or something more substantial, I was suddenly taken with the notion that I was looking into a distorting mirror.

"I believe you know more than you're letting on. It's not unprecedented for a Pixie to confide in a male human—even to take one on as a pet and lover, if she's perverted enough. Why, the Queen practically admitted as much to me tonight."

That bit of dialogue I had overheard in the club flashed back to me. Why was the word "human" an insult to Ignatz? Did Pia feel the same way? Did that mean there was no hope for any romance between us?

Before I could ask any of these questions, Ignatz made his final threat.

"We want the cooperation of the Pixies in our plans. It would make things much easier, of course, and honor the old ways. But we will not let them stand in our path. We'll use force against them if need be. And if we're willing to do that, then you can just imagine what we'd do to a mere human, if he had information we neeeded. You could end up deader than Randy Newman's career."

Straightening up, Ignatz said, "Give him a sample, boys."

The younger gnomes—Imps, I supposed, was what I should call them—crowded around me then and began to cuff and buffet me. It wasn't very painful—their hearts seemed almost not in it—and I was reminded of the rather ridiculous punishments the Goblins in the George MacDonald story Aunt Itzie used to read me would hand out. The old Imps held back until the end. Then King Bobo stepped forward and gave my nose a viscous, cowardly tweak.

I waited for the last Imp, the blind one, to administer a token blow. He fumbled closer, plainly reluctant to conform, and delivered a feeble open-palmed slap that was more like a caress. When he connected, his hand lingered for a few seconds, and I could feel a palpable shiver run down his arm.

Ignatz seemed proud of his troop. "We'll let you sit a while until you've had a chance to reconsider. Maybe then you'll even be allowed some water, say, or a trip to the toilet."

They left me alone in the room with my various minor contusions and bruises. I tried to settle down for whatever indefinite period awaited me.

It must have been only an hour or two until I awoke out of a semi-doze with a start, as the door creaked open.

In came the elderly blind Imp.

Carrying a knife.

He was next to my chair in a second, slicing at my bonds.

"Oh, my King, I'm so very sorry. Please forgive old Rufus. Once I had some stature in the court. Was I not your father's most loyal retainer, after all, his most trusted adviser? But poor Rufus has fallen far since the old days. Now he's just kept around as a symbol of the old order, something to kick and abuse and humiliate."

I stood up, stretching and then chafing my limbs. Rufus ran a trembling hand up my arm, just barely able to reach my shoulder.

"How tall the King has grown! No Imp has ever reached such heights! That's what kept your identity a secret from the others. That, plus the fact that they never held you as a babe, as I did. Without eyesight to mislead, old Rufus recognized you at first touch."

I looked down at the strange little fellow. If there was any recognition between us, it flowed strictly one-way.

"You knew my father? Who was he?"

Rufus sighed. "Good King Jad. One of the best Kings the Imps ever had. Poisoned by the treacherous Bobo! Oh, not that feeble-witted Bobo ever would have dared to on his own, weak pleasure-seeker that he is! No, it's all his ambitious son's doing! He put his father up to it, and now rules in all but name."

"Ignatz had my father poisoned? Why?"

"It's a long, sorry story, my boy. And it's hardly safe to tell it here. Go to the Queen. Tell her Rufus proclaims you the Lost Son. She'll have your answers for you. But you must warn her of what Ignatz is planning. And you must escape now, before they discover you're free!"

We began to hasten through cellar passages until we stood at the foot of a staircase.

"Will you be okay?"

Rufus sighed. "What more can they do to me? They won't even let me out of their clutches long enough to go to a doctor for these damn cataracts. And it wouldn't even cost the cheap bastards anything. Old Rufus is a veteran after all. I've got complete coverage."

I was interested in anything Rufus could tell me about my history or parentage. "Did my father fight in World War Two along with you?"

Rufus laughed. "World War Two? It was the War Between the States! Your father and I nearly bought the farm at Chickamauga. Now, run, boy. Run!"

4. IT'S A SMALL WORLD, AFTER ALL

The stairs had debouched onto a unlit alley, open at both ends. Night still held, although I thought I could see a kiss of pastels in one quadrant of the brick-framed sky-slice. I randomly darted left (wincing and revising my notion of the dawn into a bruise of colors, rather than a kiss), and ran to the street.

Water licked hungrily at the pilings of the piers extending out into the black river, on the far side of the oil-spotted cobbled boulevard. I was in the meatpacking district, many blocks south and west of where I had been abducted.

I wasted a few seconds by turning around to eyeball the warehouse where I had been held.

NAPOLEAN BRAND SARDINES
"FISH FOR A KING"

There were no taxis at this hour or place, of course, so I began to jog for the nearest subway.

I was going straight to Pia's. For answers.

I made it to the nearest underground station without any signs of pursuit. The wait for the train was interminable. I filled the minutes by turning the same speculations over and over fruitlessly in my brain.

Rufus had deemed me the fabulous Lost Son, a role that seemed to make me heir to the title of King of the Imps. Whatever that job might involve. I had a hunch that it was more like the ceremonial role of King of the Gypsies, rather than King of England. Down and dirty rather than high and mighty. But in any case, that assertion would seem to mean that I had to be an Imp. But if they all looked like Ignatz and his bretheren, then how could I be one? The only family resemblance I could see was in my rough-hewn face. After all, I wasn't bandy-legged or short—

The rattle of the approaching train cast me back in time.

The clattering of my childhood leg braces and canes—

Those doctor visits and mysterious shots through adolescence—

My Thumbelina Complex—

I was an Imp. An Imp whose identity had been stolen from him, for his own protection.

Hastening onboard the train, I ran my hands compulsively over my face, my whole sense of who I was vaporizing like a drop of Joan of Arc's sweat.

I had to know everything. Only Pia could help me.

Pia the Pixie.

At the outer door to her apartment, I leaned on the bell, number 312. Pia's sleepy voice soon sounded.

"Who is it?"

"It's me, Walter! Pia, you've got to let me in! I'm an Imp!"

There was a pregnant pause. Pia's voice was stern when it returned.

"Wally, if you've stumbled onto that silly word somehow and are trying to use it only to get in here for some reason, I just want to warn you that I won't look kindly on it. . . . "

"No, it's true! Ignatz kidnapped me! And Rufus says I'm the Lost Son!"

The doorlatch buzzed instantly, and I was in.

Up two flights I raced.

Pia stood in the doorway to her apartment. She wore a shimmering translucent gown like something from the private and unexpurgated edition of the *Victoria's Secret* catalogue. Her unbound russet hair tumbled down over her shoulders like a roan's mane. Her feet, small as a child's, with crimson nails, were shod in feather-topped, high-heeled mules.

Before I could say anything, dumbstruck by her alluring beauty, she grabbed me by the wrist and yanked me inside. Not letting go, she scrutinized my face intently. At last she spoke.

"You say you're an Imp. Then kiss me."

It was a test I had no hesitation in taking.

When our lips locked, the sensation was electric. Nuclear. It was as if someone had filled my veins with molten gold. No frustrating experiments with any big girl had ever produced this head-swirling excitement. And best of all, I could feel Pia responding the same way.

When we finally broke apart, she said, "That—that was quite convincing. But there's only one way to be completely sure. . . . "

Off came my clothes, followed by her gown.

I could almost encircle her incredibly narrow waist with my two hands.

But her heavy breasts skittered and spilled out of them.

In the bedroom, we fitted together like a rusty key and a well-oiled lock, despite our disproportions.

All my years of unease and distress dissolved when Pia squealed in climax and I bellowed my own release.

When we had stopped panting, Pia said, "It's true. Somehow you're an Imp in human form. One who's been cut off from our community. And that can only mean you must be the Lost Son. My King, my mate, my brother."

5. LITTLE WOMEN

My whole body stiffened like a timber in a kiln. I made ready to spring up from the bed, trying to picture where I had left my clothes. But Pia quickly clambered atop me and pinned me down, her breasts weighty on my lower ribs. She thrust her face as close to mine as she could get it and said, "Don't go all human on me now, Wally. You have to trust me. I know a lot more about everything then you do. And I would never do anything to hurt you." She began to grind her hips, producing implacable sensations down below where we were joined. "Is this at all unpleasant, for instance?"

I could have easily thrown her off, of course, and gone away forever.

But somehow it no longer seemed like such a good idea.

After the second finish, we lay silent for a time. Then Pia said, "Tell me first all about yourself. Then I'll hear what that rat Ignatz is up to."

So I told her my whole story, up till the time I had met her.

By the time I was done, Pia was sniffling. I had recounted my sad tale while gazing at the ceiling, cradling her in one arm. Now I turned to her in time to see her wipe tears away with two small perfect hands. I was touched that she could show so much feeling for my strange fate.

"Poor Lady Fritzie," Pia said. "Spending all those years cut off from her sisters. No Pixie-ish companionship. Nor Impish sex either, the only thing most of those jerkoffs are good for! Sorry, Wally, present company excluded, I'm sure. What a sorry way to spend one's last decades. Still, it was a noble sacrifice, since she succeeded in keeping you safe from Bobo and his faction."

"How old would Aunt Itzie have been when she died?"

"Oh, about a hundred and eighty, I believe. . . . "

Did this mean that I too would— I couldn't think about that possibility now, however, so I asked, "Was—was she really my aunt? Or maybe even my—my mother?"

"No, she was no actual relation. At least not in the human sense. All Pixies are related to one another, far back, just as the Imps are. But Lady Fritzie was King Jad's lover at the time of his death. Your real mother—our mother—was named Micola. And she and I were living safely in Mexico at the time you were spirited away."

"Is she still alive?"

"I'm afraid not. But she lived out her full span, and now, as of old, her daughter—myself—is Queen and carries forward her lineage. Just as the Imp which Micola once carried—you—must be King."

Before I could question her any further, Pia demanded, "Now tell me what kind of nonsense Ignatz is planning."

I repeated everything Ignatz had said. The effect of this story on Pia was quite different from that which my personal one had produced. By the time I was done, she was steaming mad, a pint-sized pressure cooker ready to explode. I felt like I was sharing a bed with some small and wicked animal. A wolverine, perhaps.

"Force us! Force us! Feed us drugs and force us to give birth! That bastard! I'll show that halfwit what real force is! We Pixies hold all the cards in this game! How easy it would be to kidnap an Imp or two when we needed them, milk them dry and then kill all the firstborns! Why, we could make Lysistrata look like June Cleaver!"

"Pia, please, calm down."

She suddenly took notice of me, and her eyes gleamed with schemes. "And now that we have the Lost Son on our side, we hold the final trump!"

"Now, Pia, I don't know if—"

She leaped out of bed and began dressing in the light of early morning filtering through the blinds. Ignoring my feeble protest, she said, "Get a move on. You're coming with me to the Pixie Fest. It's unprecedented, but this is an unprecedented threat."

"Pia, you were going on vacation, I know, but I can't just up and leave work without any notice."

She looked at me with a basilisk gaze. "If you ever want to see me again, you'll come along. Quickly and quietly."

I sighed. Somehow we all never thought there'd be any complications to having our fantasies fulfilled. "Where are we going?"

"Denmark. Copenhagen first."

"Let me go pack and get my passport."

"Now you're acting smart."

I wondered. I really did.

We were at the airport within a few hours. Then we were aboard a plane. As I watched the city dwindle, I felt I was leaving my whole life behind for good.

Once settled in, Pia used the hours of flight to inform me of the long, long history of the Pixies and Imps, and the final details of my own past.

As Ignatz had intimated, the origins of the Pixies and Imps disappeared into antiquity much further back than humanity's beginnings. For instance, not only did they have dim racial stories of competing with Neanderthals, but they had even more formless half-tales of watching smart apes emerge from the trees onto the African savannahs!

Throughout this long span of millennia, the Imps and Pixies managed to keep separate and unsubmerged from the common stream of mankind for one very good reason.

They—we—weren't human.

Oh, in appearance they were indistinguishable from humanity, albeit specimens from the far end of the human bodily spectrum. That was why any of their fossils that might have been unearthed had gone unrecognized as anything special. But genetically and metabolically and gestationally that was where they radically diverged.

Imps and Pixies had several chromosomes more than *homo sapiens* did. Naturally, this rendered interbreeding impossible. What was even stranger was how they did breed.

Pixies were born with the ability—or disability—to produce exactly two children apiece, none fewer and no more. Moreover, each Pixie had a little-understood ability to prevent conception psychosomatically until she so wished.

When the lucky Imp out of all previous copulations—and there had probably been quite a lot, since Pixies and Imps had very strong sex drives—succeeded in impregnating his Pixie, this was what happened:

One of the Pixie's eggs took a single sperm onboard. A sperm which bore the entire genetic complement of the father. This egg contributed nothing of the mother's genes, but served only as the matrix for embryogenesis.

Nine months later, a new Imp was born.

This Imp was not an exact clone of his father. For this reason.

The genes of the Imps and Pixies had no introns, no useless junk nucleotides. That gave them thousands and thousands of more possibilities than humanity, new patterns of brain and bone and skin being invoked every generation, in a complex dance of suppression and activation.

Upon weaning, the infant Imp went to live with his father, the mother playing no more part in his upbringing. (I was unique, it appeared, in having been raised strictly by a Pixie. Pia planned to stress this fact when she did the unthinkable by taking me to her mysterious Pixie Fest.)

Nine months after the birth of the boy, without any further coital intervention by any Imp, the Pixie gave birth to a girl-baby who carried the mother's remixed genes alone. Pixies, of course, raised these female children.

Then, in a final massive menstrual flushing, the mother lost all her remaining eggs. But not her hormonal libido.

Pia thanked the stewardess for the pillows. She put them on the floor beneath her chair so that her feet didn't dangle in midair.

"Eighteen months of being pregnant, followed by some really hellish cramps. But then all that messy stuff is over, and we can spend the rest of our lives having fun!"

I swigged my second drink, which I really needed, trying to think what to say first. "But—but that means that the numbers of Pixies and Imps must have remained stable over millions of years."

Pia looked sorrowful. "Actually, our population has diminished radically. We breed young, and we're hard to injure or kill. But fatal accidents are inevitable. We used to be much more numerous. Just look at all the old legends and myths about Fairies and Sylphs, Gnomes and Kobolds, and how they used to be everywhere. We haven't always gone by the names we use today, you know. Anyhow, the advent of human 'civilization'—something we Pixies and Imps were disinclined to invent—hasn't been entirely without its good side. It's made getting stepped on by a woolly mammoth much less likely."

I shook my head. "I don't see how such a biological arrangement could have evolved though. Speaking Darwinically. The sexes having minimal contact, the limit on births. . . . Why, it's completely unnatural!"

"I agree. We were made."

That stumped me. All I could do was echo her. "Made?"

"Bred, engineered, tailored, fabricated. Whatever word you prefer. As slaves or servants or companions or toys or tools."

"By whom?"

Pia shrugged. "Atlanteans, visiting aliens, intelligent dinosaurs, the Old Ones? Who knows? Our creators' identity is lost, but their onetime existence is something we've always just known."

Then Pia proceeded to connect my personal story with the race's history.

A Pixie named Nimphidia had been my grandmother. Our grandmother. Sometime early last century, when she had been the reigning Queen of the Pixies, she had given birth to my father, who was destined by the immemorial traditions of the race to become King Jad, upon the death of his father, Hairy Jack. Then Nimphidia had given birth to my mother, Micola, who would assume the Queenship upon Nimphidia's death.

That day came surprisingly soon. For Nimphidia failed to shed all her eggs. Instead, she became pregnant by Hairy Jack for an unprecedented third time, giving birth to Bobo, a rather feeble-minded child whose advent killed her.

The miracle was the talk of both the Imps and the Pixies for decades. Then, when no other such third births happened, it became simply an accepted one-time curiosity.

Bobo, in turn, had grown up to father (upon a Pixie named Gudgekin) Ignatz and his "sister," one Melusina, long before Jad had chosen to settle down with Micola and spawn Pia and me. Ignatz and Melusina were our older matrilineal cousins, the first such any Pixie or Imp had ever had.

"Melusina's a doll," Pia told me, sipping her Sprite. "No pretensions to the throne at all. She's too busy with her line of clothing. For petites, of course. But Ignatz is a devil of another color entirely. Ambitious and unscrupulous, he put his father up to poisoning Jad and assuming the Kingship. Although there was some resentment and anger, the majority of Imps supported Bobo's claim, for lack of any ready alternative. Now Ignatz is letting Bobo kill himself off gradually with eating and drinking, knowing that the Imps will have no choice but to name Ignatz King. And if he ever does become King, then he will carry out his crazy scheme. Which is to make all Pixies endure a third or even fourth drug-induced pregnancy, just like Nimphidia proved possible, so as to build the race's numbers up. Even if it kills all the mothers."

"But why?"

Pia waved her hand. "Oh, he has some long-range plan of taking over the planet from the humans. Doesn't like the way they're ruining it or something."

My head, already spinning at the beginning of the flight, had ended up completely awhirl. My allegiances were utterly split, my course of action unclear.

Pia seemed to have no such confusion.

"You don't have any silly trouble with us being 'brother' and 'sister,' do you? That's just a human taboo, you know. After all, we don't share any genes, and we certainly weren't raised together, even less so than any other Pixie and Imp ever were."

"No, that's one thing I'm not worried about anymore."

Pia reached over and did something beneath my lowered meal tray that I prayed no one witnessed.

"Good. Because we have a week to enjoy ourselves before the Pixie Fest."

Something Pia had said came back to me. "Uh, Pia what about magic? If you're a Fairy, where's your magic?"

She told me. In words of one-syllable and four letters.

Over the next few days, she showed me all her tantric spells.

Those few hours when we weren't in our hotel room, we did the usual sightseeing things in Copenhagen. Every now and then, across a restaurant or down some street, I'd see another Pixie, a sight that always made my heart race. Signs of mutual acknowledgement would pass between these others and Pia, along with looks of curiosity directed my way. But none of the other Pixies ever made any contact with us.

"We don't like to gather in groups or even couples," Pia explained. "It causes too much comment among the humans. That's why you'll never encounter any community of Pixies or Imps, and why the annual Fest means so much to us."

I thought of Pidge, my high school crush, and why I had had such a hard time finding her or Aunt Itzie's like.

Pia squeezed my thigh. "The Queen always arrives last at the Fest. By then, every Pixie there will know about the 'human' accompanying the Queen. When they learn who you really are, you won't be able to keep them off you with a cattle prod!"

The image was both alluring and scary. "Um, Pia, aren't we going to be King and Queen together?"

"Of course! But that doesn't mean we can't have as many lovers as we want! How boring it would be if we had to be 'faithful.'"

"You wouldn't be jealous?"

She laughed. "What a human thing to say! By the time I have our children, I'll be ready for a change."

"You're not—"

"Yes, I am. And pregnancy always makes a Pixie extra randy!"

On the fifth day we rented a car and began driving east.

Two leisurely days later found us in Jutland, outside the small town of Billund.

"Can I finally know where we're going?"

"Of course, dear. Like good tourists, we're going to Legoland."

Soon we were at the gates of the theme park. They were staffed by two Pixies, who curtsied to their Queen as she approached. Pia returned a regal nod.

"We rent the whole park exclusively for a day," Pia explained as we entered. "It's costly, but you'd be surprised how much money you can accumulate over a century or two with even simple interest. We're helping to fund the construction of another Legoland in America, so we can have a change of scenery every other year."

Soon we were among the scale models of famous buildings, all built of the colorful plastic bricks, which formed the major attraction of the park.

The toy streets were thronged with Pixies, for once looking larger than life. Hundreds and thousands of chattering, happy sisterly women of every shade and minor variation, each one of them representing my once unattainable perfect sexual object.

I broke out into a sweat. The air was thick with the Pixies' unique viburnum pheromones. I found I could hardly think.

"You can see why no Imps are permitted at the Fest. It would degenerate into an orgy. And we have business to attend to."

Pia conducted me through the crowd which parted graciously and then rejoined behind us, a mass of whispering and giggles. We approached a mini Bavarian castle; a temporary wooden speaker's platform festooned with purple bunting had been erected next to it. Pia and I ascended steps until we stood nearly as high as the top of the model, some twelve feet above the ground.

Before us stretched a field of upturned Pixie faces, eagerly awaiting the word of their Queen.

Pia gestured for silence. "Sisters, before We hear your petitions and dispense Our traditional justice, We must present a personage of great importance to us, and speak of a threat to our integrity, both bodily and spiritual.

"First, We want to introduce you to the Lost Son, King Walter of the Imps, raised as a human, preserved from assassination by Our loyal and selfless subject, Lady Fritzie de la Mare!"

A stunned silence was broken by a tentative clap or two, which soon swelled into a round of applause and shouts, as the Pixies absorbed the news. I made my best approximation of a kingly bow.

"And now," Pia began, "let Us tell you of what the vile usurper, Ignatz Lagerkvist, has in mind for us—"

An amplified shout interrupted the Queen then.

"No! She's lying! I'm trying to give you a choice and strengthen our race, and she wants to cling to her own power!"

A bullhorn in his hand, Ignatz stood atop the castle, having emerged from behind a turret. His face was brutally avid, aflame with an insane greed.

"This human is an imposter! Your Queen is a pervert! Oust her, and let Melusina rule in her place! Then we can go on to achieve our destiny!"

"No!" Pia shouted. "Don't listen to him! He killed King Jad!"

Confusion was spreading among the Pixies. "What is this Impish foolishness to us?" someone yelled. "Let them fight it out among themselves!" another said. "Stick to Pixie matters, Queen!"

"This is a Pixie matter! You don't know what the imposter intends for us! He wants—"

Ignatz landed with a thud on our platform. He dropped the bullhorn and began to throttle Pia, screaming, "Die, human-lover!"

I came out of my trance then, and leaped on Ignatz, breaking his chokehold on the Queen.

He turned his full strength on me. Small he might have been, but he was muscled like a bull.

But I was an Imp too. And had the reach on him.

Our viscious struggle brought us right up to the edge of the platform. Ignatz managed to butt his head into my chin, and I saw nebulae, lost my grip on him.

The next second, he had clambered atop the two-by-four that formed the platform railing, ready to hurl himself at me.

I threw myself toward him first.

Over he went.

But he never hit the ground.

His flailing trajectory carried him onto the next door model.

Ignatz's body lay grotesquely impaled by the torch of the miniature Statue of Liberty.

One tough little woman.

Pia's throat was already starting to show purple, but she moved under her own power to address the crowd.

"Pixies!" she croaked. "Hail the King of the Imps!"

Then she collapsed.

When I bent down to help her, amid the roar of her subjects, she winked.

My first official act as King was to make sure Rufus had his eye-surgery. The second was to get the nursery ready for my son. The third—

The third was to take extensive magic lessons, from an assortment of Pixies recommended by Pia.

I had a lot of lonely years to make up for.

And apparently quite a few, not so lonely, ahead.

Here's the B-side to "Lennon Spex." "Every generation throws its hero up the pop charts," said one wiser-than-average musical geezer. Those who hesitate to place KC on the same pedestal (or even in the same gutter) as JL suffer from an astigmatism even magical spectacles or mind-altering knitwear might fail to cure.

The Cobain Sweater

THIS TIME I'M REALLY GONNA DO IT.

I'm alone in the trailer. School was cancelled cuz of boiler trouble, and Mom's at work at the diner for the breakfast-to-lunch shift, praying the bald tires on our '85 Civic will last another day. (If the tips from the truckers and lumbermen at The Fried Owl are decent, she said, maybe we can afford to buy a couple of retreads this week.) I don't have any friends to hang with—they're all jerky granolas and jocks and geeks in this hick town we had to move to, Butthole, Washington, population ten million trees and maybe an equal number of morons. I got no money or car to make going to the stripmall in Vantage a possibility. Not even my license, if you get right down to it. I don't like to read, I've watched every one of the five videos we own a hundred times *(Pocahontas, Risky Business, Airplane!, Scarface,* and *Desperately Seeking Susan),* the TV only gets one station, and I've worn the fire button off the Sega. My face is this blotchy map of zits that makes the maps of Bosnia you see on Tom Brokaw look regular as a checkerboard. Every kid within miles hates me, I've got no girlfriend and never will have one, and the best and biggest curse of my whole miserable, stinking life is my name, the name that was mostly the choice of my moron dead father who I never knew or could ever imagine wanting to know and who was trying to brown-nose some rich old uncle who never left us a dime by saddling his kid with the lousiest name in the whole universe.

Junius. Junius Weatherall. And of course you know what all the kids call me.

June. That's when they're being kind. Otherwise it's Junie. Or even Junie-Moonie.

Can you ever, ever, ever in your life imagine getting some girl to take you seriously or romantically when you're weighed down with a name like June? There you are on a date, things are getting hot, and what does she say? "Kiss me—June!" Yeah, right. In your dreams.

I tried changing my name once, tried getting all the adults and kids I knew to call me by a better one. Nothing fancy, just James, that way I could even keep my old initials. James Weatherall, good old Jim. But no matter how hard I insisted, everyone from the teachers on down just kept right on calling me Junius or June. After a while, I got sick of hearing myself beg, so I just sighed and gave up, like with everything else I ever tried.

But anyway, none of this hypothetical stuff matters anymore, cuz this is the day and the hour and almost the very minute when I'm gonna really do it.

But unlike the rest of my fucked-up, substandard life, I'm gonna make sure all the conditions under my control are just right.

First I put my favorite Slayer tape in our crappy Wal-mart boombox and set it for continuous play. I push the volume knob up to max, and when the tin walls of our "house" are vibrating, I go into the "kitchen" (really just a different corner of the trailer). The plumbing of the sink full of greasy dishes is hidden by a raw plywood cupboard with its door missing and an old shirt tacked up in its place. Pushing the shirt aside, I take out the half-full bottle of peach-flavored brandy which Mom bought once to make some kinda fancy recipe from *Woman's World* that turned out to be like this inedible chunky slime. Carrying the bottle, I go into Mom's "bedroom," where I drop to my knees. Supporting myself with the hand that holds the bottle, I root around under the bed with my free hand, feeling for what I need among the soap opera magazines, slippers, and dust-kitties.

Sure enough, it's still there.

My worthless, had-to-go-and-croak Dad's shotgun.

With the brandy in one hand and the shotgun in the other, I get to my feet, shuffle back to the couch and plop down, my head about two inches away from the boombox speakers.

First I crack the barrel of the gun. The two shells are still in there, just like they have been ever since I can remember. Hope they're not too old to fire. Why Mom keeps the gun—why she keeps it loaded—I can't say. Maybe she's scared of living alone, with just a kid for protection. Maybe she wants to have the same option open to her that I'm gonna use today. Whatever. All that matters is that the gun is here and ready. I close it up and lay it down beside me on the couch.

Then I get to work on the brandy.

I never really drank more than a beer or two before. Maybe some champagne at a wedding once. But the brandy, which is so sweet as to be beyond nasty, goes down okay. In between swigs, I just let the music rattle me like a streetperson's cup full of change. It's kinda soothing in its own weird way. Every now and then I reach out and stroke the gun. The barrels are cold, like the railing on Zepplin's stairway to heaven, the handle is smooth like an old catcher's mitt. I wonder if my Dad ever killed anything with it. I'll use it when I finish the liquor, I figure.

The Slayer tape cycles through twice and is starting on the third time, and there's only about a quarter-inch left in the bottle. My head is spinning like a turbocharged clothesdryer and every familiar piece of junk in the trailer has acquired a twin and a fuzzy halo. The jelly jar still holding the dried dead flowers Mom picked last summer, the opened box of corn flakes, the TV with only half an antenna (except now it has two). But I'm not worried about being able to get the gun positioned in my mouth and pulling the triggers—the idea still looks good to me—cuz after all how hard can it be? I mean, it's not brain surgery, right?

Then I think, oh, yeah—it is. Funny, real funny.

I look blurrily at the nearly empty bottle, raise it like I'm making a toast to someone, then start it toward my lips. But before I can down the final gulp of booze, I start to shiver in a major way.

This shivering is not nerves. Or not just nerves, anyhow. I suddenly realize how cold it is in the trailer. I can hardly feel my fingers, in fact. Shit, our propane must have run out! Mom said she was gonna order a new tank later this week. Damn! It must be about as cold inside this dump as it is out. Hell, I could freeze to death! Wouldn't that be great, they find me stiff as a board with the shotgun ready but unused. I can see the headlines now. "Major Teenage Jerk Bungles Suicide Attempt by Freezing To Death. Those Who Knew Him Not Surprised. 'He Was Always A Fuckup,' Say Classmates."

I've got to get warm somehow, or I'm not gonna be able to stay awake enough to blow my brains out.

Looking around the trailer for the nearest blanket or coat, I spot the sweater.

Mom bought this sweater last week at the Salvation Army for maybe a dollar seventy-five. I have never seen an uglier, sleazier one in my whole life. It doesn't look even knitted so much as it looks like the hide they stripped intact off of some butt-ugly animal. It's a jacket type—what do they call them, cardigans?— but it's got no buttons or buttonholes along its edges, so I assume it was handmade by somebody's Alzheimer-type grandmother who didn't really foresee the need for buttons. The sleeves have these gay-looking ribbed cuffs on them that manage to seem both loose and confining. The whole shapeless, baggy, oversized thing is fuzzy like an angora cat that just got goosed up the ass with a zillion volts. But absolutely the worst, wormiest feature of this whole worthless substandard sweater is its color. It's a kind of puke-tinted olive, or a shit-colored beige, or a bruised-banana brown. Words fail me to describe this horrible shade.

When Mom came in the trailer with a week ago and held it proudly up, I just looked at it silently for a minute or so, then said, "Customers will definitely tip you more when you're wearing that, cuz they'll think you're a retarded feeb."

She got mad at me then and threw the sweater at me. I ducked, and it ended up half-draped over a chair, where it's stayed ever since, neither Mom nor me wanting to admit its existence. Now, too dizzy to stand, I lean across the couch, snag a corner of the sweater and pull it to me.

I must be really drunk, cuz the piece of clothing seems to crawl toward me, like something alive. I hardly use any effort, and suddenly it's in my lap.

I go to put an arm in one sleeve, then pause.

Is this really the outfit I wanna be found dead in?

But then my shivers get worse, and I realize it's this sweater or nothing, cuz I'm too wasted to reach anything else, and unless I get warm this whole farce will be over. I'll pass out and when I wake up I won't be able to shoot myself cuz I'll be sober again, and my substandard life will drag on forever, or at least till I'm thirty years old and ready to retire or something.

So soon I'm wearing the sweater, its buttonless front leaving a three-inch-wide stripe of my Stussy tee shirt showing. Man, this hideous garment is really warm ! It's like having some big ugly but affectionate dog draped over me.

Now I can get down to business.

I chug the last of the fruity booze. Then I pick up the shotgun, swing its barrels to point at myself. It's awkward holding it reversed, and my wrist start to strain, but I figure the pressure won't last too long. Holding it at an upward angle, I move it toward my open mouth.

Then a flash from across the trailer catches my eye, and I stop moving.

It's me, my reflection, in the tall skinny unframed mirror leaning against a wall that Mom uses to check herself out before work each day.

I see a guy with long brown hair parted in the middle and caught up behind his ears, an open sweater showing his tee-shirt, with something like a microphone stand aimed at his face. The sight hypnotizes me.

It is Kurt Cobain on *MTV Unplugged,* from December of 1993, when we still had cable. All that's missing is the guitar. All that's added are my zits.

Well, well, well. So that's what I was aiming subconsciously for all along. And I never even really liked his music. Too much whining. It bugs me that even my going-away-gesture is not original. At least I'm not playing one of his tapes. Oh, well, I guess there's only so many ways to do it.

I start the gun barrels moving to where I can clamp my teeth down on Death.

As I shift position slightly, the left edge of the sweater closes the gap across my chest at one spot, making contact with the right side.

Instantly, the whole front of the sweater zips closed with a sound like velcro separating. At the same time I feel a tickling at the back of my neck, where the collar touches it.

Weirded out, I decide instantly that now's the time to do it, before I can lose my mind entirely.

I mentally say goodbye, then will my fingers to squeeze the triggers.

But nothing happens.

My fingers are as rigid as frozen fishsticks.

At the same instant, words light up my brain.

Neural subject mismatch. Failure mode potential.

But it's not me thinking the strange words. It's someone—or something—else.

Accessing subject memories for historical pointers. Extremely weak referents. Synthesizing from available data. Repositioning internal chronolocator. Circa three point five years post-target-date. Acknowledged: mission failure likelihood one hundred percent. Energy reserves thirty percent. Fallback mode now operational.

While this nonsense is flashing through my head, I'm desperately trying to do something, anything! Lower the gun, pull the trigger, jump up, call for help. Nothing. I'm a zombie, trapped in my own body.

I think about the tickle I felt on my neck. Has this devil sweater put like some kinda tap into my brain? Maybe it's a new kinda Salvation Army recruitment trick. . . ?

Just as I start to panic helplessly in my head like a roach in a roach motel, things begin to happen.

My arms lower the gun to the couch and my hands drop it. I stand up. I start to walk toward the door of the trailer.

"Hey," I weakly say, and then when I find I can talk again, yell, "What's going on here!?"

We need transportation, says what I gotta assume is the voice of the sweater in my head.

"Transportation? For what? Where are you taking me?"

To the urban conglomeration known in pre-Rectification times as Seattle.

"Seattle!" I scream. All thoughts of suicide have been driven from my brain. Surprisingly so have any traces of drunkenness. "That's more'n a hundred miles from here! If I'm not home for supper, Mom will kill me!"

Hyperbole, and not relevant to the mission.

I'm still being carried by my own traitor body toward the door. As I pass the kitchen table, I helplessly witness my sneaky weasel body grabbing a butter knife.

"Mission!" I yell to the air. "What fucking mission?"

Having failed to save my primary target, I am now attempting to reach one of my secondary targets, as stored in the mission rescue-table.

My hand that's not holding the butter knife is turning the doorknob and I'm opening the door. A blast of frigid air hits me— then I suddenly don't feel the cold!

"Hey, what'd you do?"

I merely adjusted upward your threshold to external temperature conditions that would normally result in bodily discomfort.

I'm down the three steps from the trailer door to the littered snowy ground, and trotting with perfect ease toward the parking lot. A chained dog barks from across the park.

"I—I can't believe this! What the hell are you? An alien? That's it, you're some kinda evil outtaspace body-snatching thing !"

The calm mechanical voice in my head manages to sound a little peeved, like I offended its dignity. *I am of human origin, and my functions are pro-Gaian. But we need not discuss this now. My resources are low, and I must concentrate on the task at hand.*

The lot is half full of the kinda old junks that people who have to live in a trailer park usually own. Approaching the first one, I try the door handle against my will. Locked. I move on to the next. And the next, and the next—

The fourth—a twenty-year-old Toronado with its bumpersticker that says GRACE HAPPENS that I think belongs to that grouchy drunk, Mister Harris—is unlocked. I crack the door and slide in. Then my hands are busy with the butter knife and the ignition. Soon I'm twisting two wires together. The motor cranks, noisy and reluctant. Using my foot, the sweater pumps the gas, the motor catches more sincerely, I shift into gear, and start to pull out of the lot.

"Hey, I can't drive!" I tell the sweater. "I never took any lessons, and I don't even have a permit!"

But I can, it says back. *And as a Turing-level Four construct, I am automatically licensed by my manufacturer to participate in all human activities consistent with my abilities.*

We're pulling out of the trailer park lot and heading north on 243. A ways off to my right is the Columbia River, its slow cold waters shining with sprinkles of holly-jolly winter sunlight. I wish I was in the river with lead weights strapped to my body.

"You idiot!" I tell the sweater, as it accelerates smoothly, pulls the car's nose out to pass a slow truck ahead of us, and then slips back into our lane as neat as some pro stock-car racer. "You may be licensed for some grand construction tour on the fucking Planet of the Vampire Sweaters or wherever it is that you come from! But here you are riding the body of fifteen-year-old kid without a license and driving a stolen car! If a cop catches us, it'll be the freaking end of the ride! And what about your mission then, huh? How are you gonna accomplish it in jail?"

You seem worried, says the sweater, *although there is no need. The mission is solely my responsibility, although I admit that I would be stranded and helpless without the temporary loan of your somatic extensions. Would you like me to disconnect your senses? Perhaps you would worry less if you had no incoming data to misinterpret. . . ?*

"No! No!" I think about how helpless I felt back in the trailer when I couldn't even talk, and imagine being trapped blind and deaf inside my own head. "No, please don't shut off my eyes or ears or anything else! I don't need less information, I need more! I just wanna know what's going on here!"

A not unreasonable request. Allow me to gain access to the freeway first, where less of my dwindling resources will be needed for maneuvering, and then I shall explain.

I begin to relax a little, unbracing my mental muscles. "Okay, fine. Maybe we can be, like, partners, right?" I hope that sounds reasonable, and that the sweater can't read my mind. Just let me get control back, and we'll see how fast I can strip this itchy, stitchy monster off!

When the sweater replies, I think I've managed to fool it. *That is the conventional method of operation between post-Rectification humans and such as I.*

I keep quiet until we pick up Route 90 heading west. Soon we're cruising smoothly along at seventy MPH. I hope Mister Harris' ancient Toronado can take this kind of punishment, cuz I've never seen him drive it faster than thirty-five on his way to the liquor store. I realize that for the past few seconds I've actually been kinda enjoying being behind the wheel of a stolen fast car heading to a big city on some kinda mysterious errand, even if I'm not doing the actual driving. But I force myself to remember the likely consequences of this insane stunt, and my excitement disappears.

After about half an hour, when I figure I've given the sweater enough time to settle down, I say, "Um, Mister Sweater, sir, you were gonna fill me in on our mission. . . ?"

There's something like a sigh in my head. *Yes, my failed task. If I were not operating so close to my own pre-programmed extinction, I would already have dumped the whole audiovisual database into your brain, and you'd be able simply to remember it all. But as matters stand, I must converse in this time-consuming, low-energy manner. And the baud rate is appalling. . . .*

This talk about the monster dying gives me hope, but I try to hide it. "Well, I'm sorry you're not feeling better, Mister Sweater. But if you could just fill me in on the basics, like. . . ?"

Of course. The outline and implications of my mission are quite simple, although the practical details are extremely rarefied. I am a highly complex artifact constructed from the nanoscale up, originating approximately a century into your future. I was sent back in time to save the life of a certain individual named Mister Kurt Cobain. Perhaps you have heard of him. . . ?

I can't stop a laugh. "Heard of him! Of course I've heard of him! But I'm surprised anyone way up there in the future ever did."

The individual known as Kurt Cobain was a pivotal instrument in birthing the very timeline I come from. The incredible music he created in his thirties and forties, the millions of individuals he inspired, before he succumbed to one of the new antibiotic-resistant strains of tuberculosis— He was perhaps the single most influential creative individual of your era. His life ramified down the decades. But even more importantly, perhaps, was the way he raised his daughter. It was she who, as an adult, actually— The sweater breaks off.

"C'mon, man. The daughter, Beanie-weenie or whatever they named her. What'd she do that was so important?"

I am sorry. The indigenes of this period may not share that information. I have perhaps already said too much. . . .

I think about what the sweater has said. Something bothers me, and I try to put it into words. "The way you talk, Cobain lived on, raised his daughter, she did something important, your world was born. If all of that's already happened, then why did you have to come back in time to make it happen?"

Because secret records show that we—that I—did.

"Whatta you mean?"

There were sealed historical documents in our possession which offered incontrovertible proof that Mister Kurt Cobain survived only through direct chrono-intervention. We were forced to intervene because once we already had.

This is making my head hurt. "So you weren't trying to change the past, you were trying to enforce it. . . ."

Correct. And by failing to rescue Mister Kurt Cobain, I have doomed the exceedingly optimal timeline that sent me here. Doomed it, that is, unless I can succeed in saving the life of the primary backup individual.

Suddenly it dawns on me in a blaze of light. I feel humble and important all at once. "It's me, isn't it? *I'm* the backup individual. Only I can replace Cobain. Hot damn! I knew it all along! My life is gonna be legendary! I'm like the father of my country, right? The whole existence of the future revolves around me. That's why you stopped me from shooting myself."

The sweater is silent for a moment, like it's choosing its response carefully. *I am afraid to say that no information on your personal future has been programmed into me. Our meeting was strictly accidental, yet driven by a certain strange attractor. You are not the backup candidate.*

If you were, we would not be making this journey. However, this is not to say that your newly extended life has no intrinsic value or merit, on a strictly personal level without major historical significance. Remember, today is the first day of the rest of a life you would not be enjoying were it not for me.

I'm stunned. I was so sure I had the answer. Shit, shit, shit! Oh, well, what's really changed? I was a nobody before and I'm still one. Except now I'm the puppet of a wool Terminator with delusions of saving its world.

The car has just passed under a sign announcing the junction of Route 82 with 90. Traffic is light, but we've still got a long way to go, right up one side of the Cascade Mountains, through Easton, North Bend, Snoqualmie and Preston, then down the other slope and into the city, a route I've gone once before on a school trip. I vaguely wonder again if the Toronado is up to it, but I've already kinda lost interest in this expedition. What can it possibly mean personally to a nothing like me? I think about the shotgun back in the trailer and wonder if Mom will ever let me get my hands on it again, if I ever get home.

Just like it could read my emotions, the sweater pops in with a perky question calculated to snag my attention.

Perhaps you would like to hear how I failed to thwart Mister Kurt Cobain's self-extinction. . . ?

"Well, not really. But I guess you're gonna tell me anyhow."

The sweater ignores my feeble sarcasm. *I was propelled by Mission Control back in time to early in the year 1993. My spatial destination was the interior of the Cobain-Love household—a closet, to be precise. There it was assumed—quite accurately, I might add—that I would be unquestioningly adopted and donned by the subject.* The sweater's tone assumes an air of pride. *Perhaps you might have seen one of my public appearances. . . ?*

"Yeah, yeah, on MTV."

I did not make my nature known to Mister Kurt Cobain. There was no point, and it was agreed beforehand that he might be disconcerted. I could perhaps have been regarded merely as the token of a "bad trip," and discarded. So unlike the two of us, the subject and I never conversed. To all appearances, I was just a conventional nonintelligent garment. But whenever I was being worn, I was subtly rewiring the Cobain brain so as to remove his suicidal impulses.

I perk up. "You can do that?"

Certainly. That is one of my main functions. In fact, just seconds ago, when you thought about the shotgun again, I did it to you.

Suspiciously, I probe around inside my mind like a guy tonguing for a sore tooth. It seems impossible that a big urge like that can just be erased. But after a minute or so of inner inspection, I have to admit the sweater isn't bullshitting. It's true. I simply can't imagine killing myself anymore. Or maybe I can imagine it, but there's no motivation to actually do it. I don't really know whether to be grateful or angry at this messing with my head, but because it's less work to be grateful, I don't push it.

"All right, so you're not jiving me. What went wrong with Kurt then?"

Mister Cobain's suicidal gestalt was much deeper, more longstanding and intricate than yours, and was bound up with his entire being, including, or course, his artistic drive. I had to pick it apart thread by thread, if you will allow the egotistical metaphor, without damaging his musical abilities. The treatment was unfinished when it was interrupted.

I thought I had been insulted to the max, but this took the cake. "You fixed me in like two seconds, but weren't done with Cobain after a year?"

Please do not be offended. It is simply that you have no artistic abilities. Otherwise you are just as complex and worthy an individual, of infinite value to yourself.

"Thanks for nothing. You know what? I'm glad you couldn't fix him!"

Oh, but I could have, if I had not been stolen. It happened on his last European tour. A determined and tricky American fan stole me from backstage. Perhaps you'll recall Mister Kurt Cobain's deliberate yet nonfatal drug overdose during that period. . . ? Already he was backsliding without me. In any case, I was not donned by the thief—he perhaps wanted to preserve the mana *of Mister Kurt Cobain's rather vital sweat scent intact—and so I went dormant, hoping that I would later be in a position to resume my treatment. Eventually, it seems, by one means or another, I arrived back here in Mister Kurt Cobain's native state. But it was too late, as we both know.*

All this time the sweater from the future, using my handy stolen body, has been pushing Mister Harris' old Detroit iron to its limits. We've passed RV's and flatbeds full of timber, pickups and minivans, hauling ass more or less parallel to the Yakima River, zooming by the exits for Tearaway and Cle Elum. The land has been rising around us, and we'll soon be in the actual mountains.

It is interesting to note that the drier microclimate on the eastern side of this range breeds lodgepole and ponderosa pines, interspersed with grassy meadows, in contrast to the more densely ranked Douglas firs and hemlocks we shall encounter on the other side.

"School's cancelled today, so you can skip the lesson."

Although I can't move my head, I discover that the sweater has granted me a little control of my eyes which it's sharing. I figure maybe this has something to do with its limited power supply. Anyhow, looking at the dash, I can see that we're gonna need gas pretty soon. Maybe if I don't say anything and let us get stranded, I can escape somehow. . . .

But my bad luck is holding, cuz of course the sweater has seen the gauge at the same time as me.

My calculations indicate that we should be able to arrive safely at the pumping facilities in Snoqualmie before running entirely out of fuel. That is, if we maintain the optimal speed for this primitive engine.

A screaming siren suddenly cuts through the air. I flick my eyes up to the rearview and spot the cruiser, its rooflights blazing.

"Or unless we get pulled over by a fucking smokey."

This is unfortunate, but not terminal. Please cooperate.

"Like I got a choice!"

The sweater slows us down and comes to a stop on the highway's shoulder. We leave the engine running, cuz of no key.

The smokey is right behind us, still sitting in his car. I see him talking into his mike. Then he gets out.

The sweater is rolling down my window. The cop comes right up, a hand near his gun. He's big and mean-looking, wearing sunglasses and a scowl.

"Shut it down, and show me license and registration," he says, so at least I know Mister Harris hasn't woken up out of his drunk and reported his car stolen. That's good. But what's bad is I got no license.

"One moment, officer," says the sweater, commanding my vocal cords. It pops the glovebox and gets out some papers, offering them out the window. "Here you are."

As the cop reaches for them, the sweater makes its move.

Down my hand and right over the papers it flows like water, jumping across the inch or so of dead air to embrace the cop's gunhand! Then it continues up his arm, right under his shirt and jacket!

"Hey!" the cop yells, jerking back and pulling the sweater sleeve like taffy between us as he tries to go for his gun.

But then the sweater must have reached his neck, cuz his eyes roll up in his head and he falls unconscious to the ground.

The elastic sweater pulls back off the fallen cop to its normal shape. *Not the most subtle of techniques, but all I had time or energy for.*

My voice is my own again. "You idiot! What are we going to do with a zonked-out cop and his car? He's radioed the stop back already!"

No problem.

The sweater hauls me out of the idling Toronado. With strength I didn't know I had, I lift the cop up and position him in his car, arranging his limp hands on the wheel. With his shades on, he looks like he's thinking or even dozing, and I pray that none of the few dozen vehicles that have passed us saw that much, and that none of the rest to come will bother to investigate.

Then the sweater picks up the microphone. A perfect imitation of the cop's voice comes out my mouth, reassuring the dispatcher in the proper cop-talk. This last trick isn't so amazing, cuz even I could have pulled that from watching enough Fox TV.

Shall we continue?

"Oh, sure, why not? What's a little flight after car theft and assault and resisting arrest and probably kidnapping too!"

Before too long we're fully into the mountains, and the glare from the snowpack is tremendous—until the sweater modifies my vision somehow. The traffic seems like mainly sporty new cars with skis racked on their roofs. Rich people bug the shit outa me, and these are no exception. Buncha selfish jerks without any thoughts for anyone else. You think any of them would give up their own suicide to go help save the world? Fat chance!

The sweater and I don't talk. I guess we're both occupied with our own thoughts.

The sign saying that the Sonqualmie exit's coming up appears after a while. And just in time, cuz I've been trying to ignore something urgent for some miles now.

"Hey, Mister Sweater, I gotta piss!"

I can easily shut off that sensation, and we shall save some time.

"No way! I'm not gonna have my bladder burst to save you a few seconds! How long is it gonna take for me to pee anyhow?"

The sweater considers this. *Very well. We have to leave the vehicle to obtain currency in any case.*

I don't like the sound of this, but I'm not gonna argue.

The exit is jammed and we have to go slow. Local driving conditions mean the sweater has little attention for me.

The main drag of Snoqualmie is bustling with lots of happy plastic people dressed in their fancy recycled-soda-bottle ski clothes. Spotting a gas station, convenience-store-type place, the sweater pulls us outa traffic and up to a pump. Disconnecting the ignition wires stops the motor.

Now we shall fill the tank with hydrocarbons.

It feels good to get out and stretch my legs, even if they're not really mine anymore. I don't bother asking the sweater how we're gonna pay, since I figure it must have a plan.

After topping the tank off, we go inside the store and join the slow-moving line for the cashier. In front of me is a fancy-dressed babe in a white one-piece snowsuit, standing lovey-dovey close to her obnoxious boyfriend. She's carrying a Gucci purse on a strap, but the boyfriend has his own wallet out to pay.

The sweater makes me pick up a copy of *People* and hold it with both hands. Amazingly, it opens right to a page that shows Courtney Love punching someone out.

This is a good omen, says the sweater. Then, without warning, its hem starts to stretch out at one point like some kinda vine! It snakes up through the air and into the babe's purse! Without even unsnapping the catch! I hear a kind of mild rustling noise from inside the purse, and then the tendril comes back out with a wad of money clutched in its woolly grip!

At this point the babe notices something. She clutches her purse and turns to glare at me, but I'm obviously innocent, holding my magazine, no hands free to rob her. The sweater makes me smile at her in what I'm sure is a demented way. She glares some more, pulls her purse around, opens it, obviously sees her wallet intact, gives a snort, then ignores me.

By now the sweater has put the money in one of its pockets—pockets I never noticed before. When it's my turn with the cashier, I say on my own, "Um, whatever's on pump four, this magazine, and, er, ten Slim Jims."

The sweater makes my hand bring up the money.

It's a couple of hundreds, some fifties, and, thank God, three twenties.

The clerk—a guy not much older than me—looks suspicious. But in the end, he takes two of the twenties, gives me change back.

"Uh, got a bathroom?"

"Round the rear."

I leave, already peeling the cellophane off a piece of jerky.

That was draining, says the sweater. *I shall trust you to micturate on your own.*

Hungrily chewing and swallowing the Slim Jim, I try to hold down my excitement. This is it, my last chance!

In the john, I set my purchases down on a sink. I lower my hands with my own sweet willpower down toward my fly. But at the last minute I grab the hem of the devil sweater on either side and start to yank the whole thing up over my head!

Stop! Stop! This girl will die without us!

Like sunrise over the desert, my whole brain is flooded with a portrait clear as life. It's a short-haired, dark-haired white girl with glasses, just a little older than me, kinda pretty, kinda goofy-looking, freckles, snub nose.

My arms are raised up above my head, with the sweater hiding my face. Only the collar is still around my neck, making contact with my private spinal cord. I can feel the sweater trying to make me lower my arms, but I'm mentally fighting it to a standstill! I figure I can last longer than it can, so I take the time to ask, "Whatta you mean, she's gonna die?"

Simulations of her alternate chrono-vectors reveal that under current conditions the backup candidate staged a successful suicide attempt at four-fifteen this afternoon. We have less than three hours to save her.

The image of the girl is fading, but still bright. She looks so cute and helpless. "She's really gonna kill herself if we don't stop her?"

The sweater manages to sound weary. *Correct. And every minute wasted is lost forever.*

Goddamn! This is probably the one thing the sweater could have pulled that would get me to cooperate. After my own close call with blowing my own head off this morning, there's no way I can ignore this.

"All right! But after this is all over, you'd better help me straighten out the mess you got me into!"

If I can. But one would have thought that saving your life was sufficient compensation.

I let the sweater drop down around me. It flows alertly into place. "Yeah, well—"

The cashier is standing in the doorway looking at me like I've got two heads—which I more or less do.

"Heh, heh—just a little itchy under this thing." I turn around to the urinal on the wall, unzip and start to pee. When I'm done, I sidle out past his stunned face.

We get the car going, pick up 90 west again, and are soon descending the Cascades. I notice the different trees, something I never would've done if the sweater hadn't mentioned it.

Is it changing my mind further? Or am I changing on my own?

No way to really know, is there? And is there any practical difference knowing one way or another would make?

I go back to thinking about the girl. Another suicide. That makes three of us, Cobain, me and her. It's more than coincidence, that's for sure.

The sweater must be listening in, because it starts to explain.

The entire universe is determined by the quantum operations of consciousness upon it. Nothing can exist or come into existence without being observed. Perhaps you are familiar with the case of Schrodinger's Cat . . . ? Well, no matter. The termination of any conscious entity closes down a multitude of possible futures. The self-termination of an individual is a unique, somewhat paradoxical circumstance, consciousness acting to negate itself. It is almost as if a black hole were to swallow itself. Such ruptures cause the very structure of spacetime to temporarily fray, forming weak spots in the fabric of history. It is here that the course of events is most amenable to interference. Riding such gradients of self-destruction is what brought me to you. . . .

"Wow, talk about your special interest groups! We should all like form a union! 'Give me what I want, or I'll kill myself and change the world!'"

I assume you are joking. Without the benefit of hindsight and petaflop computing power to chart alternate chrono-vectors, without the ability to guage the utility and spinoffs of any individual life, such a threat would be useless.

"Well, speaking of utility, what's so special about this girl? Who is she, and what's she gonna do for you?"

Her name is Miss Ernestine Schnabel. On my original timeline, upon her graduation from the Seattle public school system next year, she became—or will become; tenses are confusing in such cases—first, the live-in governess of the young Miss Frances Bean Cobain, then later, her intimate friend and confidante. For the next fifteen years, she was—or will be—instrumental in shaping the personality of that crucial individual, second only to the child's now-deceased father. Simulations, however, revealed to us that if the suicide of Mister Kurt Cobain was successful, Miss Ernestine Schnabel would eventually become so distraught as to take her own life. Our only hope is that in rescuing her now we can somehow put her life back on the old course, and thus the life of Miss Frances Bean Cobain.

"So that crap you fed me about her definitely killing herself at four-fifteen today was just some kinda guesswork?"

Rather say a simulation with a probabilty close to certainty.

"You'd better hope so, or I'm gonna be really pissed."

Think how I will feel.

We leave the mountains behind us, only Ranier continuing to look over our shoulder like a hall monitor. Around us the suburbs of the city have sprung up like cow flops. It's past three when Route 90 carries us over a bridge onto Mercer Island, then across another and into the main part of Seattle.

When we're on Boren Avenue, heading north, I ask, "Where are we going?"

To the Space Needle.

This does not reassure me.

Traffic is thick. There's an accident at the intersection of Denny and Westlake that ties us up for twenty minutes. By the time we go under the monorail line and find a parking space near the Space Needle, it's four o'clock.

We must hurry.

The sweater sets me running. Deep breaths bring the salty smells of the nearby Puget Sound into my lungs.

Inside there's a line for tickets. I mutter, so that people won't stare. "Should I cut?"

We do not want to be ejected. Be patient. Although the observation platform is a third of a mile up, the elevator ride takes a mere forty-three seconds.

"Jesus, how can you be so calm!"

I'm counting on your help.

"Great. Put it all on my shoulders!"

That is precisely the vantage point I maintain.

When we're finally in the elevator, I step nervously from foot to foot. At least I think it's me doing it, and not the sweater. The ride itself seems to take a week of math classes.

At last, the top!

I bull my way out of the cage onto the glassed-in observation deck. I get about five seconds to take in the spectacular view of the city and the water and the mountains before the sweater says, *There she is.*

Miss Ernestine Schnabel is like I was shown, except she's wearing a long leather coat and standing by a window. I start toward her.

"Hey, Ernie!" I call, somehow knowing instinctively that that's the nickname she's been stuck with, just like my June.

It's the wrong move.

She turns to look at me, a perfect stranger, with a horrified expression of distrust and who-spilled-the-beans confusion, eyes wide behind her smudged glasses. Then she opens her coat, revealing jeans, an Eightball tee shirt—

And a sawed-off shotgun.

There are definitely too many guns in this fucked-up, substandard society of ours.

I think Ernie's gonna turn the muzzles on herself, like I wanted to.

But instead she aims at the nearest window.

The double blasts sound like a 757 crashing next door. People are flat on the floor, screaming their fool heads off, alarms are blaring, and the safety glass crunches as Ernie crosses it to the railing separating her from oblivion.

The subject was known to have a penchant for the melodramatic.

I'm on her faster than I think possible, but she's already got both legs up and over, her little butt perched on the slick railing. What feels like an arctic gale-force wind blows in.

"Goodbye, whoever you are," she says, then slides forward.

I lurch and catch her under one leather armpit with both hands, the rail gouging me in the gut, my feet flailing for a hold.

I can't pull her up. I can't pull her up!

But together, the sweater and I can.

We collapse side by side on the crunchy glass-littered floor. I keep my arms wrapped around Ernie, one cuff pressed against her neck. She seems in shock. I can hear running footsteps coming closer. Guess that lame security guard finally got his act together.

The sweater's voice is faint in my brain. *Power approaching zero. Attempting to rewire subject's neural circuitry. Results uncertain.*

There's silence, and I think it's dead. Then the sweater from the future speaks one last time.

Mister Junius Weatherall, I entrust care of the subject to you. If she exhibits signs of her malaise, you must attempt more old-fashioned cures. The future is counting on you.

"Hey, Mister Sweater, no! Don't go! You promised to help me! Mister Sweater!"

That is not my name. You never asked my name. My name is. . . . Nevermind.

And with that, Nevermind—if that was his name, and not just a last word of despair—is really gone for good.

Hands are pulling me and Ernie up and separating us, angry faces and voices are seeing if we're okay before they start to yell and threaten us, like adults always do.

Well, Ernie and I are in for an ocean of shit. But I guess we'll get across it eventually. And then just maybe she'll be a little grateful to me and won't be turned off by my zits. Ernie and June. It's so ass-backwards it sounds good. Maybe there's a future in it. Whatever.

Here we are now, entertain us.